Praise for

Keeping the House

"The novel carries us along under the power of vivid prose and complex family history. . . . *Keeping the House* is an achievement of plot and character, introducing Ellen Baker as an author who knows how to keep us turning the pages." —*Chicago Tribune*

"*Keeping the House* savors of works by Willa Cather and Marilynne Robinson. . . . It flows smoothly, and the prose is so assured, it's difficult to believe this is the author's first novel."

—*The Philadelphia Inquirer*

"Brimming with luscious details that authenticate the story's various time periods, from early to mid-twentieth century, Baker's accomplished, ambitious debut novel is a majestic, vibrant multigenerational saga in the finest tradition of the genre." —*Booklist*

"[A] sprawling debut . . . Appealing characters and a deft, nonlinear structure generate interest and suspense."

—*Kirkus Reviews*

"[A] complex, heartbreaking literary novel . . . Don't be surprised if you can't put it down." —*The Buffalo News*

"This story does what all good stories should do: It takes you places— some homey and warm, and others where you'd rather not go."

—*BookPage*

"Ellen Baker's first novel is a wonder! *Keeping the House* is a great big juicy family saga; a romantic page-turner with genuine characters written with a perfect sense of history, time and place. Baker's portrayal of the American housewife is hilarious and heartbreaking. I couldn't have liked it more!"

—FANNIE FLAGG, author of *Can't Wait to Get to Heaven*

KEEPING THE HOUSE

RANDOM HOUSE TRADE PAPERBACKS

NEW YORK

To the Long family –
with all best wishes!

Keeping the House

A Novel

ELLEN BAKER

Ellen Baker

2008 Random House Trade Paperback Edition

Published in the United States by Random House Trade Paperbacks,
an imprint of The Random House Publishing Group,
a division of Random House, Inc., New York.

RANDOM HOUSE TRADE PAPERBACKS and colophon are
trademarks of Random House, Inc.
RANDOM HOUSE READER'S CIRCLE and colophon are
trademarks of Random House, Inc.

Originally published in hardcover in the United States by Random House,
an imprint of The Random House Publishing Group,
a division of Random House, Inc., in 2007.

ISBN 978-0-8129-7784-4

LIBRARY OF CONGRESS CATALOGING-IN-PUBLICATION DATA
Baker, Ellen.
Keeping the house: a novel / Ellen Baker.
p. cm.
ISBN 978-0-8129-7784-4
1. Marriage—Fiction. 2. Wisconsin—Fiction. I. Title.
PS3602.A5863K44 2007
813'.6—dc22 2007008236

Printed in the United States of America

www.randomhousereaderscircle.com

2 4 6 8 9 7 5 3 1

Book design by Dana Leigh Blanchette

For my grandmothers,
Lila Belle and Lilly Gracia,
brave women

KEEPING THE HOUSE

Prologue

Pine Rapids, Wisconsin
August 1896

"Well, this is it, love," John told Wilma as he helped her out of the coach and onto the wooden platform at the Pine Rapids depot.

It was the underside of hell, she thought. Blackberry bushes and spindly hemlocks rustled in the scorching sun, interspersed with the remains of cut pines, stumps large enough to nap on. There was not a good shade tree or a lawn in sight. A grizzled, bearded man, missing an arm, spit on the platform. Another lumberjack, dressed all in dirty wools despite the heat, leered at her, missing teeth. The day itself felt parched, and the air smelled thick, bursting with the climax of blooms. She had to squint against the sun. The music that typically ran through her mind had gone silent. The train behind them belched steam.

That she had abandoned college, her piano, for this!

She drew in her breath at the sight of a man like a Norse prince approaching. His boot heels clomped on the boards. His dark suit was well cut, expensive. He doffed his hat, revealing thick gold curls, and grinned. "John," he called.

So this was John's brother, who, like his father, had been kept from the wedding by business concerns. Wilma's mouth was dry. Her fingers tingled in the heat.

"Gust," said John, when the man stopped before them. "This is Wilma."

"Wilma," said Gust, taking her hand and bowing to her. When he straightened, their eyes met. His were the color of a deep lake on a bright summer day.

"More beautiful than John told us," he said.

She opened her mouth to speak, but found she could make no sound.

"Take us home," John said. "We're hungry."

Once arrangements had been made for the newlyweds' trunks, Gust led John and Wilma around the depot to a lacquered black carriage. A matched set of impatient bays snorted and stomped as though they would be off of their own accord if Gust and his party didn't hurry. Gust climbed up first; Wilma looked away. When she looked back, he had turned, and held out his hand. She hesitated, glancing back at John, then reached up to Gust.

For a moment, she felt herself weightless; though she stepped up into the carriage, it seemed she'd been borne up by the inclination of Gust's arm. As he let go of her hand, she sank onto the leather seat. Her corset was like a vise around her middle, and she closed her eyes, tried to take a deep breath. She felt John settle on the seat next to her, Gust on her other side. She heard Gust click his tongue. She opened her eyes, just in time to get dust in them, as the horses jerked the carriage into motion.

She had met John her first week at Lawrence College her freshman year; he was a senior that year. He swore it was love at first sight, though she didn't believe him. He wrote her poetry all through fall term, brought her flowers daily, and listened for hours outside the practice room in Main Hall as she played piano—Chopin, Beethoven,

Liszt, Mozart, and scales, always the scales. He finally declared his love at a Christmas banquet. She held him off, giggling with her friends about his country accent, disparaging him as the son of an immigrant. But when she mentioned him offhandedly to her father that Christmas, her father raised his eyebrows and told her that John's father, Knute Mickelson of Pine Rapids, Wisconsin, was not just any immigrant. As a young man fresh from Norway, Knute had started as a dockhand in Green Bay. With pennies he pinched from his wages, he had invested in land to the northwest, unsettled areas covered thick as the hair on a man's arm with towering trees of such girth that a big man could not reach halfway around. He had logged his land himself until he could hire crews; he had sold the logs to be milled until he'd earned enough to build his own sawmill on the Bear Trap River north of Pine Rapids, which was hardly a town at all until then. Wilma's father, who was himself a paper man, said with admiration that Knute was as smart and ruthless as any Yankee, and besides that he'd married a Yankee woman who'd been born and raised in New York, a farm woman who had relished conquering the land, and rising in social status as a result, just as much as her immigrant husband had.

When Wilma told them what her father had said, her friends suddenly agreed that John was just about the most handsome man they had ever seen. So when John proposed on St. Valentine's Day, she turned him down, but hinted that he might persist. By March, they were engaged, and when he kissed her, she felt a jolt under her skin. There was no other explanation, she thought, but love.

But what had she known about love? About as much, she supposed, as the poor spinster poet Emily Dickinson, whose just-published volumes Wilma had devoured as a teenager. Her favorite lines: "Wild nights! Wild nights! / Were I with thee, / Wild nights should be / Our luxury!" But all Wilma had dreamed of then were ice-skating parties, bonfires, Hubert Graham sneaking his hand inside her muff to clutch her hand, pressing his shoulder against hers as the firelight flickered across his face and danced in his dark eyes. And then, years later, when John Mickelson had kissed her—one night even, daringly, pressing a hand to her breast—she had thought that was all there was, really.

The wedding night had been alarming, to say the least: a horrendous puncturing of her innards. She'd had no idea what to expect, and he had simply brazened ahead. (What *could* she have expected? She had no idea, now. Perhaps something more discreet? More genteel? Certainly not the heaving, painful, liquid mess it was.) Subsequent nights were less surprising, though the whole of the act was still more than she could comprehend. She bore through by focusing on one sensation at a time: his piquant smell pervading her breath; his clammy cheek pressing hers; his hand trailing over her skin; her gasp when he met the place where she parted.

The newfound knowledge clotted in her gut. Some of her turned to mist, and crept out the pores of her skin.

She blamed her father. She had counted on him to insist that she stay in school at least one more year. For as long as she could remember, he had professed that her study of the piano was his dream as much as hers. He had also always been able to construe just what she wanted, whether she told him the truth or its opposite. So, following her engagement, she hadn't hesitated to tell him—in John's presence—that she wanted the wedding to be this summer. To her horror, he voiced not one objection, and even offered to host the reception at his home! Of course, he had recently acquired a new family, a widow and her three adolescent sons; Wilma and her sisters might as well have been dust. She set her wedding for July, and made certain it was extravagant enough that the bills, at least, would not escape her father's attention.

But, in the end, she knew the blame was hers to share. She was a frog, splayed out flat with a finger pressed in the middle of its back that kept it from jumping. Lighten the pressure just by a whisker and the frog squirmed to get free. Lift the finger entirely and there was no telling where the frog would leap off to. Marriage, for example!

She did try to stay still whenever possible. True, she feared falling, tripping, other graceless mishaps. But mostly, she feared that her legs would remember the joy of running, and get away from her. As a child, she had been a top pick for neighborhood baseball games, and wrinkled her nose at her oldest sister's warnings that she was bound to be an old maid if she couldn't behave herself like a proper girl. But then, the strange summer that she was twelve, her knees melted every time Hubert Graham winked at her, and in her heart blossomed a yearning that he would see her as more than a great leadoff hitter.

With her sister's admonitions ringing in her ears, she finally set down a list of Rules for a Proper Girl, and determined to abide by them.

Though the Rules had evolved slightly in the intervening years, she continued to rehearse them, trying to keep the frog in check. *One, always be pleasant and kind; hold your temper. Two, do not exert yourself visibly. Three, do not say out loud what you really think, at least not until you have carefully considered the consequences of such a statement. Four, ignore physical discomfort; if you cannot ignore it, at least do not mention it. Five, do not indulge in licentious thoughts, especially about mill hands; they are of a lower class. Six, remember to defer to a man's point of view, even if you know he is wrong. Especially defer to your husband.*

Wilma willed the music to begin again in her mind. *Chopin's Nocturne in B-flat Minor,* she told herself, and then her hands could almost touch the swelling sad phrases, as she swallowed her nausea against the jouncing of the carriage as it rolled over jutting roots and veered around stumps that littered the roadway.

They drove past a row of tiny whitewashed clapboard houses, then made a sharp left. Visible to the right, now, across a stump-studded field, were narrow smokestacks, a large clump of buildings, and sky-high piles of planks that looked from this distance like matchsticks. The mill. She could hear the clump and drone and whine of its operation even above the staccato noises of the horses' hooves.

The carriage streamed dust as they picked up speed, approaching the town's center. They rumbled across a plank bridge above a river the width of a street, then made a quick turn to the right. They were in the business district now. Businessmen and workingmen and lady shoppers in long skirts and shirtwaists with gigantic leg-of-mutton sleeves, traversing the boardwalks in front of wood and stone buildings, turned their heads to watch as Gust sped by. Upon a closer look at the people, she spotted Native women in simple skirts and tunics and Native men, too, which surprised her. "There's the bank," John shouted, pointing at a two-story red stone structure with a corner door and cupola. "For God's sake, Gust, you're scaring Wilma to death!"

Wilma felt her sleeve brush Gust's, and he turned to grin at her as they raced away from downtown, following the path of the river.

Looking up at her brother-in-law, she was not quite conscious of the few frame houses built upon the rising hill on the left side of the dusty street, and hardly noticed a hopeful row of maple saplings. But suddenly she saw the house upon the highest hill, overlooking a bend in the river. It was majestic: three stories tall, painted a tender dove-gray and trimmed in white. In contrast to the rugged town, this house was surrounded by an immaculate lawn, flower beds, and several small trees, including a line of firs that had been planted at the western edge of the yard. It was a house fit for a prince. Someone like Gust.

"Is that—your house?" she asked him.

He laughed. "No, it's yours," he said.

"It's Pa's," John said, and Wilma felt her breath leave her, as Gust turned the horses up the street that ran to the side of the house. He reined them in at the bottom of the driveway that led up to the carriage house.

"Now, don't disappoint her," Gust said. "It's most certainly yours. All you got to do is let Pa live on the third floor. Now that Ma's gone, it's what he decided."

"Really?" Wilma said.

"And there's a whole staff that comes with it for you—two maids and a cook and a yard man," Gust said.

John broke in. "What about the little house he was building for us?"

"I'm living in it," Gust said. "I think Pa took a liking to Wilma, you know, when you sent her picture."

Wilma sensed rather than saw John climb down out of the carriage.

She looked at Gust then, caught his bright eyes. Looked away again quickly. She knew she should slide away from him now that John was gone, but she felt frozen to her seat. *He isn't a mill hand— but worse! My brother-in-law!* She turned to watch her husband, who was gazing up at the house as though he'd never seen it before. Without looking back, he began walking up the hill.

Clenching her hands together, Wilma watched him go. But she could feel Gust studying her; could feel, as she turned her gaze toward him, him opening the book of her, tracing the words there. *"Were I with thee—"*

Steady, steady, she told herself, shrinking from him. Darn that frog!—it wanted to grab the reins and slap the horses into motion, race laughing out of this terrible town, hanging on to Gust's arm.

"You'll forgive me," he said, "if I say I think my brother's a pretty lucky fellow, then."

"Oh, yes, I'll forgive you."

Ask me if I want to go for a drive, begged the squirming frog.

"Want to see your new house, then?" he asked.

"Yes," said the frog, when pressed by the finger. She took a breath, squared her shoulders. *Do not indulge—*

She watched Gust climb down from the carriage, both admiring and envying his ease. She gauged the distance to the ground, and pictured herself falling flat on her face in the attempt to reach it.

He turned, and held out his hand to her. She hesitated.

As if he understood her reluctance, he reached up, circled her waist with his hands, and lifted her down. She was mortified that she might stink of sweat; when he released her, she stumbled. He took hold of her elbow to steady her. He smelled like cigars and peppermint. He smiled. Just one of his teeth was a little crooked.

She took as deep a breath as the corset allowed, and forced herself to turn from him. She looked up the hill. Her knees felt unwilling. *You know we have to,* she scolded them.

"I'll walk you up," he said, behind her, and she knew he was more honorable than she.

One foot then the other and don't trip! she told herself. Though with her high button high-heeled shoes—not to mention the difficulty she was having breathing—tripping was a distinct possibility. John had already disappeared inside the back porch. "Does he always treat you with such regard?" Gust asked, beside her.

"What?" said Wilma, thinking, *One foot then the other and don't even look at him!*

"Nothing," Gust said.

They took a few more steps.

"It's been no different, my whole life," he said then. "He's got nothing but himself on his mind. I had hoped that with a girl like you—"

Suddenly, she felt so dizzy that she had to clutch his arm to keep from toppling over.

"Forgive me," he said, reaching out to steady her. "I shouldn't have said—"

"No," she said, needing the corset loosened; she couldn't breathe. With all her might, she was trying to abide by her Rule. *Ignore physical discomfort. At least don't mention—*

"It wasn't my place to say nothing."

Despite her efforts, her legs crumpled. He held her elbows and they sank to the ground in tandem.

"It's just that—I was—going to faint," she said. "The—heat."

"You're awful pale," he observed, and his hands slipped from her elbows to her waist.

She looked up at him, her eyes wide.

"Godsakes," he said, and sprang to his feet. He turned from her, removed his hat, ran his hand through his hair, jammed the hat back onto his head. "Forgive me," he said. "I'll help you up to the house, then. You'll be all right?"

"Yes," she said, though she knew it wasn't true. She had never been the type to faint at a little heat. She realized she'd been feeling peculiar for a couple of weeks now. And she should have bled five days ago. Until this moment, she had attributed the delay to the strain of the wedding, or to what she supposed might be her body freezing up with fear of the unfamiliar attacks upon it. The unsettledness of her stomach could be explained the same way. The tenderness of her breasts?

And now this man.

She could not have anticipated such a sudden conglomeration of disasters.

"Help you up?" he said, reaching out his hand.

Do not, she told herself, and she let him help her to her feet. She didn't dare to look at him when she linked her arm with his.

They resumed their climb uphill just as John stuck his head out the back door, wondering what was taking her so long. "The cook has coffee for us, and I want to show you the place," he called.

"Don't tell him," Wilma whispered. *One foot then the other and don't even look at him.* "Please."

"I—"

"Please."

Gust said nothing more. She could feel him like a storm beside her.

He released her at the back stoop, and faded away with a call that he would see them later. John swept her up off her feet and into his arms; Wilma's stomach lurched and she let out a whoop of surprise. John began to laugh, and soon Wilma was laughing, too. She couldn't seem to stop herself. He carried her up the steps and inside.

PART ONE

Making Marriage Work

The bride who wants to do her full job will plan from the start
to create the kind of home her husband wants, and to do it
with no more assistance than he willingly offers.

—"Making Marriage Work,"
Ladies' Home Journal, June 1950

HOME OF MRS. CECILIA FRYT
412 W. First Street, Pine Rapids, Wisconsin
Tuesday, June 13, 1950

Dolly, her brand-new sewing basket hanging from the crook of her arm, set out for Cecilia Fryt's bearing a fresh plate of Lacy Raisin Wafers, clutching a note in her fist that read "412 W. 1st." It was a perfect June day, and Dolly, having breezed through her ironing and the rest of her chores this morning, would have preferred to stay at home sunbathing in her backyard with a good book, but she hadn't dared turn down the invitation she'd received Sunday at church. Having grown up in a small town, she knew in her bones the Herculean efforts that newcomers had to make to get accepted into the best circles, and she wouldn't have her yet-unborn children suffer because she hadn't had the sense to help out the Pine Rapids Ladies Aid.

Dolly didn't know Pine Rapids very well yet, though she knew that the Bear Trap River carved a rock-stippled, elongated S through it, with a babbling rapids punctuating its eastern bend. (Everyone who was anyone, she had been told, lived south of the Bear Trap, but not *too* far south.) And to find the address on the note, she knew enough to walk straight up Jefferson Avenue to First Street, where the busy downtown hugged the south side of the river's *S*.

She turned left onto First Street at Holman's Market, hurrying along the sidewalk that ran between the storefronts and an unbroken row of Fords, Chevrolets, and Buicks that were nosed up to it. She nearly bumped into a man who was transfixed in front of the lawn mowers in the window of Wasserman's Hardware, and he turned as though angry, but once he saw her he just raised his eyebrows and smirked, tipping his hat back on his head. She blushed and walked faster, watching that she didn't collide with anyone else, though it was hard to avoid some of the women who were so intent on their shopping.

It was only three blocks before she left downtown behind, and she was grateful for the shade of the tall maples that lined the sidewalks. Scanning the house numbers, she wondered if Mrs. Fryt could possibly live in the house that Dolly had fallen in love with the day that she and Byron had driven into town in their Chrysler, pulling the trailer loaded with their belongings. She could see the house up ahead, sitting high atop the hill above the river like an aging queen on her throne, three stories of disintegrating dove-gray clapboard and melancholy stained glass, trimmed in an aged white, with a stately front porch and third-floor windows on the side and in front that poked up like pointed caps.

Of course, Byron had just snorted that day when she'd pointed it out to him. "Falling apart, looks like," he'd scoffed. "Someday we'll have a brand-new house, Doll. Modern. Nothing old-fashioned like that for my girl." But for Dolly, it had been love at first sight, though the corner of the porch was caving in and the roof was pockmarked with missing shingles. She had gazed longingly back as the house grew smaller in the Chrysler's rear window, until it slipped from view.

A block before the grand house, the north side of First Street became all brambles and birches, as the road curved to hug close up against the Bear Trap, and a hill began to rise to its south, so that all the houses were up a set of stairs from the sidewalk, first four steps, then six, then eight, then ten, as the hill got progressively higher. The number *412* hung from the railing of the last set of steps, which led to a tepid green house with a pinched look about it. To reach the dove-gray house from here, Dolly would only have to cross the avenue and run up the hill. She climbed Mrs. Fryt's steps wistfully, watching the beautiful house all the way up and even as she stood on Mrs. Fryt's porch, waiting for an answer to the doorbell.

Mrs. Fryt's door opened reluctantly, as though it was unenthusiastic about visitors, and Mrs. Fryt greeted Dolly with a grunt of assessment. She was taller than Dolly, and stout, with iron-gray hair swept up in a bun, and a face like an old potato. She looked Dolly up and down with caterpillar eyes behind her glasses, eyes that were the same color green as her house. Dolly thought the house had taken the years better than Mrs. Fryt, who must have been nearly eighty.

"Well, come in," the lady said, without a smile. Dolly obeyed and, once inside, had the immediate sensation of being flattened. Profusions of flowers danced across wallpaper as far as the eye could see, while more than two dozen spider plants dangled from the ceiling, as well as from several coat trees stationed at intervals throughout the room. Chairs, lamps, a radio, and even the upright piano, all festooned with lace doilies, appeared hard-pressed to hold their heads up in the fray; lace curtains hung bravely at the windows. On the lace-covered coffee table was an issue of *The Saturday Evening Post* and a blue glass vase filled with yellow tulips. The air smelled slightly of mothballs.

"My, what a lovely home you have," Dolly said.

"Dorothy, is it?" Mrs. Fryt said, her potato chin flapping.

"Dolly," Dolly said. Oh, this was going to be a disaster. She began to worry that she hadn't dressed correctly for the occasion: Mrs. Fryt probably didn't approve of the red ballerina slippers she had just purchased at Birnbaum's, or her glossy red fingernail polish. And her dress—white, flaring, sleeveless, trimmed in red—was probably too risqué for the Ladies Aid. Well, she was here now, and might as well make the best of it.

She smiled. "I brought some cookies for you, Mrs. Fryt."

"Why, look there! It's our newest member!" Emerging from the parlor was Corinne Olson, who had been the one to issue Dolly the invitation. Taking Dolly's shoulders in her large hands, Corinne looked down at Dolly with a wide smile that narrowed her blue eyes to tiny slits. Her hair, done up in a twist, was so fine and blond that whatever silver there might have been blended right in; a wisp of it had escaped, and skimmed the side of her powdered full-moon face. She wore a blue dress with a delicate white floral pattern, and the girdle underneath was obviously too tight for her full figure. The essence of Corinne—the delicate scent of her powder, especially—reminded Dolly of her grandma, and Dolly swallowed back a lump that rose inexplicably in her throat.

In a blur, the wafers were whisked away, and then Dolly was in the parlor, where the floral and lace theme was perpetuated, only the spider plants being fewer. A brightly patterned quilt on its frame stretched almost the width of the room, and two ladies were seated working on it, facing the parlor door. They stopped their conversation and looked up at Dolly with matching Lutheran smiles.

At Dolly's side, Corinne Olson brushed her hands together. "Thelma, Jeannette—meet Dolly Magnuson, if you haven't met her before. She and her husband are new in town—just about a month now, isn't it, Dolly? She's moved here from Minnesota and doesn't know a soul, and so, when I met her at church on Sunday, I said for her to come on over and we'd put her right to work!"

As the ladies greeted her, Dolly felt much too vivid, her hair too black, her lipstick too red. Most of all, she felt much too young—the other ladies all looked old enough to be her mother, if not her grandmother. But as Corinne Olson sat down facing the window, knees under the quilt, Dolly sat to her right, holding her sewing basket in her lap. With a glance through the fringe of lace curtains, Dolly noticed that the window provided a perfect side view of the grand dove-gray house across the street.

One of the women across the quilt stuck her needle into the quilt top and reached to shake Dolly's hand. "I'm Thelma Holt," she said, smiling warmly despite the weariness that showed in her night-blue eyes. She had stylish salt-and-pepper hair, and her elegant sapphire blue dress looked store-window perfect. Her hand was thin but strong; a double strand of real pearls encircled her wrist, and she wore a matching pearl necklace. She had the look of a woman whose husband was somehow important in town—Dolly wondered who Mr. Holt was.

The mousy woman to Thelma's right smiled a little in Dolly's direction. "Jeannette Wasserman," she said quietly, though her eyes, behind a pair of thick glasses, stayed on her work. Her nose twitched once like a rabbit's.

Mrs. Fryt was making her way around the quilt to sit next to Thelma. "Now, Dolly," she said, as she squeezed her prodigious rear end behind the quilt frame and lowered herself into a chair, "mind you aren't like some of the others and only come when it strikes you as convenient. This is important work we're doing here, making this quilt to raffle off at the fall bazaar. I'm sure Corinne told you, the fall raffle is our biggest fund-raiser of the year. And this year, we're trying to raise enough money to buy a new organ for the church. We Lutherans may be in the minority in this town, but we do what we can."

"This quilt pattern is called Wild Goose Chase," Corinne said, laughing. "Not that we think our goal is unreachable!"

"I'm sure Dolly will do just fine," Thelma said. "Do you have a smaller needle, Dolly?"

Dolly looked at the needle she held between her fingers, which was a good two inches long. It was the only size she had ever used for all the sewing she had done in her life, which admittedly wasn't much. She greatly preferred shopping at department stores to constructing her own clothes, and she had always pawned off on her mother whatever hemming and mending couldn't be altogether avoided. "Smaller?"

"Mercy me," Mrs. Fryt said. "I suppose you've never quilted in your life."

"Corinne said you all would teach me," Dolly said.

Thelma tsked at Mrs. Fryt. "Of course we will, Dolly," she said, digging into her own basket beneath her chair. She came up with a tiny needle and held it up to Dolly, who nearly had to squint to see it winking in the sunlight. "Here, use one of mine. The smaller the needle, the smaller your stitches will be. And that's what we want, small stitches." Thelma smiled encouragingly, and Dolly reached out to pinch the needle from her hand. It was no thicker than a piece of thread.

"Now, take some of my thread, too, Dolly," Thelma said, rolling a spool across the quilt. "And you'll need a thimble."

Dolly retrieved her thimble and her tiny scissors from her basket and snipped a long piece of thread from the spool. Now there was the problem of getting the thread through the tiny eye of the needle.

"What does your husband do, Dolly?" Thelma asked, Dolly imagined to distract everyone from her struggle with the needle.

"He's part owner at the new Chrysler dealership," Dolly said, poking the thread.

"Oh, yes!" said Thelma. "Roy Ostrem's new place."

"What this town needs with another car dealership, I'll never know," Mrs. Fryt grumbled. "We already had one."

"My husband was in the war with Roy Ostrem," Dolly explained. "That's why we came here." Finally, she got the needle threaded.

"Good, Dolly," Thelma said. "Now put your thimble on the middle finger of your right hand. You'll want to tie a single knot at the end of the thread, then you'll put your left hand under the quilt and use your thimble to operate the needle. You see the three layers of fabric: this beautiful top that some of the ladies pieced together, then the cotton batting in the middle, and then the backing. To start, you just put your needle through the top but not through the bottom, all right? And then pull it right back out the top. Your knot should get stuck there in the middle, in the batting. That way, we just have nice stitching showing on both the front and the back of the quilt when we're done. Why don't you show her, Corinne?"

Corinne, still trailing the aroma of powder, reached over and quickly accomplished what Thelma had explained. So quickly, in fact, that Dolly still didn't exactly understand. But she took the needle from Corinne with a grateful smile, anyway.

"Good!" Thelma said. "Now, to stitch, use your thimble to push your needle from the top all the way through the three layers, until you feel a prick on your finger below. But don't pull your thread out the bottom. Just use the thimble to angle the needle right back up through the top, and you'll do this as many times as you can at once."

"And *try* not to bleed on the quilt," Mrs. Fryt put in.

Thelma laughed at the look on Dolly's face. "You'll feel a little prick on your finger, that's all. You'll build calluses, after a while."

"Watch me, Dolly," Corinne said, and Dolly observed as with a few deft flicks of Corinne's wrist her needle sliced through the quilt's three layers, and four teeny stitches appeared. Then Corinne grasped the needle between thumb and forefinger and pulled the thread all the way through.

"There," Corinne said. "We're quilting 'by the piece,' you know, so that means all you have to do is go around the edges of each individual piece. Try to stay in about a quarter inch."

Dolly blanched. There had to be about a thousand triangles in the quilt—scraps left over from the ladies' sewing projects of the last three decades, Dolly assumed—arranged in an eye-popping pattern of lights and darks that formed diagonal lines around solid muslin squares. And she was expected to sew around each triangle?

But the women, evidently of the opinion that Dolly was now prepared for a career in quilting, had already gone back to their own stitching. Dolly inwardly sighed, and decided she might just as well try.

"Dolly's husband's just as cute as can be, by the way," Corinne said. "I met him at church. He reminds me of the Mickelson boys, you know? Blond-headed, handsome, like they were?"

"Mercy me," Mrs. Fryt said, stitching. "Do we need another thing in this town to remind us of the Mickelson boys?"

"Who're the Mickelson boys?" Dolly asked, wrestling with her needle. She had pushed it down through the three layers of the quilt, but she couldn't get it to angle back up again properly. Not even once, let alone five times.

"They were neighbors of mine," said Mrs. Fryt, jerking her head toward the window behind her.

Dolly looked out at the house she loved—the front and back porches, the bay windows upstairs and down. The missing shingles. "I saw that house and wondered who lived there," she said. "It looks almost deserted. But—I think it's the grandest house!"

"Oh, you bet!" Mrs. Fryt said. "The only house in town with its own hill to stand upon."

"They were nice Lutherans," said Thelma flatly. She had put down her needle and was touching the pearls at her neck. Dolly wondered what it would be like to go through life being so elegant.

"Oh, Thelma!" Corinne said, laughing. "You with your rose-colored glasses."

"Well, they did go to our church for many years," Thelma said, picking up her needle again. "And they did do a lot for this town."

"It's been four years since any of that family has so much as set foot in this town," Mrs. Fryt said. "Or that house. Ed Wojtas was keeping it heated in the winter and mowing the lawn and whatnot.

They kept the electricity and the water on, and every day he'd go in there, regular as clockwork, and flush the toilet upstairs and run a little water through the pipes so they wouldn't freeze. But now, of course, he passed away in April, and I haven't seen a light on in there since. They've got one of the Peterson boys mowing the lawn now. I see him early every Monday morning, out there clickety-clicking along, always in such a hurry. Heaven only knows what shape the inside of that house is in by now. I keep watching to see if someone will come back for it."

As though it were a lost glove, a misplaced handbag, Dolly thought. At the same time, a part of her thrilled that it was indeed vacant. "Well, I'd like to live there," she said. "Is it for sale?"

"Mercy me," exclaimed Mrs. Fryt. "New in town and already with designs on the Mickelson house."

Jeannette's rabbit nose twitched. "No one from Pine Rapids would want to live there."

Mrs. Fryt said, "Well, you don't live across the street from a family for going on sixty years without coming to feel they're yours for better and worse, Jeannette. At least, *I* don't."

"Mostly worse, with the Mickelsons, I would think," Corinne said cheerfully.

"Oh, Corinne," Thelma said.

Mrs. Fryt went on. "I wouldn't have minded, when I was a young bride and Amos brought me to live in this house. I wouldn't have minded one bit if the Mickelson house had fallen right to the ground. It seemed so pretentious to me, and every day when I looked out my window there was this reminder that we were *not quite.* That bay window like a little sister putting her tongue out at me: 'Look what you can't have. Look at who you aren't.'"

"Well, really, Cecilia, who else in Pine Rapids but the Mickelsons would have had marble brought from Italy for their fireplaces?" Corinne said.

"But now I'd as soon put a needle in my own eye as watch it crumbling this way, you know? So slow and painful. Despite Ed Wojtas's efforts, bless his soul. There's just no substitute for *life* in a house. I suppose I'm mellowing in my old age."

Ha! Dolly thought.

Mrs. Fryt shook her head. "A wrecking ball would be the thing, if it's got to go."

Dolly drew in her breath: just the thought of it! But Thelma and Corinne were nodding in agreement.

Mrs. Fryt pushed her glasses up on her nose and tackled her stitching again. "Well, it isn't any of our business," she said, undulating her needle through the quilt. "That's what they told us, isn't it? If not in so many words."

Dolly was just ready to ask more when Corinne broke in. "Now, let's not go airing all Pine Rapids' dirty laundry when Dolly's brand-new in town! She won't want to stay!"

Dolly knitted her brow, but decided to keep quiet. It was her first meeting, after all; it wouldn't do to ruffle feathers, and it seemed that this Mickelson family was a sore subject with the ladies. So she sat quietly and continued to struggle with the tiny needle, as conversation turned toward the best spots to pick wild raspberries, the current sale on at Wasserman's Hardware—Dolly gathered that Jeannette's husband owned the place—and the ladies' chagrin that their new young pastor was unmarried. Dolly began to imagine a discussion at the synod level of the problem of sending any poor pastor's wife to Pine Rapids to try to wrest control of the Ladies Aid from Mrs. Fryt, who, in Dolly's mind, was surely notorious. There was no chance to turn the subject back to the Mickelson house, even when the group took a coffee break. Everyone raved about her Lacy Raisin Wafers, though, until she blushed with pleasure. It was a recipe from her new *Good Housekeeping* cookbook, so she felt it a special victory that they were received so well.

The Meal Planner's Creed

My family's enjoyment of food is my responsibility; therefore—
I will increase their pleasure by planning for variety, for flavorful
dishes, for attractive color, for appetizing combinations.

—*The Modern Family Cook Book*, 1942

HOME OF BYRON AND DOLLY MAGNUSON
406 Jefferson Avenue, Pine Rapids, Wisconsin
Tuesday, June 13, 1950

In nearly two years of married life, Dolly had prided herself on never
serving Byron the same dinner twice in the same month. She kept a
calendar on which she noted each evening's fare and where the recipe
could be found, whether on a color-coded, numbered card in her
recipe box, or in one of her several cookbooks. She also jotted down
Byron's comments: "Not bad, hon"; "Tastes great, Doll"; "Mmm-
mmm." Nuanced critiques, to be sure, but Dolly noted them faith-
fully. New recipes were indicated on the calendar in red ink, and she
held herself to at least ten red notations per month. The last thing she
wanted was for Byron to grow bored with her, to find her predictable.

It was true that the stuffed pepper cups had met with little success,
and the salmon mousse had received a "We got any hamburger,
hon?" It was also true that at times he had pleaded for the familiar

solace of a pork roast. But Dolly soldiered on. Even in the midst of the move from Minnesota, she kept up her system, accomplishing it by packing her cookware and utensils last—along with two place settings—in a box labeled DOLLY—VERY IMPORTANT. This box traveled just inside the rear door of the trailer, so that Dolly could unpack it immediately upon arrival in their new home. So intent was she on accomplishing Chicken Hawaiian that evening (once Byron had unhooked the trailer, she sped off in the Chrysler to find a market) that even as she'd scrubbed the kitchen from top to bottom she had scarcely registered the red poppy wallpaper gracing the walls, the black-speckled white linoleum on the floor. A week later, though, shopping at J. C. Penney's, she had found some gauzy white curtains with red poppy appliqués to hang at the window above the sink between the cupboards. A step in the right direction, at least, but somehow the curtains didn't make her feel any better about Pine Rapids or the bungalow, either one.

Their first morning in Pine Rapids, she and Byron had gone down to Ralston's Furniture and bought a modern table, red Formica-topped, edged in stainless steel, for the kitchen. It came with two leaves and six metal chairs upholstered in red vinyl. It was at this table that they sat this evening over a supper of Tuna Noodle Casserole, with a molded peach salad on the side. Dolly had felt too done in after the Ladies Aid gathering to attempt anything more complex, though she had taken the time to adorn the table with a single red tulip from the side garden, placing it in a pewter bud vase that had been a wedding gift. She was pleased with the effect against the wallpaper—plus, in the flaring white dress with red trim, she, too, matched the table setting perfectly. In a moment of inspiration, she had even kept on her frilly red half apron—a friend back in her hometown of Battle Point had thrown her a well-attended Apron Collection bridal shower, so Dolly owned an impressive variety of aprons, nineteen in all, one to match nearly every one of her dresses—because she had read somewhere that "nothing says 'happy home' to a husband like his smiling wife, in an apron and lovely dress, bidding him come to the table, where she has a colorful, balanced, hot meal waiting." Despite the relatively humdrum tuna casserole, and even though the heat of the oven had made her sweat straight through her girdle, Dolly still thought she was a wife Byron could be proud of.

But he didn't seem to notice her, the apron, or the table setting. They were eating late again—Monday through Saturday, he rarely was home before seven. And, unlike many other husbands that Dolly knew of, he never even came home for lunch; he was afraid he might miss a sale if he left the Chryslers to themselves over the lunch hour. Dolly's suggestion that he and Roy take turns going home for lunch so the lot would always be manned had been met with "I don't think so, Doll." He had promised his schedule would ease up once the dealership was more established, but Dolly wasn't holding her breath. Well, less work for her, she supposed, since packing a lunch was much easier than having to cook a hot meal and then clean up after it. It was nice, actually, that she could get through her own work without interruption. Or so she told herself.

"I thought I had a sale made this afternoon," he was saying, between bites. "I kept telling the guy, all these new features, at this price! Well, maybe he'll come back tomorrow."

"Yes," Dolly said, stirring figure eights in her casserole.

"Aren't you hungry, Doll? You'd better eat before it gets cold."

She took a bite. She did like this casserole; she had made it four times before, according to her calendars. They chewed together in silence.

She didn't think it reasonable that this was all their life would be forever.

"Byron?" she said. "You know that house up on the hill that I like? Up at the edge of town?"

"Sure."

"I found out today that it's empty. Has Roy said anything to you about it? Do you think it might be for sale? Maybe you could get a good price on it. I could fix it up."

He squinted. "Don't you like this house? I picked it out because I thought you'd like it."

"I do, Byron," she said, looking at the swirls of casserole on her plate.

"Besides, I can't see the sense in moving when we're just getting settled here."

"But, Byron, that poor house is suffering. If we don't take care of it, who will?"

"I don't think so, Doll," Byron said, and turned his attention to his peach salad.

Dolly couldn't sleep that night. Byron's quiet breathing grated on her nerves. She flopped over and propped herself up on her elbow to look at him. Goodness, he had big ears. A cute mouth, though, and dreamy long eyelashes. But what in the world was it about him that she had been so convinced she couldn't live without?

Disgusted, she flung back the covers and threw her legs over the side of the bed. She padded across the floor in her bare feet, grabbed her robe out of the closet to cover her flimsy nylon nightgown, and went out to the living room, flopping into a chair and fishing her cigarettes out of her sewing basket. Byron didn't like for her to smoke in the house, but she lit one anyway and puffed with relish, turning sideways in the chair, dangling her legs over its arm. She thought about the scrap-book she had labored over for more than four years, which she had left back at her parents' house in Minnesota under her frilly bed. She still remembered the headline of the article, clipped from the Battle Point *Gazette* and glued tenderly to the first page of the scrapbook: BYRON MAGNUSON COMPLETES BASIC TRAINING. The date was February 1942.

Dolly had been only twelve years old when Byron Magnuson, eighteen, had lined up with about two dozen other Battle Point boys on the depot platform to bid the town good-bye in front of the train. It was a frozen, overcast day, just ten days before Christmas, a week after Pearl Harbor. The farm boys with their pink cheeks and bright eyes were puffed up to the size of real men in their plaid mackinaws and heavy boots. A few members of the high school band huddled to-gether and repeatedly blared "Over There," a song that had worked well for the previous war. Dolly stood on her tiptoes to see through the jostling crowd, her gloved hands nestled in the pockets of her wool coat. The ties of her knit hat chafed her chin. Members of the crowd surged forward to kiss cheeks and shake hands, the women fading back with proud tears in their eyes. Dolly's gaze was drawn to Byron; she thought his large ears, which were bright red from the cold, distinctive. He was smiling at the crowd, magnanimously, she thought, and the way he half closed his eyes against the cold, looking proud and invincible, caught her fancy. She elbowed her best friend,

Jane, and told her, "That's the boy I'm going to marry," pointing her chin at Byron. Jane laughed with delight. "Byron Magnuson! Sure, Dolly, and I'll marry the one next to him."

From that day forward, Dolly had combed the *Gazette* each evening for news of Byron, and each snippet went into the scrapbook. She prayed fervently for his safety, especially when word came that he was going over to Europe, and later, that his tank battalion had been involved in the fighting. She imagined various scenarios in which he came home to Battle Point, saw her on the street (or at the post office or at the movie theater or at the homecoming football game), and fell madly in love with her. As the years went by, the frequency of her daydreams did lessen, and she dated a boy in her class that she liked quite well. But, out of either habit or a lingering childish devotion, she kept up the scrapbook of Byron's exploits.

When he finally came home, just before Christmas in 1945, she was sixteen. She and Jane were trading secrets over malts at Bridgeman's when he and three other fellows, all wearing uniforms, strutted in and flopped into a booth two down from theirs.

Dolly, who hadn't seen anything in the paper about him being home, nearly choked on her malt.

"What's the matter?" Jane said, turning to look.

"It's Byron!" Dolly whispered. "Isn't it?" For despite the many hours she'd spent gazing at the grainy Basic Training photograph from the newspaper (they ran the same one every time his name got in), she couldn't be absolutely sure. He looked a lot older, for one thing, and she had never imagined him as having changed from the day she'd seen him at the depot.

"Byron Magnuson?" said Jane, much too loudly for Dolly's comfort, twisting her head again to try to catch a glimpse of him.

"Jane!"

But the boys in uniform were laughing and joking too noisily to have heard her.

"Well, you've got to go say something to him!" Jane said. She had spent four years hearing Dolly's dreams of Byron Magnuson, and was impatient for action.

"What would I say?"

"Tell him you've been waiting all this time for him to come home!" Jane giggled.

"Oh, hush," Dolly said, and quickly formulated a plan. "Come on, Jane, let's go," she said.

"Go?" Jane said. "I haven't finished my malt yet."

"Well, hurry up, then," Dolly said, tapping her fingernails on the table.

When they finally stood up from their booth and put on their coats, a waitress had just brought the boys each a hamburger. "Now, watch this," Dolly told Jane, wishing only that she was wearing pumps instead of her childish saddle shoes. As she and Jane passed the boys' booth, Dolly, walking slightly behind Jane, dug in her pocket for her gloves, dropped one, and kept walking.

She was almost to the door when a male voice called, "Mish?"

She turned. He had her glove in hand, and was just swallowing a big bite of hamburger. Then he smiled that magnanimous smile. He had a tiny smear of mustard at the corner of his mouth. "Think you dropped this," he said, holding the glove out to her.

"Oh, thank you so much," she said, a little breathless despite herself, stepping forward to take it from him. She wished she could say something else, but he was already turning away, so she turned away, too, not wanting to make a fool of herself.

Still, as she and Jane exited Bridgeman's into the starry night, she was pleased, and told Jane, "Did you see the way he looked right in my eyes? I always knew he'd be the nicest boy in the world!" She smelled her glove, and was thrilled to think it smelled of onion from his hands.

"Of course," Jane said.

Disappointingly, when questioned after their wedding, Byron didn't recall the incident at Bridgeman's, not even the glance they had shared that Dolly regarded as having moved the earth. Because, after that, there was no way she would even consider dating any other boy.

Her pursuit of Byron was subtle but plotted, involving numerous small sabotages to her father's brand-new 1946 Chrysler, which had just been purchased from Mike Sullivan's dealership. Mike Sullivan was Byron's stepfather, and it wasn't long before Dolly discovered that Byron was working there selling cars.

"I'll take the car down to have it looked at, Dad, I don't mind," Dolly would tell her father, that spring of 1946, having loosened this or punctured that the night before.

Her father would shake his head. "Just can't understand how in the world so much can go wrong on a new car."

"I don't know, Dad," Dolly would chirp, running off to fix her hair. Of course, she always waited at the dealership while the repairs were being made. At first, Byron would merely acknowledge her presence with a nod and, later, that cute smile, but toward April, he sat down and talked with her.

"You're here just about every Saturday," he observed. He looked younger again than he had when he'd just returned from the war, and handsome in his salesman's outfit of white shirt, black pants and necktie. Dolly supposed that soon he would be taking over the management of the dealership.

"Oh, my father's had awful trouble with his car," she said.

Over the summer, she cut back on the sabotages, lest anyone become suspicious, but, knowing that Sunday was Byron's only day off, she let it slip that she always spent Sunday afternoons down at the town beach. The first Sunday, he came with his friends. The group of boys set up several yards away from where Dolly and Jane lay on their towels, Dolly in her brand-new red two-piece, and only when everyone was in the water did he acknowledge her with a splash. By the end of the summer, though, they habitually set up their towels side by side, and whenever they went in the water together, he dunked her. She had her heart so set on him that, although she hated to be dunked, she would come up laughing. She loved the way he looked with droplets of water sparkling on his face and his long eyelashes, the way his smile looked in the sun.

Jane got impatient before Dolly did. "The way he treats you, it's like you're his little sister," she told Dolly.

"He's just trying to figure out how he feels," Dolly said. "He's very attracted to me, but he thinks I might be too young for him." Somehow, she felt she knew him better than she knew herself.

"Well, show him you're not, then," Jane said.

"You're not suggesting—"

"You haven't so much as hinted to him that he should kiss you," Jane said.

Jane was right, Dolly realized, so the next Sunday she let Byron chase her through the water out behind the diving platform, and when he dunked her, she came up sputtering and looking at him with big eyes.

"Hey, I'm sorry, Doll," he said, laughing, reaching out to hold her elbow. "Did I catch you off guard?"

She let the water push her closer to him, and rested her hand on his biceps. She batted her eyes once, helplessly.

"Jeez, Doll," he said. "I guess you know everyone's talking about us."

"No, I didn't know," she said, telling the truth.

"They're laughing at me 'cause they say I'm stuck on some kid. You're only sixteen."

"I'm almost seventeen," she said, and closed her eyes.

So that was that. Once he kissed her, his lips wet with lake water, the practiced kiss of an older man and not the sloppy fumblings she'd encountered with the two boys she'd kissed before, she knew she would never kiss another man in her life.

It was brief, though, and when he pulled away, he looked rueful. "I shouldn't have done that," he said, and pushed away from her, splashing water over his face with both hands. This only made her love him more.

It was three months later that he called her up and asked if he could take her out for her birthday. Apparently, whatever compunction he had about dating a sixteen-year-old was put to rest by the occasion of her turning seventeen.

Looking back on the entire episode from the distant vantage point of being twenty, Dolly, puffing on her cigarette, thought she should have realized that his caution—the very steadfastness and step-back-and-think that she had so admired—would prove an inconvenience once she was married to him.

Sometimes she just couldn't believe she had unwittingly married a man so like her father. She had spent her life subverting her father's best intentions for her, his cautionary tales of what good girls ought not to do. She would listen carefully to all his reasons why, and then go out and do exactly what he had said not to—not out of spite, but because she never found his reasons compelling enough to heed. He had been especially upset about the flight lessons—but then, so had Byron, although she hadn't even been married to him yet when she sank her life savings from seven years of babysitting into three lessons in a two-seated Piper Cub. It had been worth it, though, the feeling of soaring under her own control, even just for a moment, when the instructor had let her take it on her own. "How could you think this was a good idea?" both Byron and her father had sputtered, separately, when they'd found out, and both were deaf to her protests that the WASPs had had a fine record in the war and that, had she been only slightly older, she would have joined.

With Byron's reaction to her deepest dream, she should have realized her mistake, that the romance she had infused him with was all of her own invention.

Ever since their wedding, "I don't think so, Doll" seemed to be Byron's favorite phrase. Sometimes he'd laugh a little when he said it, as though he thought she was cute for thinking of whatever foolish thing she had just proposed. Of course, when he wanted to uproot her from her hometown, take her away from her family and friends, so he could go into business with an Army buddy, did she have the option of saying, "I don't think so, Byron"? Of course not.

Stretching her bare toes toward the ceiling, she inhaled of her cigarette. "I don't think so, Byron," she said aloud to the night, just to see how it would sound.

Decorating is the loving interest and attention given to a
home in order to bring out the beauty of everyday things.
It can be an expression of your interest in your family,
and it can enrich your family life by endowing it
with more graciousness.

—*Popular Home Decoration,* 1940

HOME OF MRS. CECILIA FRYT
412 W. First Street, Pine Rapids
Tuesday, June 20, 1950

At Dolly's second Ladies Aid meeting, the ladies gathered around the
Wild Goose Chase quilt in Mrs. Fryt's parlor in the same seats as the
week before: Corinne Olson and Dolly faced the window, while Jeannette Wasserman, Thelma Holt, and Mrs. Fryt faced the door. Dolly
was quite proud of her first row of stitching, given that this was only
her second time quilting, but when Corinne glanced over, pushing
back the wisp of silver-blond hair that had again escaped from its
twist, she said, "Don't worry, Dolly. It just takes practice."

   Thelma, looking elegant in a smooth green dress and the same
pearl necklace and bracelet, peered across the quilt. "Dolly's doing
fine," she said. Grateful for Thelma's warm smile, and for the kindness, Dolly stifled the anger that had flared up in her.

   She usually wasn't so quick-tempered, but as if it weren't frustrat-

ing enough to try to manipulate a minuscule needle through three layers of an uncooperative quilt—in truth, when Dolly glanced at
Corinne's stitches, she saw that her own were at least twice as large,
and crooked besides—Dolly was also feeling particularly homesick
today for her family and friends back in Battle Point.

She supposed her homesickness had been aggravated by a difficult
week. She hadn't had a minute to herself; she hadn't even been able
to start the new Cherry Ames book her sister had sent her. After she
finished her regular chores each day, she had so much shopping to do
to get the bungalow decorated. She had been thrilled to find at Penney's a set of bright pink towels that exactly matched the shade in the
floral print wallpaper in the bathroom. But Byron had squawked at
the sight of them, saying he refused to use a towel of that color. So it
was back to Penney's again, and again. She brought home the light
blue, the bright blue, and the green, in succession, but none looked as
good to her against the wallpaper as the pink, and the issue still
wasn't resolved. When she threatened to give up on the towels and
start looking for new wallpaper instead, Byron said he would paint
the room white, but he hadn't even bought the paint yet. Until he did,
they were getting by with their old towels—a wedding gift, they were
lime green and looked hideous with the wallpaper—because she
didn't know which color she would like with the paint. (And he'd
said: "It's going to be white, Doll! Any color will go fine with it. Just
get what color you like." And she'd said, "I like the pink.") Adding
to her frustration, she had spent hours shopping for pillows for the
sofa, finally settling on a pair with stylish buttons in their centers. But
Byron had said they were uncomfortable to lean against. She toyed
with sending him out to find pillows and seeing how he liked it, but
she discarded the idea, knowing that he would have no sense for
color. Any man who would think *white* was the solution to their
problems . . .

What made everything seem worse was her conviction that she
would have no such frustrations if she could put her creative energies
to work on a house that was worth the effort, one like the Mickelson
house. The bungalow was satisfactory, but there were dozens of
houses of the same design in Pine Rapids; even Dolly's most heroic
decorative touches would never make it exceptional. The Mickelson
house, though, was unique. It had true potential, and it *needed* Dolly,

especially since, according to the women of the Ladies Aid, no one else in town would have it. It needed Dolly before it caved in on itself from lack of care and love.

She just had to convince Byron at least to look into whether it might be for sale. All week, she had concentrated on making his favorite dinners, ones that had received at least an "Mmm-mmm" in the past. She had worn her sexiest negligees to bed, even though the summer nights in Pine Rapids were really too cool for them. She had feigned more excitement than she felt at his news that *Motor Trend* magazine had just proclaimed the 1950 Chrysler "a car of comfort and a car of class." She had listened carefully to his explanation of the Prestomatic Fluid Drive Transmission. Her plan was to continue working on him; she would know when the moment was right to broach the topic of buying the Mickelson house again.

"Isn't it nice that Cecilia got so much quilting done over the week," Corinne Olson said, breaking into Dolly's thoughts.

"Well, someone has to do it," said Mrs. Fryt. "We have to have this quilt done in a matter of weeks. And you know what happened last July and August. Everyone coming and going like butterflies, anytime they pleased. No sense of commitment."

As if on cue, there was the sound of Mrs. Fryt's front door opening. Dolly turned with everyone else to see a thin girl with short copper hair breeze into the parlor. "Sorry I'm late, Grandma," the girl said, making her way toward an empty chair. Her green dress was loose on her angular body.

"As I was saying," Mrs. Fryt said. "Here's my granddaughter, Judy Wasserman—who couldn't be bothered to come last week."

"Hello," Dolly said, glad to see another younger person, hopeful she might become a friend. "I'm Dolly."

But Judy looked down her beaky nose at Dolly and sniffed. "Hi," she said, as she sat down, and Dolly knew just by her tone of voice that friendship was unlikely. Besides, Dolly could see now that Judy was older than she had looked at first glance. There were crow's-feet at the corners of her eyes, and her skin was the hue of an unbaked pie crust; she wore bright pink lipstick that was completely wrong for her. She might have been thirty, and there was no wedding ring on her finger. Dolly suddenly felt sorry for her.

"Hello, Mother," Judy said to Jeannette, whose nose twitched in response. So, Dolly realized, Jeannette must be Judy's mother and Mrs. Fryt's daughter! No wonder Jeannette twitched! Immediately, Dolly could see the resemblance among the three of them: Not one of them had any color in her eyebrows or eyelashes, for one thing, and they all had that pie-crust pallor.

"I'm sorry about last week, Grandma," Judy said, as she got a needle out of her sewing basket. Dolly didn't think she sounded very sorry. "I told you, Dad needed me at the store."

"Judy works for her father at Wasserman's Hardware," Mrs. Fryt told Dolly. "Until she can manage to catch herself a husband."

"Grandma!"

Corinne broke in. "Speaking of lack of commitment, remember Wilma Mickelson? Every May Day, Wilma would promise to help with the fall bazaar. And then by the Fourth of July she'd tell us, 'I'm afraid I haven't the time.'"

"Quilting was never Wilma's cup of tea," said Thelma gently, touching her pearls.

Corinne laughed. "But Wilma let us down like that ten or fifteen years in a row!"

"This was the woman who lived in the house across the street?" Dolly asked.

"Yes," Mrs. Fryt said. "And an unfortunate choice it was when John Mickelson selected Wilma for his bride. She never was any sort of mother to those four children. Not that he was much of a father. He paid more mind to that bank of his than to any of those children. And Wilma was so busy playing that piano—she left the children to the maid!"

Mrs. Fryt shook her head. "And I can tell you, that maid didn't keep much of an eye on them. There was many a time I had to go out and calm them down. Oh, they were wild, always playing in the street. Football, baseball, anything they could holler about. Those boys would be out there in their short pants and their caps." She met Dolly's eyes. "Jack and Chase were the oldest, and Harry was the third boy, about four years behind Chase. You could pick any of them out halfway across town, those blond heads and that swagger they all had. The youngest was a girl, named Jinny. There were times when she was five, six, seven years old that she'd be out there with her brothers, her skirts flying up for all the world to see, sliding in at home plate. No proper mother would have let her carry on like that. But those boys thought it was the funniest thing. You could tell they were letting her get the home runs, pretending they couldn't pick up the ball and such. Chase, especially, had a soft spot for Jinny." Light glinted across Mrs. Fryt's glasses. "I wouldn't let my Jeannette play with those Mickelsons. They were too rough."

"They weren't so bad, Mother," Jeannette said.

"Jeannette," said Mrs. Fryt. "For all you've been married to Albert Wasserman some thirty years, and for all Jack Mickelson would never give you a second look, I don't think you've ever gotten over fancying him."

"That isn't true, Mother."

"Of course, Jack Mickelson thought he was too good for anyone in this town," Mrs. Fryt went on. "He always was the most supercilious boy. I'll never forget when he hit a baseball right through my dining room window. I was in my kitchen stirring up a rhubarb cake and I heard an awful crash in the dining room. I ran in there and wouldn't you know it, there was his baseball. The window was gone, and I saw children in the Mickelson yard, up there on the hill, giggling and catcalling.

"I recognized Jack with the bat in his hand, and I was not surprised. I suppose he was about nine years old then. Well, I snatched up that ball and marched right out there. And did those children run! Except for Jack. He didn't even look worried."

"That sounds like Jack Mickelson," said Corinne.

"He was just as cheerful as could be! 'Thanks for bringing my ball back, Mrs. Fryt!' he said. 'Sorry I hit it through your window.'"

Dolly laughed in spite of herself, thinking, *I'd like to meet Jack Mickelson.*

"'You ought to be ashamed of yourself!' I told him. But he just plucked that ball from me like he was picking a blueberry, and he said, 'I'm sorry, Mrs. Fryt. Send my dad the bill; he'll pay you for the window.'"

"Those Mickelsons and their money," Judy sniffed, with a little sneer of her bright pink lips.

"Yes," Mrs. Fryt said. "I wasn't about to let him get away with that. I asked to see his mother. So he called for Wilma, and when she appeared, wouldn't you know, she was wiping her hands on an apron.

Trying to keep up appearances! Even though everyone knew she didn't do a lick of work around that house—she had two maids and a cook!—and spent all day playing that piano. If only I could have had the luxury. You ladies remember, she had that haughty nose, and the corners of her mouth turned down even when she didn't intend to frown!

"Well, she came down the steps, holding her head high that way she did. You should have seen the dress she was wearing that afternoon: a high-necked sky-blue thing that looked like it wanted to go to tea with the Vanderbilts. You ladies remember the clothes she wore. Never a thing not custom made for her down at the Style Shoppe. Not until the thirties, anyway; maybe she started shopping at Birnbaum's and Penney's then."

"I'm sure she did," said Thelma.

"Well, do you know what she said, when I told her what had happened? She just looked at me and said, 'Jack is getting awfully good at baseball!'"

Dolly laughed with the others.

But Mrs. Fryt frowned. "It was Wilma that did the family in, I'm convinced of it. Almost before it even began."

"You can't blame her entirely," Corinne said.

"Well," said Mrs. Fryt, "I can tell you this much: When Wilma came to town as John's bride, and old Knute gave her and John that house as a wedding present, that was what opened up the rift between John and his brother, Gust."

"That couldn't have been Wilma's fault," Thelma said.

"Well, as I heard it," Mrs. Fryt said, "she didn't do a thing to try to ease the situation. I suppose she felt the house was her due. And then she cast her spell on Gust! You can bet that didn't help matters. Batting her eyes at her own brother-in-law."

"That was never proven," Corinne said.

"It was clear in his face. I'll never forget, I was walking downtown one day, and Wilma was ahead of me. She started up the steps to the bank, and just at that moment, Gust burst out the door. The minute he saw Wilma, he turned white. He'd been about to slam his hat onto his head, and all of a sudden he was struggling to tip it at Wilma! And, by the way, she was out to there with his brother's child! I kept walking, but I heard what he said to her, and the way he said it. 'W-Wilma! What a pleasure to see you.'"

"What did she say to him?" Dolly asked.

"She said his name, that was all, and 'Good day.' But, when I turned to look, she was blushing. It was her tone—low and cool but sweet as honey. She knew how he felt as well as I did."

Corinne sighed. "Remember that pin-striped suit from Chicago, and that gray felt bowler Gust always wore? And that beautiful carriage of his? When he drove down the street, you couldn't help but stand on your tiptoes to watch him as long as you could. And he never married!"

"Well, he was in love with Wilma," Mrs. Fryt insisted. "Why would he marry anyone else?"

"I can't believe that of Gust," said Corinne.

"Maybe the curse made him do it," Judy said.

"What curse?" Dolly asked, sitting up straight.

"Judy," Jeannette said.

The ladies studied the quilt, focusing on their stitching.

Mrs. Fryt sighed. "The story goes that some Indian chief's young daughter is buried on that hill, and the old chief put a spell on the land to keep folks off it. He said that great sorrow would come to anyone who disturbed his daughter's resting place, and it would be the deepest kind of sorrow—that caused by love." She shook her head. "Of course, Knute Mickelson didn't pay any mind to the rumors, he just went ahead and built that ridiculous house. And his wife died three months after they moved in."

I won't tell Byron, that's all, Dolly thought quickly.

"But no one knows if the story about the curse is true," Corinne said.

"Well, I for one wouldn't live in that house for all the money in the world," Judy sniffed.

"I'm sure all it needs is someone to really love it," Dolly insisted.

"Oh, they loved it, all right," Mrs. Fryt said. "And you can see where it got them."

THE MICKELSON HOUSE
502 W. First Street, Pine Rapids
March 1897

Wilma's body was utterly, painfully out of her control.

Always, she had cultivated a cautious relationship with it, distrusting it, doing her utmost to keep it in check. It frequently got out of hand when she played the piano, becoming possessed by the music, swaying and moving and breathing with far too much relish and zest. A delicious feeling, in truth, but the minute she stopped playing, she would feel ashamed, and resolve not to let the music get the best of her the next time.

But now her body's rebellion was more horrifying than ever. It had grown huge, distorted. It desired unseemly amounts of foods she had never cared for. It was too ungainly even to sleep in, and when she walked, she felt she was being pulled behind a royal entity with a will of its own. Each day when the maid Terese laced Wilma into her

dreadful "maternity corset," a complicated contraption with five separate sets of laces on the back, front, and sides, the maid was forced
to lace it a little looser around Wilma's midsection, which continued
to expand without Wilma's consent.

The worst thing about her condition was that she could hardly
play the piano. She could hardly reach it! Not a decent range, anyway. This morning, in the middle of practicing her scales, she'd
screamed in frustration, pounded the keys, and collapsed in tears
onto the piano's sturdy forehead, pressing her own temple there as
though it were a lover with whom she was trying desperately to re-
gain a past understanding. Terese had come to inquire, and suggested
Wilma go for a walk, to clear her head. "It's a lovely day out, ma'am,
quite warm, and I'm sure you'd feel better getting some fresh air.
You've been cooped up in the house all winter! Perhaps just a short
walk around the block; mind you don't go downtown and let folks
see you in your condition."

Wilma scarcely heard Terese's admonition: Cooped up, why, yes,
she had been! For months, she had endured the strict supervision of
Dr. Seguin. This was at John's insistence; most of the well-off ladies in
town waited until the last possible moment to consult a doctor, for
modesty's sake. Those who were not so well off dispensed with the
doctor altogether and consulted a midwife when the time came.
Wilma knew that most other women worked until the last possible
moment, but the doctor had suggested it would be a good idea for
Wilma to rest a good portion of each day, warning her especially not
to excite herself too much with her music. She did her best to follow
his orders, but playing the piano was another appetite over which she
had no control—just as now she could not hold herself back from the
lure of fresh air.

As Terese helped her on with her cape and her favorite green hat,
Wilma said, "You'll do me the favor of not mentioning this to Mr.
Mickelson, won't you?"

"Oh, yes," said the maid, the gray skin around her eyes wrinkling
kindly, as she saw Wilma to the door. "I know just how you feel." A
widow with five grown children of her own, who had been unable to
afford to keep her farm after her husband had died, Terese was the senior of the two maids and Wilma's favorite of the household staff.
Two immigrant girls, one Norwegian and one Swedish, were laun-

dress and cook, and there was a yard man named Nathaniel, whom Wilma avoided at all costs. He was in charge of the cistern, the boilers, and all the mysterious things in the basement, plus the horse and carriage, the grounds, the plumbing, the gas lamps—all the things that Wilma considered John's domain to supervise (indeed, John's father, Knute, supervised most such matters). Wilma stuck to the more feminine areas, and Terese was kind enough to coach her through the daily struggles of managing the household: planning the meals, overseeing the household budget, making sure that the staff was always busy accomplishing their duties, and in the proper priority.

Even when Wilma was feeling ill due to her pregnancy, she always spent two or three hours each morning, after John left for work, with her lists and ledgers, then met with Terese, who would communicate Wilma's wishes to the rest of the staff—to Wilma's relief, since the girls spoke only a little English. Sometimes Wilma supposed that Terese, to shield Wilma from the worst of the work, made many of the inconsequential decisions herself. That was fine with Wilma—she wished she could hand over all the headache-inducing, monotonous duties. Keeping the house had never interested her; even when she'd been young and her mother had tried to teach her certain crucial skills, Wilma had always had her mind on Chopin or Mozart, and had rushed off to the piano the moment her mother released her, with not a second thought to what she had just been told.

Now there were many days when Wilma, sweating over a ledger, staining her fingers with ink, hated herself for being fool enough to marry so soon, when she could have continued to study the piano. Darn her sister, anyway—she'd made her fear becoming an old maid!

If only Wilma had known the headaches involved in married life. For example, if the dinner table wasn't properly set—golden flatware properly aligned with the bottom of the gold-rimmed plate, gold-rimmed goblet set to the proper angle of the plate, and so on—Wilma's father-in-law, Knute, would raise his eyebrows and say, "I see you haven't got those kitchen girls trained yet, then, Wilma." He was awfully particular, Wilma thought, for a man who, according to his stories, had eaten off the same tin plate for six months in the woods every winter when he was young, with his pocketknife his only utensil. Now he liked things to be just so—to prove all he had achieved, Wilma supposed—and it seemed impossible to please him.

And then there was the matter of pleasing her husband! If the menu didn't vary enough from day to day—too many rutabagas night after night come January, for example—John would be sure to complain. Never mind that he expected her to achieve these spectacularly varied menus on a limited allowance, and had lectured her on the importance of never letting a morsel of food go to waste. She didn't think it was her fault if rutabagas were the only thing piled sky-high in the root cellar, while everything else had dwindled. But of course it was, they told her. It was all a question of management! Of planning!

Nearly every day she imagined packing her trunks and getting on the train to Appleton. She was certain the college would let her back in! She could just pretend that her marriage had all been a bad dream.

If not for the problem of the baby on the way.

Wilma stepped out onto the front porch and relished the warmth of the sun. As the door shut behind her, she put the worries of the household out of her mind and, beginning to imagine a theme from Beethoven's Sonata Pathétique, determined to enjoy the beauty of the new spring, which was lovely even in a town as ugly as Pine Rapids. She knew John and Knute weren't altogether happy to see spring arrive, since it meant the end of the cutting season in the forests, and huge payouts to the men who had labored for them logging all winter. This was the busiest time of year at the mill, though, and profits would follow once the felled trees had been processed.

In the distance upriver, Wilma could see the mill's smoke, and she could hear its noises, too: the pounding of the logs being shoved about, the high whine of the saws, the shouts of men and the slapping sound of the planks being stacked one on top of another. The Bear Trap River had thawed in places and the slate-colored water sparkled as it tripped over icy rocks. Last week there had been a blizzard, but today all the snow was melting into the streets and the walks and the river, and, just as Wilma made her way down the porch steps, a robin hopped across the walk in front of her, then lifted itself in flight. The baby kicked in her belly. "Hush, now, baby," she whispered, breathing in the spring-silver air. "We're going downtown. Maybe we'll order some spring dresses for Momma to wear after you're born!" She was suddenly desperate for at least a glance at something really stylish, if such a thing could even be found in Pine Rapids.

The weight of her belly threatened to topple her as she proceeded down the stone steps with her spine held stiff by her corset, but the warmth of the sun on her face was pleasing, and she went delicately. It seemed easy to forget discontents, on such a lovely spring day, and to remember only hopes and dreams. Soon, her shoes were clicking down the boardwalk, and her steps felt light, despite the ache in her back, the heaviness in her middle. The only sound was the river babbling its way around the rocks. On the hill in front of the houses on First Street, the brown earth was peeking through the melting snow, and patches of purple crocus bloomed. This spring, John had told her, the Pine Rapids Beautification Committee was distributing grass seed to every homeowner in town, and Knute Mickelson had donated money for a stump removal crew to clear the main thoroughfares—as it was, winter was the only time when people could travel easily. Sleighs glided easily over roads packed with snow, whereas in spring, the muddy, rutted, stump-pocked roads became nearly impassable. The drier seasons of summer and fall were only slightly better. Whatever improvements could be made would certainly be a relief, Wilma thought—after having grown up in well-settled Kaukauna in the east-central part of the state, Pine Rapids still seemed to her like an uncivilized frontier.

As she approached downtown, there came on the breeze the smell of thawing horse manure, and the sounds of bells jingling, carriage wheels jouncing through the muddy gravel, horses whinnying, voices calling across the street or down the block—and then it all came into view: the red stone buildings, the throngs of traffic, the businessmen in dark suits and bowlers, the draymen in working clothes, and the women in creations of all colors, many with hats rising from their heads like the plumes of birds. Wilma straightened her own hat and pinched her cheeks. She had been so excited at the prospect of an outing that she had forgotten to look in the mirror to see that everything was in order. She had forgotten that she had an image to maintain, as the wife of one of the most important businessmen in town. No matter what language they spoke—and Wilma could still hardly identify all the different languages that could be heard in Pine Rapids, including but not limited to Norwegian, Danish, Swedish, Polish, Menominee, and a great deal of German—Wilma knew everybody talked about the Mickelsons.

She glanced over at the bank on the opposite side of the street, hoping that John wouldn't happen to look out his office window and see her pass by. Then she recognized Gust's horse tethered outside.

Gust rarely came to the house, and when he did, he, John, and their father, Knute, would argue about business, the bank, the mill, their voices growing louder and louder, until Wilma could stand it no more and would excuse herself to the parlor and the piano. Yet, even as the noise of her music drowned the men out, her ears would perk up when Gust's voice came through: "... just don't see how you can ..."; "... if only you'd look at it from the other ..."

She never intended to listen for his voice, but she couldn't seem to stop herself. When he was near, she did her best to avoid so much as looking at him—not to the point of being rude, but she did try to remain distant. Yet, she so enjoyed the sight of him. She knew that if she wasn't careful she could lose herself for hours in just examining the whorls of his hair, the highlights of blond over light brown, and, in wintertime, dark brown; the unruly perfection of it as it tickled the tops of his ears and the back of his neck. She knew she could lose herself in his eyes, too, pinwheels of silver-blue. She had prayed for God to put the same light in John's eyes, but so far He had not. He was challenging her to sin, she supposed. He was challenging the frog.

The baby kicked. "Shall we go see your uncle Gust, Baby?" Wilma whispered. "Kick once for yes and twice for no."

The baby kicked once. (The baby always kicked only once, then paused, then kicked again, but no matter: She was crossing the street.)

She squared her shoulders and, clutching her handbag in one hand, lifted her skirt an inch in front with the other, as though that would keep the street's mud from getting on it. Her only intent was to catch a glimpse of him, and there wasn't anything wrong with that. Half the women she knew (church women, no less, and just as married as Wilma herself) would have crossed *town* for a glimpse of Gust Mickelson, and all Wilma was doing was crossing the street.

Her foot was on the bank's bottom step when Gust burst out of the door, his face flushed, jamming his hat onto his head. When he saw her, he stopped. "W-Wilma!" he said, fumbling with his hat. "I— what a pleasure to see you."

Someone brushed behind Wilma, passing her. Gust was standing so close, only two steps above her (now one! as he moved even closer, turning his hat around in his hands). "Gust," she said. "Good day." And she hurried up the steps, brushing past him, into the refuge of the bank, damning the frog that had so shamelessly sought him out.

The door swung shut behind her, and a lady customer, two men conversing in the corner, and the young cashier all turned their eyes toward her.

"Mrs. Mickelson," the cashier said. "You're here to see Mr. Mickelson? He's in a meeting with Mr. Mickelson, or, his father, I mean, but I can see if—"

"Oh, no!" Wilma said. "Please don't disturb him." She suspected they could see straight to the bottom of her heart.

But instead of her heart, they were looking right at her stomach. Through the folds of her cape, they could see the shape of her body. "I was just out for a walk, some air," she said, gathering her cape around her, turning to push the door open again. "Please don't disturb him."

Immediate relief: the fresh air cooled her cheeks. But then Gust was there, at the bottom of the steps. When he saw her, he smiled. She would have turned to go back into the bank had that not seemed an even more fearful choice than facing him. Oh, that he should see her in this condition—heavy with his brother's child and yet utterly foolish over him! What had she been thinking?

But she smiled, started down the steps toward him. *Steady, steady.*

"Wilma!" he said. "I wondered if you might not be too long."

"I—yes, John was meeting with your father."

"Yah," he said, with a rueful smile. "I was in that meeting until a moment ago."

She laughed. Perhaps he didn't know her feelings, and she could skate around them, even make them disappear. "So I had supposed," she said.

"In any case," he said, "seeing you reminded me of a matter I need to discuss with you."

"A matter?"

"Yah," he said. He touched her elbow and guided her down the stairs. "May I walk you home?" he said. "We can discuss it on the way, then."

"Yes," Wilma said. After all, she really didn't *need* to go shopping.

He put out his arm for her to take, and led her back across First

Street. It seemed she could feel the heat of his skin through his shirt and coat, her gloves.

Her shoes were clicking on the boardwalk again when he said, "It's about the baby, Wilma." His tone was grave, and set her to worrying immediately.

"What about the baby?"

"My brother tells me he's certain it will be a boy, and that he's planning to name him Junior."

"Yes, John James Mickelson, Junior." John had insisted on it.

"All due respect, Wilma, you can't saddle a baby with the name Junior," Gust said. "Poor child won't have a chance, then. God forbid he wants to do anything other than follow in his father's footsteps."

Wilma laughed a little and, without exactly realizing it, settled more heavily on Gust's arm. They were out of downtown now, and the houses were rising away from the sidewalk, up the hill. "I hardly think so, Gust."

He rested his hand atop hers; her heart gave a little lurch. "Wilma," he said, "don't you ever feel you're too young to have the whole of your life set out before you?"

Wilma hesitated. "Sometimes, I suppose."

"Godsakes, Wilma, I'm only twenty-two, and you're twenty-one, and chances are, twenty years from now, I'll still be working at the mill, and you'll still be living in that house and married to my brother. Only that baby will be almost as old as we are now, and maybe he'll have his whole life set out for him, too, then. He'll have the office next door to John's. Especially if he's called Junior!"

Wilma said nothing.

"Can I tell you a secret, Wilma?"

"A secret?"

"I'm restless, Wilma. I went to a dance over in Victor last weekend, and do you know I couldn't find a girl pretty enough to suit me, even to dance with?"

Something in her burned. "Of course you need a girl."

"I think I should leave this town, Wilma, and go far away from here. California. Alaska, even."

"Oh, Gust, no, you couldn't!" Then she realized what she had said. Her shoes clicked along the walk; *do not do not do not,* she repeated to herself, all the way to the bottom of the steps that led up to the Mickelson house.

They stopped there. He took her hands in his. "Stay and be uncle to your children?" he said. "And the second son?"

"Every child needs an uncle, don't they?"

He did not smile; his eyes were sharp and bright.

"Besides," she went on quickly, "it's only a matter of time before they let you have your way with the mill. John is so interested in the bank, and your father's so busy with his real estate. I overheard them talking, and your father said he thought you ought to be given full authority at the mill."

"And what did John say, then?"

Wilma looked down at their hands entwined together. "He said you were too young, and too reckless."

"I had no doubt."

"But your father will convince him, I'm sure of it."

"And what about the rest?" he said. "What do I do about not being able to find a girl pretty enough to dance with because I compare them all to you?"

She drew in her breath.

He let go of her hands, and stepped back. "Forgive me—God-sakes." He took off his hat and ran a hand through his curls.

She recovered quickly; she had to. "Oh, Gust, you're just teasing me!" She was doing her best to swim to the shore of convention, to keep from drowning in his eyes.

He smiled then, relieved. "Don't you know," he said, pretending along with her. He replaced his hat, and offered his arm to her again; she took it, and they started up the steps to the house. "And how do you think that line will work on the ladies, then?"

"Oh, wonderful!" she said, laboring up the steps. "You'll be married in a fortnight."

Though she invited him in, he bid her good-bye on the front porch. "Forgive me," he said, and she shivered at the light in his eyes. She watched him as he ran down the steps. When he reached the bottom, he turned and tipped his hat to her, then broke away into a run. The Bear Trap River babbled in the distance, and the baby in her belly kicked. *Do not*, she told herself again, and turned to go into the house, shedding her cloak, desperate to return to her piano.

The Family Hostess' Creed

Happy family relationships are part of my responsibility;
therefore—I will save enough energy to do the job of being a
happy and helpful hostess to my family day after day.

—*The Modern Family Cook Book*, 1942

PINE RAPIDS WOMEN'S CLUB MEETING
Thursday, June 29, 1950

The ladies insisted that Dolly join the Pine Rapids Women's Club,
which, according to Mrs. Fryt, had evolved out of the original Beautification Committee. "One day we noticed Pine Rapids didn't look
so bad," she explained. "So we decided we could branch out. It was
during the thirties; we raised money for needy children and such."
And, during the recent war, she told Dolly, the Women's Club had
sold an amazing ten thousand dollars' worth of war bonds.

The meetings were held the last Thursday of each month at the
town hall. Dolly was a little concerned about throwing off her schedule at home—Thursdays were when she cleaned house, and she
needed at least six hours to do everything properly—but she supposed that if the other ladies could take time away from their homes,
she could figure out how to make things work, too. Besides, all the

magazines said that community work could be a homemaker's saving grace, and after nearly two months in Pine Rapids, away from the companionship of her mother, sisters, and friends in Battle Point, Dolly was beginning to think she just might need a saving grace soon.

Mrs. Fryt was the president of the Women's Club, and, to start the meeting, she led the ladies in a rousing contralto with the singing of "Lend a Hand," a song she had composed based on the group's motto. Not knowing the words, Dolly contented herself with listening, steeling herself to be introduced. There must have been twenty ladies there, and most looked to be at least twice her age.

Only two years out of high school, and I'm already middle-aged, Dolly thought. She had actually discovered a gray hair this morning, which she had quickly attributed to an argument she'd had with Byron the previous evening.

Swiss steak, steamed carrots, and mashed potatoes with gravy had been the menu for the evening—followed by an apple pie made with a Pillsbury pie-crust mix and served with a slice of cheese. Byron hadn't seemed to notice, wolfing down his food without a word. His pie gone, he leaned back in his chair, knotting his hands behind his head. "Well, think I'll go out to the garage, Doll," he said.

She stood to pick up his dessert plate and bring it to the sink. "What did you think of supper, Byron?" she asked. She had spent a good twenty minutes tenderizing the meat; little specks of beef had littered the counter, the walls, even the floor, when she was done. Another twenty minutes had been devoted to peeling and chopping the apples for the pie.

"It was good," he said. "I always like what you make, you know that."

"Well, it would be nice if you said so," she said, sinking his plate into the dishwater. She had been enticed to buy the pie-crust mix by an ad she'd seen in *Good Housekeeping,* which promised in bold letters "'You wonderful, wonderful woman'—that's what he'll say when he tastes your APPLE PIE and CHEESE." It wasn't that she really believed the ad in a literal sense, but whenever she saw slogans like that, she just couldn't seem to stop herself from hoping that this would be the thing that would make Byron realize that everything she did was because she loved him and needed to know that he loved her, too.

"What's that, Doll?"

"You never notice how hard I'm trying," she said, hating the fact that she was close to tears. Tomorrow, she thought blackly, he'd probably go tell his business partner, Roy Ostrem, that Dolly had gone hysterical.

"I do," he protested. "I'd just like to get out to the garage. I've got to get my lures organized—I'm going fishing with Roy on Sunday, and my tackle box is a mess."

Dolly held the plate down in the dishwater like she was trying to drown it. "You don't see enough of him the other six days of the week?"

"You can come, if you want," he said. "We're going up to Pelican Lake and put his boat in the water. He wouldn't mind if you came along. Maybe he'd like to bring his wife, too."

"I was hoping we could go on a picnic together, just the two of us. A drive in the country."

"I'm sorry, Doll," he said. "I already made plans. But, if you want to come, maybe you could bring a picnic for all of us."

Dolly finally let go of the plate and took her hands from the dishwater. She could see it was futile to try to make him understand. Taking a deep breath, she dried her hands on her apron, then stepped across the kitchen and sank down at the table again. She wished she had a cigarette. "Oh, Byron," she sighed.

"What's the matter?"

It was a moment before she could speak. "I guess I just want a baby," she said. It seemed much easier to say that one true-enough thing than to try explaining the whole mess of feelings that had welled up in her—feelings she didn't even understand herself and that had suddenly made her feel all but hopeless.

Because this much was certainly true: On Tuesday night, after Byron had fallen asleep, she had gone into the hideously wallpapered bathroom and—in direct defiance of her every recent prayer—discovered blood.

She had been brought up not to question God and His plans, but she was beginning to think He had some explaining to do.

Byron got up from his chair and came around to kneel beside her. He touched her face, and kissed her lightly. "It'll happen soon, Doll," he said, smiling that smile she liked. "Want to give it a try right now?"

Men!

With the song's end, Mrs. Fryt ahemed, and introduced Dolly, then added, "I hope you ladies will take the opportunity to meet Dolly at the break or after the meeting. Next month we'll vote on the matter of her membership."

Dolly smiled weakly at the group. She hadn't been told her membership would be subject to a *vote*.

Sure enough, both at the break and during the post-meeting coffee, one lady after another made a point of meeting her and sounding out her level of commitment to the Pine Rapids Women's Club.

She was so glad to see a familiar face when Corinne Olson came up to her that she clutched Corinne's hand and took a deep breath, savoring the comforting grandmother-scent of Corinne's powder.

"How are you holding up?" Corinne asked.

Though Dolly put on a smile, she wished that Byron had never brought her to this town. Back in Battle Point, everyone knew her. She was Dr. Bronson's third daughter! Rose was the wild one, Lily was the serious one, Jasmine was the baby, and Dolly was known as "the bright one," though she had never been certain if that referred to her brains or her lipstick.

"Don't worry, Dolly, you're a shoo-in," Corinne said. "The vote is just a formality."

"That's what everyone said when I was up for homecoming queen," Dolly said. "And I lost to Betty Bowers, because she was dating Harold Anders, and everyone wanted him for king."

Dolly had never found the incident humorous, but Corinne laughed and laughed and said, "You poor girl."

Dolly walked home feeling lonelier than ever. As she kneaded together the evening's meat loaf, she watered it with two fat tears, and when Byron sat down to it later, he raved about it; somehow, that only made her feel worse.

I won't be placated, she thought, later that evening, as she stood out on the back stoop in her nightgown smoking a cigarette, the chill of the night raising the hair on her arms. She hadn't been able to sleep; Byron's steady breathing had aggravated her even more. That he could sleep, when she was so unhappy! *What's the matter, Byron?* she thought, looking up at the moon.

Married life is serious business, as living always is, but it is easier and at the same time more rewarding than single life. To be human is to be lonely. To be successfully married is to have an inner bulwark against loneliness.

—*The Good Housekeeping Marriage Book*, 1939

HOME OF BYRON AND DOLLY MAGNUSON

406 Jefferson Avenue, Pine Rapids

Tuesday, July 4, 1950

"Hurry up, Doll, Roy's got the car running, and they aren't gonna wait those fireworks for us," Byron hollered from the front room.

Dolly met her own eyes in the bathroom mirror. She could see the awful wallpaper behind her in the reflection—Byron still hadn't purchased the white paint he'd promised. She made up her mind.

She flipped off the light and went out to meet him. He looked handsome and relaxed, his collar open, his face flushed. He and Roy had been drinking beer just about nonstop since five o'clock, and the combination of their loud chatter and the shrieking of Roy's wife and two children had given Dolly a first-class headache.

"Byron," she said, "I—I'm not feeling very well. Why don't you go on without me?"

"What do you mean?"

"Really, Byron, I—I've got a headache and I just don't—I think I'd just like to get some sleep. You go on with Roy and Susie and have a good time."

"Are you sure, Doll? The fireworks only come once a year. And Susie's going to be disappointed not to have another girl along."

"I know, but—"

Outside, Roy blasted his horn.

"Really, Byron, you go ahead."

With a mournful look, he squeezed her hand. "Well, if you really don't want to go," he pouted.

She watched through the curtains and breathed a sigh of relief when the car pulled out of the driveway. She'd had about all she could take of the Ostrems and their curly-headed cherubs. It had been Byron's bright idea to invite them over to celebrate the Fourth—"It's about time you get some friends your own age in this town, Doll," he'd told her—after he and Roy had had a grand time out fishing on Sunday. Of course, they hadn't brought any fish home. Byron said they'd thrown them all back, but Dolly doubted whether they'd even cast their lines in the water. Judging from their performance tonight, they had probably been too busy drinking beer and talking about Chryslers and their old buddies from the war.

And if Susie Ostrem was all she had to choose from for friends her own age, Dolly thought she'd rather stick with the older women of the Ladies Aid. The evening had been interminable. While their husbands engaged in enthusiastic debate about the most outstanding features of their Chryslers, Dolly and Susie conducted a faltering conversation about the many uses for hamburger. And when the younger toddler smeared a handful of Dolly's Sunshine Salad on the kitchen wall, Susie had only laughed and, as she picked up the offending youngster to give him a kiss, said to Dolly, "Oh, you know how it is! If you don't have eyes in the back of your head—!" Bouncing the child on one arm, she had dabbed at the stain with a napkin, then gestured to the poppies. "Well, good thing you have such busy wallpaper!" It was the final straw.

As soon as the car was out of sight, Dolly let the curtain fall and made a beeline for her cigarettes. She went out on the back stoop to smoke. Looking up at the stars, she began to feel better, though she missed her family terribly. She had always gone to the fireworks with her sisters and Jane, after a picnic at the lake with her parents—fried chicken, potato salad, and chocolate cake. Tonight, Byron had insisted on barbecuing the chicken on his new grill. He had burned it, and that was the beginning of the end as far as Dolly was concerned. She supposed it was nice that Byron and Roy were such close friends, but she hated that she was expected to become friends with Roy's hideous wife. If this was Byron's idea of a new Fourth of July tradition, she wanted none of it. Not to mention that the holiday had thrown her whole housekeeping schedule off track, and now she would spend the rest of the week feeling off-kilter.

She stubbed out her cigarette and lit a second one—she deserved it, she thought—as the night slowly enveloped her. She was just about done with her cigarette and, with her headache feeling better, ready to go inside to *Cherry Ames, Night Supervisor*—she didn't care if the books were juvenile, at least Cherry had *adventure* in her life—when she heard the first blast of the fireworks. She was suddenly struck with a wave of loneliness, and then she got mad. That despicable Susie Ostrem was keeping her from seeing the fireworks! She dropped her cigarette and ground it out with her shoe. She walked around to the front yard, but when another firework bloomed in the sky, she knew she would have to get closer to see over the trees.

Her feet made no sound as she walked. Each time there was another explosion, cheers and applause wafted through the quiet streets and over the treetops. She walked faster, stretching herself tall to try to see. Once she was past the courthouse, she decided there wouldn't be any harm in going another block closer.

Then she realized where she would have the best view, while still avoiding the crowd: on top of the hill where the Mickelson house stood.

She had intended only to watch from the yard, but once she got there, she found that the garage, a large birch tree, and the row of shrubs at the southern edge of the property obscured her view, so she climbed up on the back porch stoop for added height, certain that Wilma Mickelson wouldn't have minded. She noticed with a twinge of anguish that, although the lawn was clipped short, the Peterson boy obviously didn't trouble about the flower beds around the house; they were thick with overgrown irises and choked with weeds.

As another red floret bloomed and faded, a cloud scooted past the moon, and a breeze rustled the leaves and Dolly's hair. Her headache gone entirely now, she breathed as deeply as she could and leaned back against the house, raising her chin toward another bright burst. The handle of the screen door prodded her back. She turned toward it, and considered it. She glanced down the hill and across the street to Mrs. Fryt's house; no light was on. To the other side was nothing but a row of fir trees and, past that, an open field.

She pulled on the handle. The screen door swung open without a peep. She grasped the glass knob of the storm door, and her stomach gave a little flip when the knob turned without resistance. *If it isn't locked, then I'm not really "breaking in,"* she told herself, and she pushed hard on the door.

It was with greater trepidation that, some time later, Dolly quietly opened the door to her own dark bungalow. The fireworks must have ended ages ago; Dolly had forgotten to pay attention. She'd been entranced by the shadow-filled rooms of the Mickelson house: the specters of covered furniture, the gentle murmur of the breeze that came in through a broken dining room window. She'd even found dusty photographs on the mantel, though in the dimness she hadn't been able to discern the shadowy faces.

"Doll?"

As Dolly's eyes adjusted, she saw Byron rising from the living room chair.

"Doll, where the hell have you been?" He came toward her.

"Oh, Byron, I'm sorry. I—I couldn't sleep, and I went out for a walk. I just—lost track of time."

"I was worried to death about you, Doll," he said. "And tonight of all nights, when there's all these drunks out running around, for you to go out by yourself! You've got to think, sometimes, Doll. Jesus Christ." He sighed deeply, then took her into his arms. He smelled of anxiety and beer. "Don't ever do that to me again."

"I won't," she said, her voice muffled in his chest.

"Now come to bed," he commanded, and she followed him.

THE MICKELSON HOUSE
502 W. First Street, Pine Rapids
July 4, 1897

After the baby—a boy—arrived, the unseemliness of Wilma's body was unbearable.

Each time she hobbled to the lavatory, she would discover brownish blood. More than once, the maid Terese had found her curled on the bathroom floor, done in not so much by the sight of the blood but by the hopeless conviction that it would never stop coming. This might have gone on for days, or weeks; she didn't know. Time had taken on a curious elasticity, a meaninglessness that she quietly savored. The Sonata Pathétique ran through her mind over and over, yet her hands felt too heavy to move. She had forsaken her household management duties, and did not even go down to dinner to defend the table settings; Terese only consulted her on major questions. Terese took care of the baby, too.

Wilma had been torn badly, Dr. Seguin had said, wiping his hands when the ordeal was over. He prescribed rest, and seemed remarkably unconcerned, once Terese had taken the squalling baby away. Wilma herself was certain that she had come close to death, and, day after day, in those weeks following the trauma, would shiver at the visceral recollection of her body raging, splitting in two, while the baby tore from her with a force she would not have thought possible. She was horrified, too, to recall her own screaming, the way she had surrendered her sensibilities—clearly breaking Rule Number Four, to ignore or at least not mention physical discomfort. She wondered how she would ever face the doctor again—or anyone, for that matter—now that it was clear she was not the lady she had always pretended to be, but merely an animal.

Whenever John ventured into the room to sit on the edge of the bed and rest his hand near (but never touching) her, she would pretend to be asleep, and keep her head turned from him, though the scent of his cologne made it impossible to pretend that he wasn't there. He would stay for a few minutes, perhaps say her name. Finally, with a sigh, he would give up, and leave her. Then she would open her eyes and study the pattern of the wallpaper, the swirls of vining roses. Her flesh ached, dreading that he would soon decide that she had been given sufficient respite from her wifely duties. Dreading, too, the moment when Terese would bring the fussing baby to her and demand that she bare herself to him like a mother pig, or cat, or dog, and let him eat off her until both her nipples were raw, for the milk of one small breast was never enough to satisfy John James Mickelson, Junior.

A month after the baby's birth, Dr. Seguin had begun to insist that she was perfectly healthy, that she ought to get out of bed and ease back into her normal routine. But Wilma couldn't muster a compelling reason to do so. From what she could tell, the household was functioning just fine without her. Her sole responsibility seemed to be to feed that rapidly growing baby, and that she could accomplish just fine in her bed.

But this morning, John had burst in on her and demanded she get dressed. He wanted his son to see the Fourth of July parade.

"You take him, John," she said, nestling deeper into her pillow, willing the music in her mind to drown him out.

"You have to come, Wilma," John said. "I've bought a carriage for Jack. We'll wheel him down and watch from the bank steps. It would look ridiculous if you weren't there. People are already starting to talk, wondering why they haven't seen you or the baby out." His tone turned petulant. "I want them to see Jack."

Wilma kept her eyes closed, and didn't answer, hoping he would give up and leave her alone, as he had on other occasions. She tried to please him; she meant to, anyway. But sometimes he seemed to ask so much.

"I'll send Terese to help you dress," he said, with an air of finality, and she heard his footsteps going away, the door click shut behind him.

So it was that by ten o'clock she was standing on the bank's bottom step in last year's dress and summer hat, squinting against the sun. Laced to her pre-baby size, the maternity corset was excruciating. She had begged Terese to loosen it, but the dress—a high-collared, elaborately trimmed affair with a bell-shaped skirt and sleeves that billowed out from the shoulders and gathered again in tight cuffs that reached halfway up the forearms—would not have fit her.

Jack slept soundly in the wicker carriage parked on the sidewalk in front of her, while John rolled it slowly back and forth, fielding the admirers who came up to peer in the carriage and exclaim over Jack. Wilma didn't recognize most of them, and she was too exhausted to try to remember their names, too embarrassed to meet their eyes. She imagined they knew the way she had screamed, the way she had bled. She tried to remember Chopin's Waltz in B Minor, closing her eyes briefly, allowing her fingers to press against the sides of her skirt to mime it. But her mind stumbled, couldn't recall.

She opened her eyes to see one of the few neighbors that she did know charging across the dusty street toward them. It was Cecilia Fryt, trailing in her wake her brown-bearded husband, Amos, who owned the hardware store. Cecilia was a tall woman, and, though Amos was taller, he always appeared stooped, compared to his wife. Cecilia wore a hat with a great plume of peacock feathers; the bellowlike sleeves on her dress made her shoulders look broad as a man's.

"Amos Fryt!" boomed John.

The man nodded in response, only the twitch of his beard betraying a smile.

"So this is the blessed mystery child," sniffed Cecilia, feathers tee-tering as she examined the baby in his carriage. "I was beginning to wonder if we'd ever see him."

"Well," John said, reaching up to rest his hand on Wilma's shoul-der, "here he is now. Wilma hasn't been feeling too well."

Cecilia's eyes bore into Wilma's. Wilma, feeling light-headed, re-called dimly that, just before Jack was born, someone at the Lutheran church had whispered that Cecilia had recently lost a baby some three months into a pregnancy. "But you know Cecilia," the church-goer had said, with a note of admiration in her voice. "She was right back out shoveling her walk the next day. In spite of what Dr. Seguin might have told her. She doesn't believe in pain, that one."

Wilma put out her chin. "I'm fine now."

"Yes, she's very well now," John said. "And have you ever seen a more handsome child?"

Cecilia looked down at the baby. "He certainly is large, for his age," she said. "Hopefully he won't turn out to be heavy." This with a glance at John's waistline, which had unquestionably widened, this past year.

Wilma sensed John step back, speechless.

"We'd best go, Cici, so you'll be on time," Amos said.

"Oh, yes," said Cecilia, with a pointed look at Wilma. "I'm carry-ing the banner for the Beautification Committee."

Wilma knotted her hands. She knew the things people said about her: that she was "too high on her horse" to notice the needs of the "common folk" and actually do something for Pine Rapids. Certain things were presumed of the wives of the town's businessmen, partic-ularly of a woman like Wilma who had household help, and Wilma had not conformed. But she had been indisposed since the day she'd arrived, with the business of having a child!

Wilma looked up and saw the peacock feathers moving away through the crowd. Of course! Cecilia Fryt always had to have the last word.

Then Wilma saw Gust, crossing the avenue toward them. She had not seen him since before Jack was born. Shamefully, though, she had dreamed of him—even, sometimes, when she was half awake. *Mean-ingless,* she had assured herself at the time. But now the sight of him made her mouth go dry. She was conscious of sweat forming under her arms.

Unaware of Gust's approach, John was talking to a couple that Wilma vaguely recognized from the church, bragging about baby Jack.

"Wilma," said Gust, as he came near. Removing his hat, he stopped before her. His curls shone in the sunlight. "It's so nice to see you up and about, then."

"Hello, Gust."

"And how's my nephew?" he said, peering over the hood of the carriage. "Sleeping soundly, I see." His movement caught John's attention, and the two men greeted each other, John quickly resuming his conversation with the couple from church.

"He's fine," Wilma said. "Thank you."

"And you're feeling well?"

"Fine, thank you," she said, though she was dizzy and short of breath; her corset was so tight!

For a moment, there seemed nothing more to say; their eyes remained locked. "I was sorry," he said finally, "that when I came to the house you were indisposed."

"You were at the house?" Wilma said.

He frowned. "Several times. You wouldn't think I'd miss seeing my nephew, now, would you? He's quite something."

"He is?" she said, then caught herself. "Oh, yes! Yes, of course. Thank you."

Gust grinned. "Jack."

She smiled. "Yes. Jack." Her smile faded; she fought the sudden, inexplicable urge to weep.

A fire wagon, pulled by six black horses shaking their manes and stomping their hooves, was leading the approaching parade.

Gust stepped up next to her, and turned toward the street. *Oh, don't—don't,* she told herself, but it was far too late. The clanging of the fire bell and the shouts of the crowd and the drumbeats of the eight-member Pine Rapids High School band grew louder and louder, and then her legs gave way, and all went black.

When she came to, she was stretched flat on a cool marble floor. Looking up into the dimness of the room, she recognized the pattern of the pressed tin ceiling. The bank. John was crouched next to her, and Gust on her other side. "Thank God, Wilma, you're all right,"

John said. "You fainted. Thank God Gust caught you. I'm sorry I brought you out today. I thought you'd feel better if you got out."

Wilma looked up at Gust. He had caught her!

He smiled. There was an unidentifiable quiver in his eyes.

John patted her shoulder, and got to his feet. "We'll go home now, Wilma. You just rest a moment, and gather your strength. I'm going to check on Jack. I left him with the Olsons, but I don't like having him out of our sight." She heard him walk away across the marble. The heavy door opened, letting in the sounds of the parade. When it closed again, the quiet was like a salve.

Wilma closed her eyes briefly. "I'm so ashamed."

Gust said nothing.

"I wish—" she began.

"Wilma," he said.

She clenched her fists against all that was welling inside her. *Steady, steady.* A tear escaped her closed eye. Still, he did not touch her. When John returned, Gust stood back while John helped her to her feet.

I wish I had known it when you had your arms around me, was what she had come so close to saying. *I wish I could know what it felt like.*

But back out into the heat and noise, teetering along under John's arm, to where their baby slept on.

HOME OF MRS. CECILIA FRYT
412 W. First Street, Pine Rapids
Tuesday, July 11, 1950

"I was wondering," Dolly said, as soon as the ladies were settled and
stitching in Mrs. Fryt's parlor. "Do you think there's any truth to
what you told me about the Mickelson house? About it being cursed,
I mean?"

Ever since her late-night adventure on the Fourth of July, Dolly
had felt lost in the dream of that wonderful house. At the oddest
times, she would recall herself back into the shadowy rooms, just as
during algebra class her senior year she had (without necessarily
meaning to) recalled herself back into Saturday night and Byron's
arms. She had felt so comfortable being in the house, she simply
couldn't believe that there was anything so menacing as a curse lurking about it.

"You just won't let that family rest in peace, will you?" Mrs. Fryt grumbled. Mrs. Fryt had grudgingly allowed the group to cancel their meeting the week before, since it had fallen on a holiday, and now she seemed to resent them all for slackers, ushering them briskly into the parlor and bidding them to get straight to work on the quilt. The room was stuffy today, despite the windows being open; the ladies and the spider plants all drooped more than usual.

"Well," Corinne said, "all we know for certain, Dolly, is that the family did have more than their share of sorrows."

"They were arrogant," Mrs. Fryt snapped. "Had no sense of their own human imperfections! That was why. And I can tell you to the day when that house started to crumble. It was the day Jack Mickelson decided to drag his brother Chase off to enlist in the First World War."

"They were heroes!" Jeannette said, surprisingly animated, among murmurs of disagreement.

Mrs. Fryt harrumphed. "Yes, heroes, of course. We all know it, and if we don't, someone else will say it to us until we do. But I still say, if Jack hadn't been so bent on outdoing everybody in town by enlisting the very day that war was declared—" She held up a hand to quiet objections. "I know, some people say he shouldn't be blamed. But I was there, and I don't see how we *couldn't* blame him. Taking Chase out of high school that way!"

"It was the bravest thing they could have done," Jeannette said.

But Mrs. Fryt turned to Dolly. "The day the boys decided to enlist, it was Good Friday—this would have been 1917. I was down at Tomsovik's Flower Shop choosing an Easter lily. Well, here comes Wilma Mickelson in the door. I still remember what she was wearing: a dress that reminded me of a silver maple leaf. Green lace over silver silk. You would never have seen that dress on anyone in this town except for Wilma. And she wore it like it was everyday! With her fancy gray coat open over it. She had a broad-brimmed hat to match, too, and even her shoes were that particular green. To wear such shoes in mud season—I couldn't understand it. Well, in she comes, with Chase trailing behind her. He had his hands shoved in his pockets and his cap pulled down low over his eyes. He was a senior in high school that year, and he always looked like he had a secret he could tell."

"Goodness," Dolly said, imagining.

"He drew wonderful cartoons for the school paper," Jeannette said, her voice low again.

"Well," Mrs. Fryt went on. "That Wilma. It wasn't enough for her to get a simple Easter lily like the rest of us. She ordered a dozen yellow roses, a dozen white roses, and three Easter lilies. She hadn't seen me when she came in, but I went right up to her. I must have asked her if she was planning to come to the Good Friday services. So what did she do but call out to Mr. Tomsovik to make it five Easter lilies. 'Two for the church,' she said. 'To set by the altar.'"

"She always was generous," Thelma put in.

Mrs. Fryt rolled her eyes. "Well, just then, the door slammed open—I still remember how loudly the bells on it jingled! And here was Jack Mickelson, skidding to a stop. I'll never forget the way he looked that day, his hair slicked back and his necktie off-kilter. I tell you, my Jeannette wasn't the only girl in the class of 1916 who spent hours fixing herself up, hoping for a second glance from him."

"Mother!"

Corinne laughed. "Even I remember that smile he had, back before the war," she said. "I was a married woman by that time, but it was dazzling."

"Well, that was the smile he was smiling that day at Tomsovik's, I daresay," said Mrs. Fryt. "A smile like he could conquer the world. And then I saw he was holding the newspaper, and I knew what he'd come for.

"He didn't have a word for his mother or me. He held up the newspaper, looked straight at his brother, and said, 'They've done it. I'm enlisting.'

"And then the littlest smile twitched on Chase's face. 'All right,' he said. 'I'll go, too.' They must have been talking about it all week long, with the president and Congress making the steps toward war.

"You should have seen the look on Wilma's face," Mrs. Fryt went on. "She went white as cream. Then, quick as that, she turned pink, and stomped her foot. She demanded to know what they were talking about, but she knew perfectly well. As though Jack didn't get his arrogance from her! Those boys left on Monday, the day after Easter, for the recruiting office, to take the tests and whatnot."

"Poor Wilma," said Thelma, shaking her head.

"Well," said Corinne, "you remember she was quick enough to turn her back on everyone whenever she didn't need us."

"I'm sure she didn't mean anything bad toward us," Thelma said. "She knit more than anyone for the Red Cross committee during the Second World War."

"Some little good it did when she didn't pay any attention to the quotas," Mrs. Fryt said. "The national chapter would put out a call for scarves, and she'd come to me with three sweaters! I was hard put to explain to the higher-ups where all our chapter's yarn was going, when we weren't meeting their quotas."

"I think she just hated this town," said Corinne. "And she hated every one of us for being part of it."

"Oh, but she tried so hard," Thelma objected.

"Don't you remember the way she was?" Mrs. Fryt said. "Letting those children run wild? Not caring what anyone thought? As though living in that house on a hill made her—well, there's no other way to say it—she thought she was better than everyone else. It was scandalous. I'd never believe she was brought up Lutheran."

Corinne laughed, then said, "Speaking of children running wild. Did you ladies hear what happened on the Fourth out at the Gronziks' farm? A bunch of kids were out there late at night pushing over the poor cows. Mr. Gronzik says he ran out there after them but all he saw were the taillights, and the poor cows on the ground."

"Mercy me," exclaimed Mrs. Fryt, and a discussion followed on the heathen qualities of the younger generation. More terrible to Dolly than what they were saying about the younger generation was the fact that they didn't seem to consider her a part of it.

"Well, I guess I really am old," she told Byron that night at supper, over the whir of the fan in the window. The skies had been darkening all afternoon, and the kitchen was dusky, but Dolly didn't want to add extra heat by turning on the light—it was bad enough she'd had to have the oven on to bake potatoes au gratin. They were having fried pork chops and green beans, too, and even as she had executed the menu, Dolly had cringed over its banality. She had planned on making stuffed pork chops instead, but, once again, the quilting meeting had sapped her verve.

He laughed. "Old? You? I don't think so, Doll. Besides, if you're old, what does that make me?"

"Ancient," she said, and whimsically flung a potato slice from her fork at his chest. It made a satisfying thwack.

He looked down at the cheesy smear on his shirt, and picked up the potato from his lap with an air of weariness. "Doll," he said. "What's gotten into you?"

She leaned back in her chair, sulking. "Nothing, Byron."

He stood up from the table and began unbuttoning his shirt. "You'd better wash this right away, so the stain doesn't set. Good thing I had my napkin on my lap, or you'd have to do my pants, too."

Suddenly, there was a great boom of thunder, and the skies opened like a dam had burst.

Byron cursed, and lunged across the kitchen to unplug the fan and yank it from the window. He slammed the window shut. Dolly leapt up, too; in a moment, tearing around the house, they managed to close everything tight, and then stood panting in the dimness of the living room, listening to the pounding of the rain on the roof. It reminded Dolly of home, of Battle Point, and she laughed. Byron, his au gratined shirt gaping open over his undershirt, laughed, too, and ran his hand through his hair, which had gotten a little wet in his battle with the windows. Ever since those days at the beach when she was sixteen, Dolly had always found him irresistible when wet.

Unfortunately, even as he removed his shirt to reveal shoulders good enough to make a girl go slack-jawed, his only thought was of the errant au gratin potato. "Here you go, Doll," he said, holding his shirt out to her. "Maybe you could get that cheese out, before it's too late."

A moment of incredulity passed, then she snatched the shirt from him and stomped to the basement.

PINE RAPIDS MESSENGER
Friday evening, April 6, 1917

UNITED STATES DECLARES WAR AGAINST GERMANY

WORLD INFORMED OF ACTION AS
WILSON SIGNS DOCUMENT

WASHINGTON, APRIL 6.—War was declared at 1.13 o'clock this afternoon.

At exactly that hour President Wilson signed the joint resolution passed by the House of Representatives and by the Senate declaring a state of war between the United States and Germany.

An hour before, the resolution was signed by Vice President Marshall, at 12.13.

These were the last formalities necessary to make the United States an ally of England, France, and Russia in the world war of democracies against autocracy. . . .

TOMSOVIK'S FLOWER SHOP
209 E. First Street, Pine Rapids
Friday, April 6, 1917

When her son Chase announced, "I'll go, too," Wilma suddenly re-called the circus she had been to as a girl: the cacophony of calliope and shrieks; the pungent scents of popcorn, sawdust, and the steaming piles that trailed the elephants; and the sequined lady who had balanced prettily on the bare back of a black horse as it galloped round and round the ring. Across the distance under the big top, the lady's gleaming smile was all that was discernible, but as the horse pranced toward Wilma's place in the grandstand, the noise of its hooves growing deafening, Wilma could see the trembling of the leg on which the performer was poised, and lines of impossible strain between her eyes.

Looking at her two sons amidst the buckets of tulips and carnations, their determined eyes locked with each other's, she suddenly knew how the woman had felt.

Steady, steady, she told herself. "What are you boys talking about?"

The matching blond heads turned toward her; their eyes were placid blue pools.

They were unfathomable, these boys, though they had been born out of her.

"Boys," she said.

They shrank in their boots, just slightly; their eyes crinkled.

"Wait for Mr. Tomsovik to get my order ready, and then bring the flowers home." Her heels clicked as she crossed to the door. "You may send my husband the bill, Mr. Tomsovik," she called, not looking back, as she stepped out onto the sidewalk.

Just like the bareback rider, Wilma thought, her brave performance was belied by trembling knees. The April air cooled her fiery cheeks; she tightened her clutch on her handbag. The muddy street was filled with cars, wagons and horses, shouting men waving newspapers, some of them cursing in German. Women were hurrying to finish their Easter shopping, palely proceeding under the pretense of nothing being out of the ordinary. *I will not faint,* Wilma told herself. She began walking toward home, her heels tapping steadily on the boardwalk, doing her best to focus on the difficult piece she had been working on lately, Chopin's Sonata No. 2 in B-flat Minor. She had first heard it in college when her instructor had played it, and she'd been working up to it ever since, finally beginning on the first movement last fall. It was that movement she rehearsed in her mind now: the resonant early chords, then the ominous theme that required the lightest touch yet the greatest intensity as fingers tangled and danced to create the most gorgeous of nightmares, with a beat like a frightened heart.

But she couldn't help thinking: *I should have known it would come to this.* The boys going to the war. It was payment for her sins.

She had always especially dreaded that some harm would come to Chase. God knew she had a bond with him that she did not have with her other children, and she supposed that He did not think well of her, as a result.

But she should have known it would come to this! She had never been able to stop Jack from dragging Chase along with him on all manner of adventures, from the time they were small: fishing, skiing, sledding, skating, sailing. When they got older, it was football, basketball, baseball, the two brothers competing to see which could outdo the other.

Chase's competitive spirit waned whenever he wasn't in direct competition with Jack; Wilma sensed that he actually preferred the solitude of his pencil and notebook. She had several of his drawings posted on her vanity mirror in her bedroom. Her favorite was a caricature of the family that he'd presented to her for Mother's Day last year, showing Wilma seated in a chair haughtily beautiful, John standing behind her impressively pompous, Jack and Chase assembled gawkily in baseball caps, Harry with hair standing on end, Jinny perched on the arm of her mother's chair. *Our Family, 1916,* he'd written in his block letters. *For Mom. Love, Chase.*

Chase kept his passion to himself; he was like Wilma with her piano in that way. Jack probably didn't even see it. And now Jack was going to drag Chase off to the war!

She stepped out into Main Avenue without looking, drawing an angry honk from a motorist. Two grinning young men ran past her, one waving the newspaper, the other shouting, "Down with the kaiser!" Their footfalls splashed mud on her skirt.

A knock at the parlor door interrupted the driving beat, the movement of Wilma's hands. When she lifted her fingers from the keys, the sudden silence pounded in her ears. "Yes?" she said.

The new maid slid the pocket door open just wide enough to put her head in. "Dinner is ready, ma'am," she said, her accent thickly Norwegian.

"Is my husband home?" Wilma asked.

"Yes, and the boys, too, ma'am."

Wilma thought there was something odd about the girl's tone, and she looked to see that the maid was blushing. She was a young girl, perhaps twenty, and too pretty, with curly golden hair and bright eyes.

Wilma wished for the thousandth time that Terese had not become too elderly to work. She was tired of these silly young maids, who came off the impoverished farms where they'd grown up, and all too easily got fancy ideas about their wealthy employer's sons. "You're discharged," she told the girl, hands still poised above the keyboard. "You may come to collect your pay in the morning."

"Mrs.—?"

"You heard me. We won't be needing you any longer."

The girl stifled a sob, and slid the door shut, leaving Wilma alone again.

She was glad she hadn't troubled to learn the girl's name. She took a deep breath and shook her head, trying to clear it. She wanted to prepare herself to argue rationally with the boys. Surely there was some way to convince them not to go.

She had to, because she had given her life for them already. Every time she'd looked out the parlor window and dreamed that her piano was on a stage and thought of the money her father had left her when he died—money she had managed to keep a secret from John by leaving it with her father's advisers—and thought of walking out of this house and not looking back, she had stopped herself. She loved her children, and her dreams were withered like old fruit, anyway. It was only the piano that made her think such scandalous things. She would force herself to get up then, to attend to the children, the drudgery of running the house, overseeing the evening's meal.

When Jack was nine, he had once caught Wilma seated at the piano in post-sonata reverie, and he'd said, "What's wrong, Mom?" She had resolved then not to play unless the parlor door was closed, shutting out the family, so they could not see that she was not what she had always pretended. She did not want them to perceive that mutinous part of her that yearned for escape. She did not want them to see that her love for them had been holding her hostage in this town, this house, for more than twenty years.

How dare those boys leave her now?

There was another knock at the door. "Mom?" It was Chase.

"Come in," she said, turning eagerly.

Chase slid open the door and stood in its frame, his hands shoved in his pockets. His handsome, narrow face hadn't changed a bit since he was about eight years old; he'd just kept growing taller and thinner, straight as a white pine.

"Is everything all right, Mom? Brita just about ran me over out there, and she was crying."

Wilma turned her back to him, straightening her music. "She's terribly upset about you boys leaving."

"Oh," he said. He sighed. "Are you coming in to dinner, Mom?"

When she looked at him again, her heart lurched, and she said, "You won't go, will you, Chasey? You're only telling Jack that to make him happy, and then you'll tell him at the last minute that you won't go?"

His blue eyes clouded over. "I've got to go, Mom," he said. Then he grinned. "Heck, someone's got to look out for Jack, and see he doesn't get himself into trouble."

She frowned, and cursed herself for not being more savvy. She might have been able to manipulate him, if she had controlled her outburst!

"We'll be fine, Mom, don't worry," Chase said. "Besides, it wouldn't be fair to let all the other boys do all the work, and us sit back and watch." Still with his hands in his pockets, he gestured with his elbow for her to come on. "Dinner's getting cold, Mom," he said, and turned away.

Wilma shook her head again. *Please,* she prayed.

It struck her that God might not recognize her.

Please, she began again, trying to sound like herself. *Not my boys.*

She got to her feet. She would work on Jack. If Jack didn't go, then surely Chase wouldn't, either.

Steady, steady, she told herself. She walked to the parlor door, bracing herself on the doorjamb a moment before crossing the threshold and heading for the dining room.

Surprise your husband with an occasional token of affection,
whether it be an unexpected kiss or a little gift
from the ten cent store or newsstand.

—"Making Marriage Work,"
Ladies' Home Journal, January 1950

THE MICKELSON HOUSE
502 W. First Street, Pine Rapids
Wednesday, July 12, 1950

Just as Dolly had feared, the rain had blown in through the broken
bay window in the Mickelsons' dining room, left a puddle on the
hardwood floor, and soaked through the large rug under the table besides.

Last night, after six tears had fallen on Byron's au gratined shirt
while Dolly removed the cheese stain, she had gone upstairs to towel
dry the windowsills. Even though she and Byron had closed the windows as quickly as they could, some of the sills had still gotten wet,
and she was wiping off the sill behind Byron's chair, where he sat
reading the newspaper, when it occurred to her what shape the Mickelson house must be in. The breeze that had been so pleasant the
night she had been in the house would translate into awful damage
with such a rain.

Though her potato indiscretion had slightly derailed her plan to persuade Byron to look into buying the house, Dolly was confident she could get things back on track. So it was that, after she had finished wiping down the windowsills, she went into the bathroom to freshen up. As always, the sight of the wallpaper made her furious, but she perfumed and fluffed her hair, reapplied her Mum deodorant and her lipstick, put on her best Hollywood starlet nightgown, and then went out to say to Byron, "Are you coming to bed?"

And so it was that, just after noon today—having rushed through the meal planning and food shopping this morning, cheating by stealing the coming week's menu wholesale off last year's calendar, the first week in June—she had slung a book bag full of rags and supplies over her shoulder and set out for the Pine Rapids Carnegie Library. At the front desk, she stopped to inquire where the back issues of the *Ladies' Home Journal* were, and requested that the stoop-shouldered librarian help her carry a tall stack to a desk in the back corner. "I'll probably be here all day," she told the woman. "I've got so much catching up to do!" It was a needlessly elaborate ruse, perhaps, but Dolly had read enough Nancy Drew to know that establishing an alibi was never a bad idea.

After the librarian had been gone a few minutes, Dolly left the magazines where they were, picked up her bag, headed down the hall past the restrooms, and slipped outside through the custodian's door. She knew that Mrs. Fryt always had lunch with the Homemakers' Club on Wednesdays, but she was still nervous about being spotted. Not wanting to appear suspicious, she made her strides even and purposeful as she walked the few blocks from the library. Then she hurried up the hill and straight in the back door of the Mickelson house.

Like a wealthy old widow dressed up for a ball, the house had been shown to its best advantage in the shadows of evening. In daylight, it was dismaying. Knowing she didn't have much time, Dolly passed straight through the dusty kitchen and into the dining room, going to work on the wet floor with the haste of an emergency room nurse. After she sopped up the standing water, though, she found disheartening evidence that this was not the first rainstorm the broken window had endured. As Mrs. Fryt had suspected, it seemed obvious that, at least since Mr. Wojtas had died, no one had checked on the inside of the house. The floor's finish was all but ruined, and, when

Dolly flipped up the corner of the saturated rug, she found that its underside and the floor underneath were dark with mold. The chair at the head of the table was destroyed, too, its golden shot silk upholstery splotched with brown patches, the wood spotted with white like a cancer.

"Sometimes you have to cut a part out to save the rest," she remembered her father telling her, but this cancer was too far gone. Even the end of the grand mahogany table was mottled with white spots. Dolly thought it was despicable that the Mickelson family had let the house go like this.

At the very least, though, she could try to prevent further damage; it would make her life much easier once Byron bought the house. She wiped dry the aged windowsill and frame, then dug in her bag, glad she'd thought to bring her hammer, tacks, scissors, and the Koroseal Strawtex fabric she had purchased with the intent of reupholstering Byron's favorite chair. Of course, when she'd showed him the Strawtex, he had laughed and said, "Baby-blue plastic? On my chair? I don't think so, Doll." (This although he was supposedly in favor of having a modern home!) Well, she was grateful now; it would be just the thing to keep the Mickelson house dry.

When the work of covering the window was done and her tools put away, Dolly sighed and took a long look around the dining room. It was plain that even during Mr. Wojtas's tenure as caretaker, he had not loved the house, only tolerated it. Perhaps he had provided it with the bare essentials—heat in the winter, a patch here or there in the plaster, as though tossing a thoughtless plate of raw hamburger to a caged lion—but clearly he'd had no real regard for the house's well-being. From the ruined rug, which was a rich pattern of gold and brown and beige, all the way up to the golden chandelier that hung dripping with cobwebs above the table, the room was all gold and should have glimmered. A rich wood—now dulled and dusty—ran halfway up the walls, framed the doors and windows, and formed a built-in buffet along the wall to Dolly's right; above the wainscoting, the walls were papered a watery gold to match the chairs' upholstery. Opposite Dolly, at the other end of the long table, was an opalescent marble fireplace; a golden candelabra, its candles tipped at drunken angles, stood sentinel on the mantel. Dust on the glass of the buffet and the cabinet that stood in the far corner obscured the dishes still stacked inside. Dolly stepped over to the buffet and pulled open one of its doors. She crouched down to examine the white china rimmed in gold, the gilded tureens, the golden sauceboats, running her fingers over their smoothness, imagining the parties that must have gone on in this house, the music, the dancing. She imagined the triumph of serving coffee to the Ladies Aid using such china. It wouldn't be as great as flying an airplane, but at least Byron wouldn't disapprove.

Another moment found her in the living room, examining the photographs on the mantel there, now that the daylight afforded her a better perception. There were six photographs altogether, four large and two smaller. She assumed that the four large ones were of the Mickelson children, and she picked out Jack and Chase in their old-fashioned uniforms, drawing in her breath at the sight of Jack's smooth jaw, long-lashed eyes, and heavy mouth. No wonder the girls had all been nuts about him. Chase had a narrower face and mouth, and an impenetrable look in his bright eyes. The third boy, with a narrow face like Chase's, blond hair that stood up thick and straight over his forehead, and a smile that said he was up to no good, must have been Harry. The beautiful blond girl with her eyes narrowed at the camera had to be Jinny. The smaller photos, one of a handsome dark-haired boy with a reckless smile in a World War II Marine uniform, the other of a pleasant-looking girl with a rosebud mouth and curly blond hair, clearly were not as old, but it was a mystery to Dolly who they could be. Wilma's grandchildren, perhaps? Dolly would have to find a way to ask Mrs. Fryt.

The rest of the living room, though it had not been rained on, looked nearly as forlorn as the dining room. The sofa and chairs were draped with white sheets, now gray with dust. Dolly's eyes swept over the photographs on the mantel. "How could you?" she said, and she made up her mind: This family, wherever they were, and whatever had happened, did not deserve such a fine house. It was up to Dolly to rescue it from their neglect.

But the truth was, Byron, with his love of all things modern and clean, would never buy it in this condition.

She was going to have to fix up this house.

She thought of the very first movie she and Byron had seen together, around Christmas in 1946. It was called *It's a Wonderful Life*. In it, Donna Reed had taken a run-down old house and fixed it up for her husband, played by Jimmy Stewart, without his knowing she was doing it. But once he saw the glow that the old house had put on his wife's face, and the home that she had created for him there, of course he acquiesced to live there. It had struck Dolly particularly, sitting there in the theater on an almost-first date with the man she hoped to marry. She had thought it a wonderfully romantic thing, to make such an effort to create an ideal home for the man you loved. And now she had the chance to do just that—and this house wasn't in nearly as bad a shape as the house in the movie.

How Donna Reed had worked out the financial end of things regarding the house in the movie was not specified that Dolly could recall. Well, she would take things one step at a time. Maybe she could fix up the house without anyone knowing, and then Byron would buy it for her. In any case, the first step was to get the house in shape for him to view. It seemed clear by the state of things that none of the Mickelsons was ever going to come back.

The first thing she did was run the water in the kitchen sink until it changed from rust-colored to clear. Like Mrs. Fryt had said, the Mickelsons had kept the water connected. Now that Mr. Wojtas was dead, Dolly would have to take over his daily duties, too.

When it was time to go home to start Byron's supper, Dolly left some supplies in the Mickelsons' pantry, packed up the rest, and tossed her bag out the parlor's side window. The parlor was her favorite room in the house, with a front window that looked out over the grand front porch, and a side window that opened onto the line of fir trees on the west edge of the property. It was papered in a misty lake-blue, with brocade draperies of the same shade. The blue rug was adorned with pink roses. In the center of the room stood a dusty grand piano, and there was an old phonograph in the far corner.

With a last look over her shoulder, Dolly slipped out the window and landed in the weeds next to her bag. She had been able to remove the screen by reaching out through a gash that ran down its center, twisting its stops out of the way, and letting it fall to the ground. Now she closed the storm window almost all the way and put the screen back in place, though she could reach only to twist the bottom stops back on. Now Dolly could come and go as she pleased, not just when she knew Mrs. Fryt was away from home. She would just have to bring something to stand on to boost herself up into the house.

It was four o'clock when Dolly headed in the back door of the library. The *Ladies' Home Journal*s were just where she had left them, and, after she sat for a moment to catch her breath, she gathered them up and brought them through the stacks to the librarian's desk, handing them over with a smile.

"Did you find what you were looking for?" the woman asked.

"Oh, yes, thank you!" Dolly said. "But I've so much more to learn—I'll be back!"

THE MICKELSON HOUSE
502 W. First Street, Pine Rapids
Friday, April 6, 1917

"Jinny," Wilma said, taking her place at the end of the table opposite from her husband, "you'll serve the dinner, please." For nearly twenty years now, at every meal, Wilma had sat with her back to the window, while John sat with his back to the fireplace; the children filled in like pegs around the table that glimmered with gold-rimmed china and goblets and golden flatware—Jack and Chase on Wilma's left, Harry and Jinny to her right, nearest the kitchen. Today, Wilma's view of John was partly obscured by a large arrangement of Easter flowers; more flowers bedecked the mantel behind him. Today, Wilma could feel her family crumbling into dust.

Jinny, who was eleven ("and a half," she would add), shook her bright blond head. "Mom, that's applesauce. Where's Brita? Or Cook? Or Thora?"

Her brothers laughed, and her father tried to look stern but didn't succeed. Wilma had talked to them all repeatedly about not encouraging Jinny's impish behavior, but to no avail.

"First of all, young lady, I am quite certain that dinner is more than applesauce," Wilma said. "I discharged Brita, and Cook and Thora have gone home early today."

"Aw, Mom! Not Brita!" said Harry. His blond hair was standing on end, as usual. Wilma had wrestled with that hair for years, and now that she had given its care over to its owner, he had little more success with it, despite frequent liberal applications of his older brothers' pomades.

Jack and Chase laughed, but they looked disappointed, too; Wilma was glad she had made the decision. She didn't know what she had been thinking, to hire someone so pretty in the first place, with all these boys in the house.

"Wilma," her husband said. "I wish you would discuss these matters with me before acting so quickly."

"What about discussing them with me?" Harry grumbled.

"That's the third one you've discharged this year, and we're barely into April," John continued.

"Poor Hare," Jack joshed his brother.

Harry's eyes flashed up. "Hey, I think she was starting to like me."

"When pigs fly!" Jinny said.

Harry reached over to thwack her with his middle finger.

"Children!" Wilma said. There was silence, and she took a deep breath. "Now, we'll say grace, and then Jinny will serve dinner. We have to go to church at seven o'clock."

Wilma looked at Chase, then bowed her head. She tried to listen while John said the prayer, but when he said something about a just war and a swift victory, she could listen no more.

The instant he was through, Harry's voice broke in. "Our victory would be swifter if I could go, too," he said. "Can I, Mom?"

Wilma held her breath.

"If I pretended I was sixteen, you could sign a paper for me, couldn't you? I could pass for sixteen."

"Like nothing," Jinny said.

"Jinny, please get the food," Wilma said, keeping her eyes on her daughter until the girl stood and went through the swinging door into the kitchen. Then Wilma turned to her youngest son. With effort, she kept her tone even. "Don't be ridiculous, Harry. You're only fourteen, not sixteen. Even if you were sixteen I'd hardly sign for you. I'm having a hard enough time thinking that Chase is old enough to go."

"I'm eighteen, Mom," Chase said.

"In the nick of time!" Jack said, grinning. They had just celebrated Chase's birthday four days before.

"You were born prematurely," Wilma snapped. "If you'd been born when you were supposed to have been, in May, you would still be seventeen, and we wouldn't be having this discussion."

"Mom, he's plenty old enough," Jack said. "Besides, isn't it best we go together? If he'd been born in May, he'd just be going next month, that's all. Or he'd be asking you to sign for him."

"Well, he could at least wait until he graduates high school," Wilma said. A flimsy argument, but her head ached and she could hardly think. She wanted simply to stand on her chair and scream bloody murder until they agreed not to leave her.

But then, looking at them, the square of their jaws, the glint in their matching eyes, she realized there was nothing she could say to Jack to change his mind. And unless he did, Chase was going to go, too.

John cleared his throat. "This is his chance to make history, not just learn about it."

Wilma glared at him. "I suppose you're all for their going!" she scoffed. "You men and your wars! Making history!"

"Mom!" shouted Jinny from the kitchen. "I can't find the serving fork!"

As Wilma got up, John said, "It's the way of the world, Wilma."

She slammed open the swinging kitchen door with the flat of her hand. It was all she could do to keep from weeping.

Homes should mean something to us humans. They are a
basic instinct. A home, with a life that centers only on food
and sleep, is not really a home, it's a house. Beauty and
graciousness, joy of living, being used in every part,
these are the things that make a house a home.

—*Popular Home Decoration*, 1940

HOME OF MRS. CECILIA FRYT
412 W. First Street, Pine Rapids
Tuesday, July 18, 1950

It was even warmer in Mrs. Fryt's parlor than it had been the week
before; the smell of the ladies' powder hung heavy in the air. Dolly
imagined that the only thing saving them from suffocation was the
hot whisper of breeze that occasionally rustled the spider plants. She
wished that Mrs. Fryt would turn on a fan, but Corinne had already
said that Mrs. Fryt, believing that fans circulated germs, didn't even
own one. As a nod to the heat, though, she had provided the ladies
with glasses of ice water—anything else might have been the pur-
veyor of disaster if spilled on the quilt. With much grumbling about
the humidity, the ladies settled into their stitching, and soon the only
sound was an occasional clinking of ice cubes when someone took a
drink.

Right away, Dolly noticed that someone—Mrs. Fryt, she assumed—had removed Dolly's stitches from last time and re-quilted all three of the triangles Dolly had spent the previous meeting working on—the blue and white plaid, the green and white polka dot, the brown and red floral. Of course, no one said anything, but it was obvious the ladies felt her work substandard. Touching the tiny replacement stitches, and looking at the many-colored landscape of the quilt, at the places the ladies had completed to create perfectly mounded little triangles within each separate triangle of fabric, Dolly could see their point. She was determined to get better, though, and she got to work on a red and white gingham piece.

Despite the heat and her frustrating lack of quilting talent, Dolly wasn't about to get discouraged. She felt as puffed up as someone newly, secretly in love. She had sneaked into the Mickelson house again on Friday—she hadn't had anything too pressing at the bungalow; Friday was her day to finish anything she hadn't managed to get to during the week, plus bake cookies and a cake, and do general shopping, and she didn't *need* to do any of that. She had spent the afternoon dusting and oiling the woodwork in the Mickelson dining room, cleaning the glass of the buffet and china cabinet, polishing the marble fireplace, knocking down cobwebs from the chandelier, and daydreaming about what living in the house would be like. When she was done cleaning, she thought the room nearly fit for a dinner party, except for the upholstery and dusty rug. Well, she wasn't about to start reupholstering things just now, and she couldn't find a vacuum in the house. She didn't know how she would possibly sneak even her Bissell sweeper, much less her vacuum, across town, so she was resigned to leaving things as they were for now. Tomorrow, she planned to tackle the parlor.

While in the house, taking breaks between tasks, she had spent more time in the living room contemplating the photographs on the mantel. She couldn't understand how all of Wilma's children could have forsaken this house—and what about those two unknown faces? The boy in the Marine uniform could hardly be older than Byron. What had happened to him? Why wasn't he here in Pine Rapids?

She looked at the ladies bent over the quilt, and cleared her throat lightly. "Did Wilma Mickelson have grandchildren?" she asked.

"Here we go again!" Corinne laughed.

Mrs. Fryt looked up from the quilt, and trained her caterpillar eyes on Dolly. "Why, yes, of course. Wilma's oldest son Jack had two children, JJ and Elissa."

JJ and Elissa. The boy and the girl in the photographs. "So Jack came home from the First World War, and he was all right? And he went on to marry and have children? Who did he marry? Where are they all now? Why don't they live in the house?"

The ladies exchanged glances. "So many questions!" Corinne said.

"Yes, one thing at a time," Mrs. Fryt said.

"You know," mused Thelma, "for some time you would have almost thought that everything was going to be all right."

"That the curse was lifted," Jeannette added.

"JJ and Elissa—Jack's children—were certainly beautiful," Thelma went on. "And Wilma and John doted on them, as grandparents do. I remember Wilma telling me about JJ, when he was about six, walking all the way across town one day to show her a frog he'd found on the riverbank. I suppose that was more than twenty years ago now! Wilma said that when she saw that frog cupped so carefully in JJ's hands, she thought it was a message from God. It seemed like, after that, she had such a light in her eyes. Especially when JJ was near her."

"JJ joined the Marines right after the attack on Pearl Harbor in 1941," Corinne told Dolly. "He wanted to do just like his father Jack had done back in 1917, when the First World War broke out."

"JJ *was* like Jack," Mrs. Fryt said. "He had the same arrogance, the same sense of entitlement."

"The same charm," Corinne added.

"Yes, JJ was a handsome boy," admitted Mrs. Fryt. "The type whose smile sends them tumbling like lawn bowls. Isn't that right, Judy? Of course, not that his charm was any good to the family—"

"For heaven's sake, Grandma," Judy broke in, her pie-crust face inflamed. "It wasn't JJ's fault. It was his awful sister, Elissa! She tore open that family just the same as if she'd taken a set of pinking shears to it! It was that boy she met during the war!"

"Oh, but she couldn't have known!" objected Thelma.

"She seemed like the sweetest thing," Corinne put in, shaking her head. "The last one you'd expect to do anything to hurt her own family."

"She wasn't sweet at all," snapped Judy. She jabbed her needle into the quilt. "She always *pretended*."

THE BABYLON BALLROOM
La Crosse, Wisconsin
Saturday, February 13, 1943

The ballroom was hot-packed with soldiers and girls, swirling, turn-ing, swinging, stomping, to music as glint-bright as the trumpets, trombones, saxophones, of the band on the red-spangled stage under blazing lights. More than one of the uniformed boys was inclined to lift his partner above his head, then swing her down suddenly, legs knifing between legs, then just as quickly lift her up face-to-face again, his smile bright in her vision. There she'd find herself clutched tight and breathless in his arms, until he spun her out again in a twirl, her skirt flaring. Oh, they were good dancers, these soldiers! The best Elissa Mickelson had ever seen. Boys from Pine Rapids were apt to drop a girl, attempting such moves.

"I told you it was the limit, didn't I?" said Betty, the cousin of Elissa's friend Muriel. Betty, a La Crosse native, had invited the Pine

Rapids girls Elissa and Muriel down to La Crosse to experience the Babylon Ballroom, and she now grabbed Elissa's elbow. Of Muriel there was, at the moment, no sign.

"Oh, yes!" Elissa shouted, still overwhelmed by the sight of it all, though they had been there more than an hour. Inside a frame of elegant arched porticos, the dance floor pulsed with the heat and movement of several hundred people, the dazzling sounds of Ben Greten and his orchestra flooding the place to the farthest corners of the viewing balcony.

A soldier appeared in front of her out of the crowd, a smile on his pink face. "Like to dance?" he said. Before she could so much as nod, he had grabbed Elissa and pulled her out onto the floor. At the mercy of his sweaty hands, she twisted, turned, and dipped, and the stranger who held her waist laughed above the music like he'd unearthed buried treasure.

"You'll love it," Muriel had promised Elissa, presenting her cousin Betty's offer last week. Elissa had lived her whole life in Pine Rapids in the house her parents had built on Rapids Avenue, and was lately considering redecorating her room. She was a senior in high school, and she'd just turned eighteen, yet her white wrought-iron bed still had a pink ruffled spread on it, and the white vanity where she was sitting had a pink-cushioned stool. Then there was the white-painted chest of drawers, the deeply piled white rug with only inches of hardwood floor peeking out around its edges. The curtains were sheer white, with pink roses on them. Elissa's doll collection was prominent on shelves above the dresser and nightstand. Elissa supposed that Betty Grable's room was much more elegant, yet a part of her didn't want to change a thing. She loved the feel of the cushy rug under her toes when she got up in the morning; still said good night to her dolls sometimes.

"Betty says there's no shortage of partners," Muriel had continued. "Every girl gets to dance as much as she likes. And they're *sweet*, too, she says. The Second Infantry Division! From the South, all of them! With those accents! Can you just imagine?" At this she had flopped back on Elissa's bed, disturbing Elissa's snoozing cat, Homer.

"Well, Muriel, I'd like to go," Elissa said, studying herself in the vanity mirror: Was that a blemish coming on? "But I doubt my dad would let me."

Muriel rolled onto her side and, resting her chin in her hand, lifted her eyes to the ceiling. "Oh, your father! When's he going to realize he can't keep you buried in this town forever?" Homer jumped down from the bed, padded across the room, pawed open the door, and made his exit, tail swishing.

It wasn't exactly fair of Muriel to say that, Elissa thought, but it was true that her parents had never taken her traveling, had never even taken her to see Chicago or Minneapolis. In fact, they never had gone anywhere at all, except to the family summer home on Lake Michigan. But that was on account of her father, Jack, having seen enough of the world to suit him when he was in the Great War. (That was just how he said it, too, if she ever asked: "I've seen enough of the world to suit me, Liss." And that was the end of that.) Now that her brother JJ was with the Marines over on Guadalcanal, she supposed she could understand her parents wanting to keep her under their thumbs, with him so far away. But she did awfully like to dance, and the idea of one-after-another dancing with soldiers was especially appealing.

"We'll just tell him we're going shopping, and staying overnight with my cousin Betty," Muriel had said, sitting up, brushing her skirt flat down over her knees. "And we *will* stay with Betty, and we *will* go shopping." She grinned. "For a dress to wear to the Babylon."

And now she was seeing the world! Seeing it suddenly, brightly, and with a certain brash confidence. Didn't the soldiers have that *way* of looking at her? That way that Pine Rapids boys, having known her since kindergarten or before, never looked at her?

Even downtown, this afternoon, after shopping at Doerflinger's (so many lovely dresses—almost overwhelming, for a girl used to Birnbaum's, downtown Pine Rapids), when they'd stopped in at a soda fountain for a malt: Three soldiers had immediately joined them, gawky, loose-limbed, laughing over the way they'd invited themselves. One—a blond roughly hewn man with an exotically droll accent (Texan, she had learned)—had taken a particular interest in Elissa and insisted on paying for her malt, fanning his wallet open so she could see the profusion of bills inside, even when she'd tried to refuse him.

"When can we see you again?" he, or one of the others, had called as the girls left, shoving arms into coats, Betty having exclaimed that they were, or would soon be, "Late! For our bus!" Betty calling back over her shoulder, "The Babylon, tonight!" All three girls giggling, running to catch their bus: such a heady excitement in the air, here in La Crosse!

So far this evening there had been no sign of those particular soldiers—but how could you find them, in such a crowd? And who cared, really, when there were so many, dressed just alike, almost all of them handsome, almost all of them looking at her that *way*?

"As though they know a little secret about me, or would like to, at least," she explained to Muriel and Betty, upstairs in the ladies' room, as they fanned themselves, refreshed their lipstick, their powder. "Don't you think?"

"Well, you're a doll, Liss!" Betty said easily. "Just look at you!"

Elissa rolled her eyes at Betty in the mirror, leaning close to apply her Crimson Blush lipstick, purchased this afternoon to match her dress, which was white with a gored skirt that flared out from her waist and ended just below her knees, with a red X of trim beginning around the neck, framing her breasts, and wrapping around to the small of her back, where it came together in a V. She would have loved to have bought a pair of red shoes to match, but she'd had to settle for wearing her familiar old black pumps, what with shoe rationing. "Some doll," she said, smoothing the golden blond curls that angled down to the sides of her neck, repinning her wavy bangs. "This hair." It had such a tendency to frizz.

"Well, I haven't noticed the boys keeping their distance from you," Betty said, without a trace of jealousy. After all, there were plenty to go around.

"Oh, boys have never been known to keep their distance from Liss," Muriel joked.

Elissa examined her red mouth critically, hoping the Crimson Blush would mask the immaturity of its form. Her mother said that she had "rosebud" lips, but Elissa thought their curves too girlish. The soldiers would probably imagine she was all of sixteen, and want nothing to do with her. Despite what Muriel said, she really hadn't had the best luck with boys to this point.

"Come on," Betty said, grabbing Elissa by the elbow and dragging her toward the door. Elissa had to strain to reach her pocketbook and grab it off the vanity. "There are soldiers in need of dance partners!"

Muriel followed. "We are here to serve!"

They made their way through the crowds on the mezzanine, where groups of soldiers and girls stood smoking and enjoying Cokes and snacks from the refreshment counter, watching the dancers below. When the girls reached the bottom of the steps, a boy was blocking their way, smiling at Elissa, and holding out his hand to her. He had black hair under his service cap, blue eyes, dimples in his cheeks. "Like to dance?" he said.

"I—I have to bring my pocketbook back to the coat check," she stammered.

"I'll bring it for you, Liss," Muriel said, taking it from her. "You go on."

"Oh, all right, Mur, thanks!" she said, and she took the soldier's hand, let him lead her into the sea of bobbing bodies. The song was "The White Cliffs of Dover," and he pulled her to him, the couples on all sides pressing them closer together than Elissa would normally have dared; a little thrill traveled up her spine as she caught a whiff of his Old Spice.

"I'm Buddy," the soldier said, with a gently Southern accent.

"Hi, Buddy," she said. "I'm Elissa."

"I ain't never seen you here before."

She smiled more deeply than she intended. "I haven't been here before. But there are so many people, how could you—"

"Oh, I'd've noticed you."

She blushed.

"Do you live in La Crosse?" Buddy asked.

"No, I'm just visiting."

"Darn," he said. "I was hoping I might get an invitation to Sunday dinner with y'all."

Elissa laughed. "I'm sorry."

"It's all right," he said. "We've got all the rest of tonight. Except, sometimes girls think you ain't serious, if you don't ask to see them on Sunday."

"It sounds like you've got quite a lot of experience."

He shrugged, gave her an adorable sideways smile. "Practice

makes perfect," he said. "But you know, you're about the most beautiful girl I seen since I left Texas."

"I suppose I hardly compare to the girls in Texas."

He grinned, and pulled her even closer.

But just as Elissa sighed contentedly, about to lose herself in him, a stocky, dark-haired man tapped Buddy on the shoulder. "I'm cutting in, private," he said.

Elissa was horrified.

Buddy scowled. "Sergeant, I ain't even had a whole song with her."

The sergeant hooked his thumb toward the edge of the dance floor. "Skedaddle, private, if you know what's good for you," he said, narrowing his eyes. He had apparently seen one too many James Cagney movies.

"I'll find you later," Buddy told Elissa, as the sergeant whisked her away.

Dancing backward, towing her along behind him, the sergeant grinned, showing discolored teeth. "Rank has its privileges, as they say," he chortled. He looked ancient, in his late twenties at least. Of all the luck. There was no way she would be able to find Buddy again, in this crowd!

"I suppose," she said politely, trying to keep the distance between them—a challenge, with the crowd pressing in.

The sergeant was dragging her far away from Buddy, toward the corner of the dance floor, and seemed to be trying to pull her closer to him, even as she strained to keep her distance. "If you don't mind, sir," she said, struggling to keep her balance.

Suddenly, he grinned, said, "Whoops!" and let her go. She stumbled backward, and bumped into somebody.

"Excuse me!" she said, turning to look over her shoulder.

The sergeant, fading into the crowd, called out, "You can thank me later, Overby!"

Just then, "The White Cliffs of Dover" ended, and, as the crowd broke out in applause, Elissa looked up into a pair of bright blue eyes that registered astonishment, then joy; then, flashing off to where the sergeant had disappeared into the crowd, irritation. Then they looked at her again and softened, and she had to catch her breath.

The soldier was tall, that was the first thing: When she'd bumped him, her shoulder had hit the middle of his triceps, and now that he'd turned around to face her, she had to tilt her chin up to look at his face. It was a good face: lean, with a strong jaw and straight nose, and a small mouth that just now was tilted in a half smile. There were little crow's-feet at the outside edges of his blue eyes; he was definitely older and more worldly-wise than Buddy, though not nearly as old as the sergeant. Under his service cap, his hair was close-cropped, blond, and looked like it would be thick and wavy if given the chance to grow.

Suddenly, she was nervous. Was he examining her as closely as she was him? She bit her Crimson Blush lower lip, and fluttered her eyes at him, without exactly meaning to. "I'm terribly sorry," she said, as the applause for the band died down. "I seem to have been tossed at you."

The soldier shoved his hands into his pockets. "That's all right," he drawled, revealing a Southern accent and a crooner's voice.

She caught herself staring at his lips. "Well!" she said, and turned to leave him, just as the band broke into "I'm Getting Sentimental Over You."

"Dance with me?" he said. His "me" sounded like "may."

She stopped, turned, took in the whole picture of him: service cap half cocked, broad shoulders, narrow belted waist, corporal's stripes. She nodded.

"I'm not much of a dancer," he told her, once they were out on the floor.

"You're doing just fine," she said, though they weren't attempting any complicated moves at the moment.

"I reckon Sarge got tired of hearing me gripe."

Elissa was as fluttery as a leaf; evidently, hearing the "I" sound pronounced as "ah" made her weak in the knees. Add to that the warmth of his hands—one on her waist, the other holding her hand—and the golden strains of a trombone, and she was really in trouble. "Why is that?" she said.

"Well, you were dancing with all them other boys," he explained.

Had Muriel been next to her, Elissa would have turned to her to share a scream. As it was, she smiled, demurely, she hoped. "You don't mean—?"

"I was watching you a mite bit," he admitted. "Sarge is always trying to keep us boys happy. He goes overboard, at times."

Onstage, the saxophones took over the lilting melody, and suddenly, Elissa knew she had fallen into the trap of the Babylon that Betty had warned of. *It's so magical there, why, you find yourself believing anything they tell you, and you tell them things, too, and at the time you even think you mean them! And maybe you do! I've heard of plenty of people who've met at the Babylon and gotten married! So don't think it's impossible for you! And these boys—they're so lonely, most of them. So far from home. You have to be careful not to feel too sorry for them—if you know what I mean. Not right away, at least.* And she'd laughed, then sighed. *Of course, lots of them only want to dance, and forget about everything for a little while. You know?*

His name was Nick Overby, and, like most of the boys at the Babylon tonight, he was in town on a weekend pass from Camp McCoy. A mere four months earlier, he told her, all the boys of the 2nd Division had been home at Fort Sam Houston, Texas, where the October wind blew a balmy 75 degrees and, even at midnight, walking home from the canteen, they'd been able to wear shirtsleeves. But then they'd been assigned to winter training at Camp McCoy, and when they'd arrived there at the end of that month, it was 25 below zero, and the supply people were scurrying to find enough parkas for all the men. Then they really loaded on the junk: mountain boots, mukluks, snowshoes, skis, ski boots, ski pants, ski poles, three pairs of extra socks. Not that he wasn't glad for it, in the cold. "What I can't get used to," he said, "is the idea that to sleep warm when you're sleeping out, you've got to take all your clothes off."

She blushed at this, but he just smiled.

He told her he was from a little town in Tennessee that she never would have heard of, Dover. She surprised him by knowing about the Civil War battle that had taken place there at Fort Donelson, and had to explain that she'd read *Gone with the Wind* three times (and seen the movie twice). "So you've got a skewed notion of the South, haven't you?" he said.

"Why? What is it really like?"

"You ought to come visit sometime, and find out for yourself."

He said that in the spring months of March and April—which Elissa quickly informed him were winter months, but never mind— when the redbud and dogwood trees were in blossom, walking under one was like walking into heaven itself. There was a redbud tree that stretched to just below his attic bedroom window, and in the spring, he told her, he would pile the quilts and feather ticks on his bed so he could leave the window open all night and let the scent of the redbud air drift in. He was an only child; his father had died before he was born, and his mother, who had never remarried, had kept boarders for as long as he could remember, filling the four bedrooms in the big old house his grandfather had built right in town on a bluff high above the Cumberland River.

"My house is on a little bluff above the Bear Trap River," she told him. "And my grandparents still live in their house above the river, on the other side of town."

"Then I reckon we got a lot in common," he said. "What's it like in your town?"

"In Pine Rapids? Oh, it's—it's home!"

"Tell me about it."

She thought a moment, then launched into a description of the Bear Trap River, how it was draped in hemlock and birch so that it looked much narrower than it was, the way the water sparkled in the spring as the ice melted, the rush of the rapids in summer, the fallen leaves sailing down it in the fall. The frozen hush of it in winter; the deer that came out of the woods and stood on its ice to sniff the white air. She told him about the arched bridge that bisected the Bear Trap and led north out of downtown to the burned-out, abandoned mill, where, as a child, she used to go and sneak in the buildings with her older brother, JJ, to prove she wasn't a scaredy-cat. She told him about how when JJ and his three pals had joined up with the Marines just after Pearl Harbor, the whole town had turned out at the depot to see them off to Basic Training at Parris Island.

"JJ was so excited," she told him. "My mom—her name is Mary—she was fit to be tied, him leaving school early, but my father, Jack, he said if he wanted to go, then they'd better just let him. I guess my dad hated it, too, but he was so proud of him, you could tell; my dad joined the Marines himself right away back when the First World War started. And everyone in town treated JJ and his friends like heroes, and gave them a great send-off. Every Sunday at church, they still say a special prayer for JJ. You can't help but be glad that everyone's behind them like that. Everyone's behind all of you boys. You know that, don't you?"

"Sure," he said. "Course, it makes a heap of difference to a guy to have a girl back home to write to, who's waiting for him to get home."

"Yes, I wish my brother did—" she said, then belatedly caught his meaning.

He let it pass with a little smile. "So Pine Rapids isn't a big town, I reckon," he said.

"Oh, no," she said, recovering. "Everyone knows everybody else's business. My father's the head of the draft board and every time he has to call up somebody's number, he can't sleep for two or three nights before and after, on account of he knows all of them, and he knows their parents, and, like I told you, he fought in the Great War himself. He doesn't like war at all, but he says it has to be done, sometimes, when there's great evil in the world."

"Well, that may be," Nick said. "But tonight I'd like to look in your pretty eyes and dance with you."

She was embarrassed; it seemed she'd been talking too much. "I'd like that, too," she said.

They jitterbugged, they danced the schottische, they waltzed. Elissa never once let go of his hand, and, for what must have been nearly an hour, forgot even to wonder where Muriel and Betty were. Contrary to what he had claimed, he was more than a passable dancer, and as he dipped her low, twirled her, pulled her in tight to him again, she felt utterly at ease in his arms and yet electrified, as though the music was coming up from the floor right into the soles of her shoes, coming through his hands straight into her pulsing blood.

"Aren't you tired of me yet?" he asked, when the band started playing "You and I" and they fell easily into step together. "I've seen some of the boys eying me and getting mighty jealous."

"I'm not tired of you. Not yet."

He laughed, twirled her, pulled her close. "I suppose you got a boyfriend back home," he said.

She shook her head. "No."

"Y'all're just saying that to make me feel better."

"No, Nick, I would never say anything just to make you feel better."

"Well, that's mighty comforting."

"Do you have a girl?" she asked, scarcely believing her own boldness; but this was war, after all!

"No," he said, "but I might look at changing that real quick, if you're agreeable."

"What?"

"Just dance with me," he said. "Dance with me till midnight, Cinderella, and tell me then if you'll leave me your shoe."

But before Elissa realized it, it was one A.M. and the band was launching into their last number, "I'll Be Seeing You." Some time after midnight, Muriel had waltzed by with a soldier and given her a wink. Other than that, all was a breathless blur of dancing. Thank goodness Betty's parents allowed a late curfew! Elissa had never been allowed to stay out so late, but this was the one night of her life that it seemed absolutely necessary.

"So," Nick said, holding her close, as the music swelled, "will I be seeing you?"

In all the times she had heard it, "I'll Be Seeing You" had never once failed to make Elissa tear up, and now was no exception. Except, this time, looking up at Nick, it was almost more than her heart could bear. She tried to speak; couldn't.

"Aw, now, don't cry," he said, touching her face. "Was it that bad a time? You'll give me your address, won't you, so I can write?"

She nodded.

"You could come down next weekend. I'd take you out for supper and then we could come dancing."

She hadn't thought of that possibility. "Next weekend?"

"You're staying at your friend's?"

"Yes."

"Can I walk you there?"

"Well," she considered, trying to keep herself in check. She was a respectable girl, after all. "Yes, if you'll escort Muriel and Betty, too."

"I'll get two of my buddies, we can all go together."

Buddy! It was the first she had thought of him since setting her eyes on Nick. Well, she supposed he had found another girl long ago. "All right," she said, feeling better, at least for the moment, prolonging the inevitable good-bye. She leaned her head briefly on Nick's uniformed chest, and she could hear the pounding of his heart.

They were a group of seven when assembled: Nick and his friends Everett and Sam, the three girls, and a soldier named Paul who had made previous arrangements to walk Betty home. As they set off down the street, Betty made a show of having two escorts, linking her arms with both of them, and then abruptly told the boys they'd have to leave the girls a block from her house.

"You mean to tell me," complained Everett, who was walking with Muriel, "we go out of our way and we can't even walk y'all up to the porch?"

The discussion continued, but Elissa, walking behind the others on Nick's arm, paid no attention. She stayed in step with Nick; he kept casting sidelong glances her way, with that little heart-stopping smile, and slowing his steps to separate them from the rest of the group. The night was frozen, still and quiet, except for the sounds of their friends up ahead and of Elissa's heels clicking down the cleared walk that tunneled through knee-high banks of snow. The houses on either side of the street were hushed and dark; the bare branches of the overhanging trees were skeletal in the moonlight. Elissa sighed, watched her breath make a cloud. Pressing her shoulder closer to Nick's, she hunched up a little inside her coat.

"I think you're real sweet," Nick said suddenly. "You're not like anyone I've met before. The way you cried a little back there. Were you crying because you had to say good-bye to me?"

She didn't know how to answer. She didn't want him to think her overly emotional, though she supposed it was too late for that.

"I'm sorry," he said, after a moment. "I reckon that's out of line. You don't need to say. But I think you're the sweetest thing, and I hope you'll write to me. I hope I'll get to see you again. I think I've been waiting for somebody like you."

"But, Nick, how can you tell?" Elissa said quickly. "It isn't possible, is it?"

"You tell me," he said.

She didn't have a chance to reply, because their friends had stopped on a corner, and stood waiting for them. "I've invited all these boys over for dinner tomorrow after church," Betty announced as they approached. "My folks always invite some of the boys who come to church, anyway, so I'll just tell them that you four are coming."

Nick and Elissa exchanged happy smiles: tomorrow!

"You can come to church, too," Betty said, with a challenging smile for Nick.

He smiled back. "What time? Which church?"

"Ten-thirty. Faith Lutheran."

"I reckon I can be Lutheran for a day," he said.

It wasn't so bad saying good-bye knowing that she would see him again in less than nine hours. He lifted her gloved hand to his lips and kissed it. "I'll be seeing you," he said.

The girls ran the block to Betty's house, the cold burning their lungs, while the boys headed off in the other direction, lighting up cigarettes, jabbing each other with their elbows, their laughter filling the night air.

HOME OF MRS. CECILIA FRYT
412 W. First Street, Pine Rapids
Tuesday, July 18, 1950

"Yes, if Elissa hadn't met that boy, things would likely have been different," Mrs. Fryt said. "But I still say it all goes back to Wilma."

"To Wilma!" Corinne said. "When it was John—"

Mrs. Fryt held up her hand. "Ladies," she said. "If you want to understand about the Mickelsons, let me tell you this one thing. Chase was Wilma's most treasured child, and she never did make a secret of it. Don't you remember? Of course, I think it's a terrible sin, favoring one child over the others the way she did; if I'd been blessed with more than one living child, you can bet your bottom dollar I'd have favored them all just the same."

"Cecilia," Thelma said.

"No one who saw them could deny it, Thelma. Wilma loved Chase more than the others. Well, a mother had to let Jack go—he was too much his own, from the time he was knee-high. But the two youngest, Harry and Jinny, she treated them like afterthoughts. Sometimes you'd swear she forgot she even had them."

"Oh, Cecilia," Thelma said. "How could a mother forget her own children?"

"I'll put it this way," Mrs. Fryt said. "In all the years of going to church when those children were growing up, Wilma would spend the whole service sitting with her hand touching Chase's hair, the first ten years of his life, at least. The only time she'd even notice Jinny or Harry is if they started to act up, and then she'd just give them one of her looks.

"Chase let Wilma favor him, but the minute her back was turned, after the service, he'd dig some treat out of his pocket for Jinny, and whisper a joke in Harry's ear, and whatever it was he said always made Harry giggly as a goose. Wilma would turn to scold them, but then Chase would give her the sweetest smile, and he'd put one arm each around Harry and Jinny, and you could just see her melt, like chocolate on low heat. Of course, by this time, Jack would have gone off to flirt with the girls."

"It sounds like Chase held everything together, then," Dolly said.

"Perhaps he did," Mrs. Fryt said. "And perhaps he could have, though it would have been a tall order even for him—dealing with that Wilma! He was only human, after all. Anyway, once Jack dragged him off to the war, Wilma was an utter wreck. You'd see her around town and her eyes were like glass. Not to be vulgar, but some of us thought she'd plain gone out of her mind. Here was a woman who'd never had to do for herself, and all of a sudden she's storming around town with baskets full of knitting and sewing and cards for the soldiers, practically trailing yarn behind her down the street!"

"Even in church, she never set down her knitting," Corinne added.

"We had to show her every bit of it, from how to cast on, to how to make a stitch, to how to follow the Red Cross pattern for socks for the soldiers," Mrs. Fryt said. "And then it was sock after sock after sock! Well, everyone was knitting socks in those days. I remember there were posters up all over town saying, OUR BOYS NEED SOCKS. KNIT YOUR BIT. Wilma took those slogans straight to heart. She knitted even more than the German ladies, who felt they had to prove their loyalty. I don't know what Wilma was trying to prove."

"Remember the sewing bees we had?" Corinne said. "Sewing kits for the soldiers? Wilma would be the first one there working, and you'd have to tap her on her shoulder when everyone else had gone, and she'd look up with those glassy eyes. She wouldn't even realize it was time to go home. And she was such a terrible seamstress! Didn't we have to redo nearly everything she did, at the beginning?"

"Yes," said Mrs. Fryt, shaking her head. "And then there was the garden."

Some of the ladies giggled. "Now, ladies, be nice," Thelma said, but even she was having trouble holding back a smile.

"Wilma had a garden?" Dolly prodded.

"Yes," said Mrs. Fryt. "A war garden, that first summer after the boys left. The government had a campaign to get everyone to grow and preserve their own food, so that farmers' produce could supply the Army. 'Can vegetables, fruit, and the kaiser, too,' was the slogan, as I remember, and Wilma took it to heart just like she did the knitting. Well, heaven knows, before the war, she'd never done a lick of work in her life. And all of a sudden, on top of all her other war work, she decided she'd tend to a half-acre plot!"

"It wasn't *that* big," Thelma said.

"It might as well have been," Mrs. Fryt insisted. "But there was no telling her any different! She wanted to do her bit, same as those boys of hers."

THE MICKELSON HOUSE
502 W. First Street, Pine Rapids
Tuesday, June 12, 1917

Under the cloud-mottled sky of a pretty June evening, John walked home from work in the shade of the greening maple trees, thinking about his sons. *Looks like we're going to join up with one of the big Divisions,* Chase had written recently, as the boys had neared the end of their eight-week training camp down at Parris Island, South Carolina. *And sad to say we won't get leave to come home.*

So his boys were going to war, going "over there." Sailing any day now, out of Philadelphia, in the first group of Americans to go over. Amazing how much of the world they were seeing: South Carolina, Philadelphia, and now on their way to France!

But Wilma! "You see, John!" she had cried, shaking one of the boys' letters in his face. "Overseas! When Chasey should be graduating high school this week!"

Well, what did she expect him to do about it? Besides, he was proud of them for volunteering, proud of them for passing the strict physical requirements and getting into the elite Marine Corps. *They say only one in ten fellows passes,* Jack had written from the recruiting depot. *Of course me and Chasey passed with flying colors. We enlisted for the duration.*

"For the duration!" Wilma had exclaimed. "What does that mean?"

"For as long as it takes," John explained, and got a withering look for his trouble, as she got up, slammed out of the room. She had not been herself since the boys had gone.

It was as if she blamed *him,* somehow, for their absence—for the entire war!

It was strange enough to have Wilma and the children home this summer—it was the first summer in years that she had not taken them to the family cottage on Lake Michigan in Stone Harbor. She had silenced Harry's and Jinny's complaints with a swift "Think of your brothers! And you think it's too much to sacrifice a summer at the lake!" The look in her eyes, they had never brought it up again. But it wasn't just having her home that was different. *She* was different.

As he approached the house towering upon the hill, as always he thought of his father. Knute had been dead more than fifteen years now, but in John's mind the house would always be his. John wondered what Knute would think of Wilma now. Knute had always said that she was a true lady, while John was merely a frog dressed up in prince's clothing. Perhaps Knute had noticed the way she paralyzed John, the way he had to buck himself up before facing her, lest he utterly collapse before her.

This was true although he had always done his best to assert his authority with her. It had been easiest in the first years: Whatever he demanded, she bowed to his will. Gradually, though, she had begun betraying the arrangement with snippy remarks. Then she began to argue with him openly at times, as though pressing to see how far she could go. He felt himself a perpetual boxer in the ring, struggling to maintain his footing against a wily opponent. But there had always seemed to be the understanding that both would play by certain rules—at least until the boys left. Much to John's dismay, the rules all changed then.

The change in Wilma was enough to bring to mind the "curse" that people in town whispered about. Knute had laughed about the rumors when he'd chosen the site for his house. But then, shortly after the family moved in, John's mother was stricken with stomach cancer. Three months later, she was gone.

At the time, John hadn't attributed his mother's death to any supposed "curse," and, in the intervening years, only the occasional outburst from Wilma or the sometime loneliness he felt like a shell on his heart had caused him to ponder—though with no real seriousness—the curse's possible veracity.

But now Wilma was acting so strangely. She had transformed herself into a paragon of matronly sacrifice and wartime purpose. Writing the boys every day, knitting, writing cards, rolling bandages, attending weekly community sewing bees to manufacture Red Cross comfort bags. After dismissing the pretty maid Brita just before the boys left, Wilma had decided against hiring a replacement for her, insisting that she would have a laundress in just twice a week and take over some of the additional work herself. So the family was left with one live-in maid, plus a cook and a yard man who each worked six days a week. John started to notice dust accumulating in the corners, a little grime in the bathtub, a little dullness to the woodwork that always before had enjoyed weekly polishing. There was simply too much work for just one maid, and Wilma didn't seem inclined to do what she had said in terms of picking up the extra housework. She was too busy with war work, from the moment she awoke at dawn until she dropped into bed late at night. She never touched her piano that he knew of.

When he suggested hiring an additional maid again, she wouldn't hear of it. In fact, faced with the new force of her, John found himself powerless to make demands of any sort. He felt that if she would grant him the smallest thing, he would be satisfied. But when he had experimented one morning at breakfast with insisting the cook prepare a roast for dinner, Wilma had responded simply, "We're having chicken. The soldiers need beef more than we do." He knew then with a frightening certainty that the war had changed her, that she was not the same woman she had been. He had to wonder: Could there be something to the notion that love was not meant to prosper in that house?

He turned up Park Avenue and walked up the driveway. Rounding the corner of the carriage house, which was now home to a 1916 Model T, he was startled to see the cook's old garden doubled in size since this morning, the exposed earth a crumbled-looking reddish-brown. And there, to his astonishment, was Wilma—in an old summer dress and high brown boots, her hair hidden under a wide-brimmed hat—smoothing the plot with a rake. Jinny and Harry were at work with hoes.

"We're doin' a garden, Dad!" Jinny cried, stopping her work when she saw him approaching. "'Food will win the war!' We're 'Soldiers of the Soil!'" She grinned, and turned back to her labors.

"Wilma?" John said, coming closer. Intent on her raking, Wilma did not look up until John had reached the edge of the plot and said her name again.

She met his eyes without straightening her back, then resumed her work. Sweat trickled down her temple. "We haven't much time," she said. "If we don't get everything planted right away, it won't be ready before the first frost."

John had trouble finding words. "Why—?"

"Haven't you heard?" she said. "What the War Garden Commission says? Everything we produce will lessen the demand on commercial supplies—so more can go to the boys! Not to mention, every dime we save by not buying food, we can invest in war bonds!"

John had seen the posters around town—Lady Liberty holding aloft a home-canned jar of vegetables underneath the slogan THE FRUITS OF VICTORY—but he had never dreamed Wilma would take the propaganda so literally. "What—what are you going to plant? You're going to fill this whole space? Why don't you have Cook do it?"

"Oh, everything!" she said. "I sent Harry to the co-op and Mr. Bertilson told him everything we needed. The commission has put out guidelines. I want to make sure they're followed to the letter, so I'm doing it myself."

"Cripes," Harry muttered, pausing his hoeing to stretch his back. His hair shone in the evening light slanting through the trees. "Isn't this against some type of child labor law? Didn't they pass those things for a reason?"

"Harry, watch your language," John snapped, automatically.

"The soil is almost ready," Wilma said.

"Well, did you fertilize?"

"Fertilize? No. I didn't see that in the guidelines. Did Mr. Bertilson mention that, Harry?"

Harry didn't look up from his hoeing.

So, without even going into the house, John cranked up the Model T and drove out to a potato farm he owned (former timber land, which tenants had painstakingly cleared of the massive stumps). He pulled up in front of the small clapboard house and got out of the car to bang on the door, interrupting the current tenant, Carl Svoboda, at his supper. John explained the situation, then took out his wallet and gave Svoboda several bills. Thus did Svoboda haul several bushels of composted horse manure into town and dump them in the plot in the Mickelsons' backyard. It was twilight when the job of spreading and blending it was complete.

"There now, tomorrow you can plant," John said to Wilma, wiping his brow with his handkerchief. The evening was growing cool, but he had been working harder than he was accustomed to.

"Life!" Wilma said, brushing a dirty rivulet of sweat from her temple with the back of her hand. "Perpetuated!"

PINE RAPIDS MESSENGER
Friday, July 6, 1917

LOCAL BOYS ARRIVE OVERSEAS

Marine Corps Privates John Mickelson, Jr., and Chase Mickelson have arrived in France, according to a letter received by their parents, Mr. and Mrs. John Mickelson, of 502 W. First Street. Both young Mickelsons are with the 5th Marine Regiment, and from their letters the hearty enthusiasm of the American contingent can be perceived. Chase says the following:

"Dear Mom and Dad, Arrived somewhere in France [censored] days ago. The trip over was grand. I would certainly recommend seeing the ocean. The only hitch was that a bunch of us got 'mal-de-mere,' as they say—seasick. I recovered just fine so don't worry. Jack was sick some, too, but by the end both of us were full of pep and rolling with the punches, you could say.

"The scene at the harbor where we landed was not like anything you could imagine. We were one of many ships to arrive at once, and all hundreds of us crowded onto the deck to see the long-awaited sight of land. I tell you Columbus himself could not have been happier to see land. All of us were looking down onto the dock, and on the dock were massive crowds of French people, all standing shoulder to shoulder. They were not cheering us, not even talking much, they were just looking up at us like they were waiting to see what we would do.

"It was some fun getting all the equipment unloaded. The Army had sent some fellows but it wasn't near enough to handle all the ships, so us Marines got going and unloaded our own ship. You've never seen such a mass of goods. They were piled on the dock almost as high as the first deck. You've never heard such noise as this impatient bunch of thousands of us boys ready to fight a war, only to be slowed down by the business of 'organization.'

"As for the rest of it, all the boys are fine, except they complain there's not enough excitement. Last night we all saw a boxing match put on by the YMCA. We hear we'll be going for more training. For now I am billeted with a nice French family and sleep in the hayloft with a bunch of other boys. The hayloft is right in the house, since there's only one dwelling for both people and animals. The priority for our comfort is only slightly below that of the animals. Jack is billeted in another part of town, but I see him almost every night when we go downtown. During the day we go on foot marches, and stand in line for food and whatever else we need.

"Mom, don't worry about me or Jack. I'm certain that once we get started it won't be long before we finish the job and are able to come home again.

"Greet all the folks back home for me. I will write again soon. Until then, Your son, Chase."

With the letter, Private Mickelson enclosed a drawing much

like those he was known for while attending Pine Rapids High. The cartoon showed a young Marine, managing to look both queasy and sheepish at once, with a steaming campaign hat overturned in his hands. The caption read: "Don't worry, I didn't get any on my shoes!"

Cultivate your capacity for companionship, for it is one of
men's fundamental goals in marriage. During courtship,
your husband thought you a desirable companion.
Do you give him reason to think so still?

—"Making Marriage Work,"
Ladies' Home Journal, March 1950

THE MICKELSON HOUSE
502 W. First Street, Pine Rapids
Wednesday, July 19, 1950

Guessing it had been Wilma's prized possession, Dolly took special
care dusting the piano in the Mickelsons' blue parlor. She wished she
could play it—she was certain it felt as bereft as the rest of the
house—but she wouldn't have wanted the neighbors to hear. Besides,
she had no talent; her mother had put the family out of its misery
after the first year of Dolly's piano lessons. She had practiced and
practiced, but somehow her fingers had always eluded her control.
Like everything else, she thought, gripping the piano's leg in her dust
cloth and sweeping down it toward the powder-blue rug.

The Ladies Aid gathering yesterday had ended unsatisfactorily
when the ladies veered from the subject of Wilma Mickelson's "war
garden" to the problems they were having with weevils this season.
Not wanting to arouse suspicions, Dolly had concealed her impa-

tience; consequently, she was left with an unsettled feeling of abject curiosity, as though Jane had written her a letter and forgotten to enclose the last two pages. Dolly had, though, managed to slip in this question: "Do you think any of the Mickelsons will really come back to Pine Rapids?"

And Mrs. Fryt had said, "Oh, no. I can't picture it."

So Dolly felt safe to continue dreaming about living in the Mickelson house, and to return there to keep working.

It was a good thing, too: Lately, no matter how hard she tried, Byron was never very pleased with her. Come to think of it, she was never very pleased with him, either. She couldn't help but imagine that if they lived in the Mickelson house—a place grand enough for their dreams—they would both be much happier. He had gotten angry with her again last night, just because she had suggested that he seemed to prefer the company of Roy Ostrem and sundry Chryslers to her. As she dusted, she reviewed what had happened, trying to make sense of it. First, he had arrived home late from work, wolfed his supper (Chicken à la King and apricot cottage cheese salad; "Great, hon"), and bolted out to the garage, where she found him later seated at his workbench sorting his screws into empty baby food jars.

"So this is what you had to do that was so important?" she had asked him, leaning against the doorjamb. She rarely ventured into the garage unless they were going somewhere in the car. Its plank walls were stained dark; it smelled of oil, earth, and mystery, and felt gloomy despite the light coming in the small windows. The Chrysler hulked in the center of it like a seed about to pop from its pod. "When I've been alone all day, waiting for you to come home, and you can't take an hour to talk to me?"

"I thought you had that quilting thing today," Byron said, tossing a Phillips head into a creamed spinach jar.

She was annoyed that he'd actually remembered; it was better to be able to get angry with him for forgetting. "Where did you get all the baby food jars?"

"From Roy." A stout little screw dropped into the former home of puréed peaches.

"I suppose with all his babies he has no shortage."

"What do you want, Doll?"

She could have screamed. "Nothing, Byron."

He held up a silver screw. "Wanna screw?" he said, and grinned.

"Don't be juvenile." She turned to go back to the house.

"Remember when we used to do it in the car?"

She stopped. "We did not!"

"Came close."

She looked at him again; he was smiling.

He looked over his shoulder at the parked car. "Want to?"

She couldn't help that her curiosity was piqued.

"We could go all the way, now," he said. "And not have to worry." He stood from the workbench, and reached out for her hand, pulled her inside the garage and shut the door. He pulled her close and kissed her. She felt her heart quicken, and savored the clean smell of his skin.

He unbuttoned her dress and slipped his hand inside. "Remember," he said, "how much I used to want you?"

"How much you—?"

He was unbuttoning her dress the rest of the way.

"Used to? Byron?"

"Doll," he breathed, dropping her dress to the floor, pushing her slip and bra straps down off her shoulder, kissing where they had made dents in her skin. She could smell the clean scent of his hair. "I used to think I was going to go stark raving mad. Remember?" He moved the other strap of her slip aside; the slip fell to the ground. "When I'd—The way you'd arch your back, Doll, the curve of your neck—you were so beautiful."

"I—was?"

It seemed she had hardly drawn a breath before she was lying on the cool leather of the backseat, with Byron leaning over her. The car smelled like trips to church, drives along the river; mixed with the heat of Byron's skin, it smelled like teenaged Saturday nights: leather and lust, perfume and sweat, hairspray, starch, Aqua Velva.

"Remember this, Doll?" he whispered. The seat stuck to her damp skin.

When it was over, he sighed her name, nuzzling her neck. He was still connected with her; how funny that part of it was, Dolly always thought, that she could almost imagine they'd fused together for good, that the heat they had made had melted their parts and their hearts all together. And then it was awful that it wasn't true, that tomorrow they'd snipe at each other about the same stupid things they always did.

She sighed, brushing her hair out of her eyes. She was growing embarrassed; married women didn't do such things, she was sure. "I always promised my sister I wouldn't lose my virginity in the backseat of a car," she said.

"You didn't, silly."

"Well, it felt like I did, the way you talked! I lost my car virginity, anyway!" she said. "Oh, I'm so stuck to this seat. Do you think the neighbors heard us?"

"Who cares if they did?"

"I'd better get my clothes," she said. "What if someone sees?"

"No one's going to see, Doll." He sounded as content and drowsy as a summer's day.

But something was gnawing at her. "Byron?" she ventured after a moment. "Do you still—want me? At all?"

"Wasn't it obvious just now?"

She struggled up to her elbows, unsticking her skin from the seat, upsetting him from on top of her. "But the way you talked, Byron— it was all about how you used to feel about me. How I used to be a virgin and I used to stop you before we went all the way."

"Sure, Doll," he said. "Isn't that how it was?"

"But I'm not a virgin anymore, Byron."

"That's even more fun," he said, running his hand over her body.

"But why did you want to marry me? I mean, when did you first have the idea you might want to marry me?"

"The first day I saw you in that red two-piece." He grinned.

"No, I mean really, Byron."

"I don't know," he said. "It just kind of got so it seemed like a good idea."

"Do you still think it's a good idea?"

He cocked his head at her, but stopped short of whatever he had thought to say. After a moment, he pushed himself up out of the car. He pulled up his shorts and pants at once, and zipped up. "Usually, Doll," he muttered then, fastening his belt.

She sat up. Her stomach hurt. She knew she was making him mad, but she couldn't seem to stop herself. "Why do you avoid me, Byron? Why do you work late all the time? And then come out here like you can't stand to be in the same house with me?"

He rested his fingers on his hips. "You don't know how it is, with a new business."

"Well, *you* don't know how it is, being left alone all the time. I used to have my family, and now you've made it so I don't have anyone but you. And you'd rather be with Roy and your cars than with me."

"That isn't true."

"How do I know?"

He looked at her, narrowing his eyes. "Put your clothes on, Doll," he said then, swooping down to pick up her panties and bra where he'd dropped them, tossing them at her so quickly she had to think fast to catch them. "Anyone could walk up and see you."

She stood up. She stepped into her panties, her shoes, then put her arms through her bra, hooked it in back, and adjusted it in front, watching as he walked around to the front of the car to pick up her slip and dress. He tossed them at her, too, then plopped down at his workbench, his back to her. A screw jangled into a jar. She put on her slip, then her dress. Another screw jingled. She began buttoning her dress. Her fingers were trembling, but she pointed her chin at his back, ready to continue the fight.

"Why don't you go in the house, Doll?" he said, tossing another screw into its new home.

As she buttoned the final button, a vision flashed in her mind: striking the back of his self-righteous head. Any implement would do.

She stifled the urge and broke into a run, weaving her way past him and out of the garage, then through their hushed little yard. She banged in the back door, and raced through the kitchen and dining room, down the hall and into their bedroom, where she flung herself onto the bed and lost count of her tears. She didn't care if it was juvenile: She missed her mother, her sisters, Jane, her father. It wasn't fair that Byron could take them all from her, and her flight lessons, too, and expect her to be satisfied with this common little bungalow in this common little town!

She had sobbed herself to sleep, thinking this way, but, after night fell, Byron came to her and woke her with a gentle hand on her hip.

She rolled over, and got lost in his moonlit eyes. "I'm sorry, Doll," he told her, running his hand down her body, kissing her. He unbuttoned everything, more slowly this time. He turned back the covers she'd flopped upon, and spread her flat on the cool sheets. His hands felt like the best dream she had ever had, and they made love slowly, deeply. "I love you, Dolly," he whispered. "More than anything. More than anything, Doll, baby."

Or had she dreamed it all? This morning over his eggs he would hardly meet her eyes. He wolfed his food again, and dashed out the door, after giving her a brief kiss. She was so confused and disheartened that she barely roused herself to come over to the Mickelson house.

But the minute she had boosted herself into the house through the parlor window, she felt better. She felt at home here. There might be sadness in the walls, but at least that meant that happiness was possible. The bungalow felt empty of everything.

She dusted off the stool and sat down at the piano, wondering if Wilma had sat here and taught her children to play. She hoped that after last night there might be a child growing inside her. She was certain she would stop picking fights with Byron if there was. If she had a baby, she was certain she would never want to fly away, then.

THE MICKELSON HOUSE
502 W. First Street, Pine Rapids
March 1899

Seated at the piano in the parlor, Wilma held little Jack in her lap, wondering if the baby she was expecting would like music as much as Jack did. After Jack's birth and that dreadful Independence Day when she had fainted in the street, her loneliness for her piano had become so unbearable that, on the fifth of July that year, she had dragged herself to the parlor and begun plunking out scales and minuets. Her hands immediately felt like themselves again; clarity was restored to her mind. Getting out of bed each morning, getting dressed, completing her unavoidable duties, and then, finally, going to the parlor, became a habit; she forgot how difficult such things had been.

In the beginning, it was the maid Terese who had insisted on bringing Jack into the parlor each time Wilma played, laying him on a quilt on the floor while Wilma lost herself in the music that her hands knew. He was a surprisingly appreciative audience, cooing and babbling happily, almost as though he was singing along, until, without fail, he would suddenly squall. She would rise from the piano, walk to the door, and pull the call bell string to summon Terese. "He's hungry, Mrs. Mickelson," Terese would almost always say when she appeared, picking up the baby and handing him to Wilma. "And I can't help him with that."

One day, when Jack began to fuss, Wilma made up her mind to handle him all by herself. She rose from the piano and approached him tentatively. She knelt beside him and picked him up. The density of his little body always astonished her. She felt his bottom. Dry, thank goodness. (She wasn't quite ready to handle *that* on her own; even in the night, Terese was always the one to change him.) Hungry, then. "Are you hungry, Jack?" she whispered. She had not addressed him directly since before he was born. She tried a smile. He stopped fussing; their eyes met. It was the first time she had really looked at him, and she was surprised by the wisdom and the fortitude in his blue eyes. Then, his face screwed up as if he would cry. "All right, all right," she told him, pressing him to her and stroking his soft hair the way she had seen Terese do. She stood and walked to the sofa with him, and undid her bodice so he could nurse. For the first time, she actually didn't mind him tugging at her. She watched him closely: How satisfied he looked, with his eyes squeezed shut. How utterly satisfied! And because of her! She choked back tears, feeling herself succumb to the willful pressure of his tiny fist, his strong mouth, weaving his life irrevocably with hers.

From that day, she did not call Terese into the parlor when Jack fussed. She would stop her music to tend to him, though she would already be wistful for the next day's session with her piano. But he was her best friend, then, and she didn't begrudge him his demands. When he was old enough to sit up, she brought him up into her lap while she played, and he watched her fingers dance over the keys and kicked the rhythm against her knees.

"Beethoven?" she asked him now, hitching him up on her lap, which was getting too small for him, thanks to his increasing size and the baby growing inside her. She loved the smell of his hair, the heat of his little body pressing against hers; she didn't like to think of the day when she could not hold him in her lap while she played.

"Beethoven!" he replied, bouncing excitedly. And so she began: the heavy chords of the opening of the Sonata Pathétique. She felt the baby inside her kicking, and, as the grave music swelled, so did the fear in her throat. This baby would be born soon, in only a couple of months. Her recollection of Jack's birth was still visceral. She could still smell the blood. Equally vivid was her recollection that, even as Terese had placed the swaddled new baby in her arms for his first feeding, she had decided he would be her only child.

But how to prevent another had been a mystery. The day after Jack's birth, when Dr. Seguin came to check on her, she asked what could be done, but he just patted her hand and said she should leave the matter to God. He said that having babies was as natural as breathing. But if that was true, why did Wilma hear of so many women who died in the process? The best she could manage was to keep John from her, but three months after Jack's birth she could hold him off no longer. She did want to be a good wife, but she had cringed as he moved on top of her, imagining the inevitable consequences. She kept from weaning Jack as long as possible—the women at church whispered that this was one means of staving off another baby—but that only made her the spoils in a war between father and son, and she felt herself torn between the two of them, Jack squalling for the milk of her breasts, John angry that the baby had command of her body. Wilma dreaded the battle with John beginning again when the new child was born—not to mention that now Jack, too, would likely resent the competition for her attention.

Yet, despite that she hadn't wanted it, and despite that she feared its birth as she feared her own death, this baby in her belly stretched and kicked as though it would swim its way up inside her heart and thus eclipse the totality of her love. He was working his magic on her the way that Jack had, but much earlier, before she had even seen his face. She worried that her heart could not stretch far enough to contain both boys. She worried that, one way or another, they would be the death of her.

With a deep sigh at the final chord of the *Grave,* Wilma launched into the *Allegro di molto e con brio* section of the sonata. Suddenly, Jack pounded his fists on the keys between her hands.

"Jack!" she squawked, stopping the piece. "Jack, no!"

"Jack play now!" he insisted, and struck the keys again. Then he looked dismayed: Why didn't it sound as nice as when his mother played?

"Jack!" Wilma cried, grabbing his hands. "Gentle! Gentle!"

"Jack play!" he yelled, struggling to free his hands from hers.

"Not until you're gentle!" she cried. She had always told him he could play when he was older; evidently, he had decided that this was the day. How would she stop him? When Jack made up his mind, there was just no arguing with him.

"Hello!" came a voice from the front hallway. Wilma's stomach lurched; it was Gust's voice. She heard the front door closing behind him, and then he was standing in the parlor door frame, his hat in his hands, his cheeks pink from the cold, snow melting from his boots. He had brought the clean smell of the winter air in with him.

"Gust," she said, as Jack held up his arms and called out, "Uncle Gus!" struggling to get down from her lap. She let him go, relieved that the battle was to be deferred, flustered by Gust's sudden appearance. She hadn't seen him in ages.

Gust crouched down as Jack toddled toward him at top speed. "Are you giving your mother trouble, Jack Mickelson?"

"No," Jack insisted, holding his arms out to his uncle. Gust picked him up and lifted him to the ceiling; Jack squealed with glee.

"You'd best not be, Jack, or your uncle Gust will get you," Gust said, as he swung Jack down, set him gently on the floor, and tickled his sides. Jack shrieked and wiggled, unable to free himself of his uncle's big hands, loving every bit of the attention.

"Oh, Gust," Wilma said. "You get him so excited."

Gust pinned Jack to the floor, letting the boy catch his breath. "Jack, why don't you run and find Cook," he said. "Have her get you a snack. Uncle Gust has to talk with your mother."

Jack tilted his head back to look at his mother. Wilma, fiddling with the brooch at her throat, nodded. "It's all right, Jack, do as Uncle Gust says. You may tell Cook that I said to get you a snack."

Gust released Jack and, when he popped up, gave him a gentle swat on the rear. Jack toddled out quickly. The only thing more exciting than wrestling with Uncle Gust was the prospect of food.

"He's grown," Gust told Wilma when Jack had gone.

"It's been so long since we've seen you," she said.

He picked up his hat from where he'd dropped it on the floor. "What, two weeks?"

"A month, at least." And it had been much longer since she had been really alone with him.

He shrugged, and put his hand in his pocket. "Time passes so quickly, you know."

"Do you really think so?"

"I haven't wanted to disturb you."

She sat up straighter, folding her hands across the baby within her. "You needn't have worried about that."

"Well, you know," he said.

He walked over to look out the front window. "It's snowing again. There's already an inch of new."

Wilma watched the square of his shoulders framed against the snowy sky visible through the window. "Did you come here to tell me it's snowing?"

He sighed. "No," he said, and turned to face her. "I came because I was just meeting with your husband. My brother. And he was intolerable as usual, begging your pardon. I thought you might be able to help me see the good points in him."

Wilma smiled. John often complained about his younger brother, saying Gust was reckless and never thought of the bottom line. Sometimes Wilma imagined that was all John thought of. "Gust, you and John are just so different. There are bound to be things you disagree on."

"Yah, that's true enough," he said, and pursed his lips. He turned from her and walked to the side window. "How do you get on with him, then, Wilma?" he said, peering out at the trees.

"Fine, I—let him have his way," she said quickly, watching the square of his jaw.

He turned toward her. "Is that the secret, then?"

She touched her brooch.

"It makes me burn inside to see the way he takes his luck for granted," he said suddenly. He threw his hat across the room, where it landed on the sofa. "Just this afternoon, he was groaning about how expensive it is to 'keep' a wife. About the clothes you order from Chicago, and the things for the babies, all the time you 'waste' on your music. I can't even listen to it."

Her hands were clenched. "I shouldn't think you would need to worry yourself about that, Gust."

"If you were my wife, I wouldn't begrudge you the *moon*, Wilma, and the children would have their hearts' desire!"

She dared not move, dared not breathe. His eyes burned on her. In the space between them hovered all that had not been said, and it was blinding. She was on the verge of going to him. He looked away. "Forgive me, Wilma," he said. "I should not have said such a thing."

She bit her lip, hard. "No, Gust."

"It seems I'm always having to apologize to you for the things that I say," he said. "Perhaps I came here intending to say such a thing, and that's even more disgraceful." He made for his hat.

"Don't go," she blurted, and he stopped, looked at her. "I don't—" Just then, the baby kicked her, and she let out a little yelp.

"Are you all right?" Gust said, starting toward her. "Is it the baby?"

She breathed, pressing her hand to her belly. "I don't know what it is. He's usually much calmer." The baby kicked again, as though sensing the unrest in her heart.

"Would you like to feel him?" she asked, recklessly.

"Wilma?" In his eyes was his shock at the impropriety of her proposal.

"I don't care," she said. "Please."

So he approached, and crouched down close to her hip. She felt him come over her like a cloak, his smell of cigars and winter, his warmth. She took his hand in hers, guiding it to her stomach, pressing it there.

"Godsakes," he said, when he felt the baby kick. She could smell the mint on his breath. "Doesn't he hurt you?"

She shook her head, trying to breathe, trying not to reach for him.

He looked up at her. Then he brushed her cheek with his fingertips.

Her eyes drifted closed, and more than just the baby seemed to shift and settle within her. There was no denying it: Gust's life was woven with hers, too. *Do not*—she warned herself, though she knew it was much too late.

Then the heat of him was gone. When she opened her eyes, he was already retrieving his hat from the sofa. "Forgive me, Wilma," he said. "I forget myself when I'm with you—"

She struggled to her feet.

"I'd best go," he said.

"It isn't your fault, Gust." She should have known better than to invite him to touch her; she should have known that there would be consequences for such an indiscretion. "I'm as much to blame—"

"I can't be near you, Wilma. That much should be clear from the way I've behaved. I'll go up to camp and cut lumber for a couple months. We must try to forget this. Pa's been after me about going up, anyway, wanting firsthand how things are going, nothing will look strange—"

"Gust, please," Wilma said, taking a step toward him. Proper ladies weren't supposed to know what went on in the wild town near the lumber camp, but knowledge of the bad women there cracked through Wilma's gut like a whip.

"I wish things could be different, Wilma. You don't know how much, how much I've suffered with it. My own brother's wife—!" He clamped his mouth closed, swept his blue eyes over her, and then he turned and was gone.

She hurried to the front window, watching as he pounded down the porch steps and slid his way down the snowy hill to his waiting horse. He climbed up into the saddle and kicked the bay into motion. She watched until horse and rider faded away into the swirling snow.

"Oh, it's an April fool," she sighed with relief after John came home one afternoon to tell her that Gust had been crushed to death up in the woods when the fall of a tree had been misjudged. She had panicked at first, before realizing it was April first, and that John was certainly joking.

"Wilma, do you think I'd fool about such a thing?" John said. "I didn't even want to tell you, in your condition, but I thought you should know. Pa's gone up to get his body. I'm making arrangements for the funeral. It's going to be on Saturday."

He caught her when she fainted. Chase was born just after midnight.

For days, she was unable to stop weeping. She clutched her sweet, uncomplaining baby to her both waking and sleeping, thinking, *My fault. Here is what happens when I disregard the Rules.*

Baby Chase was all that saved her. Gust had touched him in her womb. Her love was bound with shame, but she could not deny it; God knew the truth, anyway.

Finally, Dr. Seguin, summoned by a worried John, told her that if she didn't stop crying, her milk would turn sour and make the baby colicky. They deemed her too ill to attend the funeral.

FAITH LUTHERAN CHURCH
La Crosse, Wisconsin
Sunday, February 14, 1943

The cavernous church had been quiet when Elissa, Muriel, and Betty first arrived, but now a steady flow of people in their Sunday best, and many men in uniform, filed into the church in an almost unbroken stream. Elissa was sitting straight in the pew and trying not to be too obvious about looking over her shoulder, looking at her watch. It was 10:27, and there was still no sign of Nick.

Muriel, sitting next to her, nudged her with her elbow. "Don't worry, Liss, he'll be here," she whispered. It was all Elissa could do to manage a smile.

She had been kept awake last night imagining what she would say to him when she stepped into the church and saw him standing in the vestibule waiting for her, had practiced on Muriel and Betty the smile she would give him. ("Too much, Liss, he's not Santa Claus"; "That looks like you just ate a lemon"; until she got it right.) They stayed up late discussing the evening's events, Betty explaining that she hadn't allowed the boys to walk them all the way home in order to keep some distance and thus increase their desire. "I'll bet they're lying awake talking about us right now," she insisted, and she seemed to know about such things. Next, they debated over their outfits for church, Elissa choosing the two-piece navy dress she'd just purchased at Doerflinger's, and put one another's hair up in pin curls.

The discomfort of the pin curls, combined with the excitement of Nick, made sleep all but impossible. Elissa rose early to bathe, luxuriating in the steam until, finally, Betty knocked and told her she'd better hurry up. Thus jarred from her reverie, she dried off, dressed, and, with Muriel's help, carefully fixed her hair, gratified to see that the pin curls had worked nicely. A bit of rouge and mascara masked her lack of sleep. Then there was the time-consuming process of applying leg makeup, in lieu of silk or nylon stockings that couldn't be had. Just another thing about the war that they had almost grown accustomed to.

When the girls finally put on their coats ("You look like a million, Liss," Muriel said, squeezing her hand) and set out for church, Betty's parents hadn't even finished their coffee. Having been informed about the boys who would be coming for Sunday dinner, they made wisecracks about how nice it was to see the girls so enthusiastic about getting to church on time. "Har, har, Mom and Dad," Betty said, as the girls stepped out into the gray day. Snow drifted gently to the ground like dogwood blossoms on a Tennessee spring day (or so Elissa imagined), and as their boots made tracks in the thin layer of snow on the sidewalk, she could hardly follow the conversation. It seemed that Betty was discussing not knowing how she would ever choose between Paul and Sam, if it came to that, but all Elissa could think of was the curve of Nick's smile. But then, when they had walked up the church steps, pulled open the heavy wooden doors, and entered the vestibule, Nick wasn't there. And now, as the organ surged into the prelude, and the chattering of the congregation faded, Elissa couldn't help but wonder if all her excitement had been for nothing.

Well, at least, being a Lutheran, she could be stoic about it. She looked at her watch again: 10:29.

And then he was there, in the pew next to her, his shirtsleeve brushing hers, then his arm pressing hers, as he leaned close to her to let his friends into the pew to sit by the other girls. He smelled deliciously of soap and aftershave. The other boys greeted Elissa as they passed, settling into the pew among Muriel and Betty.

Looking at Nick, who was even more handsome today than she'd remembered, Elissa lost all control of her smile and probably gave him the Santa Claus one. He was smiling his small smile, and he winked, said, "Hello," still pressing his shoulder against hers while the last of the boys squeezed past their knees.

"Hello," she whispered back, but there was no time to say anything more; the service was starting.

She supposed she would have to say a special prayer of forgiveness when she arrived back home in Pine Rapids. Though she tried to pay attention to the service, she found she couldn't register a single word of it.

He had come in too late to get a bulletin of his own, and every time he leaned close to read over her shoulder, the scent of his aftershave danced to her nose and made her heart skip. Her palms were sweaty, her mouth dry. Her ears were unnaturally hot. When they stood to sing "Rock of Ages," his fingers brushed hers over the spine of the hymnal. He sang charmingly, drawling the words quietly, a little behind the tempo of the Northern congregation. Seated again, she watched him out of the corner of her eye, could see only his legs, his slim hands resting on his creased uniform pants. She wondered if he was scrutinizing her legs, too; smoothing her skirt over her knees, she looked over at him, and caught his eye. He winked, and reached over to brush his fingertips over the back of her hand. Her lips turned up in a little smile, without her intending it.

She had never spent a more excruciatingly joyous hour in church. When it was over, the organ's last notes sounding their finale, she turned to him, and got lost in the blue of his eyes. "Well," he said quietly. "That was mighty nice."

"Yes, it was."

"Come on, you two." That was Muriel, from Elissa's other side, already on her feet and waiting to exit the pew; Everett, Paul, Betty, and Sam were behind her.

"I reckon we'd best get a move on," Nick said, raising his eyebrows.

"I reckon," Elissa laughed, linking her arm with his when he offered it.

In the vestibule, he helped her on with her coat, and they left the church. The snow was still falling lightly. Again, they let the others hurry ahead.

"I'm real sorry we were late," he said.

"You weren't, really," she said coolly. No sense letting him off the hook entirely.

"I intended on getting you something for Valentine's Day, but every place we went was closed."

She looked at him, surprised, and he held her gaze a moment, smiling a little. Then he looked up at the sky, and stuck out his tongue to catch a falling snowflake. "I reckon it snows pretty near every day around here," he proclaimed then, as though he'd just decided it.

Her heart was drawn more and more to him; she could feel it almost like a physical thing. And she didn't like to think of him as the transient soldier he was, or to acknowledge that he might just disappear from her life as quickly as he'd entered it. If only for a moment, she entertained the dream that perhaps he would not. "Do you like Wisconsin?"

"I like it more since last night," he said.

She watched her boots make tracks in the snow, wanting to believe him. "You're an expert sweet-talker," she said. "You must meet a different girl every weekend."

"I don't even like going dancing, normally. My buddies dragged me to town this weekend. I reckon I'm glad they did." He raised one eyebrow at her. "If you are."

She looked at him, trying to judge his sincerity. Given the conventional wisdom about soldiers, she supposed she shouldn't trust him, but she could see something in the set of his jaw, and the clear blue of his eyes, that made trusting him seem the only thing to do. Besides, love didn't come complete from the start; you built it in small pieces, moment by moment, and you had to start somewhere. "Yes, I'm glad," she said.

"I'm not fooling around with you, Lissa. I just hope you aren't with me, either."

"Of course not."

"You might think it's crazy, but I have this feeling like I spent my whole life dreaming you up, and now all of a sudden here you are."

"Really?"

"You think I'm nuts?" he said.

Though they seemed contrary to what she had just been thinking, his words had immediately felt true. Perhaps love could come complete from the start. The passing of time, the creation of a history, was needed only to verify irrefutability.

"No, I don't think you're nuts," she said, wishing he would stop walking and kiss her.

But he just nodded, his mouth quirking a little. "Good," he said, making sure that her arm was entwined snugly in his, wrapping his hand over hers, as they kept on.

Married people who are happy have babies and unhappy people choose divorce instead. The fact is that babies are symbolic of the permanence of marriage.

—*When You Marry*, 1948

HOME OF MRS. CECILIA FRYT
412 W. First Street, Pine Rapids
Tuesday, July 25, 1950

The meeting in the stuffy parlor started with a modicum of chaos, as the quilt needed to be repositioned on the frame, the finished portion rolled up to leave a new row of unquilted blocks exposed to the ladies' needles. With Mrs. Fryt supervising, Corinne, Thelma, Judy, and Jeannette wrestled with the frame, tightening and smoothing the layers of fabric and finally reinserting the pegs through the frame and into the sawhorses on each end. Dolly tried to help, but to no avail—the women appeared to have a system, and she couldn't find a place in it.

"All right, ladies," commanded Mrs. Fryt, as everyone pulled their chairs up around the quilt. "Let's get down to work."

Dolly settled in her chair heavily, fished her needle and thread from her sewing basket, and began quilting a green triangle. Wild

Goose Chase, indeed—the quilt seemed aptly named, the work end-less, especially now that everything that was exposed was unfinished. Dolly wished she was at the beach. It was only four summers ago, in 1946, that she had been a carefree girl with nothing more on her mind than captivating Byron with her red two-piece. Well, that she had accomplished, and look where it had gotten her. She was toiling away every day at the bungalow and then spending this beautiful, warm summer's day indoors with a bunch of old women—and this when she still looked good in that two-piece! (Well, her legs had al-ways been stocky, but Byron never seemed to mind.) In fact, late last week, as though to prove a point, she had purchased a new red two-piece, this one with a white floral print. When she modeled it for Byron, she had barely had it on for two minutes before he was drag-ging her back to the bedroom. She tried to make him promise to take her to the beach, but he had already made plans to go fishing with Roy on Sunday. "Next week, then," she had said, surrendering her-self to him. Some little good that did, too; this morning she'd discov-ered this month's blood on her panties.

She was beginning to think that if she never got pregnant, she might just as well go to the beach as to the Ladies Aid gatherings. She was sure the beach could be a saving grace to a homemaker just as much as community involvement—why didn't the magazines ever mention that? And after all, what was the point of community in-volvement if she had no child in need of social advancement? Since she and Byron hadn't been born in Pine Rapids, it was hopeless to think that they would ever belong to the upper crust themselves. Even if they did end up living in the Mickelson house.

"Our little Dolly's looking down in the mouth today," Corinne said, jarring Dolly from her thoughts.

"Indeed," said Mrs. Fryt, pursing her lips as she started a line of stitching.

"Oh, I'm sorry—" Dolly said.

"Aren't thinking of quitting, are you?" Mrs. Fryt said. "Days like this are when we always lose the youngsters."

"Oh, no, I—"

"For heaven's sake, Cecilia," Thelma snapped.

For a moment, uneasy silence reigned. No one knew what to make of such an outburst from mild, elegant Thelma.

"What's the matter, Thelma?" Corinne said finally.

"I'm sorry, ladies," Thelma sighed. "I suppose I'm tired. I was up half the night with George. He had a terrible cough."

"Is he better today?" Jeannette asked.

"He seems so," Thelma said. "I've finally convinced him to go to the doctor, though. You know men, they'll never go of their own free will."

"Isn't that the truth," Mrs. Fryt said.

"And we women will go at the slightest hint of trouble," Corinne said. She laughed, clearly trying to take Thelma's mind off her troubles. "Especially when Dr. Seguin was our doctor. He was so handsome! Of course, after he delivered all three of my children, that pretty much ruined the romance."

"I suppose Judy and Dolly are the only ones here that Dr. Seguin hasn't delivered of children," Jeannette said, her nose twitching.

"Did he deliver Wilma Mickelson's babies?" Dolly asked. If the children were born in the house, she wanted to know all the details.

"She never gets enough," Judy muttered. Dolly glared at her. This week, Dolly had even more reason to dislike Judy than ever: During church on Sunday, she'd caught Judy making eyes at Byron. Dolly supposed Judy was desperate for a husband, but setting her cap for an already married man was despicable. Fortunately, Byron hadn't noticed. It was perhaps the first time that Dolly had been pleased with his obtuseness.

"Yes," Mrs. Fryt said, "Dr. Seguin delivered all four of Wilma's children, and her two grandchildren, too. She had a hard time with her third, Harry. He came in the middle of a bad storm at the beginning of January. Jack couldn't have been more than five years old, but they sent him out for Dr. Seguin, in the middle of that raging blizzard."

"Didn't they have a telephone?" Dolly asked.

"Oh, of course the Mickelsons did, but the line was dead that night, with the storm," Mrs. Fryt explained. "I said later, why didn't they just send Jack over to get my husband? He would have gone for the doctor. But no, that little boy ran downtown, and when he didn't find the doctor at his office, he ran all the way to his house. Thank goodness Dr. Seguin was home. He dragged Jack up in the saddle with him and they rode right over, lickety-split. I heard that Harry didn't come for hours, though. He might have been breech, I don't remember."

Dolly shuddered. Sometimes she was glad that she couldn't seem to get pregnant.

"Goodness, that Jack," Thelma said.

"Yes, he always was that way," Mrs. Fryt declared. "There was just no stopping him. Like I was saying about him taking Chase off to the war. Once Jack made up his mind, that was it."

Corinne sighed. "When I think of Wilma now, and how awful that time must have been for her. Remember how we were talking about her garden last time? I don't think any of us really understood, then. Of course, now some of us have experienced that, our boys going off to war. But then, Wilma was different from the rest of us, wasn't she?"

"*I* still can't understand the way she let her irises go, there on the side of the house," said Mrs. Fryt. "Planted them all in a fit one day, and then forgot about them. It used to make me want to cry, the way those irises begged to be divided."

"She was doing the best she could, wasn't she, Mother?" Jeannette said. "You always say, some people aren't made as strong as others."

"Yes, but most people don't bring their families crashing down around them, either."

"Wilma sure made good sweet pickles, though," Corinne said, laughing, doing her best to lighten the mood. "She brought them to the Thanksgiving potluck that year. I remember because we all commented on it. We were afraid they were going to be just awful!"

"Well, consider the source," Mrs. Fryt sniffed.

At the other end of the quilt, Judy was pursing her bright pink lips and shaking her head. "You're wrong about Wilma Mickelson, Grandma," she said, almost under her breath, not looking up from her quilting. "In the end, everything was Elissa's fault. The way she chased after that soldier—"

THE MICKELSON HOUSE
502 W. First Street, Pine Rapids
August 1917

Early in the summer, Wilma had subscribed to *Good Housekeeping*, thinking it would assist her with advice on preserving the food from her war garden. She was hung up on the idea of making pickles, and the magazine afforded her what John viewed as a perilous amount of information. "For sweet gherkins, the cucumbers must be between one-and-a-half and three inches," she told the family one night at dinner, as though she was quoting from an article. "Can you imagine? Just one-and-a-half inches! Imagine something that small being of any use at all." John shared skeptical looks with Harry and Jinny; they all doubted she would go through with it.

But they had forgotten: This was a new Wilma, and there was no stopping her.

Some mornings John would watch her from the back porch. Wearing a broad-brimmed straw hat, with a basket hooked over her arm, she would tiptoe between the rows of cucumber plants, lifting the wide, prickly leaves to peek for pickle-size product. When she saw something, she crouched to wrestle it from the plant, and John could observe her conversion in the way she examined each cucumber before setting it in her basket, like they were holy relics, evidence of God.

Day by day, she lined the cucumbers on the counter in the pantry, first one dozen, then two, then three. Soon there were too many to fit on the counter, and Wilma sent Harry to the co-op for bushel baskets. The peas and beans were coming now, too, and even a few tomatoes, and they'd already enjoyed a couple weeks of fresh radishes, beets, and spinach.

Finally, the time was upon them for the first batch of pickles: sweet gherkins. From what John could surmise, the process of making them took her the better part of a week, during which time he, Harry, and Jinny were told in no uncertain terms to stay out of the pantry. "And if you *must* go *in* there," she told them, "don't touch a thing!" He couldn't resist, at midnight one night when he tiptoed down for a glass of milk (Wilma fast asleep on their bed, snoring in sheer exhaustion), sneaking in to peer under the lid of the crock. In the darkness the contents looked like a witch's brew, whole cucumber flesh bobbing in dark, sweetly vile liquid, among mysterious flecks of other matter. Though the spiced vinegar smell made him shudder, the concoction was strangely captivating. Harry, down for his usual midnight snack, discovered his father hovering over the crock, and let out an accusing "Aha!" John had to promise to take him out in the car for a driving lesson in exchange for his silence.

After the cucumbers had cured for the appropriate amount of time, Wilma canned eighteen pint jars of sweet gherkins, the steam filling the kitchen (to hear Harry tell it; John was at work) thick enough to choke a person. The following week, she was on to dill pickles, dismissing the cook for the day so that she might have full use of the kitchen. Over a cold supper on the night the pickles were finished, Jinny reported that Wilma had let her help pack the cucumbers (which had been soaked overnight in brine, again with strict instructions to the family to *keep out*) into the hot jars lined up on the kitchen counter. Wilma had poured the boiling mixture of liquid and spices into all the jars; Jinny had followed, putting on the lids. Then Wilma had lowered the jars into boiling water, while Jinny was the official clock-watcher, telling her when it had been twenty minutes exactly. "You shoulda seen Mom, Dad," Jinny announced. "It was like she'd done it a million times before." A sharp gleam of pride shone in Wilma's eyes.

The next evening, watching Wilma at supper while Harry gave a play-by-play account of the afternoon's baseball game, John reflected that he was glad to see her finally coming into her own as a woman, accomplishing concrete things. Though her ethereal nature had always magnetized him, he realized now how maddening it had been. It was nice to think that she had finally joined him in the real world. She was a better mother to their children, and was contributing more to the household. She never played the piano anymore. If only she would grant him the pleasures of their bed, he decided, he would be entirely satisfied with her.

After supper, Wilma announced that the two dozen quart jars of dill pickles had cooled sufficiently and that she would be lining them up in the pantry. John offered to help. "You've been working so hard, Wilma, just let me do this one thing," he told her, following her into the kitchen. He hoped that she might reciprocate the gesture with favors in the bedroom.

"You really don't have to help, John," she told him. "The maid can help me when she comes down to do the dishes. Why don't you go sit and read the paper?"

The kids had scattered off, banging out the door as soon as they were excused from the table. It was a warm summer evening, and a gentle breeze that smelled of hemlock and slightly of manure wafted through the screens, mixing with the scents of dill and vinegar that lingered in the kitchen. "It's all right, Wilma, I'm glad to help," John boomed, feeling it true, lifting one of the jars with both hands. Her handiwork: He would be careful.

He stepped aside at the door of the pantry so she could get out (she smiled up at him; his heart fluttered a little, as though they were courting again!) and he stepped in, placing his jar on the pantry shelf next to where she had placed hers.

Returning from his ninth trip, he took her in his arms and began waltzing with her.

"John!" she said, her waltz step clumsy with surprise at first, then melting into grace as she set the jar of pickles she had been carrying on the butcher block in the center of the room. "What's gotten into you?"

"It's the summer, Wilma," he said. "Having you here in the summer. It's like we're young again." *Or, could be,* he added, to himself.

"It isn't either, John," she scoffed, but she continued dancing with him.

"It is," he insisted. "And we're not that old, really, when you think of it."

"Speak for yourself."

"I will. I'll say you're just as beautiful now as you ever were."

She laughed. "John."

"I'm glad you made pickles, Wilma. You seem happier now. Just be careful that you don't overdo."

"That would be impossible. As long as the boys are over there, I can't do enough."

"Still, though, Wilma, they wouldn't want you taxing yourself like this."

"Well, I have to do *something*!"

"Yes, but—" Mid-waltz, he felt the back of his hand brush against the cool, firm surface of a canning jar. There was a terrific crash. Liquid splashed onto his ankles.

"Oh!" Wilma said. She dropped his hands and sank to the floor. "Oh."

"Wilma," he said, crouching next to her. For a moment he thought the pickles might be salvageable. He would run to the store, get a new jar, they'd repack them, good as new. Then he saw the shards and crystals of shattered glass mixed with the pickles as finely as spice.

"My pickles, John," she said. "I worked so hard."

"Wilma, I didn't mean to," he said. "It's just one jar. I'll clean it up." He reached for the metal band around the lid; the top half of the jar was still attached, hanging from it with jagged edges. He picked it up quickly, and just at the same time, she reached for it. A bottom edge of the glass sliced her palm like a knife; a breath later, bright blood showed in a thin line.

"Wilma!" John said, straightening quickly to his feet, broken jar still in his hand. "Where's a towel? We have to stop the bleeding."

"Don't," she said.

He looked down at her. She had closed her hand into a fist over the shattered pickle jar and was watching it. A drop of blood fell from her hand, mixing with the liquid on the floor. "Wilma, we have to get you a bandage."

"It doesn't matter," she said.

John panicked: the ethereal tone of her voice. Had he lost her again? "Of course it does!"

"It's just God's way of showing us," she said. "That we haven't any control."

"Don't be ridiculous, Wilma." John set his part of the broken jar in the sink, started pulling out drawers, slamming them shut. He couldn't remember where the towels were. "It was just an accident. Now let me get something to wrap your hand with." As he turned toward her again, he saw another drop of her blood fall from within her fist into the pickle juice on the floor. The smell of the pickles was wafting upward, their sweet-sourness burning his throat.

"It doesn't even bother you," she said. "Does it? That they're gone?"

He looked at her; had finally had enough. "I'm proud of them, for God's sake! And so they're gone. They'll be back!"

"People are dying over there, John. Thousands of people are dying."

"Not Americans."

"You can't honestly believe we'll get through this whole war without any Americans—"

"Not my boys."

"How do you know, John? Did God tell you?"

"Well, apparently, He's been talking to you."

"I've tried. I've made bargains with Him. If I sew this many kits, the boys will be all right. If I give up my piano, if I stop being so selfish, plant a garden, be good to Harry and Jinny, then the boys will be all right."

"Good Lord, Wilma," he said. So this was the explanation for her change.

"I never should have been a mother, John," she said. "I was never meant to be a mother, and here I am, four times over. Do you know what it's like? Knowing they came out of *me*? Everything they do, it's like they're plucking these little pieces right out of my body. Carrying me away with them. Those boys!—not realizing that when they go off to the war it's like they grabbed my stomach and are hauling it along with them, trailing my intestines across the ocean! I swear to you, John, if something happened to them—"

"Nothing's going to happen to them."

"You talk as if you could never be wrong," she said. "You've been wrong about me. All these years, you've been wrong. You didn't know I never wanted them. I never wanted them! I just wanted to play the piano. I was such a fool! I believed you when you told me I could have it all, my music, and you, and some beautiful life with everything I wanted—well, I *can't.* It's taken me long enough to realize it, hasn't it? Or maybe I realized it years ago, but it was already too late. And now I'm stuck here in this disgusting town where everyone hates me, stuck just praying my awful heart out. And I would give my life for these ungrateful children, when I was tricked into the whole thing, this life, motherhood! I didn't want them! I didn't want them!"

"You—" John started to say, but a part of him had heard the small gasp from outside the kitchen door. Wilma looked back at the door. She had heard it, too. She pressed her fist to her mouth.

John's shoes crunched on the glass as he crossed the room in three strides, walking through the open door between the kitchen and porch just in time to see the tail end of Jinny's skirt and little shoes flying around the corner of the house. "Jinny!" he called, banging out the screen door and stumbling down the back stoop after her. He meant to catch her, but when he rounded the corner, he could not see where she had gone. He was out of shape, couldn't run. He stood in the side yard, gripping his head in his hands. "Jinny! Come back!" he tried again, but there was no sign of her.

HOME OF JACK AND MARY MICKELSON
505 Rapids Avenue, Pine Rapids
Monday, February 22, 1943

After school on Monday, a week after their La Crosse trip, a downhearted Elissa and her best friend, Muriel, were just about to trudge up to Elissa's room with hot cocoa—they had much to discuss—when Elissa's mother Mary looked up from the pie crust she was making and said, "Oh, Liss, you got a letter."

For a moment, Elissa scarcely dared to hope.

But then her mother smiled. "I expect it's something to do with that shopping trip to La Crosse you wanted to make."

Elissa and Muriel looked at each other, squealed, dropped their cocoa mugs on the counter, and raced to the front hall. The letter was waiting on the sideboard.

Elissa had been unable to think of anything but Nick the entire seven days since she had left him. Only seven days! It already seemed an eternity. She kept replaying in her mind all the moments she had spent with him, and especially the Sunday afternoon good-bye scene at the La Crosse depot. "Good-bye" had never seemed so dreadful a word! And yet, after church and dinner with Betty's family, there had been no choice but to go to catch the train. Nick and the other boys offered to escort her and Muriel; the eight-block walk had taken far too short a time. Then, as they stood on the platform together, it was difficult to know what to say. Elissa didn't remember what sort of idiotic small talk she'd ended up making, when there was so much that she wanted to say and was afraid to. And then came the call: "All aboard!"

"Well, I sure hope you can come down next weekend," Nick had said to her then, kicking at the platform, adding with a little grin, "and that you'll still like me all right." He lifted his hand and brushed her cheek with his knuckle; she felt her knees tremble. The train whistle blew. Muriel called to her from the steps of the coach.

When Elissa stepped away from Nick, up the steps into the car, and he let go of her hand, she felt like she'd been torn in half. It seemed impossible that she had met him only the night before; she felt so suddenly incomplete, leaving him. He smiled at her, shoving his hands into the pockets of his overcoat. She stayed standing in the doorway until the train started to move; her last vision of him was blurry with tears. Finding her seat next to Muriel, she was experiencing a peculiar mix of clammy hands, burning throat and eyes, cheeks aching from smiling too big for too long. Muriel made an immediate diagnosis: "You're in love," she declared, squeezing Elissa's arm. "Isn't it swell?"

Elissa had long wished for something romantic to happen to her, but she'd had no idea of the pain that would be involved. "Oh, Muriel," she'd sighed. "I just *have* to see him again."

But when she got home to her parents, her father had absolutely refused to let her go back to La Crosse the following weekend for more "shopping." He said that the trains were crowded enough with the war, and one frivolous trip was more than enough for the year. Then he lit his pipe and disappeared behind the newspaper, putting his feet in their ratty old slippers up on the ottoman. Her mother shot her a sympathetic look, but they both knew there was nothing she could do. Once Jack Mickelson made up his mind, that was it.

"For the *year*!" she'd exclaimed to Muriel over the phone that night. "What am I going to do?"

"You could always tell him the truth, tell him about Nick," Muriel suggested.

That was out of the question. "Oh, no, then he'd never even let me out of the house!"

Elissa's father had not allowed her to date at all until she was sixteen, and he only agreed to that after a year-long campaign she began the day she turned fifteen. (Fortunately, her mother and her brother, JJ, had both taken her part, or she probably still would not be allowed.) And still, as a prelude to the first date, each boy had been subjected to at least a half hour in the living room with Jack, who would sit in his chair by the fireplace wearing his old slippers, smoking his pipe, and staring at them with his icy blue eyes. The boys, making faltering stabs at conversation, would be met with only silence and cool, appraising looks, puffs of smoke. Most were soon reduced to cold sweats, flushes, indigestion. After all, Jack was a legend at Pine Rapids High: His 1915 rushing record still stood, and his Great War uniform and record of service were prominently displayed in the front foyer. This was the man in Pine Rapids whom a boy's father, when in need of a favor, went to with hat in hand.

Needless to say, Elissa didn't have many dates, and, of those boys brash enough to ask for one, few asked for a second. And now Jack was standing in the way of things with Nick. Elissa felt her life was utterly hopeless. Her father was just so *old*—she imagined he always had been—and obviously had no idea about romance or anything that was important. And the worst thing was, he didn't even *try* to understand!

Muriel told her that she would just have to write to Nick and hope that she could persuade Jack soon to let her take another trip to La Crosse. So, with a heavy heart, Elissa had done so, still wondering if perhaps she had imagined the whole experience, the entire realm of feelings. It wasn't possible that Nick could feel such unreasoning excitement and anguish about her—was it? Plagued with such doubts, she hedged her letter a bit, was friendly but not gushing. She was apologetic, even regretful, but took care not to let any of her tears fall onto the letter. She did not put a lipstick print on the envelope. When she mailed it, she was as depressed as she had ever been in her life, and spent the next few days hollow-souled, bereft. She had supposed he would not even bother to reply, since it was unlikely they'd ever see each other again.

But now: a letter! She tore it open; Muriel read over her shoulder.

Hello, sweetheart, I was sure sorry you couldn't come down, it said, his handwriting a narrow scrawl. *I hope you don't mind me saying so, but ever since you got on that train, I've been missing you. If it's all right with you, and your family, I would like to come see you next weekend. I could come Sat.* A.M. *(the 27th) and leave Sun.* P.M. *We're going up to Michigan on maneuvers in March, so if I don't come now it will be some time before I am able to. Or if you don't want me to come, just say so, and I won't. But I would sure like to look in those pretty blue eyes again. Maybe we could even go dancing again, if you don't mind me stepping all over your toes! Ha ha. Just let me know. Yours, Nick.*

"He wants to come visit!" Elissa whispered, wide-eyed, to Muriel.

The battle that evening had all the earmarks of a family legend in the making.

Finally, all rational arguments failing, Elissa burst into tears and sobbed for what must have been an hour. And her parents, seeing there was no other way to stop her tears, relented—if grudgingly.

"Well," Jack grumbled finally, leaning back in his chair, picking up the newspaper. He always had to at least act as though he had gotten the last word, so he added, "As long as he's in the Second, I suppose it's all right." Jack and his brother Chase had been Marines with the 2nd Division in the Great War when it was first formed for service in France, composed of one brigade each of Marines, U.S. Infantry, and artillery. "See what he's made of, anyhow. See what his intentions are," he muttered, rustling the newspaper open. "Although I don't like it one bit, you know," he said, more loudly, peering around the paper to flash his eyes at his wife. "The way she went behind our back. And him being in the Army—I know what those guys are like."

"I know, Jack, and I don't like it, either," Mary said, "but you'll be here to keep an eye on him." Elissa's mother was next to Elissa on the sofa, rubbing her back while she hiccuped. "Besides, it looks like it's too late for us to stop it. And she'll hate us if we try. Chances are, it will burn out on its own."

Elissa hiccuped again. "Just wait until you meet him! You'll see."

There was no response from behind the newspaper; a warning glance from her mother.

But Elissa didn't care. She would fight for Nick. She knew he was worth it. "Excuse me," she said then, with all the dignity she could muster. At least her hiccups had faded. "I have to go write to Nick." She stood, intending to make a haughty exit.

But however much she wished she was that sort of girl, she wasn't. So she leaned down to hug and kiss her mother. Then she walked over to stand beside Jack's chair. "Dad?"

Jack looked out from behind the newspaper.

"Thank you, Daddy," she said.

She thought he almost smiled. "You could bring me my pipe," he said.

HOME OF MRS. CECILIA FRYT
412 W. First Street, Pine Rapids
Tuesday, July 25, 1950

"Judy, you're overly dramatic," Mrs. Fryt snapped at her copper-haired granddaughter, and Judy glared at her grandmother, then turned back to work on the quilt, yanking her needle through like an ill-tempered maestro marking beats.

Dolly, having finished quilting the green triangle and moved to the blue one next to it, decided it was a good thing, after all, that she was here and not at the beach—knowing the story of what had happened in the Mickelson house might help her to understand why the family had left it to fall into disrepair. Besides, hearing about the Mickelsons gave her a funny little thrill, when she hadn't been thrilled about much of anything lately.

"The truth is," Mrs. Fryt continued, "regardless of that soldier and Elissa, that Mickelson house would have fallen in on itself. I saw everything, all those years—and the truth is, no one in that family had the least bit of faith in their own two feet standing on the ground. They believed themselves helpless, and that house just fell down around them, piece by piece, while they sat there and watched like their hands were tied! And I'll tell you when it went from bad to worse: the minute Wilma got the news about Chase. You ladies remember! How Wilma became a perfect monster. And at the moment her family needed her most! I can hardly blame John, looking back on it. You ladies remember the way she slammed the door in my face when I brought the pound cake."

"Haven't you forgiven her for that yet?" asked Corinne.

"As a matter of fact, no," Mrs. Fryt said. "I don't see why I should—why I didn't deserve to be treated with decency, when I was reaching out to her."

"What news?" Dolly asked nervously.

"Haven't you seen the statue on the courthouse lawn?" Judy said. "It's a likeness of Chase. They only added the second war's names to it."

"You don't mean—" Dolly had seen the statue of a soldier from a distance across the courthouse lawn, but she had never approached it, assuming she wouldn't know any of the names on it. Apparently, she had been wrong.

Mrs. Fryt turned to Dolly. "When the news got out about Chase, everyone was beside themselves, of course. It was in the newspaper, but still no one could believe it. John admitted they'd gotten the telegram, but Wilma wouldn't show her face in town. It was several days that went by, and finally I decided I couldn't let it go any longer. So I made up one of my special pound cakes, and when it cooled I put it on my best plate and marched over there with it. And do you know what she said when she answered the door? Well, first she said nothing at all, just stared at me, and I told her, 'We're all so very sorry to hear about your son.' She said, 'I don't believe that he's dead, thank you,' and slammed the door right in my face. She wouldn't even take the pound cake."

Thelma shook her head. "She was in denial for the longest time."

"Oh, well, of course!" Dolly said, having a hard time herself accepting the news.

"It took her years to accept it, years!" Mrs. Fryt said. "And I don't know that she ever forgave Jack. It was his idea, after all, them both going to war."

"They might have been drafted," Corinne pointed out. "And everyone admired them so for choosing to go like they did."

"But if they hadn't gone so early, they might not have gotten into the thick of that battle. Not many did, you know." Mrs. Fryt shook her head. "I'll never forget the sound of her screaming, that June day when she got the telegram. Enough to curdle cheese, that sound. It carried all the way over here and it made the hair on the backs of my arms stand up. Do you remember that, Jeannette? You heard it, too, and you came downstairs to the kitchen. You were pale as a ghost. I suppose we knew what it had to be."

"It was a few days before we found out for certain," Jeannette said. "And when a day had gone by and we hadn't heard anything, I told myself maybe she'd seen a mouse."

"A woman doesn't scream like murder over a mouse," Mrs. Fryt said.

"Well—I hoped!"

PINE RAPIDS MESSENGER
Friday, June 7, 1918

SEA SOLDIERS ADVANCE AGAINST FIERCE ATTACKS

YANKEES DASH INTO FRAY YELLING
LIKE INDIANS—NO QUARTER

*Germans Put Up Stout Resistance, Officers Urging Them
On—Impetuous Onrush of Marines Completely Overpowers Enemy*
(By Associated Press)

WITH THE AMERICAN FORCES ON THE MARNE, JUNE 7.—
The American Marines who began a second attack on the German lines late yesterday captured the village of Torcy and drove
their way into Bouresches, northwest of Château-Thierry. This

morning they were holding Torcy in the face of repeated counter-attacks and were pushing back the Germans through the streets of Bouresches. Virtually all their objectives in this attack were attained. . . .

The one point where the objective was not reached was on the right of the attack in the Belleau Wood. The fiercest fighting is continuing here. . . .

FIRST NATIONAL BANK OF PINE RAPIDS
101 W. First Street, Pine Rapids
Monday, June 24, 1918

A June day, so glorious that all the bank's windows are open, even the windows in the conference room where John Mickelson is meeting with his vice president, Odell Drake, and cashier Hal Lundholm. A warm breeze—like a miracle, after the long, frozen winter—dances through the building, tickling customers and tellers into laughter, friendly conversation. Everyone feeling looser, more at ease, really beginning to thaw. One of the first truly warm days they've had, warm enough that John has removed his jacket and rolled up his shirt-sleeves, and he can't help but feel the fortune and glory of living.

But it's easy enough to feel fortunate when you're president of the First National Bank of Pine Rapids and watching your numbers climb steadily up, since Secretary of the Treasury McAdoo has been telling Americans to borrow from their local banks to buy Liberty bonds. "A man who can't lend his government a dollar twenty-five per week at four percent interest is not entitled to be an American citizen," the secretary has said, and movie stars such as Mary Pickford and Douglas Fairbanks are saying the same thing, inciting rallies to such patriotic fervor as has never been seen. Even here in Pine Rapids, people are buying bonds at a rate John would not have anticipated. The First National Bank of Pine Rapids happily lends citizens the money to buy all the bonds they want, and then happily rediscounts the same bonds at the Federal Reserve district bank downstate. It is much more profitable than financing the small farms in the area that almost invariably fail.

John has hung a service banner with two blue stars in the bank's window, representing Jack and Chase, and makes it a point to personally thank each person who comes in to buy a Liberty bond, on behalf of his boys. Everyone wants to know how the boys are doing, of course, and John's pride is expansive, thinking about, talking about them. "They're doing great! Having a grand time!" he was able to report, throughout the past winter. "Seeing a lot of France! Meeting so many French people! They're billeted in a new place just about every week, with a new French family, and marching all day every day, you know, training, getting in shape. They say the French people are wonderful! They've heard the sounds of the guns at the front lines a few times, but they haven't seen any action yet."

In the letters the boys wrote, this past winter, they couldn't reveal where they were, exactly, but from the newspaper John was able to gather that the Americans were massing to the south and west of the lines, waiting until they were substantial enough in number to get into the heart of the fray as an independent American force.

But, just as the first spring robin appeared in Pine Rapids, and patches of gray began to appear on the thawing river, the news was dramatically *not good* for the Allies. The Germans had launched a tremendous offensive and, according to the papers, had advanced thirty-seven miles in five days, driving back the Allies and nearly separating the British from the French. Reports indicated that some Parisians were fleeing to the south, and the French government was considering relocating to Bordeaux. The Americans were needed, desperately, and General Pershing finally ordered some of them to help the French reinforce areas of their lines.

It was unclear, back in Pine Rapids, just exactly how the boys were involved, just exactly where they were. "I'm sure they wouldn't go into the fighting without telling us first!" Wilma exclaimed, knitting needles flying, one spring evening in the living room as John read aloud pieces of the newspaper and the latest, disappointingly vague letter that had arrived from Chase: "*The worst thing,*" John read, "*is seeing the gray faces of the French people—women and children and some old men—who are walking one way down the road while we are walking the other way up it. All that's left of their worldly goods is packed into wagons or carts, and they creak along like a long, broken-down train. In the really unfortunate cases, all they have is tied up in kerchiefs and clenched in their fists. It is terrible to think of all the people who have lost their homes, and I can't imagine what it would be like if a war was fought right in Pine Rapids like it is being fought in the backyards of these folks—*"

"But what about him?" Wilma broke in. "Does he say where he is? What he's doing? Is he in danger? Is he getting enough to eat? Is he warm enough? Has he seen Jack?"

"He says he's fine, that's all," John said, skimming over the rest of the letter. "More about the French people and the way the land looks. Some about the other boys in his company. Here's a drawing of a peasant woman."

"Let me see that," she said, getting out of her chair to snatch the letter and the drawing from his hands, trailing yarn behind her.

The hardest thing was the not knowing. What they were doing. Where in the world they were. "Somewhere in France!" As though that phrase were enough to calm a parent's worried mind.

But now it's a glorious June day and John Mickelson with his sleeves rolled up is full of optimism, full of an extravagant sense of the justness of his life and business in wartime America. Not only are things going well at the bank, but he has also had the foresight to diversify his other interests. He is out of the lumber business entirely—he had never liked it—and now owns a creamery, a cheese factory, and a resort some fifteen miles north of town, all managed by men so capable that John rarely troubles even to visit them. These things are the future of Pine Rapids, now that the white pines are long gone; true, the three establishments together don't employ near the number of men that the mill did, but a man has to do what's best for himself and his own. John has also invested heavily in the stock market, and watches with awe as his money increases with no effort whatsoever on his part.

Wilma, too, has been a stellar wife these last months, since the bitterness of the pickle disaster has ebbed. It's true that if John had been asked on that terrible day whether he would ever again feel tenderness toward his wife, he would have answered with an unqualified no. But now, nearly a year later, the episode has receded in his mind. Sometimes he even imagines it must have been a nightmare. Wilma now is pleasant, droll, warm toward him and the children. Still diligent about the garden and her war work, but lacking the frenetic air of obsession that possessed her the first few months of the boys' absence. Worried about her children overseas as any mother would be, but pleasant about it, admirable, brave. Meek now, too, toward her husband: roast when he wants it, and pleasures in the bedroom, too. He is king of his home once more, and so great are his wife's ministrations that he feels himself (and his boys, too) invincible. If he thinks of the "curse" at all, it is only to chide himself for ever giving it any measure of credence.

In fact, on a glorious June day like this, John can almost forget, even, that these last couple of weeks have put his gut on edge. No letters from the boys. News that the Germans have again made a push toward Paris and at long last the Americans have been getting into some heavy fighting. News that the Marines have been involved in the heaviest of it, along the Marne. They're in the middle of it, in fact, and have been for two weeks or more, and John knows from the newspapers it's in a small place called Belleau Wood. His boys are almost undoubtedly there, though Wilma maintains the hope that they have become separated from their brigade, or that their particular regiment or company has been held back in the rear. John doubts that this is true.

But a June day like this makes a man happy just to be alive, making good money, married to a good woman, father of four extraordinary children. True, Wilma has been on edge lately, despite that he's kept the newspapers away from her, has told her only the bare minimum; she's developed a bit of a twitch, of her lip, at times. At least she can laugh about it, a small, skittering laugh. Saying, "Just think of it as a smile!" And true, Wilma and John have both been having trouble sleeping; he encountered her at three-thirty this morning when he went downstairs for a glass of milk. One small lamp shining on the work in her hands, she was sitting in the living room knitting, needles clicking, and she looked up with frightened eyes when she heard his footsteps. Almost before he recognized the motion of her face as one of her incorrigible twitches, she had turned it into a small (if fluctuating) smile. Neither spoke; he crossed to her and kissed her forehead and walked on into the kitchen, the clicking of her needles following him like a pack of yippy dogs nipping at his heels.

But on a June day like this—who can worry at all? In fact, John, sitting in the meeting with Odell and Hal, finds himself recalling his childhood: rambling down by the waterfront, fishing on Green Bay, lost in his own boy world, when entire afternoons could center on the capture of a dime-size brown toad, the perfecting of a duck call using a blade of grass.

John is half listening to Hal's numbers, and half thinking about buying a new fishing pole, when his son Harry bursts into the conference room. Harry, fifteen, growing taller by the day, his handsome face now white as one of the puffy clouds floating across the sky this beautiful day.

"Dad!" Harry yelps, interrupting Hal. All three bankers regard him with surprise, indignation.

"Dad, you'd better come home. We got a telegram. It's Chase."

His own heavy feet, crunching the gravel of the road with each quick step, Harry urging, "Come on, Dad. Mom's not doing so good."

He's left his papers strewn on the conference table, left Odell and Hal standing with their knuckles on the table, mouths gaping. He has not stopped for his jacket, is barely conscious of the stunned silence in the bank—tellers, customers, his secretary, all standing with knotted hands and brows, watching as he follows Harry out with matching long strides.

A block from home, John has to stop to catch his breath. The leaves on the sheltering maples rustle like a dance line; clouds explode against the bright blue sky. Harry strides on. "Harry!" John calls after him.

The boy turns, his mouth grim, hair gleaming in the sun.

"Harry! What is it? Is he—injured?"

"No, Dad," Harry calls back.

John feels his throat constrict. "Well, then—killed?"

"Yeah, Dad," Harry says, and turns and runs toward the house.

When John walks in the front door, the house feels paralyzed. There is no sound—no chattering from the kitchen, no ticking of a clock. Nothing.

Then John hears Harry's voice in the dining room: "Mom?"

But John is mesmerized by the rectangle of paper he sees on the hall floor. He can read the block letters across the top: WESTERN UNION. He bends to retrieve it, begins to read. It is addressed to Mr. and Mrs. John Mickelson, Pine Rapids, Wisconsin.

REGRET TO INFORM YOU
YOUR SON CHASE G. MICKELSON
KILLED IN ACTION JUNE 6
BELLEAU WOOD
STOP
LETTER TO FOLLOW
STOP

"Mom!" comes Harry's voice again from the dining room, but John does not go to his wife and son. *Now we have a hero in the family,* he thinks. Strange, though: In his mind's eye, Chase is still ten years old. John simply cannot conjure a picture of him any older than that. Amazing thing to contemplate, a ten-year-old war hero! He stares at the telegram, registering each word.

CHASE.
KILLED.
JUNE 6.
BELLEAU WOOD.

Their son has been dead a good two weeks, without their even knowing it! While John has been foolishly whistling over his good fortune, over the Americans making a good showing in the battle. His horror muted by shock, he wonders if their other son, if Jack, is dead, too. Would the world allow such folly on the part of a father? Would it allow that level of self-absorbed ignorance?

"Dad?"

He looks up at Harry.

"Dad? Mom's in here at the table. She won't say anything. She's just—" Harry looks back over his shoulder. "Just sitting here. She doesn't look good, Dad."

John takes a last look at the telegram, folds it and stuffs it into his shirt pocket, then gets up to telephone Dr. Seguin. He has no trouble with the operator, but once he gets Dr. Seguin on the phone, it is all he can do to croak, "Doc. John Mickelson. Please. My wife—" No more words will come; he replaces the earpiece on the cradle, sets the phone back on its table. Then he goes, finally, into the dining room. Wilma is seated in one of the side chairs, her elbows on the table, fists pressed to her face. Her eyes are closed.

"Wilma?" John ventures; she does not move. Feeling Harry's eyes on his back, he crosses the room to where she sits. He knows he has to take control, or they will not get through this day. He crouches next to her chair, slides one arm behind her back and the other under her knees, then stands with her cradled to his chest. Her eyes flash up at him, desolate, angry. She covers her face with her hands, lets out a low moan. He bites down on his lip before turning back to Harry.

"I'm going to take her up to bed," John tells his son. "Doc will be coming. Send him up when he gets here. She'll be all right, son," he adds, passing Harry by, unable to feel where Wilma's trembling stops and his begins.

After John lays her on the bed, Wilma will not speak to him, will not open her eyes or move. He doesn't know what to say to her, anyway; he sits slumped in the chair in the corner. He feels like he has terrible heartburn.

Only when Dr. Seguin arrives do Wilma's eyes open. Her first words: "I've done all I could do. And still He saw fit to punish me."

"No, Wilma," John objects, horrified.

Her eyes snap gray onto him. "How would *you* know?"

Dr. Seguin lays a comforting hand on her shoulder and gives John a pacific look. "Now, Mrs. Mickelson, you just rest," the doctor says, his eyes telling John that she'll be back to herself in no time. It's been a tremendous shock, certainly, but she'll be just fine in no time at all.

But, judging by the glint in her eyes, John does not believe it.

Doc administers a sedative. When he leaves, John charges Harry with looking after Wilma, and goes outside to find Jinny. She is up in her tree house and won't come down. John has little energy for cajoling; finally, he just sits down at the foot of the birch, leaning his back up against its sturdy trunk, facing away from Wilma's garden, toward the fir trees that line their yard to the west. He sighs deeply, feeling the ache of his knees, thinking, *Someday soon I am going to die, too.* Thinking, *It is not true it is not true my son how can it be?* Extracting the folded telegram from his pocket and spreading it open across his knee. *There must be some mistake, this cannot be.* With his little daughter twelve feet above his head, the rectangular paper held flat by his palm, he sits there long enough to watch the day fade away, the sun sinking and spreading its red light like fire between the trees.

When he comes back [from the war] it may take a few years for
him "to find himself"—it's [your] job—not his—to see that
the changes in both of [you] do not affect the
fundamental bonds between [you]. . . .

—"What Kind of Woman Will Your Man Come Home To?"
Photoplay, November 1944

THE MICKELSON HOUSE
502 W. First Street, Pine Rapids
Wednesday, July 26, 1950

It was in a dispirited frame of mind that Dolly, toting a book bag full
of rags and supplies, boosted herself up once again through the parlor window and inside the Mickelson house. She still hoped that the
house could become a home for her and Byron, but finding out that
Wilma's favorite son Chase had been killed couldn't help but cast a
shadow of doubt: Was it possible that there really was a curse on the
house?

Walking home from the Ladies Aid meeting the previous afternoon, Dolly had crossed the courthouse green to the bronze statue of
Chase Mickelson, which rose high above her head, resplendent in the
summer sun. The artist had done a remarkable job creating Chase's
likeness; she recognized the line of his jaw, and the determined look
in his eyes, from the photograph on the mantel in the big house. She

reached up and rested her hand upon his sun-warmed bronze boot. CHASE GUSTAF MICKELSON, USMC APRIL 2, 1899–JUNE 6, 1918, read a plaque on the statue's base. Below that, a plate had been added with the heading PINE RAPIDS HONOR ROLL WWII, five names standing out in relief, the bronze unbearably bright and new.

It was the cross of every generation, Dolly supposed: boys who left and never came home. She knew that there were causes worth fighting and dying for, but she wished somehow that Chase would have been all right. That all of the boys could have been all right. That there was not such cruelty and terror in the world altogether. Like the death camps in Europe, for one thing, news of which her parents had tried to shield her from when it came out in 1945. They had thought she was too young to be faced with such horrors, though children much younger than herself had suffered through them, had died as a consequence. But Dolly had learned—only a little, but some—and then in the middle of the night one night in the first year of her marriage, Byron had awakened in a cold sweat, mumbling. It was only then she'd learned that he had seen one of the camps, had been present at its liberation. He would not say what he'd seen, but he held her so tightly that she almost couldn't breathe, and they had never spoken of it since, not that next morning, not ever. She yearned to know what he had experienced—to really understand him—but she had been afraid to ask, afraid to try to knock down the walls he'd put up, visible in his otherwise inscrutable eyes.

She was relieved to see that JJ Mickelson's name wasn't on the World War II Honor Roll plaque. She walked home, determined that she would find out from the ladies what had happened to him.

The problem of finding out what had really happened to her own husband loomed larger. She believed she could be a better wife to him if he told her, but because she was trying to be a good wife, she hated to press him. It was one of those perplexing conundrums that seemed to present themselves often in her dealings with Byron.

Well, at least she was making tangible headway with the Mickelson house—once she had boosted herself up through the window and taken a look around the parlor, she began to feel better. The piano gleamed, the chandelier sparkled. She decided that it simply wasn't possible that such a lovely place could be cursed.

This morning, she had hurried through her meal planning and grocery shopping at the bungalow, planning this afternoon to start on the Mickelson kitchen. She had finally received a response from her mother to a plea for cleaning tips fired off two weeks before. *I'm happy that you're so content keeping the house, Dolly, and wanting to learn all you can,* her mother had replied, along with the requested information. *But some of the questions you asked made me wonder what kind of place Byron has you living in. You should not have severe problems with mold, and is the wood really in such bad condition?* Well, Dolly would explain later—if things worked out with the house, anyway.

Dolly hadn't told anyone about what she was doing with the Mickelson house, not even her best friend, Jane, back home in Battle Point. Her family and Jane all would probably just shake their heads: "Oh, that Dolly! Always coming up with some new, impossible scheme." Her older sister Lily, if she found out that Dolly had taken her inspiration from *It's a Wonderful Life,* would be sure to tell her, "This is *real life,* Dolly, not the *movies.*" Well, Lily had told her that during the war, too, every time she'd caught Dolly working on the scrapbook about Byron—"This is *real life,* Dolly, not the *movies.* You can't just *decide* you're going to marry some boy and then have it all *work out.*" Dolly, to show she had no hard feelings, had named Lily as a bridesmaid when the time came to plan the wedding. But this time, she didn't want to listen to the opinions of her family. She was simply determined that her life and marriage would not be "one of countless thousands that settle into a routine, then gradually stagnate," according to an article she'd seen in the *Ladies' Home Journal.* The article had gone on to indicate that in many cases a "triangle" would develop when an "interesting third party" happened along, "because the marriage offers too little competition."

The thought of Byron becoming interested in another woman made Dolly nauseous. Well, she already was making her best effort in the bedroom with her Hollywood starlet nightgown and at the supper table with her apron. If she could keep all of that up, plus perfect this spectacular home for him, surely he wouldn't stray in search of excitement.

If only she could get pregnant—children would strengthen the bond between them for sure.

Well, she couldn't think about that just now. For now, it was enough that she felt armed to tackle the dusty kitchen cabinets and cobwebbed stove, the moldy refrigerator, the filthy linoleum floor.

For a moment, Dolly stood, simply taking it all in. The kitchen was at the rear of the house in the western corner. There was a large butcher block in the center of the room; counters and cabinets formed a horseshoe shape around it. The sink was in the center of the horseshoe—the window above it must have provided beautiful sunset views through the trees that lined the western edge of the property—and the stove was directly opposite that, on its own wall, with a door on either side leading out to the hallway. Across the hallway was the pantry.

Dolly preferred the more subdued, just-right décor in this kitchen to the over-the-top poppies in the bungalow. Here, the walls were painted light green, the cabinets and butcher block white, and the wall behind the stove was wallpapered in a tiny green and yellow floral pattern. The curtains were sheer white (or had been, before dirt darkened them) with embroidered daisy trim. The linoleum flooring, in a white and green block pattern, was a sure indicator that the kitchen had been "modernized" twenty or thirty years earlier; it was exactly the same flooring Dolly's mother had had in her kitchen all Dolly's growing up years. It was the perfect reminder of home—and a good sign, Dolly thought.

She would want new appliances, of course, but otherwise, she thought the kitchen would do very nicely, once it was spiffed up a little.

She set to work on the stove, which, fortunately, had been clean when the Mickelsons left it. Not so fortunately, her cramps suddenly felt terrible and she was bloated as sin. She was reminded of Jane, who had written in her latest letter that she'd felt "puffy" for the last month solid. Jane had just discovered she was expecting.

Really considering the matter for the first time, now that she had time to think, Dolly despaired, wiping the stove in slow circles. It was impossible not to worry about it: All of her friends from high school were having babies—even Jane, now—and here was Dolly, married longer than any of them and still babyless. As Byron always said, it wasn't for lack of trying, but—what could it be?

It was miserable, that was what it was. Everyone knew that to be a wife you had to have a baby, preferably several. Not only for your husband's sake, so he could show his virility and carry on his name, but for your own. "Because, as much as you'd like him to be, your husband will never really be yours," her mother had told her, while pinning the hem of Dolly's wedding dress, Dolly standing on a chair, pirouetting slowly; wondering, suddenly, what exactly she was getting herself into. "You will be his," her mother had gone on, "but he'll be his own, and the only way you really have anything is to have your children."

Well, her mother had been right about Byron not being hers, that much was certain. No one had ever told her how dreadfully lonely marriage would be, and, truthfully, until moving to Pine Rapids and leaving her family and friends behind, she really hadn't noticed. But now, she thought, if she had a baby, at least there would be someone who needed her, who really thought she was important. She could tend to a child night and day, and never think at all about what she really wanted.

Wait, what do you mean? she asked herself, stopping her dusting mid-circle.

And just then, she heard something. It took her a moment to identify the noise. Heavy footsteps, and then: a key jiggling in the back door's lock.

PART TWO

The Bane of Man

Curiosity has long been the prerogative of woman and a woman's curiosity the bane of man. It seems likely that women have earned this reputation for nosiness not from any genuine bent for being curious but simply because of the kind of questions they *will* ask. Women ask questions for all sorts of inconsequential reasons—the desire for information is not of prime importance. And the results are none too good. Progeny have left home and husbands run screaming because too many thoughtless interrogations on the part of their womenfolk have knocked the props from under their morale.

—*Good Housekeeping*, May 1950

Pine Rapids
Saturday, February 27, 1943

Elissa could hardly believe that Nick Overby was really here, in Pine Rapids, sitting next to her in a booth at Sullivan's lunchroom in the Pine Rapids depot. She kept stealing little glances over at him to make sure she wasn't dreaming. Each time, she was so thrilled at the sight of him that she had to look away to keep from grinning.

Her father, Jack, had insisted upon coming with her to meet Nick at the train, and now sat across the pockmarked table from them, a hard-eyed half smile on his face. Elissa had seen that look on her father's face before; his way of softening someone up before he moved in for the kill.

Jack had been insufferable about the whole idea of Nick visiting, spending the whole week making up a list of special rules for the visit and lecturing Elissa about what unreliable boyfriends soldiers made.

At least he let him come, she kept telling herself. Just feeling Nick's arms around her that moment when he stepped off the train had been worth putting up with her father's behavior the past week.

"So, tell me about yourself, Nick," Jack said.

"Well," Nick said, "I'm from Dover, Tennessee."

"Yes, I know," Jack said impatiently, lighting a cigarette. Embarrassingly, he had not removed the battered hat that he'd had practically since before Elissa was born; the brim shadowed his face as he smoked. "Lissa told us. How long have you been in the Army?"

"Thirteen months."

"All with the Second?"

"Yes, sir. Well, Basic, first. Then I was at Camp Barkley in Texas, for training."

"You're a corporal?"

"Yes, sir."

"Infantry?"

"Yes, sir. Medic."

Jack scowled. "You aren't one of those they put in that slot because you object to killing, are you?" he said.

"Dad!" Elissa said.

"No, sir, I don't reckon I am," Nick said. "But I reckon they thought since I was the assistant to Doc Lidge there in Dover I might just as well be a medic."

Jack brightened. "So you were working in medicine in civilian life!"

"Well, for horses and cattle and such," Nick said.

The scowl came back. Jack smoked. "How old are you?"

"Twenty-three, sir."

Elissa drew in her breath. What a thrilling number! Her father gave her a stern look over his cigarette.

"So before you joined the Army, you were an assistant to a cow doctor," Jack said. "And you've never been to college."

"No, sir."

"Elissa's going to college in the fall," Jack said.

"I think that's great, sir," Nick said, with a warm glance in Elissa's direction. "When the war's over and I get out of the Army, I reckon I might go, too. For medicine, or veterinary science."

"I'm going into the cadet nursing program," Elissa said.

"You're going to be a nurse?" Nick said.

She nodded.

"Apparently you two haven't gotten very well acquainted," Jack grumbled.

Elissa looked at her hands. Her wool sweater was starting to make her itch; a woodstove flaring in the corner made the lunchroom too warm.

Jack went on. "Which brings me to my next question, Nick. What do you have in common with my daughter?"

"In common, sir?"

"Yes."

Nick smiled. "Well, I reckon her and me both come from real nice families."

Jack raised his eyebrows, and took a final puff of his cigarette before squashing the butt in the ashtray. "And your father's a stellar character like hers, I suppose."

"I never knew my daddy, sir, but my mother tells me he was. He passed on before I was born."

"I'm sorry to hear that," Jack said. "What family have you got, then?"

"Just my mother, sir, there in Dover, and a heap of cousins and such."

Jack folded his arms, giving Nick a cool, appraising glare.

"Dad—" Elissa broke in, but when Jack's eyes shifted to her, she couldn't say anything more.

"My wife," Jack pronounced, "told me that since Lissa's always been a good girl, we should give you two a chance. I'm not happy about the way you met. And I'm sure as hell not happy about my daughter being interested in a boy whose family I don't know. Especially an older boy who happens to be a soldier. My son, JJ, is over on Guadalcanal with the Marines."

"Yes, sir."

"Do you know when you might be sent overseas?"

Nick folded his hands together on the tabletop, glanced at Elissa. "No, sir."

"Soon enough, I'd bet, and who knows when you'll be back, or if. But Elissa's mother told me I had to get used to the idea that she's eighteen now and has the right to make her own decisions, so you're here. But as long as you're under my roof, we're going to have some rules."

"Yes, sir," said Nick. Elissa stayed silent, while her father dug in his pocket for his list.

When the waitress brought their lunches, Elissa was too distracted to eat, only picked at her food and cast sidelong glances at Nick, while her father reviewed his rules.

"Elissa will have a curfew of ten o'clock tonight. You will have dinner at Elissa's grandparents' at six. Nick will be staying there tonight. You both will attend church tomorrow morning. You will not be allowed to use the car." On and on he droned. Elissa finally stopped listening.

The ordeal of lunch complete, it was off to the house so Nick could meet Elissa's mother, Mary.

Mary seemed to like Nick right away, greeting him with a gentle smile and strangely bewildered eyes. For his part, Elissa thought, Nick was utterly charming. But she was impatient to be alone with him—if there was an all-encompassing rule stating they were not to be alone in any circumstances, she hadn't heard it—and suggested they go ice-skating. Though Jack objected, Mary was all for the idea, and jumped up to get JJ's old skates from the back porch. While Elissa went upstairs to change into her snowsuit, Nick tried the skates on and pronounced them a perfect fit. "I've never been on skates before," he was saying, looking up at Mary from his seat, as Elissa came downstairs.

"Mary, I told you I didn't want them going off by themselves," Jack said.

"Jack," Mary snapped. "Just let them go. You kids be at Grandma's by six for supper, all right?"

"All right, Mom." Elissa quickly gathered her skates, hat, gloves, and put on her boots. She could feel the tension between her parents, her mother silencing her father with a glare, but she didn't look at them. She and Nick went out, suddenly, blissfully free.

Pine Rapids was postcard-still under a snow-colored sky, houses and trees bearing up under heavy loads of snow, lights burning in windows. Only an occasional car purred past on the white-frosted streets. The sidewalks were mostly clear, and their boots made no sound as they walked.

Elissa apologized right away about her father, but Nick told her he didn't mind. "Sweetheart, you're worth it," he said. "Besides, he's not wrong. I don't know where I'm going, and I don't know when I'm coming back. That's not fair to you."

"I don't care," Elissa declared, boldly adding, "as long as I know you'll come back."

"I promise I'll do my best to," he said, reaching for her hand.

Elissa was kneeling in front of Nick helping him lace his skates; she could feel him gazing down at her. Securing the laces in a knot, she glanced up past his elbow to the edge of the park. Just then, a familiar 1936 Ford Tudor pulled into a parking spot on Sixth Street facing the ice rink, positioning itself so that the spruce and maple trees studding the park didn't obscure the driver's view of the rink. The car was a good twenty yards away, but Elissa recognized her father behind the wheel. Her astonishment negated anger and bashfulness both. "Good heavens!" she said, and told Nick. "He's enough to drive me crazy, sometimes!" she added.

"He doesn't give a guy much of a chance," Nick acknowledged.

"If he had his way, I'd never even be allowed to leave the house."

"Well, maybe he'll keep all them other fellows from you while I'm gone."

When she looked up at him, he was smiling that little smile she loved. Then his smile deepened into a grin. "I might should kiss you," he said. "And see what he does."

Elissa blushed. "He might not like that." She tied the second of Nick's laces in a double knot.

"Would you?" Nick said.

Elissa stood, turned, skated a fish hook. Stopped and looked at him. Nodded. Couldn't keep from grinning.

"I don't mind one bit," Nick said, the third time she tried to help him to his feet and they landed together on the ice in a laughing heap. "I mean, I'd roll around in the snow with you all day."

"Nick!"

"But—I'm worried your daddy might get the wrong idea," he said, sobering. "He might think I'm doing this on purpose. Heck, I wouldn't trust me, either, pretty as you are."

She glanced toward where her father still sat in the car. Nick was right: Too much more of the two of them landing in each other's arms and he was bound to explode out of that car and send Nick packing. "We could go to Emory's," she said. "Want to?"

They unlaced each other's skates, and he rubbed her sock-feet between his hands to warm them.

The warm smells of pie and coffee hung in the air at Emory's, and the place felt cozy after the white chill of the outdoors; they'd walked the nine blocks from the ice rink, after Elissa had stopped to talk to her father. To her relief, he had agreed not to follow them to Emory's.

The restaurant was long and narrow with a counter and stools up one side and five oak booths down the other. The walls were barely visible behind a profusion of framed photographs: school teams from all the way back before Elissa's father's time, fishermen with their prize-winning catches, mill crews and railroad crews, summer baseball teams, portraits of all the boys in the service. Somewhere there was a picture of the parade the town had had for Elissa's father when he'd arrived home from the Great War, the huge banner hanging over First Street declaring, WELCOME HOME, JACK.

Elissa and Nick removed their coats at the door and hung them on the coat tree, then settled into the center booth.

"This is something else," Nick said, indicating the engravings of initials and numbers that covered the wooden tabletops, benches, and wainscoting throughout the restaurant.

"Yes, it's a tradition," Elissa explained. "Everyone carves their initials and class year when they graduate. My dad says he was the one who started it, but I don't know if I believe him. Look," she said, pointing to a *JJM '42* in the wainscoting. "That's my brother, JJ. He didn't actually graduate, but they let him do it just before he left to join the Marines. My dad's right there by your elbow."

Nick quickly moved his elbow, making Elissa giggle. Then he found the carving. "This must be him. *JJM '16.*"

"Yes, that's right."

"Where's yours?"

She knotted her hands atop the table. "Well, I have to wait until I graduate this spring." She sighed. "You probably think I'm such a kid. I didn't know you were twenty-three!"

"I did."

"Well, yes, I know, but—Oh, it's this war, isn't it? Doesn't it make everything seem crazy? Here I never would have met you except for the war, and yet because of the war—I don't know if I'll see you again. How could something be so lucky and so unlucky all at once?"

"Aw, Lissa. I think you'll see me again. I don't think I'll be that easy to get shed of."

Then Mrs. Emory was there, standing at the end of the booth. "Didn't see you kids sneak in," she said. Mrs. Emory was one of the more glamorous fixtures in Pine Rapids; people said she looked like Hedy Lamarr, and she was originally from Minneapolis. She was modest, though, and always looked out for everyone. "How are you today, Elissa? Who's this with you?"

"This is Nick," Elissa said, smiling, her eyes locked with his.

"Just look at the sparks fly between you two!" Mrs. Emory said. She scrutinized Nick. "You *look* like you could be a local boy, but— you aren't from here, are you?"

"No, ma'am."

"Oh, I can see why you'd fall for him, Lissa, that accent! And calling me ma'am. He certainly isn't from Pine Rapids, at that."

Elissa laughed, loving the curve of Nick's smile. She couldn't wait for their first kiss. And after that—who knew what might happen? Why, anything might, with the war on, and that look in his eyes!

THE MICKELSON HOUSE
502 W. First Street, Pine Rapids
Saturday, February 27, 1943

As the family sat down to dinner that night, John Mickelson was fuming. John never had liked anyone to divert attention from him, and Nick had thoroughly charmed Wilma, Mary, and Elissa. While Elissa's brother, JJ, had always been their grandma Wilma's favorite, Elissa had always been closest to Grandpa John. But now Elissa was so caught up in Nick that she barely had a glance for him.

Watching Elissa, Jack realized that his daughter was clearly enraptured. What Jack had seen of Nick so far hadn't set off any warning bells, but Jack couldn't help but despise the situation that Nick was putting Elissa in. Nick had no idea what he was getting into, what war was like, what it could do to a man. Jack couldn't understand why his mother, Wilma, especially, would accept this soldier with open arms, knowing full well what might happen to him, and to Elissa if she hooked her dreams on him.

It was pure selfishness, Jack thought, to get a girl's hopes up and then go off to war to get yourself killed. Ruining her life for the sake of your vanity. Jack's own brother Chase had done it to the woman Jack himself had finally married, Chase proposing to Mary in a letter in 1917, writing her from Parris Island that he loved her and it would sure make a heck of a difference to him to know that she was waiting for him when he came back. *But if you say yes, Mary, let's not tell our families, let's leave it a great surprise for when I get home.* Jack hadn't known about it until long after Chase was dead; Mary had shown him the letter just once, a long time ago, but he'd never forgotten the raked-over-the-coals look in her eyes, and he'd be damned if the same thing would happen to his own daughter. Especially at the hand of some Southern kid who wouldn't fit in the family to begin with. But, watching the way Elissa looked at Nick, Jack knew that Mary was right when she said there was nothing Jack could do to stop Elissa from feeling the way she did. She might get hurt, Mary said—but hadn't they all been hurt, when they were young?

As dinner went on, Jack couldn't deny that Nick was strangely endearing. Maybe part of it was that he reminded Jack a little of Chase: something in the set of the mouth, the corners of the eyes, the way he held his shoulders. Jack wondered if his mother had noticed it, whether that was why Wilma seemed to like him so well. She certainly seemed to melt before the kid. When Nick had blurted that he'd never before eaten with a golden fork, she had grinned, her eyes alight; Jack couldn't recall the last time he had seen her smile like that.

Jack's father, on the other hand, seemed suspicious, asking Nick many of the same questions that Jack had asked, wanting to know all about Nick's family and origins.

"Well, my daddy was from Wisconsin, if you can believe it," Nick said.

"Is that so?" John said. "And your mother?"

"Born and raised in Dover, just like me."

John narrowed his eyes. "How did your parents meet?"

"Well, my daddy was a photographer. He went down to take pictures of the battlefield at Fort Donelson. His daddy had fought there on the Union side. He wanted to make a picture book, my momma said. But instead, he met my momma, because he stayed at her momma's boardinghouse. He'd go out making pictures and taking notes all day, and then come back home at night and there'd be my momma waiting for him. She said she was bedazzled by him, because she'd never met a Yankee before."

Elissa giggled.

"Is that right?" John said, sawing at his venison.

"Yes, sir. Course, when she set her mind to marry him, her momma about had a conniption. Because my momma's daddy fought at Fort Donelson, too, only on the Confederate side. He got taken prisoner and suffered terrible. Never was the same, and died young. So momma was marrying the enemy, far as everyone around home figured it."

"Oh, dear," Wilma said.

"How do they feel about Yankees now?" Jack wanted to know.

"Well, sir, they're still not fond of them in general," Nick said, with a little smile over at Elissa. "But they haven't met Lissa yet."

"We've got to send him away, by God," John said, as soon as he'd closed the door behind him. "He's going to break Lissa's heart."

After dinner, John had called Jack away from the table and into his office off the living room. Nick was still charming the women with stories about the horses he'd encountered in his work with the Dover veterinarian, as they lingered over the last of the coffee they'd had with apple pie.

The office had always been Jack's father's domain; only on very serious occasions had Jack or any of his siblings been called into it. One time in particular stuck in Jack's mind: At the age of eighteen, just done with high school, he had told his father he didn't want to work at the bank. John, who argued that Jack needed to be groomed as John's successor, for the good of the town, had kept him in that office until Jack had relented, though Jack had said at the time only that he'd try it out. Of course, look where that had gotten him: Almost thirty years later, he was still there, still the so-called vice president, since his father refused to retire.

The office walls were the same brownish-green now that they had been then, the heavy drapes the same velvet-gold. John crossed to his rolltop desk, took out a cigar and lit it, turning toward Jack with the same steely blue gaze he'd had all those years before. In the dimness of the room—a green-shaded lamp on the desk emitted the only light—Jack could almost believe that nothing had changed at all. Just some pounds added on his father now, the hair silver instead of light blond.

Jack stayed near the door, folded his arms across his chest. "I don't know, Dad," he said. "You saw the way they look at each other. I don't know what I can do about that."

"This is war, Jack," John said. He puffed his cigar, paced from desk to bookshelf and back again. "You know how it is."

Was that *pleading* in his father's eyes?

"Look, Dad, I know Lissa's always been your girl, and you don't like the idea of getting replaced by this kid."

John shook his head. "Your mother," he sputtered, gesturing with his cigar toward the dining room. "Wilma seems to think he's the best thing since shoe leather, for God's sake. I can't have her getting attached to him. What if something happened to him?"

"I know," Jack said, though at the moment he was less worried about his mother than he was about his daughter. It could be said— and was, around town—that Wilma had lost her mind over Chase's death, but she had been healthy for years. In 1923, when Jack raised the money as commander of the Legion to put the statue of his brother Chase in the courthouse square, Wilma's pride in it had seemed to help the scar tissue harden over her heart. JJ was born that same year, and Wilma doted on her grandson the way she'd doted on Chase, and seemed the better for it. A few years later, she'd gone with a group of Gold Star Mothers to visit the graves of their sons in France. She'd come back a different woman. Now, having JJ away, with the Marines on Guadalcanal, was difficult for her, but she seemed to be bearing up well, and once again was so involved in war work that she rarely was seen without her knitting. It was Elissa that Jack really worried about. She was so young.

"And Lissa," John said. "By God, I couldn't stand to see her heart broken. And you know how these guys rush things. I mean, physically."

Jack started. Not that he hadn't thought of it himself, but—shocking to hear it mentioned out loud, and by his father.

"Look what a handsome kid he is," John went on. "It wouldn't take much. He'll ruin her life."

"Not Lissa," Jack said.

"Hell, Jack, you know how it goes. You were in the service. It's war! Everything's up for grabs. He'll make her all kinds of promises, and then he'll meet some dame at a nightclub in New York or some English broad. You know it as well as I do. They won't keep it going—and that's if he lives through this thing. This now, it's just getting her hopes up. Besides, do you want the girls all wringing their hands about another one, with JJ already overseas? You know your mother barely survived it when you and Chase were over there in the first war. And then, when the news came about Chasey. Well, you wouldn't have wanted to see her then." He took another puff of his cigar. "Hell, Jack, I haven't told you this before, but for months afterward, she'd pluck, pluck, pluck at the front of her dress. Just a nervous habit, I thought. But then I asked her about it one day, and she looks at me plain as day with those big eyes of hers, and says, 'Why, I suppose I'm trying to tear out my heart.'"

Jack flinched. He ran a quick hand through his hair. "Christ," he said.

"We've got to stop this, Jack. *You've* got to. She's your only daughter, for Christ's sake. Are you going to let him ruin her life?"

Just after eleven that night, Jack found a parking spot outside the movie theater, turned off the car, and waited for Elissa and Nick to emerge. After dessert at his parents' house, Mary and Wilma had prevailed upon him to allow the kids to go to the movies, even though it meant that Elissa wouldn't get home until after eleven. He'd finally thrown up his hands, said, "Fine! But I'll pick them up after the movie!" Jack's father had shaken his head glumly, but then said, to Jack's bewilderment, "Let me take your picture. To commemorate the night. After he's gone, Liss, you'll want his picture, won't you?" So they had waited while John went for his camera; he took three shots of them standing near the front door.

After the kids left, cheerfully waving good-bye, Tommy Dorsey and his orchestra playing on the radio was the only sound, along with the clicking of Wilma's and Mary's knitting needles. John put away his camera and poured himself a liberal drink from the decanter, liquid tumbling noisily into the glass, while Jack smoked and looked at his watch. He couldn't help feeling restless in his parents' house, itchy to get out of there. Around ten, he told Mary he would take her home.

"Keep an eye on things, Jack," John intoned as they left.

Sitting in the car now, blowing into his gloved hands to warm them, Jack reflected that John had often taken this same tone. From the time Jack was a little boy, Jack had known that people in Pine Rapids liked John Mickelson even less than they had liked John's father, Knute, and Jack had always thought that perhaps it had something to do with John's *tone*. As a child, Jack had hated it. As the years went by, he despised it more and more. There was nothing profound about it: The tone simply said, *Because I'm bigger than you and I said so.*

People had been willing enough to give John a chance, in Pine Rapids' early years. His father had done well by the town, after all, building the mill and giving first a few, and then many, men good jobs, processing the fruit of the land, the massive white pines. It was safe to say that Pine Rapids wouldn't have been much of a town without what Knute Mickelson had invested in the mill, without what he paid its workers.

But by the time Jack was a boy, the white pines were almost exhausted. Some of the lumber mills were adapting to process hemlock. Though it was not as straight and strong as the white pine, hemlock had bark that was used in tanning leather, and was becoming more and more in demand. According to what Jack's mother had told him, Jack's uncle Gust, seeing the supply of white pine dwindling, had been adamant that the Pine Rapids mill had to move toward hemlock. John and his father had hesitated, not certain of the comparable profitability of such a venture. They wanted to stay with the white pine as long as possible, or diversify into other hardwoods. They were looking toward acquiring new land in Michigan's Upper Peninsula. Gust argued that they were already sitting on a gold mine of hemlock, and they were foolish not to cash in.

After Gust was killed, Wilma had told Jack, Knute began to see merit in the hemlock idea, especially now that the rough lumber itself was in some demand. John dragged his feet, but eventually gave in. The mill was adapted for processing hemlock.

Jack had little but a vague recollection of his grandfather Knute, who had died when Jack was only five, but he did distinctly remember the springs and early summers of his boyhood, going out to the mill with his father and Chase. The boys would scamper away when their father wasn't looking, Chase always trailing a little behind, and together they would climb the slabs of bark that were piled to cure. The delicate edges sometimes gave way beneath their toeholds, sacrificed to the boys' ascent, falling like clods of earth to the ground.

When they reached the pile's top, the brothers would settle on the rough surface, watching the men at work below them peeling the logs, inhaling the heady smells of the bark, while spring burgeoned brightly green around them. Later, when Jack saw the bodies of men decaying on the battlefield, or stacked along the trenches like sandbags, he would think of the trees at the mill, of those piles of bark, of the discussions he and his brother had had. ("Don't the sun and the moon like each other, Jack?" "Of course not, Chasey. The sun is the boss and the moon works for him. The moon works the night shift because the sun doesn't want to.") There were points, Jack had realized, at which life and death commingled.

Just after Jack's twelfth birthday, late one May night, the ringing of the telephone woke him from a dead sleep. He heard his father running down the stairs; only then did his brain register that the fire bell was clanging in town. He jumped out of bed, shoved his legs into pants and his feet into shoes, then ran across the hall and woke Chase. They ran downstairs and out to the garage, cranked the car for their father, and jumped in behind him. John drove as fast as the car would go, down First Street, across the bridge, out the Mill Road. Jack and Chase exchanged glances, thrilled at the speed, the looming adventure, their arms in goose bumps not just from the chill of the night air. On the horizon, they could see the orange heat leaping against the darkness.

They stayed at the mill until the fire had been extinguished and dawn emerged with its revelations. The shells of the buildings remained, soot-crusted, stinking, and soaked with water that had been pumped through the fire department's hoses out of the millpond. The mill was clearly a total loss. "I'm sorry, son," John said, laying his hand on Jack's shoulder; for years, John had been telling Jack that he would run the mill, when he was old enough.

After the excitement of the fire, the gray dawn was like a wet rag on the back of the neck. Jack's eyes were itching from fatigue; if he was like his brother, the soot on his lashes had something to do with it, too.

The fire chief, whom Jack recognized even through the smut on his face as one of the men who bossed the other men at the mill, came up beside Jack's father. "You'll rebuild, won't you, Mr. Mickelson?" the chief said, wiping his blackened hands on a rag.

"We'll have to see, Karl," said Jack's father.

Using that tone.

When it got out that John Mickelson had taken the insurance money and invested it in stocks for himself rather than rebuilding the mill, some of Jack's classmates at school looked at him like they would spit on him if they dared. In truth, the mill's time had passed; all over the region, the grand old sawmills were closing their doors, as the supply of lumber dwindled with the forests. The people in town didn't see things that way, though, and the fact that John quickly built a new creamery and a cheese factory made no difference, especially since both only employed a few people. When school started again in the fall, most of the mill kids were gone, their families having moved to Wausau or Merrill for the jobs that could be found there. In the north part of Pine Rapids, the homes they'd left behind sat vacant, were vandalized (sometimes by Jack and his friends, in truth; they were just that age). John Mickelson and the village council felt that these tumbling clapboard houses that had been home to the mill workers were eyesores, since anyone coming into town by train would have to pass them to get from the depot to the nice part of town. By the time Jack got home from the war, many of them were gone, as if they had never been there at all.

As for the mill itself, most of the damaged buildings were taken down immediately, though for several years John left standing the ones that were not so bad off. John was a forward-looker, not one to clean up his messes or even waste time discussing them, or the past. It wasn't until Jack's own children were in school that finally the last of the buildings was demolished, after a kid crushed his toe under a beam that shifted while he was in there messing around. The millpond had long since turned to a swamp, a haven for frogs and heron, and for fish who needed a breather from the fast pace of the

Bear Trap River, which rushed on past as though it, along with the rest of the world, no longer had much time to spend in Pine Rapids. John Mickelson's fault, everyone said. Pine Rapids really could have *grown into* something.

As a young man, Jack had heard whispers around town: People hoped the curse was true, that John would get his comeuppance. Knowing how the town felt about his family and the big house on the hill, Jack had made up his mind to leave as soon as possible. He'd been working up the courage to squirm out from under his father's thumb when the war broke out. And then when he'd arrived back home, in May 1919, and the town had put on that big parade for him, he'd been furious: that big banner strung over First Street in front of the bank, proclaiming WELCOME HOME, JACK, people lining the route all the way from the depot to his parents' house, waving flags, congratulating him, not even mentioning the brother who hadn't made it back home. He'd wanted to leave town for good then, and not look back. It wasn't until years later that he realized the parade had been the only thing they knew how to do for him; that they had forgiven him, for the moment, for being his father's son.

Because soon after that parade, it was summer, and he'd gone to the family summer home in Stone Harbor, his mother insisting that he have some time before going back to the bank as his father wanted. Jack was not saying much about anything at that point, but he went to Stone Harbor, and then he noticed that the girl in the cottage next door, Mary, had grown into a beautiful woman while he was gone. By the end of the summer, he was determined to marry her. But when he found out she had been secretly engaged to Chase, he was so angry, and his pride was so wounded, that he'd almost let her get away. Fortunately, he'd finally garnered the sense to go after her, following her to Chicago to beg her forgiveness, promising he would provide for her if she would only have him. She was the only peace he could find, then; still was now, for the most part.

But marrying Mary meant taking the one job he knew he could have, and coming back to the bank and Pine Rapids. Oh, he could have done something else, he supposed, but he was so tired from the war, and his father had told him it would be best for everyone if Jack carried on the family legacy. John had said it would upset Wilma if Jack went away again, and she was already so upset about Chase.

"Someday you and Mary will have this house, and your children after that," John had said, to press him further. "The house your grandfather built. Your mother and I insist on it. You'll stay at the bank, Jack, and fill my shoes when I'm gone. You're the oldest, and you know as well as I do that your brother Harry isn't the type for it. And this town needs us, Jack."

Needs us like it needs a hole in the head, Jack had always thought, but he went to work every day and didn't make a fuss, all these years. He guessed he could have taken over his father's cheese factory or creamery, but he knew nothing about either and had no desire to learn. There was a university-certified master cheesemaker at the factory who would surely resent the intrusion. Besides, the offices at the bank were nicer. And it turned out Jack had made the right choice, because both the factory and the creamery had been burned in the 1933 milk strikes by arsonists, farmers angered by falling prices and rising production costs. So that was the end of the Mickelson family's foray into the dairy industry. Things being what they were, John had decided not to rebuild, though others had continued to expand the industry in town, and, recently, with the war, it had boomed.

The bank wasn't so bad. Jack guessed it had been in part due to his efforts that they had kept it afloat during the Depression, with his father distraught over his personal misfortune in the stock market crash. Jack didn't really find the work interesting, but what was the difference, really? He brought home a good paycheck, and made a stable home for Mary and JJ and Elissa, which was what mattered. Jack adored his wife—the way she loved him despite himself, the way she steadied him with her quiet grace. And when first his son, JJ, and then his daughter, Elissa, were born, he thought to himself, *This is why not me; this is why I made it through that hell, for them.* Appreciating the miracle of their tiny hands sculpting him into someone real again, when they touched him.

And now, though the Depression had indeed taken a bite out of the family's wealth, Jack's children still stood to inherit tidy sums, especially since his father had often commented that Jack was the only one of the Mickelson children to have paid his dues to the family, suggesting that Harry and Jinny wouldn't get much of the family's money.

In his own eyes, though, Jack was like a wooden toy train, his wheels set in their grooves, going round and round a short track. He hated that everybody in town thought he was *like his father,* hated that they thought he was a *son-of-a-bitch,* a *hero,* an *eccentric,* one of those men who came back from the war and was *not the same,* a man to be feared, perhaps scorned, perhaps idolized. Not a human being, but a mythical figure of their own creation. Something children might dress up as on Halloween.

But of course he was *not the same,* and anyone in town wouldn't have been either, if they had seen the things he had. If they had lived in the mud and stench of the trenches and hung their helmet on a foot protruding from the wall of dead human beings that protected them, trying to get a little shut-eye, trying to sleep sitting up with their butt three inches deep in water and muck, while shells burst overhead and every five minutes there were screams, muffled sobs—like trying to sleep in hell itself. And the next morning, busting out of that trench and running headfirst into a storm of fire, screaming like a banshee because you were a Marine and (you were told) didn't feel fear.

No, Jack was not the Jack Mickelson who had left town in 1917, the Jack Mickelson whose greatest trial had been the big football game against Merrill his senior year. He'd continued to play after breaking a finger, winning Pine Rapids the game with a fifty-seven-yard rush. But Jack didn't even know that intrepid, proud "Jack Mickelson" anymore.

Sometimes he couldn't help but feel it would have been better if his brother Chase had been the one to survive the war. Surely Chase, great artist that he was, would have brought more to the world than miserable old toy-train Jack Mickelson, whose best days were behind him.

In fact, since the war, Jack hadn't been proud of much of anything, except for fathering two great kids and being, he hoped, a passable husband, despite his nightmares, despite the horrific things he'd done. He certainly hadn't been proud recently when the county had asked him to be head of the draft board in this war, saddling him with deciding the fates of all the county boys. He rarely slept; when news came that one of the boys he'd classified as 1-A had been killed or wounded, he didn't sleep at all. And he didn't sleep when he thought of his son, JJ—Jack knew that JJ had joined the Marines both in spite and because of Jack, and he knew JJ was on Guadalcanal learning the same unspeakable lessons about life and death that Jack himself had learned in France.

Jack wished he was a praying man, and indeed he tried to pray for JJ, but in truth he mostly went to church to keep up appearances. Unable to find peace enough to sleep at night, most nights he'd sit up doing crossword puzzles, drinking hot cocoa, leaving the pan with its scorched-on milk on the stove for Mary to find in the morning when she came down in her pink bathrobe to make the coffee. She would look at him with sleep-mussed honey-blond hair and those exasperated blue eyes he so dearly loved, one arm folded across her stomach, the other hand holding the pan out for him to see. "Jack," she would say. "How many times do I have to tell you? Just soak it, at least."

"Sorry, hon," he'd say, and suddenly he'd be unable to keep from smiling. Though every morning his reflection in the mirror looked older, the hair another shade grayer, he was at his happiest in such moments of pure domesticity with Mary. He was happiest, until the inevitable wave of guilt came that it was he and not his brother who was sharing this life with her.

Mary told him he was foolish to think that way; she had made her peace with God. But she was never truly angry with Jack; she knew his nightmares, his grief, his fears. She knew because she shared them. She knew that sometimes he couldn't bear to stay in the house, that he would go out and walk up and down every street in town. He liked Pine Rapids at night: It was peaceful, and he could pretend that no one knew him. But sometimes the cops out patrolling would stop and chat for a half hour, and he had to oblige them. Others up too late would see him go by, and recognize him by the shape of his old hat. He knew the gossip was that Mary and Jack had made a mistake, marrying each other. That Jack left the house at night because he couldn't stand to be in bed with a woman who would rather have married his hero brother, Chase. That they really didn't love *each other* at all.

That told you how much people knew, Jack thought, stepping out of the car to look for Elissa and Nick as people started to emerge from the movie theater. Some of the crowd were laughing, but a few had tears glistening in their eyes.

THE MICKELSON HOUSE
502 W. First Street, Pine Rapids
Wednesday, July 26, 1950

How silly of them to use a key! Dolly thought first, clutching her rag against the stove top. *Don't they know it isn't locked?*

Then, suddenly, realizing she was about to be discovered, she panicked. Looked around for someplace to hide. The door was opening. There was nowhere. And a man came in.

He was wearing a black hat, a white shirt with its sleeves rolled up to his elbows, a loose brown necktie, tan pants. His steps were uneven. When he listed toward the kitchen and saw her, his eyes were a piercing blue, sullied only by the dark shadows underneath.

Her smile trembled into place, faltered under his gaze.

The man's brow furrowed in puzzlement. His square face was handsome, shadowed with a day's stubble. Though he looked much older than in his photo on the mantel, she was sure she recognized him.

"Hello," she squeaked. "JJ?"

Pine Rapids
Sunday, February 28, 1943

The cold was stiff as a starched white sheet; the sun was shining in a bright sky. The fresh inch of snow that had fallen overnight shimmered on everything, and crunched under Elissa's boots as she walked, trailing behind her parents down Sixth Street toward church.

The church was ten blocks from their house and they usually drove, but her father, Jack, had said this morning that the car was almost out of gas and he couldn't get any more ration stamps until tomorrow. Knowing that Nick would be waiting at the other end, Elissa didn't mind the walk. Last night had been perfection. The way he had charmed the whole family at dinner—even Jack was softening toward Nick, she could tell—and then pressed his shoulder sweetly against hers throughout the entire movie, sneaking his hand over to hold hers. His touch made her breathless, and when he moved his fingers in little circles on her palm she was certain she would faint. But she sat very straight and still, part of her wishing she were the type of girl who could lean over and kiss a boy of her own accord, instead of waiting for him to make the first move.

They had waited until the last credits had rolled, then walked out together slowly, Elissa wishing they could go to Emory's again. She hadn't wanted the evening to be over, plus she'd thought it would be nice to show Nick off to the whole senior class, likely to be gathered there on a Saturday night. But Jack, of course, had insisted on driving them home immediately following the movie.

"I wish the day wasn't over," she'd sighed, as they meandered up the aisle of the now quiet theater.

"Me too," Nick said. "I don't like to leave you."

All day long, they had talked about nothing, everything; it had seemed to Elissa she had known him forever, that they fit together like long-lost puzzle pieces finally reunited. And when he looked over at her after the movie, the look in his eyes was full of the stars and, it seemed suddenly to Elissa, forever.

Or was that just her imagination?

She didn't get a chance to find out, because the minute they stepped out into the theater's lobby, her father was there waiting for them. "I was beginning to wonder where you were," Jack said. His eyes looked sad. "Come on," he said, and turned. They had no choice but to follow. The ride to Elissa's grandparents' house was less than a minute; with her father there, their goodnight was nothing like it should have been.

Still, though, her heart was wildly content, and when she crawled into bed a little while later, she lay awake dreaming of Nick for a long time. The way his eyes crinkled when he smiled; the warmth of his hands; the way their legs had tangled together when they'd fallen at the skating rink. Just before finally drifting into a restless, happy sleep, she decided: No matter how long he was gone, she would wait for him.

But when Elissa and her parents arrived at the little white church and stepped into the warmth of the foyer, John and Wilma were waiting for them without Nick. Clutching her handbag with white knuckles, Wilma looked pale, and her mouth was turned down.

Elissa knew right away: Something was terribly wrong. "Where's Nick?" she said.

John looked at her. "That damn kid," he said.

"Grandpa!"

John held up his hand. "Now, Lissa. Sometimes these things happen. You know how soldiers are."

"Grandpa?"

John sighed. He gestured for them to come closer, and when they circled around him, he spoke in a low voice. "I was hanging up his coat last night after Jack dropped him off, Liss, and a letter fell out of the pocket. Your grandma had taken him in the kitchen and was making him hot cocoa. I took a closer look at it and—well, I couldn't help noticing the handwriting on the envelope was feminine. And there was a lipstick print right on the front of it. The return address was Dover, Tennessee."

Elissa felt ill.

John sighed again. "I waited until your grandma went to bed, and then I confronted him about it. I asked him if he had a girl back home. He denied it at first, but—well, he admitted it, finally. Then he told me he didn't see what the harm would be in having a little fun while he was up north. He said he liked you a lot, but—he's engaged to this other girl, Lissa."

Everything swayed and trembled before Elissa's eyes.

"He said he's known her since the first grade."

"John, please!" Wilma said, too loudly, snatching at John's arm.

John cleared his throat. "Sorry," he said. "Well, I told him he wasn't welcome in my house. Not when he was just using you. I put him on the one A.M., sent him right back where he came from." He reached out and touched Elissa's face. "I'm really sorry, Liss."

"Goddamn it!" Jack said.

"I only found out this morning," Wilma said. "Oh, Lissa, I know how much you liked him. I, myself, I waited up to make him that cocoa! He seemed like such a nice boy—"

Elissa broke away, pushed her way through the crowded foyer and into the bathroom, just in time to stumble to the toilet, vomiting and sobbing at once.

Her mother was waiting at the door when she came out. The foyer was empty, the service having started.

"Lissa," Mary whispered, hugging her, quickly pulling away. "Oh, honey. Are you all right? You're so pale." She wiped her thumb against Elissa's cheek, as if there were a tear remaining there. Elissa knew there wasn't, though; she had cleaned herself up entirely, though of course she couldn't get the red out of her eyes.

"I'm going home, Mother," she whispered.

"That's fine, honey," Mary said. "I'll go with you. And we don't have to go to Grandma and Grandpa's for dinner. I'll make you whatever you want at home."

Elissa nodded, pressing her lips together.

"Honey, don't take this personally, all right? He—It's just the way soldiers are, sometimes. You're such a lovely girl, I'm sure he just—couldn't help but want to spend time with you. These boys, they—take advantage sometimes."

Elissa bit her lip. She wished she were the type of girl who could scream at her mother, "Be quiet! You aren't helping!"

Instead, she said, "Mom, I'd like to be by myself, please." Then she pushed her way past Mary and out of the church. The cold air felt good: clean, like maybe if she stayed out in it long enough, it would freeze away her anger, bitterness, self-castigation. And then she could start over again. Perhaps. She knew she had to, anyway. *And next time I won't be so stupid,* she told herself, choking back a sob as she ran down the steps of the church, forgetting until she was almost home that she had missed the chance to pray for her brother, JJ, with the congregation. When she thought of that, she couldn't hold back her tears any longer.

Pine Rapids
Friday, March 5, 1943

My heart is broken and I don't think I'm ever going to recover, Elissa had written in her diary that cruel February afternoon that she had learned the truth about Nick, flopped on her bed, leaning on her elbows and clutching a doll under her arm, snuffling back tears.

That day and for many days following, Elissa tortured herself with memories, writing in her diary the whole of the brief romance, with analysis, her hand cramped, the script tiny, wounded, not at all like her typical flowing style. *That last night, he said he didn't like to leave me, and he seemed almost like there was something more he wanted to say. Was he planning to tell me the whole, bitter truth? Of this girl waiting for him back home? Or p-haps he thought he was doing nothing wrong. I cannot believe that someone could so despicably lead a girl on the way he did—recalling, for example, the way he*

pressed his shoulder against mine while we were at church in LaX.
He arrived late, must have been debating whether he should come to
see me in light of his f., but decided to play me for the fool I so clearly
~~am~~. Was, I mean. As God is my witness, I shall never be foolish
again.

Everyone in school knew of her folly, of course. It had been big
news, Elissa and Muriel's trip down to La Crosse, then the subsequent report of the boys they had met, and, most excitingly, the fact
that a soldier was coming up to visit Elissa. Talk had been that she
was practically engaged to him already. And then, to have everyone
find out she'd been duped! To have the entire saga spread so gleefully
by the likes of Judy Wasserman! "He already had a fiancée back
home! And she thought she really had something! Isn't it the limit?"
It was mortifying, the whispers she had sensed behind her back that
dreadful Monday following the Betrayal, as it came to be known between her and Muriel. She faked sick Tuesday through Thursday—
giving her plenty of time to flesh out the saga in her diary—but her
mother finally made her go back to school on Friday, and Muriel
dragged her to Emory's after school. "You've got to face everybody
sooner or later, Liss," Muriel reasoned. "Why let 'em see you're
down? You've got to hold your head high. It's his loss, after all."

Elissa would have liked to see what Muriel would have been acting like, if the same thing had happened to her. But she went along to
Emory's; what else could she do?

The minute they were seated in a booth, Mrs. Emory asked about
him. "How's that soldier boyfriend of yours, Lissa? I suppose he had
to go back?"

Elissa's eyes filled with tears. *Fool,* she told herself, but she
couldn't stop them.

Muriel spoke to Mrs. Emory in a confidential tone. "She's quite
sensitive about it, Mrs. Emory. Perhaps it would be best just not to
mention him again."

Mrs. Emory felt so bad for upsetting Elissa that she brought her a
free chocolate malt with the cherry Cokes they had ordered. "Young
love," she sighed, patting Elissa's hand, before moving on to the other
kids that were gathering in booths and at the counter.

"See now, things aren't so bad," Muriel said. "Any day you get a
free malt has to be a good day, right?"

Elissa sniffed, and picked up her spoon. She dipped it into her malt and lifted it out again, watching the ice cream stream from it. "I'm not hungry," she said.

"Not hungry!" came a voice behind her. "Why, whatever could be the matter?"

Elissa looked over her shoulder. It was copper-haired Judy Wasserman, her bright pink lips looking to Elissa like a cruel slash in her face. Her cronies huddled around her, giggling.

"Unlucky in love, could it be?" Judy said.

Elissa turned back to her malt. Judy and her gang scuttled past, hiding their laughter behind their hands, heading for a booth in the back.

"They're just jealous," Muriel assured Elissa loudly, but that only made the other girls laugh harder.

"Oh, I'd just *love* to find out I'd set my cap for another girl's fiancé," Judy said.

"Hey, Judy," came a boy's voice from behind Elissa. The whole of Emory's seemed to shush.

Judy stopped, turned. "What is it, Ty?"

"What's this I hear about your boyfriend Hank winning a date with that Rockette on that radio program out in New York?"

Judy flamed pink. "It's a lie!"

"Oh, yeah, I know, he spends all his free time dreaming of you," said the boy. There was a loud chorus of laughter throughout Emory's.

Judy shot a death look across the restaurant, then turned and went toward the rearmost booth, her friends scurrying along behind her.

Elissa looked back over her shoulder. Her benefactor was Ty Lofgren, also a member of the class of '43. He caught her eye, and winked.

She blushed, and gave him a little smile back.

All the underclass girls were wild about Ty. He dated several of them nonchalantly, and was always kind to them, which kept their hopes up. He was cute: dark brown hair flopping into his long-lashed brown eyes; strong, square face; dimples.

Elissa watched as he put on his cap, said something to his friends Pete and Carl. The three boys headed out the door, the bell jingling.

When Elissa looked back at Muriel, Muriel raised her eyebrows, as if to say, *What was that all about?*

Elissa could only shrug. She spooned up a bit of her malt, considering it. She had known Ty forever, of course, but they had never been close. The lines had been drawn in the earliest days of kindergarten, when she had shyly spent what seemed like weeks working up the courage to invite Ty—who even then had possessed admirable long eyelashes—to play in the sandbox with her. Unfortunately, just as she was approaching him, trowel in hand, he became an unwitting participant in Cowboys and Indians when Carl Olsen "shot" him with a loud "BANG!" Ty's death was so histrionic that he immediately became a favored player, and his acceptance in Carl's group was sealed for life. He ultimately became the joker of the class, the actor (he had given a heartbreaking performance as Romeo last fall, and was Gloucester in *King Lear* the year before that). He was the boy everyone felt they could talk to but no one exactly knew. Elissa had always liked him well enough, but she was at as much of a loss as Muriel to explain why he would so publicly take her part in a fight that had nothing to do with him.

"That was certainly interesting," Muriel said.

Elissa, her sadness flooding her again, just sighed, watching another tiny stream of her malt cascade from her spoon. She thought of her brother, JJ, on Guadalcanal. She knew she was pathetic to feel so sorry for herself as the result of a little romantic trouble, when her brother was living in mud and terrible danger with nothing so comforting as a chocolate malt anywhere in sight. She forced herself to take another bite.

A house, exactly like a dog, must be loved before it
will show the best side of its nature.

—*Popular Home Decoration*, 1940

THE MICKELSON HOUSE
502 W. First Street, Pine Rapids
Wednesday, July 26, 1950

He had seemed to bring heat into the kitchen with him. Not light, just
an intense heat, like campfire embers. Dolly felt a flush rising in her
face, and wondered how long he would stare at her before speaking.
She could think of nothing to say. What would he do? Call the police?
Have her arrested for trespassing? She despaired: If that happened,
her children would never achieve Pine Rapids' upper crust.

Finally, to her relief, he flashed her a small grin. "You have the advantage," he said. His voice was gravelly, like a movie gangster's, and
sent a little chill up her spine.

"Oh, I'm sorry," she said quickly. "Dolly Magnuson." Only after
she said it did it occur to her that she probably should not have given
him her real name.

"My dad must have hired you."

"I'm sorry?"

"To clean the house."

"Oh! Yes, of course." That lie came easily, and seemed much simpler than trying to explain what she was really doing there.

JJ looked around the kitchen. "You haven't done a very good job."

"I just started in this room," Dolly said, defensive despite her nerves. "I did the dining room and parlor before this. It isn't easy, you know, when the place has been let go like this."

JJ sighed, and stepped unevenly into the room, looking up at the kitchen ceiling.

Why, there's something the matter with him, the way he walks, Dolly realized.

"My dad didn't tell me he was getting help for me," he said. "I guess it's a good thing. I guess he figured I'd need it."

"Oh!" Dolly said, taken aback.

"Would you make up a bed for me on the couch in the living room?"

"Of course," Dolly said, and quickly turned from him.

She found a spare set of sheets in a linen closet upstairs, and started down with them clutched to her stomach, hoping that JJ wouldn't ask too many questions and catch her in her lie. But if he really thought she was there working for his father, how was she ever going to get out of it? Not that she wanted to give up on the house—but continuing to work on it with JJ Mickelson present was going to be awkward, to say the least.

Descending the stairs, she noticed with dismay the dust lurking in the corners of the front room and weighing down the velvety maroon drapes. There was so much to do to get the house in shape, but now that JJ was here, Dolly couldn't help but realize that her efforts to prepare the house for Byron were presumptuous. The pictures of the Mickelson family came easily to her: Wilma sitting on the end of the burgundy couch talking on the telephone; Chase running down the stairs for dinner or a baseball game. She had claimed the house and the family's stories for her own, and it was discomforting to encounter someone to whom they really belonged.

When she reached the bottom of the steps and turned to walk down the hall toward the living room, she saw JJ straight ahead through the door, standing at the mantel, his hands shoved in his pants pockets, staring at the portraits lined up there. She could see by the way he held his shoulders that he had his own share of memories, and she felt a curious swell in her heart, watching him. He'd taken off his hat, exposing his thick, dark hair. He was nearly as thin as the POWs in photos she'd seen after the war. Picking up one of the portraits, he furrowed his brow.

He seemed both dangerous and pitiful, like a hurt stray dog. She pressed herself to continue toward him, and passed behind him with the sheets, noticing that he had taken all the covers off the furniture and left them in a heap on the floor. Typical.

"Do you think he's better-looking than I am?" he asked, turning toward her.

She looked; he was holding out the picture of the man she had figured was his uncle Harry. As she picked up the sofa pillows and dropped them onto the floor, she laughed, determined to act cool. "Oh, no," she assured him, though the image of Harry showed an innocence that JJ clearly lacked. "No, he's handsome enough, but *you* could be in the movies." She didn't meet his eyes, or mention that he would have to play an unhealthy, troubled fellow, the way his eyes were shadowed and his waist was so thin.

"I've wanted to," he said, and when she looked, his face was brighter, his eyes almost sparkling. "I mean, I've thought of it. My aunt Jinny," he said, gesturing toward the picture of Harry's sister, "she was in the movies. Mostly on the radio, but she was an extra in a couple of movies. She went out to California before the war. She got me a couple of parts on the radio, when I was in Chicago, summers."

"Really! Well, you do have a wonderful voice." She unfurled the sheet over the sofa, and began tucking it in around the cushions, watching him out of the corner of her eye.

He replaced Harry's picture on the mantel. "I played a cop, one time. My line was 'We found him just like that, sir.'"

Dolly smoothed the sheet. "I bet you were wonderful."

"Another time," he said, "I was this guy at a party. Know what I said then? 'Don't they have any good bourbon? This stuff is rot.' Speaking of which!" He began his uneven steps toward the dining room. "Maybe there's some of Grandpa's old booze around here."

The naked desperation of his tone was alarming. Her father had talked often enough about the problems of old soldiers; she had even seen it among Byron's friends—though not, thank goodness, in Byron. She straightened up, pushing a stray lock of hair off her face. "Wouldn't you like to check on the house?" she suggested, tossing the pillows back onto the sofa, watching his back as he limped into the dining room. "The electricity and water are on, so you shouldn't have any trouble staying here, but a lot of things have been let go. You can see the window's broken in the dining room. I covered it."

"I'll look at things later," he said, out of sight now. She heard a cabinet door open.

"There's a lot I could show you that needs to be done."

The cabinet door closed, and he came limping back into the living room, a glass in one hand and a half-full decanter in the other. "Look," he said. "My dad isn't paying you to boss me around, who-ever you are."

"Dolly," she said.

A disconcerting light had come into his eyes with the acquisition of the decanter. "Right. Dolly."

She watched as he crossed the room and flopped down into an armchair. He poured himself a drink, set the decanter on the table next to him, and loosened his necktie further.

He took a sip of his drink, leaning back in his chair. He began massaging the thigh of his bad leg. "Did my dad tell you I was com-ing?"

"Um, no," Dolly said, then quickly added, "I mean, he mentioned you *might* be, but I didn't know—"

"That's all right. I was just wondering." JJ sighed, and took an-other sip of his drink. "Can you do me two favors?"

"All right."

"Would you not tell anyone I'm here? They'll just come bothering me. And the second thing is, right now, I'd like to be alone for a while. Could you call it a day?"

Dolly put her hands on her hips. It was true that she had no appar-ent right to be in the house. Maybe what she'd been doing was nuts. Yet it was just like Mrs. Fryt had said: Somehow, Dolly could sense disaster hovering. She couldn't help but think of the curse. She was suddenly afraid JJ would be the house's—and the family's—final ca-tastrophe.

She had to believe there'd been some reason she'd felt so drawn to the house. Maybe God wanted her to save it—maybe for her own sake, maybe for the sake of the Mickelson family. She would wait and see about that; the important thing for now was to make sure that JJ didn't make matters worse. "But there's so much to be done," she told him. "How do you think this house feels, left alone for so long?"

He considered her for a moment. "You're right," he said with a smirk, reaching over to pick up the decanter. "I'll bet the house needs a drink, too." He pulled the stop, and began tipping the decanter over the arm of the chair.

She lunged, yelling, "No!" She caught his wrist in one hand and the decanter in the other; after a moment of struggle, he relaxed, laughing. She was crouched in front of him, close enough to smell the cigarettes and booze on his breath, and to see the depths of his shadowed blue eyes, the prickly hairs of his emerging beard, the dryness of his lips, the conflicting whorls of his hair.

"It was a joke," he said.

She gathered the decanter to her, leaning back on her haunches. She was trembling. "It wasn't funny." She got to her feet, stumbling a little as she backed away from him. She thought maybe God had overestimated her, pitting her against this man.

Superior, Wisconsin
Tuesday, November 6, 1945

The sleet-snow mix slanting through the frigid air stung Harry Mickelson's cheeks as he stepped out into the darkness of the early morning onto the landing outside his second-floor apartment. He slammed the door behind him, making sure the lock caught. He could feel it in his forty-two-year-old bones that the coming winter would be a bad one. Of course, most winters in Superior were bad ones; he'd learned that much, the five years he'd lived here. He shrugged his shoulders to make sure he was as far into his coat as he could get, pushed his hat down lower on his head, and shoved his hands deep into his coat pockets, realizing he'd forgotten his gloves again. He wasn't one who liked to retrace his steps, though, or waste time on regret: easier just to run the six blocks to the office.

He thundered down the wooden stairs to the backyard, avoiding patches of ice with quick feet like the athlete he'd once been. His loafers crunching in the shallow snow, he loped around the corner of the house and through the narrow side yard. Without a backward glance at the white clapboard house where he'd rented for the last two years, he veered onto the sidewalk and set an easy pace, the icy ore dust air burning his lungs.

He hadn't run a block down the narrow street through the close-set, stout houses when his knee began to ache. Another block, it felt like little men were pounding his knee with silver sledgehammers, mining for his blood. He had to slow to a walk. He cursed under his breath, limping a little. At least Uncle Sam had known what he was doing when he'd classified Harry 4-F. Harry shrugged deeper into his coat, dug his hands deeper in his pockets. Funny how a guy could still be feeling the effects of a high school football game almost twenty-five years later.

Despite the pain in his knee, Harry didn't mind these early morning walks; he liked to imagine that in each house with yellow light glowing through the curtains there was a housewife in her bathrobe boiling the coffee, getting ready to face the day. It seemed to him that every one of the houses in his neighborhood was home to people who believed in working hard and, like him, not wasting time on regret. Maybe that was why he wasn't as restless here as he'd been in every other town he'd ever lived.

He supposed one could call it a series of failed love affairs, his relationships with the small towns where he had lived. Pine Rapids, for starters, his hometown. And then, after college, Little Chute for two years, Osseo for one, Alexandria for four. Then three years in Moose Lake, one in Pine City, and four in Stone Harbor.

Though he tried not to think of it, he supposed there had been a pattern to each relationship. Each place had taken a shine to him, and he to it, in the first rosy days, weeks, even years of his residence. He'd usually started out as a buck reporter, getting sent out to all the city council meetings and the two-A.M. accidents. He'd worked his way to editor in Alexandria and Moose Lake, started out that way in Stone Harbor. Jobs like that, it was his responsibility to get to know everyone in town, to form relationships. And he was damn good at that, rubbing elbows with mayors, police chiefs; charming the old guard of the Women's Christian Temperance Union, the Lutheran church, to the point that they brought him Jell-O salads and invited him to their coffee klatch to introduce him to their unmarried daughters. How he adored the towns, then, hearing each side of each story and then taking a stand on issues ranging from the paving of streets to the ordinance restricting chickens in the city limits. Fielding calls from irate citizens who had been certain he was on their side. "Turncoat!" they called him, while he grinned, elated as only a man in love could be.

But then there would come a time when Harry would grow bored: in Alexandria, factions had argued for weeks about whether to paint the water tower to look like a fishing bobber. Harry had been so agitated about the time lost at three consecutive city council meetings that he'd finally stormed out, and got a good talking-to from Berglund, the publisher. The pattern, he supposed, was growing resentment, discontent. He would feel walls start to close in on him. Every place in every town that had once been exciting, fresh, and bewitching would begin to feel garish, repulsive, as with a lover who'd always seemed beautiful in candlelight whom you now saw naked in sunlight, eyeliner caked into crow's-feet, blotchy skin, swirls of light brown hair all over her body.

Disgust boiling until it finally bubbled over, Harry would lash out with an editorial that alienated half the town. There was always a woman, too, who, when confronted with the full measure of Harry's boredom and disgust, would run out sobbing, handkerchief clutched to her mouth. (He'd lost more handkerchiefs that way.) Until, finally, one day he would type up a brief letter of resignation, slap it on some bigwig's desk, and walk out, catching a train to the next promised land, suitcase in one hand, typewriter in the other. He imagined that someday, when he was a famous novelist, they would paper a museum wall with his letters of resignation.

He'd been in Superior now for five years—longer than he'd lasted with any other place. Maybe it was on account of the war that he wasn't itching to leave yet—this rumbling port town was a great place to see the action from if you were 4-F. But then, maybe Superior held his interest more because of its mood swings. He couldn't abide those gentle towns that tried so hard to please, with their prim little bungalows and sculpted downtowns, their gentle rains and snows, their flowers. As though they were mewling, "Make me your home; we'll be so happy!" Superior simply barked, "Stay if you want to; I don't give a damn," blaring its boogie-woogie music out of its Tower

Avenue taverns late into every night, stretching awake before sunrise again the next morning with the clank and whine of metal, the whirring of pulleys, the shouts of bleary-eyed men.

Superior was a tempestuous lover, to be sure, howling and spitting and wearing away a man's morale one minute, caressing him and murmuring sweet nothings the next. Spring, summer, fall, it could be so sweet a man never wanted to leave it. Of course, Harry reflected, burrowing his chin down closer to his neck, squinting against the spitting sleet, those three seasons typically accounted for only about six months of the year.

But, at least for the time being, he was content enough. From his third-floor office window at the Superior *Gazette,* as long as it wasn't foggy or snowing a whiteout, he could see the hills of Duluth, Minnesota, rising up on the opposite bank of the St. Louis River. When his windows were open, he could hear the whistle and clatter of trains, the blasts of ships, as they moved their cargo that would ultimately reach nearly every part of the world. The stirring within him was placated by the knowledge (fanciful as it might be) that, any day he wanted to, he could stroll down to the harbor, stow away in the hold of a ship, and soon be halfway around the world. Oh, just knowing that the getting away would be so easy!

Harry took the marble steps in the *Gazette* building two at a time, ignoring the jouncing ache of his knee. The flight of stairs leading to the second floor was massive, directly in the center of the building's large foyer. At the second floor, a 180-degree turn was necessary, either to the right or to the left, to reach one of two narrower flights that led to the third floor. Harry always turned to the left, since the newsroom and his attached office were in that direction.

"Morning, Maggie," Harry said, bursting into the newsroom. "What's new?"

"You tell me," his assistant said, continuing to type. She was wearing her blue dress today, Harry's favorite. She had worked for him for three years and he'd never told her.

Several of his reporters, not shown to their best advantage in the garish overhead lights, were already at their typewriters, with cups of strong coffee, smoking, trying to get their copy pounded out. The phones would be quiet for a couple of hours, probably long enough for them to get through the six o'clock staff meeting, and then all hell would break loose. The society desk alone usually took twenty calls in a morning, everyone wanting to get their party listed or, these days, the families of men getting home from the service wanting arrivals announced, and plenty of weddings. Tinnanen at the news desk would get his share of calls: There would probably be a traffic accident, an incident at one of the grain elevators, and maybe a crisis at Central High, all before nine o'clock. Their deadline was eleven-thirty, and the paper would roll off the press in time to get packaged up for the delivery boys who came after school to do their routes, for the truck to take it around town to the drugstores and restaurants and hotels and whoever else would sell it.

Harry laughed. "Same old line! Never gets old, does it?"

"If only your readers were so easily amused," Maggie said.

Harry took off his coat, and hung it on the coat tree that stood in the corner of the office. "Ain't that the truth," he said. He was plopping his hat onto the coat rack when he heard the closest typewriter—Maggie's—stop.

"Mr. Mickelson," she said. "When you're ready—there is someone here to see you."

Harry turned. The young woman seated in one of the chairs by the door got to her feet. His heart skipped when he recognized her.

"Hello, Mr. Mickelson," she said. Her eyes were a warm green, her hair a deep red. "I'm sorry to drop in unannounced. I—Do you have a moment?"

Harry rubbed his chin, wishing he'd taken the time to shave that morning, and smiled. "Miss Wallace. For you, of course." He gestured to his office with a wide sweep of his hand. He didn't miss that Maggie rolled her eyes, or that Tinnanen, across the room, raised his sparse eyebrows. Anne Wallace smiled a little, her cheeks pink, as she walked toward Harry. When she passed him, he caught the scent of her: vanilla spice cookies mixed with jasmine.

Harry followed her into his office and closed the door behind him, shutting out the noises of the newsroom. He straightened his tie, noticing the way her dark purple hat set off her hair and her matching suit accentuated her slim waist. The small slit in the back of the knee-length skirt drew his eye to her real silk stockings, the seam running up the back of each leg.

When she reached the corner of his desk, she turned to face him. Something in him capsized. The previous two times he had met her, she had been wearing her Red Cross uniform, and she had been stunning then, but today she was an absolute knockout. Her lips were a dewy brick red.

He gestured for her to be seated, and walked around to his own chair. He took satisfaction in its important-looking size, settling himself into it. "Well, you're up early, Miss Wallace," he said.

"I wanted to be sure to catch you, Mr. Mickelson," she said, and smiled. Even her teeth were perfect, he thrilled. "It's kind of you to remember me. I won't take much of your time, I know how busy you are. It's just—I need to ask you a favor."

"Of course. What can I do for you?"

"Well, Mr. Mickelson, there's been quite a decline in donations to the Red Cross, now that the war is over. People don't seem to understand, there's just as much that needs to be done now as there ever was! I suppose I shouldn't have come here; the chapter president will be furious if she finds out. But I just thought—you were so nice, before, and after those two stories you did about St. Francis, I understand there was—well, a spike, they said, in donations. And I thought perhaps if you could—let everyone know that the chapter still really needs the money and even the time—we've lost so many volunteers, people getting back to their old lives, you know. And there are so many people who still need the chapter's help!"

Harry, watching her lips move, had heard perhaps half of what she had said. "Are you still volunteering at the hospital?"

"Yes. Yes, I am."

"Well, maybe I could come out and visit you, then. People liked those stories I did on you—on the hospital. Especially they liked the follow-up, because they felt they already knew you."

"Oh, I don't mean it has to be a story on me."

Harry dismissed that with a wave, sat forward in his chair and picked up a pencil. "Of course it does. The readers loved you. They'll want to know what's happened. So, let's start with some preliminary questions."

"Well, all right," she said. "If you think it's the best way to raise money for the chapter."

"All right, then." He chewed briefly on the end of his pencil, straightened his tablet on his desk. "As I recall, you were engaged to be married to a pilot over in the Pacific?"

She cast her eyes down at her hands, which clutched her purse on her knees. "Yes," she said. "You have a good memory."

"You've got to, in the newspaper business," he said. "So—is he—?"

She looked up. "He was killed."

Harry swallowed. "Cripes. I'm sorry," he said, leaning back in his chair. "How long ago—?"

Her lip was trembling. "May."

"What was his name?"

"Bobby Granholm. Robert."

The name rang a bell. "I remember when that happened. When we heard, I mean. We ran it on page one."

"Yes. Thank you." She smiled a little.

Harry sighed, threading his pencil between his fingers. He certainly had grown sick of every week having to run another story about a local boy killed in action. Even last week, there'd been a story about a boy who'd been a Jap POW over on Bataan since 1942 whose family had had every reason to think he was still alive, as they'd received a postcard from him in August. But last week they had learned that he'd actually died of starvation in March. Harry had sent Tinnanen out to get a quote from the mother and father; he hadn't had the stomach to face them himself.

He looked up at Miss Wallace. "Is your brother all right?"

She smiled. "Yes! Yes, thank you. He was wounded, but not badly, we don't think. We're expecting him home any day."

"That's great," Harry said, meaning it. He sighed again, then stood. "Miss Wallace, I've bothered you with enough questions for today. Why don't I come out to the hospital—tomorrow? Will you be there?"

"Yes, in the afternoon."

"Four o'clock all right?"

"Yes, that will be fine." She stood, held out her hand. "Thank you, Mr. Mickelson. For taking time in your busy schedule."

He grasped her hand a moment. "No trouble," he said. He walked around the corner of his desk to lead her to the door, which he then opened for her, letting in the tumult of the newsroom again.

She stopped, looked up at him with another pretty smile. "See you tomorrow, then, Mr. Mickelson."

"Sure thing." He watched her walk across the office, open the door, walk out. When the door closed behind her, he realized that Maggie had been watching, too, from behind her desk.

"Isn't she a little young for you?" she said.

Harry ignored the rib. "That's the Red Cross girl from St. Francis, remember? Anne Wallace. We did the two features on her, last November and last April. She's asked me to do another. She said they need to raise more money."

"Oh!" Maggie said, returning to her typing. "Well, in that case, she must have her finger on you. Knows just who to come to for a good, sappy story."

Harry narrowed his eyes. "She lost her fiancé. Killed over in the Pacific."

Maggie stopped typing and looked at him a moment. "You're quite a pushover, Mr. Mickelson," she said.

He smiled, then turned and went into his office.

A moment later, as he was sitting at his desk trying to get his notes together for the morning staff meeting, his telephone rang. He snatched it up. "Mickelson."

"Harry?" The voice was faraway, scratchy-sounding, but he recognized it.

"Mom?"

"Harry! How are you?"

"I'm good, Mom. Everything all right?"

"Oh, yes. It's nice to hear your voice, Harry."

"You too, Mom."

"We haven't seen you in so long."

"I've been pretty busy up here."

"I'm sure you have been. Harry, I know we can't stay on the line long, but I wanted to let you know. We just found out! JJ's coming home!"

"Cripes, Mom, that's great! He's doing all right?"

"Yes, well, you know he's been in the hospital quite some time now, over on one of those islands, then in Hawaii, and then in California. He's—Well, from what they tell me, he's doing as well as can be expected. They say he walked a few steps the other day! It hurt an awful lot, but he's pushing on. You know, after all he's been through."

Harry bit his lip, then said, "Well, when's the big day?"

"It depends on when he can get a flight. He thinks he can get one from California up to Chicago, and then he'll likely have to take the train from there. Can you come down, Harry? I know it would mean so much to him to have us all here."

"I'll do my best, Mom. Will you give me as much notice as you can? So I can make arrangements?"

"Of course, Harry. Well, we'd better get off the line. You take care, Harry. I'll call you again as soon as we know."

"Thanks, Mom."

"Bye-bye, Harry." And the line went dead.

Harry replaced the handset in its cradle. He leaned his elbows on his desk and covered his eyes with his fingertips. As he always did when he heard his mother's voice, he remembered the summer he was sixteen, the reason why he hated to go home, and the reason why she drew him there like a moth to a flame.

John Mickelson had insisted that the family return to their cottage at Stone Harbor for the summer. They had stayed home in Pine Rapids the last two summers, but now the war was over, Jack was home, and John said it was time that everything return to normal, at least as much as possible.

Wilma said she never wanted to go back to Stone Harbor again.

John said it would do her good to relax, and called Dr. Seguin, who prescribed more sedatives. The next thing Harry knew, John was taking the family and their trunks to the Pine Rapids depot and putting them on the train to Green Bay, where they would catch the boat up to Stone Harbor. John was staying behind to work, and would come later in the summer for two weeks. John had wanted

Jack to stay behind, too, to begin working at the bank, but Harry figured Wilma must have won out on that point, because Jack was coming to Stone Harbor.

Jack hardly said a word the whole time on the train, staring out the window and smoking cigarette after cigarette. Over Harry's protests, Jinny sang the song "K-K-K-Katy" over and over again until he finally kicked her shin. She just glared then, and started singing "Oh, How I Hate to Get Up in the Morning." Wilma slept, crushing her fine hat against the window.

Jack had been home for less than two weeks, and he was like a stranger. His eyes were flint, his mouth a hard line. Harry had seen him once in his undershirt and had been shocked at how thin he was. His left biceps had a scar on it like a hard white spiderweb; his right had a tattoo, an anchor with the letters *USMC* across it. "Mom know about that?" Harry had asked him, trying to joke, even though he felt a strange lump in his throat. But Jack hadn't answered, had just lit another cigarette.

The Mickelsons' Stone Harbor cottage was tiny compared to their house in Pine Rapids. It was one level, and included three bedrooms, a bathroom, kitchen, dining room, and front room. All Harry's life, he had shared the narrow north bedroom with his two older brothers; there were two twin beds pressed against the side walls with a small aisle between them and one bed at the foot of the room that the door barely cleared. (Now, Harry supposed, they could get rid of one of the beds, but they didn't.) Jinny had a small room, and the master bedroom was about a third of the size of Wilma and John's room in Pine Rapids. The dining room was just big enough for a table that sat eight. The best part of the whole place, though, was the front room, which featured a stone fireplace and windows all around, providing a stunning view of the bay out through the cedar trees and the large porch that ran the length of the cottage's front. There was a piano in the front room, too, which, in the past, Wilma had played every day. This summer, she didn't touch it.

The slightly smaller cottage next door was home in the summers to the Howard family from Chicago. The oldest girl, Mary, was eighteen, two years younger than Chase would have been this summer.

The middle girl, Stacy, was fifteen now, a year younger than Harry; and the youngest, Alice, was just Jinny's age—thirteen.

As far as Harry could tell, the trouble started one afternoon down on the dock. The two families had barely been in Stone Harbor a week, and Harry was with Stacy, watching Jack swim, when Mary came down, spreading out her towel near Harry, sitting down.

"You'd never know he'd been shot, would you?" Harry said, watching Jack's arms slice through the water.

"Do you know what happened, Harry?" Mary said.

Harry shrugged. "It was after Chase got killed, that's all I know. A few months after, I mean. They were in the same regiment, but I guess Jack's company stayed behind when Chase's went over the top that day at Belleau Wood. They stayed there for days, just shooting at anything that moved in their direction through the wheat field. That's all I know. That's all he'll say about any of it."

Mary sat there with her arms crossed over her drawn-up knees, chin resting on her arm. "Oh, poor Chasey," she said, finally, like a sigh.

Stacy shot Mary a look. Harry said nothing, though he knew that the last summer the two families had been in Stone Harbor—1916—Chase and Mary had been sneaking around and falling in love or something. Seventeen and fifteen at the time, they had done their best to keep their relationship a secret—particularly from Wilma, who had a tendency to get angry if Chase paid too much attention to any one girl. Harry had seen signs of it, though, including the letters that had arrived from Mary that fall and all the way through when Chase had left for the Marines in the spring of 1917. Harry had tried asking Chase about it several times, teasing, cajoling, trying to figure out how serious things were between the two of them. But trying to get personal information out of Chase had been like trying to get a pearl out of a sunfish—it just wasn't going to happen. And Harry wasn't about to ask Mary now and bring up something that did no good to talk about now that Chase was dead.

"You'd have to ask Jack about it, though," Harry said finally. "Maybe he'd tell you, you never know."

Harry's eyes were drawn to Jack then, who'd swum in and was pulling himself up onto the ladder at the end of the dock, streaming water from every square inch, brushing his wet hair back off his face, grinning. Harry hadn't seen Jack grin since he'd returned from the war. "Did you see that?" Jack said. "This arm's never been so good!"

"That's swell, Jack," Harry said.

"Wonderful," said Mary, smiling at him; Stacy's eyes were glued to him, too.

But Jack's eyes had shifted to Mary and he was looking at her like he'd never seen her before in his life. The grin stayed on his face, but got a little softer, and his eyes bore into her.

Mary said, "Oh," and a tiny smile spread across her face, as Jack watched her. Summers before the war, Jack had never had a minute for any of the Howard girls—or his own younger siblings, for that matter—but it seemed that was about to change.

"Come on, Mary," Stacy snapped. "You have to come up with me. Mother wanted us to help her with the vegetables for supper."

Mary looked up, surprised.

"She told me earlier and wanted me to tell you. Come on!" Stacy stomped up, and shoved her feet into her shoes.

With a quick slide of her eyes over Jack, who still hung there on the ladder with his grin, Mary got up, picked up her towel, and followed Stacy.

Jack shook his head after them. He climbed the rest of the way out of the water and went to pick up his towel where he'd dropped it at the middle of the long dock. He rubbed his face dry. Harry saw him sneak a look up toward where the Howard sisters had disappeared into the trees. Then he laid his towel out on the dock and stretched out, toes toward the water. He took one last look over his shoulder.

"So," Harry said finally. "Your arm's feeling all right, then?"

"Harry," Jack said, turning his head to look back at the shore again. "Why didn't you ever tell me that girl was so beautiful?"

"I think your head's just addled from that time you spent at the war," Harry said, but Jack kept looking back over his shoulder. It gave Harry a funny feeling in his stomach to see Jack get it in his head to steal Chase's girl—even if Chase was dead, it just didn't seem like something a brother should do.

But no matter how Harry felt about it, that June and July, Jack and Mary seemed to be falling hard for each other.

It was impossible not to notice that Jack felt a lot better when Mary was with him. At night, Jack had trouble sleeping; when he did sleep, he had nightmares, and would wake up the rest of the family with his yelling and crying. All the Mickelsons were starting to look a little rough around the edges from the sleep they'd lost. So if Jack could find some peace during the days with Mary, Harry was glad of it—but thinking that made him feel disloyal to Chase. But what choice did Harry have, really? Jack and Mary were going to do what they would do; he might as well just accept it, he figured.

Then, toward the end of July, Wilma got a letter from John back in Pine Rapids saying that he'd told the maids to go through all of Chase's things, and that he was going to have Chase's room redecorated.

"Why would he?" Wilma said to Harry that afternoon, as he sat at the kitchen table, watching her pacing, her hands clenched at her sides. "How could he?"

"I don't know, Mom," Harry said. He had a rotten feeling in his stomach again.

"I wonder if he'll open the box!" Wilma said, and Harry remembered how she'd been when Chase's "death effects" box had arrived at the door from the Marines. Tight-lipped and gray-faced, shaking her head, saying, "No! No one will open that box. Not while there is *life in my body*." So John had carried it into Chase's room, and there it sat patiently all year, like it was waiting for him to come home.

Harry figured that, if John was having Chase's room cleaned out, something would have to be done with that box. But he said to Wilma, "He wouldn't do that, Mom."

She glared at him, and left the room.

Three days later, Wilma told Harry that she had written John to go ahead and burn Chase's things. "Isn't it about time, I told him!" she said, laughing. Pain burning his gut, Harry wondered which doctor in Stone Harbor was feeding his mom something.

When John arrived in mid-August to spend the rest of the summer with the family, everyone—including the Howards—met him at the boat dock. John brought with him a heavy trunk, which Jack and Harry lugged the half mile to the cottage. When they got it inside, Jack said, "Let's take this back to the bedroom, Harry."

But John called after them. "Bring it into the living room, boys."

"John?" Wilma said. She tried to smile; faltered.

Harry and Jack set the trunk down in the middle of the front room. John held up his hands. "I'll tell you all now—I think the Howards will want to hear, too." He cleared his throat. "Wilma, you said you thought I ought to do what I thought best with Chase's things. And the more I thought about it, the more it came clear to me. We'd open them here, together, his family and our closest friends, in this place he loved."

A silence. Then: "John? Do you mean—?"

"I haven't opened a thing. The box they sent from France is here in my trunk."

Harry saw Wilma's lip start to tremble; John stood there like he was waiting to be thanked. Harry began kicking the trunk with gentle rhythm: *thump-thump-thump.*

"Well, can we open it now?" Jinny said, excited. She knelt in front of the trunk and started to fumble at the latch.

John slid his hand into his pants pocket. Keys jingled. "I don't see why not," he said. "If it's all right with your mother—"

"Is it all right, Mom?"

Wilma pursed her lips, silent, gray-eyed.

So they went ahead and opened the trunk, and Jinny took out the small cardboard box that sat on top. When she opened it, the smell of dust filled the room.

There was a small piece of fabric—from a uniform—right on top.

Jinny smoothed the fabric across her lap and reached in again, everyone watching.

"Look, Mom, it's a letter for you," Jinny said, taking out a flimsy Red Cross envelope and holding it in her mother's direction. Wilma was standing straight and stiff, gripping the back of a chair with both hands, pale as a cloud.

"Oh, I—I couldn't—" Then her eyes changed, and her gaze on the letter was hungry. She looked at Jack, but Jack was looking at the floor. Then she looked at Harry. "Harry? Would you?"

Harry felt his teeth clench, but he reached out his hand and took the envelope when Jinny gave it to him. He extracted the thin sheet of paper and unfolded it. "*June tenth, 1918. Dear Mrs. Mickelson,*" he read. *"Here is the best part of your boy's uniform that we could send. I cut this out of his sleeve before he was buried to send to you, as we didn't have much time. You don't know me, but Chase was in my company and even though he was a quiet sort of a fellow, I know you know like I do that he was a real fine fellow. Ma'am, I want to tell you, you can sure be proud of your boy. We were in this company together for some time and he never showed any fear. He was just in a hurry to give 'em some heck—if you'll pardon the expression—and get home as quick as he could."*

Harry stopped to clear his throat, blink his eyes. *"So you may know that he never had a moment of fear or doubt and he was brave to the very end. He never knew it when he died, just like the rest of us never know when our time will come. You can surely be proud of him. I feel lucky to have been in the same company with such a fine Marine. We all wished we could have been so brave and cool as him. God bless you, ma'am. Nels Iverson, USMC.*

"P.S. This is all the gear that he had in his pack—it wasn't much because we've been on the move and can't carry much."

There was nothing more.

John cleared his throat. "Thank you, Harry," he said. Wilma's eyes were glazed; she was seeing nothing.

Harry busied himself folding the letter back into the envelope.

Jinny was digging in the box again. "Aw, it's just a bunch a dirty ole Army stuff," she said, like a kid disappointed at Christmas.

"Jinny!" John said.

"Well, it is!" she said. "I don't see who'd ever want it!" Then she burst into tears.

Harry crossed the room and walked out the door, clutching the letter in his hand.

No one came after him. He didn't expect them to. He wasn't the one who'd been a hero. He'd never been a hero in his life. He'd never died for his country. How could he ever match that?

His mother had never seen him and she never would.

He went down to the dock and sat hugging his knees, watching the water, which was calm tonight, almost lavender in the light of the setting sun, the voice in his mind saying, *She never will and I don't care; he's not coming back and she never will.* After some minutes, there came a voice behind him. "Harry!" He turned. It was Stacy. She was holding what looked like another letter in her hand, and marching toward him like a fury. "Did you know about this?" she said. "About Chase and Mary?"

So there had been letters from Mary in the box. Harry turned from Stacy, and looked out at the water. "He's dead," he said. "My brother Chase is dead. Haven't you heard?"

But Stacy ignored him. "She talked herself out of this mess, like she always does," she said. "'Oh, we were just good friends!' They all believed her! But, Harry, in this letter it says they were *engaged*!"

Harry turned, surprised.

"Yes! Engaged!" Stacy said. "I didn't say anything, but—but she's pretending to Jack like it never happened, like she's only ever had eyes for him! But I don't see how she ever *could* love Jack—not if this letter is the *least* bit true—We have to do something, Harry. Don't you think? We can't let Jack get hurt; we can't let Mary have Jack when she doesn't deserve him! She's been lying to him this whole time! You have to help me."

Harry shook his head. "You know Chase died? He died, so what the heck does it matter about any of it? So what if your sister loved him and now she loves Jack. What do you know about any of it, anyway? About what it's like to really lose somebody. To love somebody and lose them. How would you know what that's like? How would you know if Jack would even give a damn about it, what with all he's seen, all he's done? How would you know?"

"But she couldn't love Jack, not if this letter is true! And it must be true, because here it is! Don't you think Jack has the right to know?"

"I don't care, Stacy. I don't care what Mary does, or what she did. Chase *died*, Stacy. Goddamn it, he died! The least you can do is let the rest of us alone!"

Harry turned back toward the water.

After a moment he heard her say, "Fine. Fine, Harry, if that's the way you feel."

He's not coming back and she never will she never will and I don't care I don't care I don't! until he heard footsteps, leaving him alone.

But Stacy ended up showing Jinny the letter from Mary to Chase. Harry gathered it was full of a bunch of lovey-dovey stuff, plus some detailed plans for an elaborate wedding, apparently part of a game Chase and Mary had played in every letter, trying to outdo each other with more fantastic dreams for their future. Jinny told Jack about it.

Jack was furious at them all for keeping him in the dark. Evidently, he'd been under the impression that Chase and Mary had been nothing more than pen pals, and his pride couldn't stand the truth. He broke up with Mary, wouldn't talk to anyone.

Harry thought that if Jack had any real brains he'd be furious with himself, too, for having paid so little attention to Chase that he had no idea of Chase's dreams. Jack had plugged his own ideas of Marine glory right into Chase's life without ever asking if it was what Chase wanted. If it wasn't for Jack, Harry thought, Chase might not have gone into the Marines at all. He might still be alive. It was hard not to hate Jack for being so selfish, not only about Chase, but about Mary, too, when you saw how broken and sad she looked, now that she'd lost not just one but two brothers. Harry didn't blame Mary for loving both of them; he blamed them for taking her for granted. Darn Chase, anyway, going off to war when he had a girl like that pinning her hopes on him. Darn Jack for being a blind, arrogant fool. If Harry ever had a girl like that, he'd stay with her, and that was that.

But Harry said nothing to Mary about it, or to the rest of them. He started spending all his time down at the Yacht Club or Bronson's ice cream parlor with his friends. He took up drinking, some, and smoking, a lot.

The day before the Mickelsons were going back to Pine Rapids, Harry came home late at night—they hadn't even left a light on for him—and went in and flopped on the couch in the front room to smoke a last cigarette by the light of the moon, knowing that even if his parents smelled the smoke they wouldn't come out. They'd think it was Jack smoking; or even if they thought it was Harry, they wouldn't care.

The box of Chase's things was still there on the floor. Nobody had touched it since the day they'd opened it, almost two weeks ago.

Harry pulled the box over to himself and pawed through it. He picked up Chase's dog tag and looked at it. It was strange knowing that somewhere in France his brother lay in a grave wearing the matching tag. Harry ran his thumb over the letters pressed in the aluminum: CHASE G. MICKELSON 1917 USMC.

"Harry?"

"Mom?" Harry was so busy trying to hide the dog tag that he forgot all about trying to hide his cigarette.

Wilma was in her robe and nightgown, and in the moonlight with her hair wispy around her face she looked old, almost tattered. "What are you doing, Harry?"

"Nothing," he said. "I just got home."

"What are you doing with Chasey's things?"

"Nothing—I just—Nobody had done anything with them. I was just—"

"I don't want you touching them. We're going to leave them where they are."

Harry stubbed out his cigarette in the ashtray on the table; it had burned down to his fingers. He clutched the dog tag in his fist. "It doesn't change anything, Mom."

"What?"

"Even if you don't touch them," Harry said. "He's still dead."

She narrowed her eyes; he felt himself shrinking from her. "Do you think I don't know that? You little smart aleck. As if I haven't been punished enough, as if I haven't had everything taken from me, you—"

"For Pete's sake, Mom," Harry broke in. "Jack came home, didn't he?"

"You don't understand, Harry. You couldn't understand."

Harry felt his eyes going blurry; he blinked to clear them. "What about me and Jinny?" he said, despite himself. "You've still got us, don't you? And Dad?"

She looked at him a moment, and finally sighed. "You're like me, you know, Harry. Always trying so hard. My poor boy." She came to him then and took his face between her hands, kissed his forehead. "My poor sweet boy," she said.

He felt like he'd been granted a reprieve. But the sad way she looked at him, shaking her head a little, was a dismissal, too. "Good night, Harry," she said, sliding her hands down his face and away. She turned and walked back toward her room. Her footsteps made no sound.

Later, it would seem to him that it was the first and last time she had really seen him. Just that one fleeting moment—if he hadn't dreamed it. But he had worn Chase's dog tag around his neck for years, as if to prove to himself that night had existed; that his brother, too, had existed.

Dream or real, it had been enough, over the years, to kindle the hope that Wilma would one day see him again. Just as he did his brothers, Harry loved her and hated her at once. She was blind and arrogant, too, he thought, though it made his eyes blur again—made him feel worthless and guilty and shot to hell—to think such things about his own mother.

In your preoccupation with the practical demands
of homemaking, don't overlook your husband's
need for your understanding and love.

—"Making Marriage Work,"
Ladies' Home Journal, March 1950

PINE RAPIDS WOMEN'S CLUB MEETING
Thursday, July 27, 1950

"You ladies won't believe me when I tell you," Mrs. Fryt said, joining
Dolly and Corinne Olson near the refreshment table at the back of the
town hall following the Women's Club meeting. Dolly had been unan-
imously approved for membership, only one anonymous woman ab-
staining. Dolly, though exhausted from worrying all last night about
what would happen now that JJ Mickelson had discovered her in the
Mickelson house, was pleased enough, but she knew she would always wonder which paragon of Pine Rapids thought she didn't quite
measure up. After the meeting, to perk her up, she had helped herself
to a gingersnap and a cup of coffee. After all, she had a lot to contend
with this afternoon. Between the chores waiting at the bungalow and
that impossible JJ Mickelson being convinced that she was now in his
employ, it wouldn't do to let one abstention wither her.

Mrs. Fryt wore her fanciest hat today, and another wild floral dress. "Maybe my eyes were playing tricks on me," she declared, tugging on the peplum of her dress, "but I would swear I saw a light in the Mickelson house last night."

Dolly choked on her gingersnap; coughing, she spilled coffee on her hand.

"Dear, dear," said Corinne, patting her on the back. When Dolly's coughing was under control, Corinne said, "Are you certain, Cecilia? What time was it?"

Mrs. Fryt tugged at her peplum again. "It was late. I couldn't sleep, so I got up and sat in my rocker by the window. It was just for a moment, in their living room window, a flare, almost like someone had struck a match. And then it was gone."

"Maybe you were dreaming," Dolly croaked, and coughed again. Her hand stung where the coffee had spilled on it.

"I am not *that* old, miss," Mrs. Fryt snapped. "I know when I'm awake and when I'm asleep."

"Maybe it was a ghost," Corinne laughed. "Old Knute himself, I bet."

Dolly stayed quiet, clutching her stinging hand.

Dolly soon escaped, after making sure that Mrs. Fryt was still engaged in conversation and wouldn't be at home to see Dolly walking straight up to the Mickelsons' back door. Dreams of creating the perfect home for Byron aside, she had no choice but to return to the Mickelson house. If she didn't, JJ Mickelson was apt to report to his father that "the housekeeper" hadn't shown up to work. Then the truth about Dolly breaking in would come out and she would really be in trouble.

But she couldn't deny, too, that she felt herself drawn to JJ like a passerby to a car wreck. Yesterday, after she'd taken the decanter from him, the look he'd given her made her skin crawl—yet, when he'd told her, "Come back tomorrow," she had said, "Yes, all right." She supposed she was foolish not to run from him. Maybe she had read too many Nancy Drew stories, after all, imagining she could descend into the mystery of the Mickelson house and emerge unscathed.

On the other hand, this was the first excitement she'd had since arriving in Pine Rapids. She wasn't about to shrink from it.

On her way to the Mickelson house, she stopped at the bungalow to pick up a plate she'd made up of last night's leftovers: salmon patties, parsley-buttered potatoes, and creamed peas. When she'd asked Byron how he'd liked it, he'd said, "Just fine, Doll," which meant he didn't like it at all. She'd been about to throw the extra two patties in the trash when she thought of JJ. There was no point in letting good food go to waste when there was a wifeless man across town.

Retrieving the plate from the refrigerator now, she decided to heat it in her oven—she liked excitement, but she was a little nervous about returning to the house, too. Last night, she had tossed and turned for hours, worrying about the mess she'd gotten herself into. The harder she squeezed her eyes shut and tried to stop thinking about it, the more images of JJ Mickelson flooded her mind. His flinty eyes, his chapped lips, his stubbled chin. The way he'd looked at her when she'd taken the decanter from him. She couldn't help but imagine him sitting alone in that big house on the hill with his liquor, bent on the obliteration of consciousness that sleep would not provide him, for she was sure she had seen nightmares in his eyes. Was he getting drunk with the intention of doing something awful to the house? Or to himself? Would she be the one to discover his destruction?

As Dolly's mind raced, the heat of Byron's body and the contented sounds of his sleep had been well nigh unbearable. His every breath seemed to accuse her of a kind of unfaithfulness, saying, *It's our house you should care for. What about our house? What about me?*

All she had wanted was to do her best for Byron, and look where it had gotten her. She was neglecting the cleaning at the bungalow, repeating last year's menus—what was next, allowing plants to go unwatered, socks undarned, shirts unstarched?

Well, there was nothing to be done about her shortcomings just now. She pulled the warm plate from the oven, covered it, and set out.

From the outside, the Mickelson house looked the same as it had yesterday. But what might she find inside? Her steps slowed at the bottom of the driveway, but she forced herself on. Her calves strained as she climbed the hill, and she ascended the steps to the back stoop, her legs feeling heavy. She knocked on the porch door.

No answer.

Holding the plate of leftovers in one hand, she pulled open the door, slipped inside the porch, and knocked on the door to the house. She bit her lip, looked around. She hoped Mrs. Fryt hadn't arrived home yet from the Women's Club meeting. She tried the door. It was locked.

She knocked as loudly as she could, and waited.

Then, there came the sound of a bolt shooting out of the lock, and the door opened.

JJ was bleary-eyed, his hair mussed, on crutches, wearing a white T-shirt and blue and white striped pajama bottoms with the left leg pinned up above where a knee should have been.

She did a double take, gaping at the empty space.

He said nothing.

"It's—afternoon!" she managed finally. "You're not dressed!"

"Guess I had you fooled yesterday, with my fake leg," he said. "Good party trick, huh?"

"I—I'm sorry!" she said, forcing herself to look at his face.

His mouth twisted; he shrugged. "You can come in if you want."

As he turned from her on his crutches, her nostrils caught a whiff of the whiskey stink emanating from his skin.

"I—brought you some lunch," she said to his back, but he didn't turn to acknowledge her.

She followed him down the dim hallway, his crutches thonking on the dusty wood floor. His missing leg, his strange attitude—not to mention the smell of him—inspired a surge of longing for the dull, safe little bungalow. But she still had that car-wreck feeling of fascination —plus, she was determined to play her "housekeeper" part to the utmost. So she pressed on, following JJ into the living room.

The sight of it was a shock. Shards of broken glass glittered on the floor in front of the fireplace. The portraits on the mantel lay face-down. Clothes were strewn across the backs of chairs, and the sheets on the couch were twisted into ropes. JJ's prosthesis lay at an unsettling angle under the bay window, like a casualty of war. Cigarette butts spilled over the ashtray onto the mahogany coffee table. The room stank of smoke, a desperate night, and the bourbon that had spilled on the rug.

"Oh, my," Dolly breathed. Suspecting something and knowing it were drastically different, and now she didn't know what to do.

"I wanted to keep you busy, I guess," he said, like a joke, but he still had a strange grimace on his face.

She stared at the mess a moment. Then she rallied. "Well! Your father certainly didn't tell me that cleaning up after you would be part of my job!"

Hurt showed in his eyes. He closed them briefly, lifting his hand and rubbing the bridge of his nose, wincing, like he had a headache. "You won't tell him, will you?"

Considering matters, Dolly set the plate of food down on the end of the coffee table. Then she folded her arms. Though JJ's impression that Jack Mickelson had hired her was what was trapping her here, she decided to use that same idea to her advantage. "I don't know," she said. "I might have to tell him."

"I don't even remember doing it," JJ protested. "It's not like I did it on purpose. The last thing I remember is going out to the trunk of my car and carrying in a couple bottles of Jack Daniel's."

She pursed her lips, and looked away.

"I'm sorry," he said. "Please, don't tell my dad."

"How do I know you won't do this again?"

"I won't! It's just, my head gets—messed up, sometimes."

Her skin was tingling; she prayed he wouldn't see through her lies.

"I'm not planning on staying long, anyway," he said. "I'm just supposed to check on the place. Looks like it was doing better before I came."

She looked at him then, and pity washed over her; his eyes were small pools of misery. "I'll clean this up," she said finally. "I won't tell your father."

JJ smiled, his relief evident. He was as transparent, and as changeable, as a child. "'Who is 't can say, "I am at the worst"?'" he said then, in a resonant stage voice. "'I am worse than e'er I was. / And worse I may be yet; the worst is not / So long as we can say, "This is the worst."'"

Dolly looked around the room. "Well, it's pretty bad," she said.

He laughed. "You know, you're awfully cute for someone who doesn't know Shakespeare when she hears it."

She touched her throat. "I—I'm married!" A reflex, as much as if he'd tapped her knee and she'd kicked him. But her heart had taken off like a horse out of the gate. *Stop that,* she scolded.

"I saw your ring," he said. "I meant in a little sister way. Besides, I never mess with married girls. It's a rule I have. You don't have to worry about me."

She sighed. "Oh. All right, then." She straightened her spine and took a deep breath. "Well, I should get to work. Please—eat." She gestured to the plate.

He picked up a near-empty pack of cigarettes off the coffee table, extracted one, lit it. She noticed a tattoo peeking out from the sleeve of his T-shirt, but she couldn't tell what it was. "Thanks," he said.

Superior, Wisconsin
Wednesday, November 7, 1945

After meeting the day's deadline and taking a little catnap at his desk, Harry drove the *Gazette*'s 1928 Ford truck through freezing rain out to St. Francis Hospital in Superior's East End. Anne Wallace was waiting for him at the front desk, and greeted him with a smile when he came in. She was dressed in her crisp gray and white uniform with a Red Cross patch on the sleeve and a starched white cap. When he saw her, he felt his heart and breath quicken, but he just smiled, shook her lovely little hand.

For the next three hours, he shadowed her through the hospital's four wards, listening while she read to patients, watching as she fluffed pillows, observing the way the patients' eyes sparked when she stopped by their bedsides and they had a chance to tell her their latest news. While they moved between patients, she told him again the difference between the Gray Ladies and the Nurses' Aides. "The Nurses' Aides have more training, and they really step in for the nurses, since there's been such a shortage on account of the war. We Gray Ladies mainly make sure the patients are comfortable, and try to help them pass the time." She also spoke of the splendid work that the Superior Chapter Production Corps had done. "They've made more than a thousand items of clothing to be sent overseas, to European civilians and servicemen. I knit, too, in my spare time," she confided. "I've made three OD green sweaters and two pullover vests to send overseas."

Harry scribbled furiously in his notepad.

"Oh, dear," she said, checking her watch as they entered the foyer. They'd just spent a good twenty minutes talking with a woman who was expecting her first child at any moment. "It's seven. The end of my shift. I—hope you have enough information?"

Harry nodded, still writing as he walked. "Thanks, Miss Wallace. I have just a couple more questions for you. Maybe we could get a cup of coffee?" He looked up.

"All right," she said. "We can go to Joe's; it's just a couple blocks away. Do you want me to ask Miss Ludczik if she can come, too?"

"That's all right. I got enough chance to talk to her earlier. The story'll be mostly about you, so naturally there are just a couple of details to fill in."

"All right," she said. "I'll get my coat." He watched as she walked into an adjoining office. Thinking of her green eyes, he scribbled a few more notes.

She linked her arm with his as they hurried through a biting wind past the church and around the corner into the East End business district. Despite the cold, Harry was a little disappointed when they reached Joe's Café and she let go of him.

He opened the door for her, and followed her into the bright room, breathing in the warmth, the smells of meat and bread that had been fresh that morning.

"You kids go ahead and have a seat," a waitress called to them as she hurried by. Joe's was a small place, with red vinyl booths along either wall like piers, and rectangular tables scattered in the center like flotsam. A counter ran the width of the back, with a view into the kitchen. The wall by the door was full of autographed portraits of servicemen. Three old men were eating pie and slurping coffee in one of the booths; a group of girls giggled over milk shakes in another.

Harry held out his hand for Anne to go ahead, and followed her to a booth in the front corner of the café. They took off their coats and hats and hung them on the pegs provided. "Have you ever been here, Mr. Mickelson?" she asked as they sat down across from each other.

"No, I haven't. I spend most of my time downtown."

"Oh, yes," she said. "I suppose you would."

"Do you come here a lot?"

"Since I was a little girl. My mother even waitressed here for a while, during the Depression, when my dad was always getting laid off from the railroad. Plus, I've been volunteering at the hospital since my senior year of high school, and Joe's is so convenient. The other girls and I come here all the time after our shifts."

Harry turned to dig his notebook and pencil out of his coat pocket from where his coat hung behind him.

She laughed. "You aren't going to write that down, are you?"

"Always on the job," he said, grinning, turning to a blank page.

The waitress, a stout woman with grayish-blond hair pulled up into a bun, stopped at their table. "Hi there, Anne," she said. "I see you've finally got your mind off Bobby enough to get yourself a cute date. Bit older than you, if I had to guess, but age doesn't matter, if you find common interests. My sister's married to a guy twelve years older and it's always been just peachy for them—"

"Dolores! No! This is Harry Mickelson, the editor of the *Gazette*. He's interviewing me for a story about the Red Cross. Remember when I was featured last year? He's the one who wrote the articles!"

"Guess I spoke out of turn, then," the waitress grumbled. "So, what can I get you?"

"Oh, I'll just have a piece of pie, and coffee," Anne said.

"Anne Wallace," Dolores said. "I know you've just got off a shift at the hospital and probably haven't eaten since breakfast. You'd better have the meat loaf, with mashed potatoes and gravy and a side of green beans." She nodded to herself, wrote it down on her tablet. Harry glanced at Anne, who had opened her mouth as though to object.

Dolores went on. "And then pie for dessert, where it belongs." She made another note, then looked up at Harry. "And you?"

"Sounds great. I'll have the same," he said, folding his hands atop his notebook.

"Coffee for you both?"

They assented, and Dolores made a note, then walked away, calling, "Joe! We need two loafs with mashed and beans!"

"I'm sorry about that," Anne said.

Harry laughed. "I didn't mind," he said, picking up his pencil again.

"But your wife—"

"Nothing to worry about, Miss Wallace. I'm not married."

She glanced up with big eyes. "You're not?"

He shook his head.

"Oh! Well, forgive me. I naturally assumed—"

"That's all right."

"The girls aren't going to believe it," she said.

"What's that?"

She met his eyes. "Last year, when you came to the hospital those couple of times, all the girls had the awfullest crush on you, and Yvonne said she'd heard you weren't married. But I told them you had to be, because you were the most perfect gentleman to me, and single men never are!" She laughed. "I'm afraid I dashed all their hopes."

"Well, I'm flattered, I think."

"I shouldn't have told you that. That's me—always opening my mouth when I shouldn't."

"I wouldn't say that," Harry said.

Dolores appeared with their coffees, setting one before each of them without comment; they thanked her.

"All right, then," Harry said. "I just want to make sure I got this all straight. You've been volunteering as a Gray Lady at St. Francis since just before you graduated high school?"

She nodded.

"Which was what year?"

"1942. I was in the Junior Red Cross while I was in high school, too. I was president of our chapter my senior year. We raised over six hundred dollars."

Harry nodded, scratching out his notes. "So, was it Bobby who in- spired you to keep working for the Red Cross? Was he in the service back then?"

She shook her head. "Oh, no. I didn't even meet Bobby until I started college. He was from Superior, but he went to Central and I went to East."

"So was he a freshman at college the same year you were?"

"No, he was a sophomore. We dated that whole school year, and then in June he left for his pilot's training. He proposed to me just be- fore he left. I only saw him twice more after that, but we were en- gaged for over two years before—" She stopped.

"That's a long time to be apart," Harry said.

"We wrote letters almost every day," she said. "It helped us to feel—close, still. We always wrote about what we'd do when the war was over."

"What were your plans?"

"He was going to finish college and then go to law school. He wanted to go to the University of Minnesota, and then we were plan- ning to move back to Superior."

"What about now? What are your plans now?"

"I don't know," she said. "I'll be graduating from college this spring. I suppose I'll try to get a teaching job here in Superior. The only problem is—sometimes I still can't believe that Bobby isn't com- ing home, and I don't want to make any plans without him." She hes- itated, then looked up and met Harry's eyes. He could see her deciding to trust him. "His body was never recovered. When his plane was shot down, he was able to bail out, but he landed in the ocean and the seas were high. Another crew watched him drown. There was nothing they could do. His whole crew was lost, either in the explosion or in the water. So—there was no question. I mean, there should be no question. His family had a memorial service for him. But—I don't know."

"I'm sorry," Harry said.

She smiled a little. "Would you like to see a picture of him?"

"Certainly."

He expected her to pull one from her purse; instead, she looked to- ward the opposite wall, where the servicemen's portraits hung. Harry stood with her and she led him over to a small framed portrait that hung amidst others over the unoccupied middle booth. A broad-shouldered blond man in a uniform and a pilot's leather jacket looked out at them from under his cap with a friendly smile. On the photo was written with movie star flourish, *All the best to everyone at Joe's, Bob Granholm.*

"That was taken during his flight training," Anne said. "He signed it here on his last leave home."

Harry recognized the picture. It was the same one the family had provided to run in the *Gazette* with the story about Granholm's death. "Handsome guy," he said.

Anne smiled. "I always thought so."

Dolores's voice came from over by their booth. "Meat loaf's getting cold!"

Harry touched Anne lightly on the elbow, and she smiled up at him. There was pain in her eyes, but not hopelessness. They turned and went to sit down, as Dolores waited, a platter of steaming meat loaf held aloft in each hand. As he slid into his seat, Harry moved his notebook from the tabletop to the bench next to him.

"You know, Anne," Dolores commented as she clunked their loaded plates down in front of them. "I knew Bobby. He wouldn't expect you to mourn him forever. It's been what, six months now?"

"Thank you, Dolores," Anne said, looking at her meat loaf. "This looks delicious."

Dolores sighed, put her hands on her hips. "Anything else, then, kids?"

"No, thank you," Harry and Anne both said. Dolores scooted away.

"Well, Mr. Mickelson," Anne said, picking up her fork. Her tone of voice had changed, and he knew she had replaced her armor. She seemed not to like to show weakness, and he was surprised she had shared as much as she had with him. "Now that I've bared my soul—is there anything else you need to know?"

He didn't want barriers between them. He wanted her to trust him entirely. He didn't know if it was possible. "Why don't you call me Harry?" he said, lifting his fork to take a bite of his meat loaf.

"Is that a question, or a request?"

He smiled.

"Well, if it's a question, the answer is because you're a newspaper editor and I'm just a college girl, and my mother taught me it's polite to respect your elders." She said this with a gleam in her eye, and he knew it was a playful jab.

He laughed. "All right, then, how old do you think I am?"

She took a bite and chewed, looking up to the ceiling as though deep in thought. After she swallowed, her eyes flashed back to his. "Well, that's kind of a tricky question, Mr.—Harry. If I consider your esteemed position in the community—"

Harry raised an eyebrow.

Anne laughed. "No, no, hear me out. I'll bet it takes some time to get enough experience to become a newspaper editor. I can assume that you've been to college—?"

Harry nodded.

"And you probably had to work as a reporter for some time before becoming an editor. Because it's obvious you're a good reporter, with all the questions you've been asking me!"

He laughed.

"So if I had to guess, I might say, thirty-five? Thirty-six?"

He grinned.

She pointed her fork. "But then there's a spark in your eyes! Which makes me think you're—thirty-two? But then I'd have to wonder why you weren't in the service."

"Well, I can answer that for you," he said quickly. "Knee injury. Back from my high school football days."

"Oh, dear. I'm sorry."

He shrugged. "In any case, you've got quite the powers of deduction, there, Miss Wallace. If you're looking for a job after graduation, maybe I could hire you as an investigative reporter."

"Wouldn't that raise some eyebrows!" she said. "A woman reporter!"

"It's all over the country now, Miss Wallace, with the war. Many women doing a fine job as reporters. Even editors."

"Yes, but now that the war's over, they're going to get sent back to their kitchens, aren't they?"

"I suppose they are."

"Well, I'd accept the offer, Mr.—Harry, but I guess I have my heart set on being a teacher. And you didn't tell me if I was correct."

"You'll have to do some more investigation."

She made a face.

"So, what do you want to teach?"

"First grade," she said, serious again, swirling her fork through her potatoes.

He was struck by her certainty. "Why first grade?"

"Because it's such a place of—beginning!" she said.

Harry speared three little green bean logs onto his fork. "I guess it would be nice to work in a place like that."

"How did you become a newspaperman?" she asked.

"Well," he said, "when I was in college, I majored in English. Decided I wanted to be a writer. Pictured myself the next Hemingway, you know. Newspaper reporting gave me a way to support myself."

"Oh!" she said. "So, have you written—books?"

"A couple," he said, with a small smile.

"How exciting! Do they have them at the library? I'd like to read them."

"No. They're just in my closet."

"In your closet? Do you mean—you mean they haven't been published?"

"That's right."

"Well, what a shame! Have you tried?"

He shrugged. "Not much. Been too busy."

"Well, why not? To have a great talent and then not even try to share it! It seems such a shame."

He laughed. "It's charitable of you to assume that I have great talent."

"Of course you do," she said. "I can tell just by the way you look at me."

"By the way I look at you?"

"Yes! You're sizing me up, but not the way that most men do."

He set down his fork and leaned back, embarrassed.

"Most men," she continued, "just look at the outside. But you— you look as though you're trying to see right through me. As though a million little questions about me are running through your mind.

What does she like to read? What does she think about when she's walking in the rain? Does she stomp in puddles or avoid them? Does she wear pajamas or a nightgown to bed? Is she messy or is she neat? Does she wear a sweater all summer or go swimming in Lake Superior the first of June? All of that! And at first I couldn't understand why you'd want to know all that, but now that you say you're really a writer, well, I understand perfectly! My brother is a writer; he writes short stories. He explained this to me, one time before he left for the war. It was when he was still in high school, and I was, oh, thirteen, I guess. I've always remembered it. He's written wonderful stories about his experiences in the war that he sent home to my mother for safekeeping. Wonderful and terrible, too, of course."

Harry leaned forward and picked up his fork again. "Well?" he said.

"What?"

"Do you stomp in puddles or avoid them?"

She smiled. "It depends on which shoes I'm wearing."

It was past nine when, having polished off their suppers and two large pieces of chocolate chip pie, they finally rose to leave. "Goodness," Anne said, putting on her coat. "I think I ate enough to last me the week."

Harry smiled as he buttoned his coat. "Looks like Dolores knew best after all." He paused, then went ahead and asked, "Can I give you a lift home?"

She adjusted her hat. "I live up by the college. Is that all right?"

"Of course. I'm heading that direction anyway."

"All right, then."

Dolores trundled toward them, a rag in her hand. "You kids stay warm out there, now," she said. They were the last ones left in the restaurant, and Dolores looked as though her busy day had caught up with her.

"Thank you, Dolores," Anne said.

"Thanks, Dolores," Harry said. "Supper was just great. The pie, too."

"Good, good. You kids come back soon," Dolores called after

them, as Harry held the door open for Anne and followed her out into the cold night.

The wind had died down and a gentle snow was falling, settling like a clean bedsheet over the quiet street. All the shops had closed up for the night; only two cars remained parked on the street. Harry hoped Anne would take his arm again, but she didn't. In contrast to their hurried walk over from the hospital, though, she strolled slowly along.

"I love snow this time of year, don't you?" she said, looking up at the drifting flakes.

"Better than in March, that's for sure," Harry said.

She laughed.

"So you live up by the college? I thought you said you were an East Ender," he said. "I've got it in my notes!"

"Yes, I grew up here, but I rent a room at a house near the college. It's so much easier; I can run back and forth to campus anytime I want to."

"So you're out on your own?"

"Almost like a grown-up!" she said, laughing. "Dolores is right, though, I don't eat nearly as well as I would if I lived with my mother."

"Well, that makes two of us."

"Oh, did you grow up here, too?"

"No. No, I've only lived here a few years. I grew up in a little town called Pine Rapids. You've probably never heard of it. My parents still live there."

"Are you able to visit them often?"

"Not really," he said cheerfully.

She laughed, and the sound thrilled him.

He touched the small of her back lightly to turn her so they could cross the street to where the truck was parked. They cut across, leaving tracks in the snow.

"Actually, I might be going home soon. My nephew is getting home from the war."

Her shoulder brushed his as they walked. "That's wonderful," she said.

He didn't know why he had told her.

When they reached the passenger side of the truck, she waited for him to open the door for her, and when he did, she let him help her up into the seat. "I have to apologize," he told her. "I'm sure this isn't the most luxurious form of transportation you've ever seen."

"Don't be silly! It's awfully exciting, riding in the *Gazette* truck."

He grinned, then shut her door and walked around the front, opened the driver's door, and hopped up into the seat, pulling the door shut behind him. He pumped the clutch and turned the key, and the truck roared to life. He rubbed his hands together to warm them. "You must think I'm an awful slacker," he said.

"What do you mean?"

"Well, here your fiancé was killed in action and your brother's a big hero and I'm just this broken down no-good 4-F." He cocked his head at her, still rubbing his hands together.

"I think you're a very important man," she objected. "Why, I don't know what people in this town would do without you! I can't tell you the number of times I've gotten into discussions with other students about things that had run in the *Gazette*, especially your editorials. Now that I know you better, I'll pay even closer attention, but everyone on campus always reads the editorials. You really keep a close eye on this town, and that's important. Otherwise, who knows what folks would try to get away with?"

"Well, you're right there," he acknowledged.

"Of course I am! And furthermore, it isn't as though you wanted to avoid serving." Indignant, she straightened her hat, removed her gloves.

He was, for a moment, too pleased to speak. He turned on the lights and the wipers, put the truck into gear, and pulled away from the curb.

She spoke up. "When my brother comes home—maybe you'd like to interview him? For the paper? He was at Normandy and the Battle of the Bulge and everything."

Harry smiled to himself, feeling the tires trail through the wet snow. "You'll have to let me know when he comes home."

"I will. Thank you."

"I'll give you my direct number; you can call anytime."

"Thank you," she said again, then leaned back in her seat with a sigh. They had gone a block before she spoke again. "You know, I haven't thought about Bobby for at least an hour. I can't remember when that's ever happened."

He looked over at her, and caught her in profile. For an instant, everything stopped. He swallowed. "Is that good or bad?"

"I don't know," she said, her smile nearly imperceptible.

After he dropped Anne off at her house, Harry drove downtown, parked the truck in its customary spot next to the *Gazette* loading dock, and let himself into the building with his key. The sound of his whistling echoed through the empty foyer as he tramped up the two flights of stairs to his office, unlocked the door, and went in. He flipped on the light in the empty newsroom, hung his coat and hat on the rack, pulled his notebook out of his coat pocket, then opened the door to his own office. Soon he was settled behind his desk, a cigarette dangling from his mouth, enjoying the clean look of a fresh sheet of paper in his typewriter. "ST. FRANCIS PATIENTS REMAIN IN CAPABLE HANDS OF RED CROSS VOLUNTEERS," he typed.

Despite his best intentions of getting the article written while the information was fresh, his mind wandered. He'd felt like a kid at the end of their evening together. When he pulled up to the curb in front of the house she indicated, he offered to walk her to the door. She said he didn't need to, but he insisted. He held her elbow all the way up the slippery walk, and they exchanged witty repartees about Superior's fine weather. When they reached the bottom of the porch steps, though, he didn't know what to do. The urge to touch her face was so strong that he shoved his hands into his coat pockets.

"Thank you for supper," she had said, smiling up at him. "And for doing the article, too. I can't tell you how much I appreciate it."

"Sure," he said, wanting to ask if she would go to supper with him again. But the words stuck in his throat: He was afraid she would laugh, or slap him, or say something like, "You're old enough to be my father!" The best he could muster was to dig in his lapel pocket for one of his cards, and hold it out to her. "Here's my direct number. Give me a call when your brother gets in. Or—anytime you want." He grinned. The picture of the pathetic, scrounging, older bachelor, he supposed, upon reflection.

But she took the card, smiling. "Thank you, Harry. You've been so kind."

He shoved his hands into his coat pockets again. "Good night."

"Good night," she said, and turned, walked up the steps.

The lovely Miss Anne Wallace, whom readers will remember, he typed, reflecting that he couldn't recall the last time he had hesitated to ask for a date if he wanted one. Usually he didn't give much of a damn either way. If he asked someone out and she said yes, great; on the rare occasions he was turned down, he wasn't usually too bothered. He couldn't remember the last time that his gut had gnawed with this anxiousness to see someone again.

Escape into a substitute relationship is a going back to the dreamlike
stage of late adolescence, putting new promises ahead of present
performance, and attempting to make life stand still, so that
one may continue on the threshold of maturity without
ever stepping over into the place where one
must make good one's promises.

—*The Good Housekeeping Marriage Book*, 1939

THE MICKELSON HOUSE
502 W. First Street, Pine Rapids
Thursday, July 27, 1950

JJ sat on the sofa, not saying a word, smoking and watching Dolly
clean up the mess he had made. First, she opened the front and back
doors and all the living room windows, to let in the fresh air. Then
she swept up the glass shards—they made a pleasant tinkling sound,
like wind chimes—and righted the portraits, dusting them and the
mantel. The portrait of JJ himself was missing; she couldn't bring herself to ask him what he had done with it.

She did ask him, "Aren't you going to eat?" She gestured to the
plate she'd brought, which was still sitting on the coffee table.

"Maybe in a little while," he said, smoking. "Thanks."

She folded the sheets that had been covering the furniture, which
he had thrown on the floor yesterday. She wiped down the marble
fireplace, dusted the baseboards and the windowsills and the carved

backs of the chairs. When she got to the sofa, he obliged her by leaning out of her way so that she could dust behind him; when she
leaned near him, her nose picked up the traveling-salesman-suitcase
smell of him: spilled whiskey, used tobacco, the stale air of loneliness
and unwashed shirts. She wrinkled her nose and quickly moved away,
feeling his eyes on her.

But she found the work satisfying, his attention strangely gratifying. Not to mention, the Mickelson house showed such appreciation!
The change in its mood was palpable as it began to gleam—unlike the
staid bungalow, always so indifferent to her constant efforts. She
yearned for a vacuum for the living room rug. She began to think: *If
I can catch JJ in the right mood—if it seems like he really isn't going
to stay—I'll ask him if they might sell.* She wouldn't feel right kidnap-
ping the house if it was wanted; adoption, though, was another matter.

She was running an oiled rag across the strip of wood that divided
the upper half of the walls from the lower when she noticed JJ crutching his way toward the parlor, his pants slung over his shoulder. "Can
you bring me my leg?" he called back to her.

The minute he came out of the parlor, dressed and walking on two
legs, he pushed open the screen door and stepped out onto the front
porch overlooking the highway and the Bear Trap River.

She followed him, keeping her body inside while her head poked
out the door. "Aren't you worried someone might see you?" she whispered. "I thought you wanted to be left alone."

He took a cigarette from a pack at his biceps, got his lighter out of
his pocket, shielded the cigarette as he lit it. He clumped over a few
steps, and leaned his back against the house.

She eased out onto the porch, cushioning the door as it closed behind her. The last thing she wanted was for Mrs. Fryt to see her. "The
neighbors will start talking," she warned him. "Mrs. Fryt already
told me this morning she thought she saw a light in the house last
night."

"She's still alive?" he said.

"Oh, yes, very much."

"How about that," he said, tapping ash from his cigarette onto the
porch. "Well, then, everyone will know soon enough, won't they?

About me being home." He laughed. "That old lady used to think she knew everything that went on over here."

"Well, she did know an awful lot," Dolly said. "She's been telling me all about it. And she's been keeping her eye on the house to see when one of you would come back."

"Oh, she has?" he said. "She hasn't sucked you into that Ladies Aid thing of hers, has she? You go to our church?"

"Why, yes. I'm new in town."

"My mom hated that group. So did my grandma. She said her ears would burn every Tuesday afternoon all summer long, because she knew they were sitting over there looking at this house and talking about her."

Dolly looked at her shoes.

"So, what have you heard about my family?"

She looked up again, and met his eyes. "Well, I've heard about your great-grandpa Knute, your grandma Wilma and grandpa John, and your father, Jack, and your mother, Mary, and about Chase—and I'm so sorry—and then they've been talking about your sister—about Elissa—lately. But I haven't found out what happened. Judy says it was her fault, but the rest of them say she couldn't have known. Something about that boy she met during the war—"

Taking a last drag of his cigarette, he limped to the front edge of the porch. He stubbed his cigarette out on the railing, tossing the butt into the garden below.

"I wish you wouldn't do that!" she said, stepping up next to him.

He looked at her, his face pinched in a scowl, his eyes rife with evil, goodness, and desolation. So unexpected was this glimpse of his essence—as clear as if he'd hollowed himself out with a spoon and spread the contents before her—that she was stunned into silence. She clutched the porch railing in both hands and looked out across the highway toward where the Bear Trap glinted through the trees, conscious of his hands gripping the railing next to her, feeling at once gratified and a little queasy with fright.

Pine Rapids
Spring 1943

Suddenly, it seemed that Ty Lofgren was everywhere. Elissa saw him between almost every class period, after school at Emory's, Saturdays when she went to the library or the market. There he would be, pulling his cap down low over his eyes, giving her a wink and a smile. She wondered if he had always been so present in her life, and she just hadn't noticed, or if lately he was somehow contriving to put himself in her path.

Muriel encouraged her to acknowledge the possibility. "He's cute, isn't he? Even if we have known him all our lives, you've got to admit he's turned out all right. And Nick's out of the picture, Liss. You've got to move on. I know you thought you were in love with him, but you have to face the fact that it's over."

Elissa tried, but every time Ty caught her eye, she just felt embarrassed, and she could never think what to say to him. She blamed everything on Nick, for making such a fool of her. She had lost all confidence.

Besides, she explained to her diary, *he probably just feels sorry for me. Everyone knows what a fool I've been.*

Then came the Saturday in early April when Elissa bumped into him as she came out of Holman's Market, on the corner of First Street and Jefferson Avenue, laden with a brown-wrapped roast that her mother had sent her to pick up for tomorrow's dinner. Grocery shopping had just been made very complicated with the beginning of meat rationing a week before, and Elissa, the roast tucked under her arm, was busy counting out her stamps, wondering how much more meat they would be able to get this month now that the three-pound roast had cost them six ration points and one dollar and eleven cents. Nobody quite understood the point system yet, not even Mr. and Mrs. Holman.

Engrossed in the problem of the stamps, she was just out the market's corner door and about to turn south down Jefferson when her shoulder bumped against someone. Fortunately, the roast was wedged tightly enough under her elbow that it stayed put. She looked up, and saw Ty Lofgren's brown eyes.

"Excuse me!" he said.

"Oh, pardon me. I wasn't watching where I was going."

It was a typical early-April day in Pine Rapids, the melting snow adding a pleasant moistness to the air and the streets, the damp surfaces and shrinking piles of snow all seeming to glitter a bit, reflecting the sun, the warmth of which could be sensed on face, hands, and hair, despite the coolness of the air. Cars tooled by on First Street in no particular hurry, tires sluicing through puddles with a joyful noise. Elissa had left her coat unbuttoned and wasn't wearing a hat or gloves. Similarly, Ty's jacket was unzipped, his head and hands bare. His brown hair was a little messy from the breeze. It was true that Elissa had volunteered to go to the market—perhaps, though she would not have admitted it even to herself, in anticipation of such a meeting.

He looked as though he was happy to see me, she would write later in her diary, *and altho' I dreaded what he might say, I found myself holding my breath, almost I guess you could say nervous, beyond*

descrip.! Would he have an explanation for all the strange coinci-
dences of late, for example running into him in these circumstances
(how could he have known that I would be at the market at that time,
and yet didn't it seem p-haps suspect that he of all people would be
the one I would literally physically bump into)? And would he finally,
now, speak to me, to tell me why he had been winking at me across
whatever room in whatever circumstances for more than a month,
ever since the Betrayal was known to All? Was he laughing at me,
pitying me? Or was it something more literally fantastic? (& for
heaven's sake, what in the world was I hoping for, given the present,
i.e., broken, state of my heart?)

"No, it was me—me entirely—I wasn't watching," he said.

She didn't know what to say. *As usual.*

"Are you heading home?"

"Yes."

"Can I walk you?"

"Of course, yes," she said, too quickly, then smiled.

So they fell into step together, turning down Jefferson and shortly leaving the bustle of downtown behind them. Birds hopped across the walk, fluttered up to the bare branches of trees, chirped and sang. April seemed full of possibility.

"So," he said, "I heard you're going to be a cadet nurse."

"Yes," she said. "At the University of Minnesota."

"That's great," he said. "I'd like to have you for a nurse—or—" She looked up in time to see him flush. He recovered, grinned. "I mean, I'm going in the Army," he said. "Just got my orders yesterday."

Elissa was taken aback by his news. It wasn't surprising, exactly—all the boys were going into the service, and many from the class of '43 had left already—but, to think, the class's sensitive Romeo! In the Army! "Will you be going soon?"

"Right after graduation."

"I'm glad you don't have to leave right away."

"You are?"

She blushed. The odd angles of his hair were quite adorable. And those eyelashes!

"I'm glad I bumped into you," he declared. "I always see you at school, but I don't ever get to talk to you."

"Well, I never knew you wanted to," she protested. *Perhaps too vehemently,* she would describe it later.

"Well, I did."

"What did you want to talk about?" she challenged him. She was in no mood for dissembling, after all the times he had winked at her.

"How about—Well, how about a date?" he said. "Friday night."

It would be an exaggeration to say that the heavens broke into song, yet p-haps I did feel a lightening of my soul, and the sun seemed to shine a little brighter when he said it. P-haps an explanation of the events of the past month with him? Yet, one has to wonder, what about the Betrayal was inspiration to him, what about it attracted him to me? I still say he's sorry for me, yet looking in those brown eyes I found myself I guess you could say melting, like a pile of snow in the April sun, to risk a mawkish simile.

"Friday night?" she said, a little coyly. "Let me think. I don't think I'm busy."

"Want to go to a movie, maybe? I could pick you up at seven."

She smiled. "All right."

Talk turned to other things; she found herself wishing she hadn't let him get away so easily in kindergarten.

He is smart, & very sweet, in fact walked me all the way up to the front porch and went over details of Friday and gave me a terribly sweet look before parting. Yet strangely I left him in a state of almost disappointment, I guess you could say. Suppose all the mystery is over, now it's on to typical movie dates, and him trying to sneak his arm around me, etc., him nervously wanting to kiss me and etc. while I pretend coyness, or feel conflicted (he's so sweet but should I, etc.), & matters proceed in the typical pedestrian manner, tho' in defense I am truly beside myself and don't know why I am bothering when it can only end in disaster (love or lack of it??) as ever.

Everyone was surprised when they found out that Elissa and Ty had started dating. Both prominent members of the senior class, they had one minute been as separate as oil and water, and the next, it seemed to everyone, they were all but fused, seen together before school, after school (him leaning on her locker, chucking her under her chin, looking back over his shoulder as he walked away from her, as she pretended not to notice), Friday nights, Saturday nights, Sunday af-

ternoons. Judy Wasserman in particular was vexed, even though, before Elissa took an interest in him, Judy hadn't bothered with him
at all.

To Elissa's surprise, her father, Jack, after some initial grumbling,
had very few complaints after he met Ty. She supposed it helped that
he had known Ty's father for years; Jack bought all his insurance
from Mr. Lofgren. Or maybe her mother, Mary, had prevailed upon
him with something like, "She's going to end up with someone; at
least he's a hometown boy." Though Elissa knew that her mother
wasn't too happy about Ty getting so serious about Elissa when he
was heading off for the Army in a couple of months. Her grandfather
John, on the other hand, seemed very pleased when Elissa told him
about Ty, while Wilma gave very little reaction at all, just an "Oh,
how nice," with her eyes looking glazed. Elissa wasn't quite sure how
to take that.

In fact, from the varied reactions of everyone around her, Elissa
wasn't at all sure how everybody expected her to feel about Ty.
Mostly, she was just as surprised as everyone at school about the way
things had gone. From the first, Ty had treated her with delicacy and
great care, and on their third date, over milk shakes at Emory's, he
had asked her to go steady.

It had seemed awfully sudden; she'd hesitated.

*Wondered immediately if a good idea, with him leaving for the
Army so soon and me still so uncertain after the Betrayal. Could our
relat. withstand a long separation? Did I even want to try? Not sure
why I chose the particular objection to voice that I did.*

"Oh, Ty, I don't know," she demurred. "You've got so many other
girls you're dating, what about all of them?"

"Elissa, I don't want to date anyone else. Not anymore. When I'm
with you—I can't even remember any other girl's name," he said.
(The sophomore class was devastated, when word of that line got
out.)

*So I said yes, of course. Vindication, of a kind. (& sweet besides.)
J. Wasserman is beside herself. "Are you in love?" Muriel asks. "Wait
and see," I tell her.*

The proof is in the pudding, as Dad so often irrelevantly says.

> Express your wishes as requests, your advice as suggestions,
> rather than issuing orders or instructions.
>
> —"Making Marriage Work,"
> *Ladies' Home Journal,* January 1950

THE MICKELSON HOUSE
502 W. First Street, Pine Rapids
Friday, July 28, 1950

After Byron went to work and Dolly finished washing the breakfast dishes, she vacuumed the bungalow. It was a task she'd planned for yesterday, but between the Women's Club meeting and the time she'd spent over at the Mickelson house, she hadn't managed to get it done.

She was feeling short-tempered, and as she worked she found herself getting aggressive with the furniture, shoving chairs and end tables here and there so she could properly vacuum, getting so angry when Byron's favorite chair wasn't far enough out from the wall that she slammed the vacuum into its leg to move it aside. Then the vacuum made a crackling noise, a sure sign of crumbs underneath the chair, meaning Byron had been eating his late-night snacks there again. Dolly had spent two years of married life telling him to eat at the table; that he would so deliberately flout her made her teeth clench. And he *still* hadn't made one move to paint the bathroom! Spent, she shut off the vacuum, sat down on the sofa, and buried her face in her hands.

She knew she was supposed to be happy, that she *should* be happy, with her lot in life. She had a handsome husband who provided her with all her material needs. She knew it was her job in return to provide him with a well-kept home, as well as with the support he needed in order to conquer the world of work and continue providing for her and the children they were supposed to have. That was what everybody said, anyway, and, when she was in high school, that was what she and her friends had always discussed and expected— except when they'd discussed the things they might do if they *could*. Dolly had wanted to become a pilot, Jane a doctor. But they had yearned for husbands and children, too, and knew in their hearts that it was impossible for both dreams to come true. So they had pursued the more acceptable choice.

But now Dolly couldn't seem to stop herself from asking, *Is this it? Is this my* life?

After her first set of flight lessons, she had in no way imagined that she would never again fly an airplane. And, try as she might, she couldn't seem to resign herself.

Yesterday, when Dolly was on the porch of the Mickelson house with JJ, the depth of his eyes, the way he had looked at her, had seemed to reveal that life could be a sonata; she'd been so busy plunking out "Three Blind Mice" that she hadn't even stopped to wonder over other possibilities. Looking in Byron's eyes had always been like standing on the shore of a calm lake: pleasant, but inscrutable. You knew there were things under the surface, but the glint of the sun kept you from seeing anything but the blue calm. And she had allowed Byron to define her world—from the time she was twelve years old, really! Now that she'd seen a kaleidoscope of passionate possibilities, she feared what she might do.

But at least I'm not attracted to JJ Mickelson, she told herself. *How could I be, when Byron is so much more handsome, and whole, and well-fed? Thank goodness! I'll get over this! I'll get pregnant soon, and that will calm me down.*

After noon, she walked over to the Mickelson house, again bearing a plate of leftovers for JJ: creamed chipped beef on mashed potatoes, with glazed carrots and cold cucumber salad on the side. (Byron's tepid comment: "Nice job, Doll.")

She had to knock four times before JJ finally answered the door. When he did, his eyes were bleary, and, like yesterday, he was still on his crutches, one leg of his pajamas pinned up, despite its being so late in the day. He looked terrible.

"I thought you'd be up by now!" she said.

He looked at her long enough to make her nervous. "Well," he said. "If it isn't my little housekeeper."

"I brought you some lunch," she said.

"Thanks," he said. "You can come in." He turned, and began crutching his way down the hallway. She shut the door behind her and followed, trying not to breathe too much; he was trailing that terrible traveling-salesman-suitcase smell.

When she reached the living room behind him, she stopped in her tracks. The ashtray was overflowing again; next to it, an almost-empty bottle lay on its side. Next to that was the plate she'd brought him yesterday, scraped clean. The sheets were twisted on the sofa, and JJ's prosthesis was resting at an awkward angle near the radio on the opposite side of the room. There was broken glass on the floor again.

He turned to her with a sheepish smile. "Didn't want you to get bored."

She found room on the coffee table for the plate of food, then walked over to the window, opened it wide, and turned back toward him, surveying the mess. "I thought you said you weren't going to do this again."

He ran his hand over his hair. "Look, Dolly, I'm sorry. Just—do whatever my dad said to. I'll stay out of your hair. Forget I'm even here."

But when he looked up, his eyes seemed to say that was the last thing he wanted.

Or was she only imagining things? Still, she felt strangely powerful, strangely keyed up.

She worried what she might do with such a strange feeling, and decided she'd better put the brakes on whatever was in the air between them. "I'd better do the kitchen today, after I get this cleaned up," she said. "I never got a chance to finish the other day, when you came."

"All right."

"It's very important, this house," she said, reminding herself, too.

"Sure, Dolly," he said. He flopped onto the sofa again, looking as spent as if he'd just run a marathon, and reached for his cigarettes.

A little later, while she was scouring the kitchen sink, she heard his uneven footsteps approaching. She looked over her shoulder.

"How's it going?" he asked. His eyes were glossy, and, even from across the room, she could smell the alcohol on him. She wondered where he had his supply stashed.

"Fine, thanks!" she said; a reflex. In fact, though she'd been laboring to stifle her foolish conceit, she hadn't succeeded in ridding herself of the powerful feeling she'd had when she'd gotten to be the one to disapprove. She had cleaned the refrigerator—a particularly odious task—and wiped down the countertops and now the sink. If she washed the cupboards and the walls and still felt proud, she dreaded what she would do when she got home to the bungalow. Pick a fight? Slack on Byron's supper? Smoke in front of him? It could be all-out war, if she didn't get hold of herself.

"That's good," JJ said, taking out a cigarette.

She went back to her scrubbing.

"So, Dolly," he said. "How'd you get roped into this job, anyway? How'd you meet my dad?"

She kept her head down as she scrubbed. She felt sweat pop from her pores. "Oh, you know," she said breezily. "Church."

"I didn't think he'd even been back here in a couple years."

"Oh, well, you know," Dolly said, scrubbing. "He wrote to the church and asked them to find someone, I think. Something like that, anyway."

"I'm just surprised he didn't mention anything about you. Especially when he asked me to come up and look at the house." JJ laughed. "What he said, actually, was, 'You're not doing anything this summer, are you, son?' Summer's his busy time with his sailing business in Stone Harbor. So I figured, what the hell? I hadn't been back here in a couple years myself."

"Really!"

"Sometimes I can't believe I ever lived here at all."

She stopped her scrubbing and looked over her shoulder at him again.

He waved his cigarette hand, leaving an arc of smoke. "Hell, listen to me," he said.

"It's all right," she said, turning to face him. A drop of water fell from her sponge onto the floor. "I don't mind."

His only response was a twist of his mouth. He smoked for a moment, and watched her. She met his gaze.

He spoke first. "What does your husband think of you spending all this time over here?"

She turned and resumed scrubbing the sink. She felt her pride deflating—a relief, really, though she was wistful for it before it was gone. "He—he works a lot." She concentrated hard on a dark spot on the sink.

"Was he in the war?" JJ asked.

"Yes!" she said. "He was in Europe, in a tank battalion."

"See some action?"

"Yes, I—I think so. He doesn't talk about it."

JJ didn't answer.

After a moment, slowing her scrubbing, Dolly spoke again. "Do you ever talk about what happened to you?"

"No," he said.

She heard his footsteps again. She turned just in time to see his back framed in the door as he left the room.

She could have kicked herself.

Some time later, as the kitchen started to show its true colors, she was getting her hopes up about the house again, though she still felt bad for having upset JJ. Suddenly, she heard his voice behind her. "I'm going downtown," he said.

He had given her quite a start, and her heart took off again. Then she thought, *What if he says something to someone?*

When she turned to look at him, he was smiling, just as though nothing had happened between them, just as though she had never stuck her foot squarely in her mouth. But he smelled even worse than before.

"Don't wait for me, all right?" he said.

"Oh," she said, her mind racing. "All right. Um, JJ?"

"What?"

"Could you do me a favor and not mention to anyone in town that I'm working for your dad? My husband—he—well, actually, he doesn't know. I thought it might hurt his pride, you know? It was just—I wanted to buy him an extra special Christmas present this year, using my own money." When that came out of her mouth, Dolly was actually impressed with her improvisational skills.

JJ winked, and nodded. "I see," he said. "No problem, Dolly." He made no move to go, just stood there looking at her.

She decided to take the opportunity—he was seeming so friendly. "Say, JJ?"

"Yes?"

"If you're not staying—do you think your family would ever considering selling this house?"

A shadow crossed his face; he ran his hand over his hair. "My dad would be the one to ask about that. I don't know anything about it."

"Oh," she sighed. "Yes, I suppose. I'm sorry. It just—it seems sad, left alone like this."

He quirked his mouth, but all he said was, "Well, see you tomorrow?"

"It's Saturday tomorrow," she said. Real housekeepers didn't work on weekends, she was sure.

"Monday, then?"

"Yes, all right."

Pine Rapids
August 1943

Ty had been gone since June, at Basic Training, and Elissa had spent most of the summer volunteering for the Red Cross: rolling bandages, knitting, fund-raising with her mother. They wanted to do their part; plus, they kept busy to keep their minds off things. JJ was somewhere in the Pacific. According to his latest letter, his unit was busy getting ready, though for what he could not say, if he even knew. Elissa wrote to her brother every week, to Ty every day.

Since Ty had left, they had been counting down the days until he would have a two-week leave. *Only three weeks till I see you. Only two weeks and one day till I see you.* Still, Elissa could hardly believe that the day was here. She had bought a white suit to wear to the train to meet him. The day was sizzling, and the blackberry bushes across the tracks bristled with the heat. Even the hemlock trees seemed to be staying still as a matter of defense. Elissa, though, paced back and forth on the platform, her red broad-brimmed hat trembling. A few other people stood in clusters waiting, too, but Ty's family hadn't arrived yet.

Alone, she thought of the day two months ago when she had bid Ty good-bye. For the first time, he had told her that he loved her, and she, astonished, had said, "Why! I love you, too, don't I?"

He had grinned, and said, "I hope so," and had given her a kiss that had made her toes curl in her shoes. All of this right in front of his parents and three older sisters, who had just laughed and nudged one another with their elbows (except for his mother, who had visibly steamed).

She couldn't help but be reminded, too, of the time, just six months ago, when she had been waiting on this very platform for Nick. She knew that the 2nd Division was still at Camp McCoy, and she wondered if Nick had found another Northern girl to have fun with. Just the thought of it made her furious, and she paced faster. But then the train whistle blew in the distance, and she composed her face, brushed off her prim white suit, straightened her hat. When the train creaked to a stop and Ty came down the steps of the car, looking very broad-shouldered in his khaki uniform, she ran to him with a great smile, and landed happily in his arms.

She was proud to be seen with him around town, as they made the rounds from his family to hers to the end-of-summer parties their friends were having before everyone headed off to the service or college. He was as sweet as ever, though he seemed different from how he had been, too. Before, he had worn his heart on his sleeve, and she could read his eyes like an old farmer reading sky. Now a curtain had drawn over them, and he seemed to be carrying secrets. Still, he made her feel like a princess, and she wished that his two-week leave would last forever. When it was over, he would be leaving for the Army for good, and she would be going off to Minneapolis to start cadet nurse training. Nothing would ever be the same. *Still, tho',* she wrote in her diary, *I am resolved to make the best of ev'thing these two weeks, for example not talking to him about any of my fears regarding what might occur in the next months (years?), or even speculating out loud when the next time we see each other will be. I am living every mo-*

ment for itself, and I guess you could say he is, too, because we haven't had one cross word between us, and, funny tho' it sounds to say, when we're together he acts as though he's standing in a down-pour with his head tipped back and his eyes closed and his mouth wide open, just that thirsty for me.

"You look happy," Muriel said to Elissa when they ran into each other at Pete Schiemmer's farm two nights before Ty was to leave. Some of the boys—including Ty—were swinging from the rafters of the barn, while Glenn Miller blared from a phonograph and the girls stood in cliques sipping bottled beer. The barn was pungent with the smells of hay, horse manure. "Have you—?" Muriel cut herself off before finishing, but raised her eyebrows meaningfully.

"No!" Elissa said. "Good heavens."

"Well, I know it's getting serious with you two. And he's leaving, what, tomorrow?"

"The day after," Elissa said.

"Are you going to give him a going away present?"

"Muriel," Elissa said, clenching her teeth. Actually, she wished she could ask for advice, but she was afraid someone would overhear. It was true he'd gotten her a little riled up, these past few nights, parked out by Heron Lake, the way he had kissed her, held her, his hands fumbling under her blouse, his fingers sweaty and tentative creeping under her skirt, though never roaming farther north than mid-thigh. She couldn't help but wonder what would happen if he moved his hand a bit higher. Would she have the strength, then, to stop him?

"Hello, Liss," he said, sweeping in on her and kissing her full on the mouth, in front of everyone, his arm locking around her waist. She could taste the beer on his breath.

"Ty!" she said, pushing him away. "You're drunk."

"I ain't so very drunk, Melly," he lisped. A line from *Gone with the Wind;* her heart melted. He grinned, knowing he had her. "Want to go for a walk?"

She nodded, ignoring Muriel's arch glance as they set off.

They walked out the barn's wide door into the mild night, heading toward, and then into, the Schiemmers' hay field. It was late, perhaps eleven, and the stars glittered above, growing brighter as Elissa and Ty left the light and noise of the barn behind them. His hand was warm in hers, and the tilled earth soft under her feet. With every step, its fecund smell drifted to her nose, and soon the chirping of crickets was louder to her ears than the music and shrieks of the party.

They passed two haystacks before, at the third, Ty stopped, and pulled enough hay out of the stack to make a nice bed on the ground. "Ty, all Mr. Schiemmer's hard work," Elissa protested, but he just grinned, held out his hand. Next thing she knew, she was lying in the hay and he was on top of her, kissing her, tasting like beer, the sweet, rich smell of the hay surrounding them. It was heavenly, and she was a little disappointed when he rolled off her onto his side. "I'm going to remember this forever, Liss," he whispered. "The way the moonlight looks on your hair." He kissed her softly. "The way your eyes are shining."

"Ty," she sighed.

His fingers caressed her neck, and trailed down to rest over heart. He kissed her again, pressing his body close to hers. "Promise me—promise me you'll always remember this, too," he said.

Ty seemed nervous when he drove her home, and was largely silent—unusual, for him. She hoped she hadn't offended him when, ultimately, she'd squirmed out from underneath him, brushing the hay from her sweater, and insisted they go back to the party. His hand had wandered farther up her skirt than ever before, and had made her nervous, and then he had pressed himself heavily against her so that she could feel his desire—he had never done that before, either. The heat of him, and her nerves, sparked, burned, became unbearable, and though part of her wished she were the type of girl who could just lie back and—well, she wasn't, and that was all. They had spent the rest of the evening avoiding each other's eyes.

"Lissa," he said, when they pulled up to the curb at her house. "I hope I didn't—upset you?" His eyes flashed to her, luminous in the moonlight.

"Oh, Ty!" she said. "No! I—I was hoping that I didn't upset you!"

He slid toward her, holding out his arms. She snuggled into his embrace, not wanting to think that in less than two days he would be gone again. "No, Liss," he said. "I'm sorry if I—It's just that you're so beautiful and—well, I don't expect you—I mean, if you want to wait—well, I understand."

She sighed, and held him tighter. He really was a wonderful boy.

He walked her to the door, and gave her a kiss good night that made her knees buckle. "See you tomorrow," he whispered, giving her hand a little squeeze.

She watched him as he sauntered out to his car, thinking how difficult it was, sometimes, to stay a good girl.

The next morning, just before noon, Elissa was up to her elbows in sweaters and skirts, trying to decide what to bring with her to Minneapolis—she was leaving the day after tomorrow—when the doorbell rang. She ran downstairs to answer it; her father was gone at work and her mother was busy in the kitchen.

"Ty!" she said, when she pulled open the door. He was in his uniform, holding his service cap in his hands, his dark hair slicked back. She was delighted to see him, but horrified at the same time: She didn't have any makeup on, her hair was held back with a ribbon, and the frayed blue shirt she was wearing untucked over shorts had long ago been relegated to stay-at-home status. "I thought we were getting together this afternoon," she said, smiling despite herself.

"I couldn't wait that long," he said.

She called to her mother that Ty was there. "Is it all right if he comes upstairs with me? I have to get my packing done."

Mary appeared in the kitchen door frame, wiping her hands on her apron. "Hello, Ty. Yes, I suppose, Elissa. We'll be having lunch in a few minutes, Ty, if you'd like to join us. Jack will be coming home."

"Thank you, Mrs. Mickelson," Ty said, and followed Elissa upstairs.

He had never been allowed into her room before, and immediately teased her about her dolls. Blushing, she cleared a pile of skirts off the pink-cushioned stool so he could sit down. "I'm never this messy," she said. "It's just because I'm packing."

He made a skeptical noise, and when she looked at him, his eyes were sparkling.

"Well, I'd like to see your room," she rejoined. "I bet you have hockey skates piled in the corner, and stacks of books to the ceiling." He had no response but an arch smile.

She stepped into her closet, and pulled down another stack of sweaters from the upper shelf. "You have to help me decide which ones to bring," she called.

He laughed. When she came out of the closet, he was just crossing his ankle over his knee. His face was flushed.

She hoped she hadn't left a pile of underwear out for him to see, and took a swift glance around the room. It looked like everything was all right. She dumped the sweaters onto her bed, and went back to the closet for more.

"I won't be much help," he said.

She came out of the closet again, and dropped another pile of sweaters onto her bed.

"Which of those are you going to bring?" Ty said.

She turned to the pile, picked up the old green one on top, and held it up, turning toward him. "What do you think?"

"Try again."

When she picked up the next sweater, a little black velvet box tumbled out of the pile onto the bed. "What in the world?" she said. When she looked at Ty, he had a funny smile on his face.

She picked up the box. "Is this—?" she said, but couldn't finish the thought. When she lifted the lid of the box, there was a ring with a tiny diamond sparkling on it. "Ty?"

He had dropped to his knees before her, and now looked up at her with those eyes that she couldn't resist. "I'm not one of those guys who—" He shook his head, started again. "I mean, it isn't—Will you, Lissa? Marry me? When I come back?"

"This isn't because of—last night, is it?"

He shook his head. "No, Lissa. I bought the ring the first day I was home. I've just been waiting for your father—I mean, not that I—I just wanted to do this right. I've been meeting with him every day—he's been asking me all kinds of questions—you, too?"

It was true: Every night since Ty had been home, Jack had had some kind of question about him—how he treated her, how she felt about him, what she thought he was planning to do with his life after the war.

Ty went on. "Just this morning he finally said it was all right, so I came right over."

"Really?"

"Yes, Lissa. I love you. I'd marry you today, if—"

She sank to her knees to face him, and held the little box out to him. "Will you put it on my hand?"

> The time to put on the brakes in checking runaway
> emotions is before they gain momentum.
>
> —*The Good Housekeeping Marriage Book*, 1939

THE MICKELSON HOUSE
502 W. First Street, Pine Rapids
Monday, July 31, 1950

Dolly marched up the Mickelsons' back steps late Monday morning carrying a basket that held four small foil-wrapped packages. One package contained four cinnamon rolls from the batch she'd made yesterday; another, several slices of yesterday's ham; another, a baked potato; and the last, steamed broccoli. She had warmed all four packages in her oven before leaving the bungalow.

She let herself in the back porch and knocked on the door to the house, swallowing the trepidation that had been swirling within her all weekend. Considering the damage JJ had done each of the two nights last week, she hated to think what he might have accomplished over the weekend.

Yesterday after church, Mrs. Fryt had been atwitter because Jeannette had told her that Albert—Jeannette's husband, who owned

Wasserman's Hardware—had helped JJ on Saturday pick out some sandpaper, varnish, and a set of brushes. "Something about a table he was going to refinish, I understand," she told Corinne and Dolly, the fresh daisy atop her hat trembling. "Apparently he looks just awful. Thin as a rail and pale as death, and he smelled worse than a lumberjack—alcohol and cigarettes and like he hadn't had a bath in days—and the way he walks, it's just pitiful, Jeannette said. He might have even been drunk, but he was so *charming* that Albert couldn't say for sure." She emphasized *charming* as though it was a distasteful thing to be.

Dolly wished she could sock Mrs. Fryt and send her ridiculous flowered hat sailing. Instead, she changed the subject, and Corinne, fortunately, backed her up.

When Byron returned to Dolly's side—he had, after the service, gravitated toward a group of men discussing hot fishing spots—Mrs. Fryt and Corinne were going on about the troubles they were having with their tomatoes this year. Happily, the subject of JJ Mickelson didn't come up again, because the ladies would have been surprised to hear from Byron that they had arranged for Dolly to work for JJ.

Well, she'd had to tell Byron something, before he heard from someone else that she was hanging around the Mickelson house. But when she had told him at supper on Friday night that JJ Mickelson had hired her, he'd looked at her and said, "I don't think so, Doll." Of course, he had no idea that she had been sneaking into the Mickelson house for almost a month as it was.

"But, Byron—" She was trying hard to behave herself—no matter how gratifying it had been to act prideful with JJ. It was important to make Byron think that she wouldn't dream of doing anything he didn't approve of first.

"I make enough money. You don't have to work." Byron stopped to consider, and added, "I won't *have* you working. Cleaning someone else's house!"

So she'd had to think fast. "It's just a favor for him! Through the church! I volunteered! The church asked for someone, and then he offered to pay me. Or, I mean—if you don't want me to take the money . . ." She glanced up hopefully. JJ still thought that his father was paying her, so there would be no money coming to her. She should have told Byron in the first place that she was volunteering. It made a much better story.

Byron considered it. "Well, volunteer work, through the church. And it's just temporary?"

She nodded.

"Well, all right, then, as long as you don't spend too much time there," he grumbled, and went back to his Deviled Hamburger Toast—a recipe out of the Quick and Easy section of her cookbook, since she had arrived home too late after finishing up the Mickelsons' kitchen to make the pork roast she had planned.

"Oh, I won't!" she said.

She had seduced him Friday night, Saturday night, and Sunday night, too, praying that a baby would catch. *"Three Blind Mice" is a wonderful song,* she repeated to herself like a mantra, but she still kept thinking about the Mickelson house, about the look in JJ Mickelson's eyes, about the way she'd felt being in control, if only for a moment.

Glancing around with her accustomed furtiveness—she couldn't get used to her visits to the Mickelson house being on the up and up—Dolly was about to raise her fist to knock again when the door swung open. She drew in her breath at the sight of JJ.

His clothes were the same, khaki pants and a white T-shirt, but they were *clean,* the white of the shirt practically gleaming, and he was freshly bathed and shaved, and standing on two legs. His usual sour odor was nearly masked by strong aftershave and whatever he had used to slick back his hair. He grinned, and his eyes managed a sort of brightness, even through their hazy film of leftover inebriation. "I cleaned the bathroom," he said.

"Oh! Oh, my goodness. I never even thought—I should have cleaned that the minute you came—"

He waved her off. "Don't worry about it. Come on, let me show you the rest."

As if the sight of him hadn't been stunning enough, the living room actually gleamed, just as it had when she had left on Friday. Nothing was out of place. He had even folded his bedding neatly on the end of the sofa.

"Does this mean you're staying?" she asked him finally, taking it all in.

He ignored her question. "I've been checking things out around here," he said. "Everything's in pretty good shape, really, considering no one's lived here in four years. I guess it was lucky my dad had hired someone to keep an eye on things, to keep the heat on in the winter and everything, keep the pipes from freezing. Oh, I talked to a guy about getting the window fixed in the dining room. Thanks for covering it up—it must have broken after Mr. Wojtas died. Anyway, the guy said he'd come and look at it."

"Goodness!"

Then JJ noticed the basket in her hands. "What did you bring me today?"

"Oh, well, some cinnamon rolls, and leftovers from our dinner yesterday."

"Really!" he said. "Cinnamon rolls! I bet you made them yourself, too."

She nodded.

"I missed your cooking this weekend," he said. "I had to go down to Shorty's Pub and eat burgers. But don't worry, I didn't tell anyone that you're working here." He grinned. "Even though I wanted to brag about what a good cook you are."

She tucked her hair behind her ear. "Should I put this in the kitchen?"

They ate cinnamon rolls standing at the butcher block in the kitchen. She hadn't planned on joining him, but he insisted. "Take a break, Dolly! Besides, I can't eat all of these myself." She felt somehow flattered, picking up a gooey roll. After a moment, emboldened by his affability, she asked what had caused him to take such an interest in the house all of a sudden.

He gave her a sheepish smile. "I guess it's why I'm here, right? So, what the hell?"

She licked a smear of icing off her finger. "But you don't—care?"

He shrugged.

"Well, I've told Byron—that's my husband—I've told Byron that I'm helping you clean the—or, I mean, that I'm going to be working more hours for your father, on account of your being in town. I certainly would appreciate any help you might—" She let her voice trail off; he was looking at her and seemed amused.

If that's how he's going to be!

After they finished their rolls, he made a show of stocking the refrigerator with the foil-wrapped packages Dolly had brought. "My first food!" he said, positioning the packages on the middle shelf. "Almost like I live here."

"Would you like me to go shopping for you?"

He waved her off. "I don't want to bother you with that. I'm not much of a cook, anyway."

"Just some bread and meat for sandwiches, maybe?"

He looked at her a moment. "Yeah, okay. That would be nice." Then he smiled. "Not to say I don't want you to keep bringing these leftovers. I tell you, that husband of yours doesn't know how good he has it."

She couldn't help it: She blushed.

He closed the refrigerator door. "Want to see the upstairs? I want to show you how good I did on the bathroom."

"Oh," she said, more pleased than she should have been. "All right."

He told her to go on ahead to the second floor. He could manage stairs; it just took him a little longer.

The bath suite upstairs was a series of small rooms with heavy oak doors between each. The first room off the hallway had a porcelain sink to one side, and on the other side was a little closet enclosing a toilet of the old type, with the water tank high above and a pull chain for flushing. Next was a dressing room, with a vanity along the far wall, and a linen closet, and plenty of hooks to hang towels, robes, and clothing on. In the third room was the copper bathtub, encased in oak, with a copper tank at its head. A small stained-glass window looked out at the west lawn and the line of fir trees. The light fixtures and the window were dusty, and there were cobwebs in the corners, but the fixtures were sparkling. She could hardly believe JJ had actually cleaned. She would have fainted from shock if Byron had ever done such a thing; he hadn't even managed to paint the bathroom at the bungalow yet, though it had been six weeks since he'd promised her he would.

She could smell JJ's sour-sweet-spicy scent when he came into the tub room behind her. She turned, and was astounded again at how breathtaking he was when clean. Then she detected the sharp odor of new whiskey on him again; he must have sneaked a drink before starting up the stairs.

He gave her a disarming grin. "I know it's your job to clean the place. I hope you don't mind I stepped in. I decided I better take a bath before Mrs. Fryt smelled me on the breeze and called the cops."

"No, I don't mind!"

"Some bathroom, huh? I guess my great-grandpa Knute had a thing for them. This was the first house in town built with indoor plumbing." He rapped the copper tank with his knuckles. "This tank was for heating the water after it was pumped upstairs from the cistern in the basement. There's two more of these in this house, tubs and tanks, I mean. I guess old Knute liked to take a bath almost every day. He said he was rich enough. That's what my grandma told me, anyway. She said even after she and my grandpa moved into the house, old Knute used to sit in the bath every day long enough to smoke a whole cigar."

"Goodness!" Dolly said. "Do you have to pump the cistern to take a bath still?"

"No, my grandpa had an electric pump and stuff installed when I was a kid, and hooked up to city water."

"Well, you certainly smell better!" Dolly blurted, and then she blushed. "Or, I mean—"

He laughed. "That's good," he said. For a moment, he held her in his gaze.

She blinked, and quickly stepped away. "I'd better get to work!"

He seemed to sigh a little, but he said nothing as she scooted past him out of the room, telling herself, *The house, Dolly! That's all!*

Superior, Wisconsin
Thursday, November 8, 1945

"You had the truck last night, didn't you, Mr. Mickelson?"

Harry looked up from his copyediting, rubbed his right eye with his knuckle. He'd fallen asleep at his desk the night before and hadn't awakened until five in the morning, when Maggie shook his shoulder, saying, "Mr. Mickelson? Mr. Mickelson, you've got to stop doing this!" She brought him a cup of coffee to camouflage his sleep-tainted breath; he'd combed his hair in the men's room, and made a mental note to bring in a toothbrush and razor from home. The day had flown by in a whirl of deadlines, strewn papers, arguments, spilled ink. Now it was three P.M., and Harry was still at his desk, editing some of Tinnanen's copy for tomorrow's edition. No matter how many times Harry told them, it seemed the staff wouldn't stop ending sentences in prepositions. It gave him a headache.

"Yeh, I did, Jorstad, what's the trouble?"

A grin split Mike Jorstad's stubbled face. In charge of delivering the *Gazette* to vendors around town, he was dressed in his typical denim coveralls; he doubled as the old truck's mechanic. Jorstad tossed a black glove onto Harry's desk. "Entertaining one of your lady friends?"

The glove sprawled on the desk. "This was in the truck?"

"Passenger's side floorboard. Belong to someone you know?"

"I suppose it must."

Jorstad shook his head. "It's quite the life you lead, Mickelson," he chuckled.

"Thanks, Jorstad," Harry said, dismissing him.

He tried to get back to work, but the words swam before his eyes. Before long, darkness began to fall outside. He was sore from the night spent hunched over his desk. And thoughts of Anne kept surfacing with the bright persistence of dandelions in a lawn. He surely did want to know whether she slept in a nightgown or pajamas.

Maggie came in to say good night; no matter what he said, she insisted on working hours almost as long as his.

"Night, Maggie," Harry said. "Say, can I ask you something?"

"What's that?"

"If you left your glove somewhere, and someone found it, would you want them to go out of their way to bring it to you?"

She gave him a look like he'd gone off his nut. "Of course! What kind of a question is that?" She left shaking her head. "See you tomorrow," she called over her shoulder.

He lit a cigarette, plowed through another page of copy. Left it strewn across his desk and got up to go home and get cleaned up, clenching Anne's glove in his fist as he walked through the biting dark.

He climbed the porch steps and rang the doorbell at the house where he'd said good night to Anne just a little less than twenty-four hours before. He'd been to his apartment, taken a bath, shaved, and put on fresh clothes; his aftershave-scented cheeks burned in the cold air. The night was clear, star-filled. He held Anne's glove firmly within his pocket.

A bright-eyed blonde answered the door. "Yes?" she said, smiling at him.

Harry treated her to his most charming grin. "Is Anne Wallace home?"

"Anne? Sure, wait just a minute." With another cute smile, she shut the door gently.

Taking a deep breath of the cold night air, Harry waited a moment before ambling toward the other end of the wide porch, crossing in front of a picture window that emitted soft lamplight. He stopped when he reached a wooden chair that sat next to the far railing. A table in front of the window held an ashtray containing two lipstick-stained cigarette butts. Evidently, the landlady didn't allow her girls to smoke in the house, whatever the weather. He turned and ambled back toward the door, just in time for it to open.

There stood Anne. The look of surprise on her face quickly turned to a smile. "Harry!"

"Hello, Miss Wallace," Harry said, appreciating the happy, warm look on her face—and the curves filling out her green sweater and herringbone tweed skirt. "I hope you don't mind my stopping by."

"Of course not," she said. "Won't you come in?"

"Thank you," he said. When he stepped over the threshold, she did not immediately step back. He imagined he could feel the warmth of her body. He pulled her glove from his coat pocket. "You left this in the truck last night," he said, handing it to her.

"Oh, I did! I've been wondering all day where it was. Thank you."

"No trouble," he said, smiling down at her. Her lips were the same brick red as the other day.

She stepped away, setting the glove on a sideboard that appeared to be the landing for various lost gloves, textbooks, scarves, lipsticks, purses. "It's very kind of you to bring this to me," she said, straightening the stray items self-consciously. "I guess I'm awfully silly, not keeping track of my things."

"I wouldn't say you're silly," Harry said. "I suppose you have a lot on your mind."

Her eyes flashed up, and she smiled. "Well, yes, that's true." She paused a moment, considering him. "Would you like to stay for a cup of coffee?"

"If it's not too much trouble."

"Would you like to hang up your coat?" She indicated an overburdened coat tree that stood to his right, at the foot of a flight of stairs leading to the second floor.

"Nice place you have here," he said, as he took off his coat and balanced it atop the mountain of girls' coats that threatened to topple the stand. He then balanced his hat on top of his coat.

She laughed. "I'm sorry, we weren't expecting company. Mrs. Hanson tries to get us to clean up after ourselves, but usually we only manage it about fifteen minutes before one of the girls has a date."

"Well, it's my fault for dropping over unannounced."

"It was awfully kind of you to make a special trip just to return my glove," she said. She turned; he followed her into the living room, which was the source of the warm lamplight he'd appreciated out on the front porch.

She bid him sit on the davenport and promised to be back in a moment with his coffee. He sat forward with his elbows on his knees, his hands tented in front of his chin, wondering if he was ridiculous or just felt that way; not caring. Listening to the clink of dishes from the kitchen at the back of the house, the murmur of feminine voices.

The room appeared to have been decorated forty years before, with patterned wallpaper and an abundance of lace doilies and bric-a-brac. But it was pleasant and cozy, with reading chairs on either side of the table lamp shining in the front window, a coffee table in front of the davenport on which he sat, a fireplace on the far wall. A piano was situated directly opposite, an oval mirror above it. He stood, walked over to the mirror and straightened his tie, checked his profile. He was sitting again, wondering how Mrs. Hanson enforced the absence of coed detritus in this room, when Anne came in, carrying a tray.

"I'm sorry it took so long," she said, negotiating her way through the furniture with the loaded tray. "When I told Mrs. Hanson you were the editor of the *Gazette,* she insisted on sending out some of her molasses cookies." Anne set the tray down on the table in front of Harry.

"That's awfully nice of her," he said. "They look delicious."

But he was more conscious of Anne sitting down next to him, reaching for the coffeepot. He watched her hands, the stream of coffee tumbling from the china pot into the delicate cup. "Yes, she is nice," Anne said, pausing the stream, shifting the spout over the other cup and tilting the pot again. "Though she did remind me that all gentleman callers have to be out of the house by ten o'clock. House rules."

It had been a long time since Harry had had to be concerned about curfews. He fumbled for a witty remark, didn't find one. "I suppose you're used to that," he said.

Anne set the coffeepot down on the tray. "Well, I haven't had many callers."

Harry leaned forward to collect his coffee cup. "That's hard to believe."

"Well, there's a bit of a shortage of boys with the war," she explained, picking up her cup. She continued to sit forward, her knees angled toward his. She took a sip of coffee.

"Ah," Harry said, though he was certain she wasn't telling him the whole story.

Realizing his skepticism, she laughed a little. "Well," she said, "maybe I haven't exactly encouraged anyone. Since—you know."

Harry sipped his coffee.

She glanced up quickly, flushed. "You must think I'm—I don't know. I don't know what in the world you could think of me." She set her coffee cup down and stood, pacing over to the piano.

Harry set down his cup, too, and followed her, stopping close to her side with his hand on her elbow. "Anne, I—"

"You called me Anne."

"I'm sorry," he said, drawing back his hand.

She smiled. "No, I'm glad you did," she said. She held his gaze a moment, then stepped away and sat down at the piano. "I'm afraid I'm about to make a fool of myself," she said, and began to play a bright, jazzy tune.

He watched her a moment, listening to the music her hands made. Then he went and sat to her left on the bench. She scooted over so he would have more room.

"Do you play?" she asked, continuing her song.

"Not for a long time. My mom gave me a few lessons as a kid, though. She was quite the virtuoso herself."

She stopped. "Play me something," she said, smiling sideways at him.

He ahemed and stretched his fingers, then plunked out a simple minuet that somehow he still remembered after thirty years. His arm pressed hers as he played. She applauded when it was through. "Harry, you're too modest!" she said. "That was wonderful! Play something else."

He gave her a mischievous smile. With one finger, he began plunking out the melody of the Gershwin tune "Embraceable You."

Her eyes widened as she recognized it. She jumped up from the bench, crossing the room to sit again on the davenport. Her china cup tinkled nervously against its saucer as she took a sip of coffee.

Harry stood. "Anne," he said, crossing to her. "If you won't make a fool out of yourself, then I guess I'll have to make one out of me."

She looked up at him.

He sat down next to her. His nerves were worse than a schoolboy's. "I know you lost Bobby not too long ago, Anne, and I know it's been hard. But unless I'm dreaming, I think you're starting to like me a little bit."

A small smile raised a corner of her lips.

"But unless you can sneak something of yours into my coat pocket before I leave tonight, I'm just about to run out of excuses to see you again."

Her smile broadened; she looked at her coffee cup.

"So I guess I'm just going to have to come right out and ask you if you'll let me take you out for dinner tomorrow night."

"Oh!" She set her coffee cup on the table, smoothed out her skirt. Then she looked up and met his eyes. "Yes. Yes."

You'll be surprised at the number of table mats, napkins,
curtains, and sport things that have to be ironed,
even with only two in the household. . . .

—*Good Housekeeping,* January 1950

HOME OF MRS. CECILIA FRYT
412 W. First Street, Pine Rapids
Tuesday, August 1, 1950

Rain came in the middle of the night, and lasted all morning. Dolly
was exhausted from all the work in the Mickelson house bath suite
yesterday, plus from staying up late to finish her laundry, then getting
up early to get started on the never-ending ironing before making
Byron's breakfast. Still, the change in the air and the smell of wet
hemlock lifted her flagging spirits; she was light on her feet the whole
way to Mrs. Fryt's under her umbrella.

Unfortunately, Mrs. Fryt was of the school of thought that windows must be closed tightly against even such a gentle rain; her parlor
was miserably stuffy, the windows covered in steam. As Dolly settled
around the Wild Goose Chase quilt with the other ladies, in her sleeveless white dress with the red trim and her red ballerina slippers, her
mood languished again, as she began to feel sticky immediately.

A sense of apprehension only made matters worse. Though she didn't know how the ladies would respond, she had decided she'd better tell them something about her and the Mickelson house. She hadn't been able to stop worrying over what conclusions Mrs. Fryt might draw, and what rumors might take flight, if Mrs. Fryt saw Dolly going in there.

As everyone was threading their needles, she blurted, "Well, JJ Mickelson has hired me to help him clean the Mickelson house."

The ladies raised their eyebrows. Mrs. Fryt shook her head. "Mercy me, child, now you're going to have trouble for sure. How on earth did you get into that?"

"Oh, well, I bumped into him downtown, and he asked me," Dolly said. She had planned her story in advance, but she had no idea whether they would believe the particulars.

"Why you, of all people?" said Judy Wasserman.

"Because he didn't know me."

"Oh ho," said Mrs. Fryt. "He's still trying to keep that family's secrets from us, is he? What are their plans for the house?"

Dolly's heart raced. "I don't know," she said.

Mrs. Fryt harrumphed. "Well, of any of them, I didn't expect *him* to be the one to show his face in this town. Such a *hero* in the war that he didn't have the time of day for us when he got back! Never even came to church so we could give him a proper welcome home!"

"Mother," Jeannette said, "he did have a difficult—"

"Of course, he is his father's son," Mrs. Fryt interrupted. "Not to mention that the weekend he did come home, that Thanksgiving in 'forty-five, was the weekend that everything went to pieces. I suppose that doesn't sit too well with a proud boy like that."

Dolly drew in her breath; she hadn't known that the family's demise could be traced to a particular weekend. "What happened?"

The ladies shifted in their seats, looking anywhere but at one another. Mrs. Fryt's caterpillar eyes shone behind her glasses. "Well, JJ came home on leave from the hospital, and everybody came to see him. And then, lo and behold, here came that boy Elissa had met back in 'forty-three, who the whole family thought they'd seen the last of." Mrs. Fryt shook her head. "The saddest thing is to look back and realize how they were all bound for their own destruction, and didn't even know it! They thought the worst was over, and it was only beginning! Harry was the one who brought everything to light. Made John steam like a teakettle! But then, Harry had always had a knack for that—"

"Mother," interrupted Jeannette. "What's the difference, if JJ's back now? Shouldn't we welcome him? Bring him a casserole, or something? Let him know we're glad he's back."

"But what *happened*?" Dolly said.

Mrs. Fryt turned to Jeannette. "I'm not sure I *am* glad he's back," she said. "He was so young when he left, I can't judge him but to say that, if he's like his father and grandfather, he's going to be nothing but a headache for this town. Thank goodness Jack sold the bank after John died, or we'd likely have JJ taking over as we speak."

"He isn't like them," Dolly blurted. Her vehemence surprised even herself.

Mrs. Fryt raised her eyebrows. "Oh, he isn't? And how would you know, having never met them?"

"Well, he isn't like you say they are! Maybe they weren't like you thought, either!"

Mrs. Fryt laughed, and went back to her stitching. "Now the child tells me I don't know my own neighbors, my own neighbors I've lived across the street from for near sixty years!"

Thelma and Corinne cast Dolly pitying looks.

"I know JJ Mickelson," said Judy. "He's just like anybody else with too much money, thinks he's entitled to whatever he wants. His sister Elissa was the same way. It served her right, what happened. It served them all right."

Dolly glared at Judy. If the ladies only knew that yesterday JJ had spent two hours with her, telling her a detailed history of Henry VIII and his six wives, as she'd scrubbed the walls and floors of the bath suite and wiped down the oak doors with lemon oil. Or the way they'd smoked side by side on the front porch again when she'd finished her work, and how he'd walked her to the back door and bid her good-bye with a wink and a (was it hopeful?) "See you tomorrow?"

But she knew it wouldn't do any good to tell the ladies about what JJ was really like. And she wasn't about to quit the "job" now, not when the house was starting to look so good, and not when she and JJ were getting along so well—which might work in her favor when the time came for the Mickelson family to sell the house. Besides, what would JJ do if she quit? With his drinking, there was still the danger he might harm the house. And he would almost certainly talk to his father about her.

She knew she was walking a fine line; no doubt the less she told the quilting ladies, the better.

After the meeting, with her sewing basket hooked on her arm, Dolly dashed across the street under her umbrella and ran up the steps and into the back porch. She set down her basket, leaned her umbrella in the corner so it could dry, and fluffed her hair with her fingers.

He should have been expecting her—she had told him she would stop by after the quilting meeting—but he didn't answer the door. She finally gave up pounding on it and let herself in. "JJ?" she called. It was quiet in the back hallway, and the air was damp and musty. She could hear the rain coursing through the gutters outside. "JJ?"

She took a few steps down the hallway toward the living room. Her heart seemed to be holding out judgment, paused in mid-beat.

The oak pocket door at the end of the hallway was half closed. She tiptoed up to it and peered into the living room.

He was sprawled on the couch, in yesterday's clothes, and seemed to be sleeping, his mouth hanging open and his breath noisy. His prosthesis lay on the floor next to the couch, near an empty bottle. There was an empty glass on the coffee table, and the ashtray was full of cigarette butts again. At least he didn't appear to have broken anything this time. She took a tiny step; the floor creaked under her weight.

His eyes flew open; panicked, he struggled to sit up. But then he recognized her, and eased back down again. He gave her a bleary smile, and raised his hand to rub his temples. "My little housekeeper," he said. "Come to set everything right."

She eased into the room. The smell would have been horrible had he not left the side window open a crack; the sound of the rain was gentle in here. "It's two-thirty in the afternoon," she told him, taking on a forceful air despite her nerves. The sight of him waking was distressingly intimate. "I told you I was coming."

"So you did," he said, closing his eyes. "But I was having so damn much fun last night I didn't stop till this morning."

She stood still, arms folded, holding her breath to see what he would do. As she watched, he creaked up into a sitting position, then leaned against the sofa's back, tilting his head back over the top of it.

"Christ," he muttered.

Seeing him like this made her stomach ache. "Why are you doing this to yourself?" she blurted.

JJ looked at her then, and the sadness in his blue eyes made her heart stop for an instant. He creaked forward to pluck his cigarettes and lighter from the table. He lit one, inhaled, blew out smoke, then dropped the pack and lighter back onto the table. "I bet you don't know what pretty legs you have," he said.

Her eyes opened wide.

"I'm serious," he said. "Did you ever just appreciate them? I hope you don't mind me noticing."

Dolly shook her head finally. "That's all right," she said. "It only makes sense you would notice things like that."

He took a puff of his cigarette. "Look, just don't tell your husband I said so. I didn't mean anything by it." But when he met her eyes, his look again belied his words.

Or was that just her unruly imagination talking? *Stop it*, she told herself. "Are you hungry?" she said. "I didn't have a chance to get to the store yet, but I can go if you'd like."

"Don't worry about it," he said, leaning back again. "I'm not hungry. I've got some of that ham and stuff you brought yesterday, anyway."

"All right."

"So you're going to make me up one of the upstairs bedrooms today?"

They had discussed it the day before; he had said he was tired of sleeping on the couch, and would manage the stairs from now on.

"Of course. I'll bring your things upstairs so you can really get comfortable."

He laughed. "Well, I don't know how comfortable I want to get, Dolly. I don't even know why I've stayed here this long."

"You don't?"

"No. Why, do you?"

She drew back, surprised. "No."

"You ever hear of the curse on this house?"

Dolly fidgeted. "They may have mentioned something about it. An

Indian princess was buried on this hill? I don't believe in curses, though."

"Know how this princess died?"

"No."

"Story goes, she killed herself when she found out her lover was cheating on her. Broken heart. Threw herself right in the Bear Trap. Drowned herself in shallow water. The curse I guess said that anyone who disturbed her resting place would be as unlucky in love as she was."

"Goodness!"

JJ reached forward and stubbed out his cigarette in the overflowing ashtray. He almost seemed to be smiling.

"What's funny about that?" Dolly objected.

He leaned back, folding his hands over his stomach. "My grandpa used to say there was nothing to it."

She took a deep breath. "What happened, JJ? To cause your family to leave this house?"

When he didn't answer, she pressed him. "Was it Thanksgiving? 1945?"

He laughed. "I see those ladies have been talking. Why don't you have them tell you? Since they know so much."

"But they *don't* know, JJ. They only think they do, and first they tell me that Wilma's to blame, and then someone else says your father's to blame, and then they say Elissa's to blame, and then they say it started the minute Wilma set foot in this town, or when Chase was killed, or that it all happened the one weekend, the Thanksgiving you got home from the war. Maybe it's *your* fault, I don't know. Don't you even want to defend yourself? Or tell your side of it?"

JJ shook his head. "Look, Dolly, it doesn't matter anymore. If they want to talk about it, fine. I suppose they don't have anything better to do in this town. The thing is, no matter how much you look at the past, you can't change it. So why waste your time?"

"But you don't really believe that, JJ! Or else why would you have brought up the curse? I think you want to talk about it!"

He shook his head. "I don't think so, Dolly."

She winced. "I was starting to think you were different," she said. She turned, and ran upstairs like there were wolves snapping at her heels.

Anne Wallace was a little embarrassed about having dropped her glove in the cab of the *Gazette* truck. It really was an amateur trick. Linda had shrieked with laughter when Anne had told her about it the night before.

"You dropped your glove in the truck?" she'd howled, wiping tears of mirth from her eyes. "Subtle, Wallace, real subtle."

Who's laughing now, Anne thought as she closed the door gently behind Harry after they'd said their good-byes for the evening and made arrangements for him to pick her up at seven o'clock the next night.

"Linda! Oh, Linda!" she sang up the stairs.

Linda's bedroom door opened and out she came, her face lit with a bright smile, blond hair poufing out behind her as she thundered down the stairs to clutch Anne in a hug. Trailing two steps behind and piling on to the hug was dark-haired Janice. The three of them had been inseparable since meeting the first week of freshman year, and together they'd been through six-and-a-half semesters that had been a roller coaster of excitement, laughter, boredom, agony, grief, and, sometimes it seemed, starting over again and again.

"We heard the whole thing!" Linda exclaimed. "We listened at the grate."

"Yes, the music was much to our satisfaction," Janice said, "but then suddenly it stopped!" Her dramatic tone made all three girls laugh.

Linda grabbed Anne's elbow and pulled her up the stairs; in a moment the three were heaped onto Linda's bed, plumping pillows in preparation for the full debriefing.

"Well, you're right about one thing," Linda said, flopping onto her stomach with a pillow under her folded arms. "He's an absolute dreamboat!" She turned to Janice. "Think of a cross between Jimmy Stewart and Gary Cooper, but with blond hair. You know, the tall, gangly type, but with a killer smile and bedroom eyes."

"Linda!" Anne said.

"So, tell us what happened," Linda prodded.

"Well, he's going to take me to Vinzetti's tomorrow night."

"Vinzetti's!" Linda said.

Janice whistled. "That's high class, right off the bat. And you haven't even gone on a date since Bobby—He must really be something special."

"He's—different from any man I've met before," Anne said. "He's funny, and very nice, and he's been taking all sorts of trouble to get to know me. He isn't just concerned about looks, and it doesn't seem to matter to him whether I disagree with him or say something out of turn—"

"One thing you couldn't say about Bobby," Linda put in.

"I don't mean to imply anything bad about Bobby, I don't," Anne said. "But Harry's so thoughtful. And even though he's such a success, he's not pompous like some men. And you should have heard how cute he was! He said, 'Unless you can sneak something into my coat pocket, I'm running out of excuses to see you again'!"

"He did know about the glove, then!" Linda said.

"I don't know," Anne said, smiling. "Maybe he suspected a little."

"Anne," Linda said. "I think this is wonderful. Bobby would have wanted you to be happy."

"I suppose," Anne sighed. "Though there's a part of me that can't help but feel unfaithful."

"Don't be silly, Anne," Janice said. "He's been gone six months. I've read about girls out in California who didn't even wait two months after getting the telegram to *marry* someone else."

"Anne," Linda said, "you were grade-A faithful to Bobby the entire time he was away, and now for six months after—Well, he'd want you to be happy."

"I just don't want to rush into anything," Anne said. "I don't know why I dropped my glove. It was like I just couldn't bear not to see him again. It's the strangest thing."

"Oh, no!" Linda assured her, and Janice added, "I think it's terribly romantic."

Anne smiled.

"Now, come on," Linda said, patting her hand. "We have to get your outfit ready."

Before long, Linda's bed was piled high with dresses from all the girls' closets, and Janice was rushing in and out of the room, pulling selections from Anne's closet and her own for Anne to try on. They finally chose a navy-blue dress of Anne's that had a sleek, fitted long-sleeved V-necked top and a knee-length gored skirt. "Perfect!" Linda declared. "Glamorous but—practical, too!"

Once the dress had been selected, there were the matters of jewelry, shoes, a hat. It had been so long since Anne's last date—even an old-hat date with Bobby, much less a first date—that the flurried debate of choices, combinations, and potential consequences nearly overwhelmed her. But when they had selected the final ensemble, Janice and Linda agreed: She would be stunning. Gazing at her reflection in Linda's mirror, Anne thought they might be right, and hoped so.

At five after seven, Anne was in her room in front of her mirror, adding a dab of perfume behind her ear, when she heard the knock at the door.

"He's here!" Linda shrieked. She ran past Anne's room and down the stairs—she had insisted on answering the door so Anne could make an entrance—while Janice poked her head in. "Are you all set?"

"I think so," Anne said. Janice grinned, gestured *V* for Victory, and scooted back to Linda's room so she would remain out of sight.

Anne heard her friend open the door and admit Harry. She picked up her purse from the vanity and crossed to the door. All the girls' rooms opened out onto the landing, so the minute Anne stepped out, she could see Harry waiting just inside the front door, at the bottom of the stairs. He saw her, too, and grinned. She smiled, noticing that he held a wrapped package of flowers.

He watched her the whole way down the stairs; fortunately, she didn't trip. When she reached him, she found herself body to body with him, looking up into his eyes.

"Hello," he said. Bedroom eyes! Linda wasn't kidding about that. And Anne liked the square of his jaw, the shape of his mouth, his straight, perfect nose.

"Hello."

"It's nice to see you."

"It's nice to see you, too."

"These are for you," he said, handing over the wrapped flowers.

"Thank you," she said, taking them, peeking under the paper. "Roses! How beautiful." She held the open end of the package to her nose so she could smell them.

"Yellow ones, for friendship," Harry said. "So they tell me."

She smiled up at him. "Yes, I know."

Linda broke in. "I'll take them and put them in water, Anne."

"Thanks, Lin," Anne said, handing the flowers to her friend, who made a hasty exit toward the kitchen.

A moment later, Harry had helped her into her coat, and they stepped out into the brisk evening.

Vinzetti's was located downtown. It was owned and operated by a husband and wife who had come to Superior from Italy more than thirty years before as a young couple. They had transformed an old vaudeville hall into an Italian courtyard, ripping out the auditorium seats and painting scenes from their home village on the walls, draping the scenes with plush red curtains. The only light in the place emanated from a series of sconces along the wall, and a tuxedoed man sat at a grand piano at one corner of the old vaudeville stage that doubled as a dance floor; sad songs billowed from his fingers. The floors were tile, the booths were hand-constructed by the husband and stained a dark walnut, and the wife did the cooking, using recipes she'd learned from her mother in the old country. At Vinzetti's, there was a palpable sense of love, and even a touch of homesickness, in the tender amalgamations of garlic, tomatoes, peppers, pasta, bread, and wine that were presented to guests.

Anne had never dined at Vinzetti's before. East Enders rarely ventured downtown, and the college crowd only came here for special occasions like marriage proposals; Bobby had proposed one afternoon at the airport just after he'd taken her up for a ride in a Piper Cub. Seated in one of the handmade booths, watching the couples dancing onstage, Anne was inspired to order a glass of red wine, though her experiences with wine had heretofore been limited to communion and a sip or two on Christmas Eves. Harry ordered a locally brewed beer. After scanning the menus, they both decided on the lasagna, and, once they had placed their order with the waiter, were left gazing at each other over their drinks.

"Well, Anne Wallace," Harry said.

"Well?"

"Mind if I ask you a few questions?"

She laughed. "Haven't you asked me enough questions these last few days?"

He leaned back, took a sip of his beer. "Fair enough. You want to ask me something?"

"Well, yes," Anne said. "You know all about me and I don't know a thing about you."

"I wouldn't say that," Harry said, setting his glass down on the table. "But all right—what do you want to know?"

She thought for a moment, then said, "Tell me why you're not married."

He laughed. "You would make a good reporter, wouldn't you? You just cut right to the chase."

She laughed, too, and took a sip of her wine. "I'm sorry," she said. "I told you—I'm always blurting out things I shouldn't. But you can't blame me for wondering."

"Are you afraid I'm not the marrying type?"

She met his eyes. They were warm, easy to get lost in. "I was just wondering."

"Do you want to get married?"

"Well, I was expecting—Now, wait, I thought I was asking the questions!"

Harry laughed. "I'm sorry. You want to know why I'm not married."

She nodded.

"I guess I've just been waiting for the right girl to come along."

"So, you would like to get married someday?"

"Maybe," he said. "Is that a proposal?"

"I'm not busy next Saturday," she joked, but when he didn't laugh, she blushed. "I'm just kidding," she said, and took a sip of her wine, chastising herself for not thinking before she spoke. Now he was going to think she was some marriage-crazed girl desperate for prospects.

"I don't think I'm busy then, either," Harry said.

She looked up, startled, then quickly looked down again into the dark swirls of liquid in her wineglass. She decided she'd better change the subject before she really got herself into trouble. "Have you heard when your nephew's coming home?"

"Not yet. Have you heard anything about your brother?"

"No. You said your nephew grew up in your hometown?"

"Yes, my brother Jack and his wife, Mary, live there. My brother's the vice president at my father's bank."

"Oh, I didn't realize—" She cut herself off.

"Didn't realize what?"

She looked in her wineglass again. "That you came from a wealthy family. Not that it matters, it's—Well, I guess I should have known, since you went to college in spite of the Depression and all. My brother should have gone to college, he's so smart and such a good writer, but he had to go to work on the railroad until the war—and he was lucky to get that."

Harry reached across the table and touched her hand with his fingertips. "Anne, there's something you should know."

"What is it?"

"First," he said, "my family's not that wealthy anymore, and even if they were I wouldn't get a cent of it. And second, I graduated from college in 1925. Twenty years ago."

"You—what?" She tried to do the math, but she couldn't make sense of it.

"I just want to be honest with you, Anne. I was flattered the other night when you guessed I was—what was it, thirty-five? Thirty-two?"

"Well—I didn't know."

"But the truth is, I'm forty-two. That probably sounds old as a dinosaur to you."

"But you don't seem that old!"

Harry laughed, and withdrew his hand. "Well, it's the truth. My older brothers fought in the Great War, and I was just a couple years too young to go with them. My nephew, JJ, is the same age as you, and my niece Elissa is only a little younger."

Anne looked at him carefully. "But you don't—think I'm too young?"

"I think you're perfect," he said. "But I wouldn't blame you if you thought I was too old."

She paused, considering it, then said, "Why would a number change my mind? I thought you were a dreamboat before and I still do. My friends do, too!"

He laughed. "A dreamboat? You're kidding."

"Yes. Or—I mean—no, I'm not kidding. I'm just glad you aren't one of those men who's more worried about what people think he is than about what he really is. You have—substance."

"Substance and experience," Harry joked, taking a sip of his beer.

Anne laughed. "Yes, just think of all I could learn from you."

Harry raised an eyebrow and smiled a little. "I've never been called a dreamboat before."

"I'll bet you just didn't know it. No other girl was bold enough to say it to your face. I'll bet you've been one your whole life."

"My whole, long life."

"Yes, your whole, long life," she said, laughing.

Their lasagna came and, while they ate, Anne set to work finding out all she could about Harry. "You've lived twice as long as I have," she teased him, "so I have twice as much to find out!" He rolled his eyes, but seemed to enjoy telling her stories about his various newspaper jobs in small towns around the region, and about college in Appleton. But when she asked about his family, his face clouded over.

"You said you have two brothers?" she asked.

"Well, I had two brothers that fought in the war. One of them didn't make it home."

Her face fell. "Oh. I'm sorry. That must have been terrible."

"My brothers are both big heroes in my hometown. They've even got a statue of Chase on the courthouse lawn. He died in the battle of Belleau Wood. And my other brother, Jack, he's the oldest in our family, he's been the president of just about every club in town, VFW, American Legion, you name it."

"So you're the wanderer in the family."

"I guess. My sister, Jinny, she's kind of the same way. She's an actress on the radio in Chicago. She tried to get into the movies some years back, she went out to California, but she only got a bit part or two and decided to go back where she was wanted. You might have heard her, if you listen to the soap operas. She calls herself Jennifer Michaels."

"I'm sorry, I don't listen to those shows."

Harry grinned. "That's probably a good thing. I catch them every now and then, just to listen to my sister. But I don't hear from her much, only if she needs money."

"Doesn't she make a good salary, being on the radio?"

"Oh, sure, but there's an image to maintain! When she goes out to clubs and such, she's got to have the right clothes. And she's got to have the right address."

"Oh!"

"So, that's my family. Jack's the only one who's ever made anything of himself."

"Harry, I can't believe you would say that, when you have such an important position."

He scoffed. "An important position, maybe, but I'm never going to be president of any VFW or Moose Lodge or anything. Everywhere I've gone, I've been an outsider."

"Well, you're afraid to stay long enough to really belong, aren't you?"

"What?"

"Two years one place, three years another, one year? Of course you're going to be an outsider, if you never stay long enough for folks to get to know you."

He waved that away. "It's just the way things are. Anywhere you go, if you weren't born and raised from diapers on Main Street, you aren't ever going to be one of the ones that matter. And in my town, there was only room for my two brothers, the one living and the other dead. Especially after I hurt my knee."

"What do you mean by that?"

He shook his head. "Oh, I don't know. I always thought—See, after Chase died, I was coming up through high school, and everyone got the idea I might be as good as my brothers. You know, football, baseball, basketball. And since Chase missed the baseball season his senior year by going off and joining the Marines, everyone had this sense of incompleteness, I guess. So I was supposed to fill in and make everyone feel better, especially my dad. But then I hurt my knee the second football game my senior year. Couldn't finish the football season, or play basketball or baseball. My dad pretty much washed his hands of me then."

"And you've never forgiven him."

"Well, I—" Harry stopped, looked up at her. "You really do cut right to the chase, don't you?"

"Well, am I right?"

Harry poked at his lasagna with his fork. "Well, maybe, but I wouldn't say it's all just in the one direction. I don't think he's forgiven me yet, either."

"What has he to forgive you for?"

"For not being any kind of a hero." And he looked up at her with a biting, crinkle-eyed, sad smile.

As soon as they were finished eating, Harry patted his mouth with his linen napkin and, with a mischievous glint in his eyes, excused himself from the table. Still sipping the same glass of wine, Anne watched him as he wove through the tables and climbed the steps onto the stage. He made his way through the few couples dancing and leaned over with a friendly hand on the piano player's back, said something, slid some money from his pants pocket into the tip jar. The tuxedoed man nodded, mid-flourish, and Anne watched as Harry made his way back toward her, an impish smile on his face as he met her eyes. She was not exactly conscious of the fact that she hadn't felt so vivid in ages, the back of her neck tingling with the freshness of possibility.

As soon as Harry slid back into his seat, the pianist began playing "Embraceable You."

"Well, what do you know about that," Harry said. "Looks like they're playing our song, Miss Wallace."

She couldn't help smiling. "What a coincidence!"

"Like to dance?"

She nodded.

He stood, and held out his hand to her. She took it, and let him lead her through the restaurant and up to the dance floor. He found them a cozy spot in the stage's far corner, turned to face her, and took her in his arms. She was only as tall as his chin, and she tilted her head back to look up at him, liking the warmth of his hands, one at the small of her back, the other holding her hand. Resting her other hand on his shoulder, she imagined she could feel his solid warmth through the fabric of his suit coat and shirt, and she felt somehow at home with him.

"I suppose you know you're the most beautiful girl here," Harry said.

Anne felt herself flush, and looked down her arm at the scuffed hardwood floor. "Oh, no," she said, shaking her head.

"It's true," Harry insisted. "In fact, I think you're the most beautiful girl in all of Superior. I'd go so far as to say in all of Wisconsin. I don't know what you're doing with me."

She looked up into his blue eyes; was mesmerized, helpless, just for a moment. But she recovered quickly. "Well, I felt sorry for you," she said, smiling beatifically.

He laughed, and pulled her closer.

The pianist obliged them with several lush Gershwin tunes, and they didn't let go of each other until Harry happened to glance up and see another couple being seated at their table, the woman with a look of confusion handing Anne's purse to the waiter. "Uh-oh," Harry said, and led Anne down off the dance floor to confront the waiter, who apologized profusely, saying he was certain they had left. Mr. Vinzetti, seeing the commotion, came over and offered free dessert and coffee; Harry said they would take a rain check. Anne reclaimed her purse, and Harry paid the bill and got their coats. As he helped her into hers, Anne heard the waiter behind them, defending himself to Mr. Vinzetti, sputtering, "The table was empty for half an hour, what was I to think?"

"Were we really dancing for half an hour?" she asked Harry as they settled into his borrowed Buick, which was considerably colder than it had been prior to dinner.

He grinned at her as he turned the key in the ignition. "I wasn't checking the time."

"Well, it's all right," Anne said. "I suppose it wasn't fair of us to take up a table when we were finished eating."

"Want to go for a drive? Maybe out to Wisconsin Point?"

Anne laughed. "Harry Mickelson! Worse than any college boy! Usually they wait until at least the second date before they ask a girl out to Wisconsin Point!"

"Well, you know, being older, I don't have as much time to waste."

"I suppose that's true."

"I'll be good as gold. I just thought it might be a nice place to talk. Besides, we have to celebrate gas rationing being over. I mean, even though it's been over three months."

She relented, laughing.

They drove through town, out into the darkness of the countryside, and down the rutted road that led out onto the Point, following the narrow beams of the headlights through tall brown grasses that shimmied in the breeze. Anne had the strange sense they were descending somehow, traveling to a place other than anything she had known before. It seemed that perhaps there would be no return. But she had no regrets. In fact, her skin seemed to hum with anticipation—exactly for what she didn't know, but she had the feeling that finding out would be its own reward.

The water off to the left—the harbor's narrow little finger—shone black in the night. To the right, past the trees and over a sand dune, was Lake Superior. Occasional cars were pulled off the road into parking spots that had been created through persistent use. When Harry found a vacant one, he pulled in, and the Buick rolled to a hushed stop.

"Want to get out and take a look at the lake?" he asked.

She weighed the idea, then nodded. She had always felt that the lake could almost baptize her, when she needed it to. She supposed she had been avoiding it these past few months, because she knew it would access that place deep within her that mourned, the place she kept buried under obligations of classes, friends, volunteer work. But she knew the time had come. She was glad that Harry had brought her here, and found herself wondering, *How could he have known?*

He shut off the car, then came around to open her door for her, and she stepped out into the cold air gusting off the lake. She could hear the waves rolling on the shore as she took his arm and followed him onto the dune, holding on to her hat, struggling to keep her footing in her heels. When they reached the dune's apex, they were met with the vista of the black expanse of the lake meeting the strip of white sand, all topped by an endless cloud-striped sky. She caught her breath. Like a string that had been plucked, her grief reverberated within her, loudly at first, and then fading to almost nothing. She tasted a snowflake that landed on her lip. It seemed that the end of something had come.

"You all right?" Harry said. "Want to go back?"

She smiled up at him, trying not to show her trembling. "No, let's walk out a little farther," she said, and stopped to take off her shoes. She might ruin her silk stockings, but she felt the need to touch the sharp edge of a new life. To see what the lake could show: that there was more to the world than it might sometimes seem.

"Anne!" Harry said. "Your feet are going to freeze!"

She smiled up at him. Underneath her hat, strands of her hair snapped across her cheek. "It's just for a minute."

He cocked his head at her. Then he stepped toward her and, in one motion, had picked her up off the ground. Surprised, she let out a little cry as he settled her in his arms. They both laughed; it seemed that small shards of her grief were sailing away on the wind.

"I won't be responsible for you catching your death of cold." His smile was close, warm. "Running around barefoot in the middle of November!"

She sighed and looped her arms around his neck, trying not to bump him with the shoes that dangled from her hand.

"I'd think with you working at a hospital you'd know better," he said.

She smiled, looking out at the black water lapping against the shore. Another snowflake fluttered onto her lip and melted, and she turned her head back toward Harry. He was close enough to kiss.

So, feeling grateful to be alive, she brushed her lips against his.

This was not like her at all, and she drew back, hot despite the cold wind. But he was smiling, and she got lost again in the warmth of his eyes, and smiled back at him.

She hoped she hadn't given him the wrong message, and was a little concerned that he might try to take advantage once they got back to the car—he didn't seem like a wolf, but you just never knew with men. She couldn't believe she'd been swept away in the moment like that. But she let him carry her away from the vista and back over the hump of the dune, and when they were settled in the Buick again, he smiled over at her and said, "If you swing your feet up here, I'll warm them up for you."

Still filled with that strange recklessness that had overcome her on the beach, she leaned her back against the passenger door and stretched out her legs. Harry took her feet in his warm hands and carefully lowered them onto his lap. Enveloping first one and then the other in his hands, he massaged them gently, watching her with soft eyes.

Anne, sinking farther into the seat with each press of his hands, had never known that her feet were so sensitive; she felt the warmth traveling slowly up her legs and melting her middle, felt her heart catching itself in mid-beat.

"Better?" said Harry.

She nodded, thinking of Bobby. He was the only other boy she'd ever been out to Wisconsin Point with, and he certainly hadn't wasted any time touching her feet. Yet, Anne couldn't remember feeling quite like this even when he had touched her in bolder places. She sent him up a little apology, then wondered what Linda and Janice would say. She was quite certain they'd never experienced a man having his way with their feet.

She sighed, and wondered if Harry might seduce her and then skip town; maybe this was just a more subtle approach than most men would take. Men as a whole were not to be trusted, her mother had always taught her. "Especially with your looks, Anne! You have to be constantly on your guard!" And Anne had been, maintaining her virginity even in the face of Bobby's pleas that he might die. Even when, one sweaty night, he had said he would marry her the next day, if she wanted! But, in soberer moments, he'd insisted that, if he were to be killed, better that she not be a true widow. "But—in my heart, I would be!" she had promised him, and that was the compromise they had settled upon, for lack of any truly satisfying option.

Only now, she reflected that it really wasn't the same. If she had married Bobby, she wouldn't be in school. She might have had a baby. She might be living at her mother's house, a young mother herself, with no prospects for the future but a string of dirty diapers and no man to bring home the bacon. And what man would want to marry a woman who had already been through the mill? One thing was for sure: If she had married Bobby, she wouldn't be spending this November night with her feet in Harry Mickelson's lap. *I'm sorry, Bobby,* she told him again silently, relishing the warmth of Harry's steady hands, her grief lingering like mist after a storm.

Harry went to work early on Saturday morning and was done by noon, the presses downstairs churning out the weekend edition. He threw on his coat and hat, and hollered good-bye to Maggie, who was just pulling on her gloves. He ran down the stairs loose-limbed like a kid, whistling a jaunty version of "Embraceable You."

Anne was waiting for him in the lobby, and looked up, smiling, when she heard him coming. Neither had relished saying good night the night before. They had stayed out at Wisconsin Point for perhaps two hours, and Harry had held her feet in his lap the entire time, only removing his hands occasionally to turn the key in the ignition so the car would warm up again. Moments of conversation had alternated with moments that were made of just their contented breathing, and her little feet nuzzling his hands. "I—I wish I could invite you in," she had told him as they stood under the porch light at Mrs. Hanson's, and he had brushed her cheek with his finger, and finally kissed her, at the outer corner of her eyebrow. He'd been astonished out at Wisconsin Point on the beach when she had kissed him, so astonished that he'd quickly disregarded it, thinking maybe she'd just slipped or something. He didn't want to rush things; he was still afraid of seeming like a lecherous old man if he came on too strong. But that didn't stop him, saying good night, from asking her, "When can I see you again?" and adding, "Tomorrow?" as sort of a joke, but she'd looked up and nodded. "You aren't like anyone I've ever met," she told him, before closing the door gently between them.

Waiting for him now at the base of the stairs, her maiden's armor was back in place: sharp, lovely eyes, bright smile. He called to her, "Hello, beautiful," and liked the way her smiled deepened. When he reached the bottom of the stairs, he crossed to her quickly, touched her elbow. He was shy and grinning with elation, a little short of breath at the sight of her.

"Hello," she said. She was wearing her navy-blue hat and coat, clutching her black purse in her gloved hands.

"I hope you haven't been waiting long."

"Just a couple of minutes."

"Are you ready for lunch?"

She nodded. He held the door for her; once they were out on the sidewalk, she linked her arm through his, and he had that feeling of capsizing again.

They walked quickly the block to the Capitol Tea Room, where Harry often ate his lunch. He exchanged greetings with several of the patrons and servers as they walked in, then helped Anne off with her coat, appreciating again the slim curves of her body. Today she wore a russet-brown wool skirt and a creamy sweater. He hung up their coats and hats, and then guided her to a vacant booth toward the back. It was a younger crowd this time of day on Saturday, and he imagined every pair of eyes in the joint following her, the boys with desire, girls with envy. When they sat down across from each other in the booth, he was glad to see that her eyes did not wander from his; he couldn't resist reaching out to rest his hand over hers on the table. He wished they were alone.

After they had finished lunch—burgers, fries, and Cokes—they walked out arm in arm and determined (at his suggestion) that they would go to a movie.

More than once during lunch he'd lost the train of conversation in the curl of her hair, the curve of her ear, the quiver of her smile. She made him feel like a kid again, awkward and unsure, so he figured he might as well take her to the movies, where he'd perfected the yawn-and-stretch move about twenty-five years earlier. Feeling so jittery was ridiculous for a man his age; he imagined that once he really kissed her—no more of this timid fooling around—he would be restored to his old, jaded self again. This peculiar effervescence that he felt when he was near her was almost unbearable; he hadn't felt such a thing in decades.

He didn't figure it could last long, at his age.

But he half hoped it would.

"Do you know what's playing?" she asked, holding her hat against the wind as they hurried along.

He laughed, feeling caught in his adolescent plan. "No," he admitted. "But we can try the Palace or the Beacon, there's bound to be something good."

"It doesn't matter," she said. "I was just wondering. Let's go to the Palace."

"That's fine with me," Harry said. Just then, he felt her steps slow, and her weight dragged at his elbow. He turned toward her.

"Look," she breathed.

What had caused her to slow her steps was a display in the window of Thomas Jewelers. A poster showed a handsome young man preening in a suit; behind him were a plane, a tank, a ship with rows of indistinct soldiers and sailors disembarking. In the lower corner was a pretty young woman with an expectant look on her face. JUST GET HOME? barked the caption. GIVE HER A RING TO SHOW HER YOU NEVER WAVERED! In front of the poster were laid out more than two dozen sparkling diamond rings on an artistically draped American flag.

"Anne," Harry said, taking her shoulders in his hands and turning her toward him. She looked up; he hated the inexorable grief he saw in her eyes.

"I'm sorry," she said, smiling a shaky smile. "I'm sorry, Harry. I— I thought I was going to be all right."

And then his effervescence settled into something else, and he felt the simple necessity of their fusing. Certain as breathing, he knew that, without her, his life would continue to spiral away from him with nothing to show for it; he would only grow older and lonelier, ending up with his sole legacy a box of dusty papers that no one would bother to read.

Emboldened by the conviction, he leaned down and brushed her mouth with his. Her lips gave way; when he kissed her again, they bloomed with desire. She needed him as much as he needed her, he realized, a little surprised, relieved, thinking, *Maybe she did mean it, last night.*

On a runaway train, he lifted his head and tipped her chin up with his finger so he could look into her eyes. "Anne, sweetheart, do you want one of those rings?" he said. "Will you let me buy you one? I know I'm not—what you were hoping for. But if you'd let me, I'd—take really good care of you. I promise."

Her eyes were wide. "You're not—serious, are you, Harry?" she said, sounding a little afraid.

A week ago, if he'd even managed to get himself into such a situation, he would have laughed it off, and proceeded to the movie as planned. But Anne had made him want everything he'd never quite been conscious that he was missing. "Yes. I'm serious, Anne. I'm crazy about you. I've fallen in love with you."

"In—love?" She clutched the sleeves of his coat in her fists, as though afraid if she let go she would blow away down the street.

He extricated her hands from his coat, and took them in his. He sank to one knee, careless of his coat and pants, of the discomfort of the sidewalk under his knee. "I'm in love with you, Anne," he said. "Will you marry me?"

For an agonizing moment, her green eyes were inscrutable; puzzled, if anything. Then, a smile began to spread across her face.

"You can't blame me for asking," he said lightly, still holding her hands. He was trying to put the brakes on the train a little, afraid she was going to say no and he was going to crash and burn.

"I didn't mean for you to feel sorry for me," she said, the unsure words not matching her happy smile.

"Anne, I don't. I don't."

She laughed then, and it was a joyful sound of release. "Yes, Harry," she said. "Yes, I'll marry you."

In an instant, he was on his feet, and he took her in his arms and kissed her, scarcely conscious of the smattering of applause and cheers from the small crowd that he hadn't realized had gathered around them. An enterprising Mr. Thomas, who had been watching through the window of his store, stepped out and joined in the applause.

As soon as they had their wits half about them, the jeweler swept them into the store with a grand gesture and a slightly smug smile. Together they chose her ring, a simple princess-cut diamond set on a narrow gold band. Harry wrote a check and Anne wore the ring out of the store, admiring its lovely glint. "Everyone is going to be so surprised!" she said, as the Thomas Jewelers doorbell jingled and they stepped out onto the street. Harry laughed, hugged her tight enough to lift her off the ground, and kissed her again, reveling in her sweetness, in his good fortune.

The Cook's Creed

A well-prepared dish and an appetizing meal is
a creative achievement; therefore—I shall
derive happiness from work itself.

—*The Modern Family Cook Book*, 1942

THE MICKELSON HOUSE
502 W. First Street, Pine Rapids
Tuesday, August 1, 1950

Dolly was frustrated the whole time she was cleaning the upstairs
bedroom in the Mickelson house and making up the bed for JJ. That
he would respond to her suggestion to talk about his past with "I
don't think so, Dolly"!

When she finally went back downstairs, he seemed eager to apologize, and asked her if she would come back again tomorrow. Still
peevish, she snapped, "Probably," and rushed out. Even as she said it,
though, she knew there was no way she could stay away from the
house. Or from him, for that matter. Upset with him, she had felt
lonelier than ever. Even shaping up another room of the Mickelson
house hadn't been satisfying, when she was on the outs with JJ. She
knew it was wrong to be developing such an irrational attachment to
a man who was not her husband—to feel that way about him and

then not make every effort to steer clear of him. In fact, to seek him out the way she was doing! Especially considering that he wasn't exactly moral, what with his drinking and all his problems. The truth was, though, that she was more like JJ than she wanted to admit: alone. A little lost.

Such thoughts just worsened her mood. She didn't want to give up the Mickelson house and go back to the limited life she'd had before. She knew she was being selfish, and flirting with danger. She knew she should be putting her energies into improving life at the bungalow with Byron. But JJ had said he wasn't staying long, so what was the harm in spending a little time at the house while he was in town? She still hoped she could convince JJ to sell it to Byron. A case of the ends justifying the means if ever there was one, since owning the Mickelson house would undoubtedly improve the Magnuson marriage.

To ease her conscience further, she decided she would stop bringing JJ home-cooked meals. Even if they were just Byron's leftovers, it was too wifelike an act, now that she was getting attached to JJ. She would bring meat and bread from the store, and doughnuts for breakfast. She would not want to be accused of taking equally good care of a stranger and her husband.

As she neared the bungalow, Dolly fantasized about surrendering to her foul mood and flopping on the couch with her Cherry Ames novel and a big piece of chocolate cake to soothe her. But there were things there that needed tending to—of course! She decided she would cut corners on supper so she could finish her ironing before beginning cooking. She had been planning on stuffed cabbage rolls, but Hamburger-Tomato-Macaroni Medley would work just as well, and use many of the same ingredients, and it was much less time-consuming. Byron would never know the difference, and even if he did, he would probably be relieved to be spared the cabbage.

Once home, she headed straight for the basement, finished the rest of the ironing, then ran up to the kitchen to boil the macaroni, brown the hamburger, chop the onion, and open the can of tomatoes. By six-fifteen, the table was set and all the ingredients were mixed together and simmering on the stove. Since Byron wasn't home yet, Dolly decided to try to get the meal planning and shopping list for the coming week done—it was tomorrow's job, but if she could get it done tonight, she would have more time to spend at the Mickelson house.

Leaning against the kitchen counter, she pulled the 1948 calendar from the drawer and randomly turned to September.

Thursday, she wrote in her notes, then copied the notation from the second Thursday of September on the old calendar: *Breakfast (Byron): Poached eggs on toast, grapefruit. Lunch (Byron): Meat sandwich, banana, cookie. Lunch (Dolly): Carrot sticks, raisins, banana. Dinner: Meatballs with sauerkraut, creamed potatoes, green beans, whole wheat bread with butter.*

Seeing the menu from her first year of marriage made her melancholy. She couldn't help but recall that, back then, she had thought she knew what married life was all about. She had thought that if she prepared the right meals, looked the right way (lipstick in place, a starched apron to match her dress), she would somehow feel perfect satisfaction inside, too. After all, in appliance ads, the model women glowed from the inside out, merely because their refrigerators were modern and sparkling clean.

Dolly had known enough to know that life wasn't like an appliance ad, but always before she had imagined that that glow of pure satisfaction was actually possible to achieve through homemaking. All she had to do was just try hard enough; if she wasn't satisfied, it was her own fault. Back then, she had been busy learning, and spending most of her time with her mother and sisters and friends in Battle Point. She had never been lonely there the way she was in Pine Rapids, and homemaking had seemed a fine career choice.

So she had never until now had occasion to wonder: If this life she'd chosen was meant to fill her like water filled a vase, why did she feel so empty? Was she a flawed woman, a *cracked* vase? What if she was on the wrong track, trying to get the Mickelson house for Byron, trying to get pregnant? What if the house and babies weren't enough to fill her emptiness? What would she do then?

"Hi, Doll."

Dolly looked up. Byron had come in the back door without her hearing. He looked exhausted. He really did work hard, she knew; she really did want to do her best for him. "Hello, darling," she said, and went to kiss him. "How was your day?"

When they sat down to supper, Dolly, with her doubts and worries nagging her, had trouble following the things Byron was saying about his day down at the Chrysler dealership. When he lapsed into silence, she blurted, "Byron, have you ever considered what you really want in life?"

He looked up, startled. "Sure, Doll. Plenty. Especially during the war, I did."

Dolly held her breath. Was he going to tell her something about the war?

"I wanted what I have now. A nice wife. A nice job. A nice house. We've got it a lot easier than my folks had it on the farm, you know. I never wanted to work seven days a week like my dad did. But then, once you're in a war, you don't stay too picky about much anymore."

Leave it to him to prick guilty holes in her dreams and dissatisfactions. "Do you want children?" she asked.

"Sure. Isn't that what we've always talked about?" His eyes opened wide. "Do you mean—?"

"Oh, no. No, nothing like that. I'm sorry."

They were silent a few moments, the only noise the clinking of utensils against plates. Then he said, "Aren't you hungry, Doll? You're just picking at your food."

"No, I'm fine, Byron." She took a bite of the Hamburger-Tomato-Macaroni Medley to prove it, though it stuck in her throat going down.

ON THE TRAIN TO PINE RAPIDS
Wednesday, November 21, 1945

He could see Buck's eyes. Shining white in the filthy face.

Numberless nights. Crouched in their foxhole anticipating a Jap bayonet charge, dungarees stinking, skin smeared with filth and foul with scabs. Their boondockers crusted with the mud they'd slogged through that day and all the days before. Hollow-eyed, more gaunt by the day. Atrabine-yellow skin. Teeth clenched, mouths foul. Their rasping breath tasting the rank air; their ears tuned to every screech of the jungle, every whir of insects, every scuttle of lizards. Knowing there were Japs out there, creeping toward them.

He could hear Buck's voice. "You couldn't tell this if you wanted to. There's no beginning or end. It's the rest of our fucking lives. Not in a line like you think of life, but pinging around inside a goddamn circus fun house we can't get out of."

Buck had died on Tarawa in 1943.

JJ opened his eyes, blinking against the lights of the train.

Someday, he thought, he would read a history of the Pacific War and try to put his memories into order. Surely, someone had to know what had happened out there, and why, and when.

He checked his watch, foolishly, as though it would give him some measure. But all he could tell was that the train seemed to be running right on time.

He was getting a bad cramp in the leg that wasn't there, and shifted his weight to try to curtail it. It did no good, of course.

Phantom limb pain, they were told it was called. They were told they weren't crazy. When Dixon had been in the bed next to his in California, the two of them had had good laughs about it. "Phantom pain," one of them would call out, and the other would answer, "Phantom, hell, mine *hurts*!"

He would miss Dixon, he thought, and the nurses on that ward. If he was counting right, he had been in that hospital since May. He had spent weeks in traction and had had two stump revisions. Finally, he had been fitted with a temporary prosthesis, which tonight was traveling in the baggage car; it was too painful to wear. Besides, he was better at getting around without it, despite all the practicing they had made him do. His nurses had threatened not to have his doctor sign his leave papers—they said he wasn't ready to travel. But when they learned it was going to be his birthday and he hadn't seen his mother in three-and-a-half years, they settled for making him swear on his life to rewrap his stump every two hours. They had him practice and practice until they were certain that he was correctly adjusting the bandage's tension. After his Thanksgiving leave, he was to report to the hospital at the Great Lakes Naval Station. He wasn't out of the woods yet. They made sure he knew that. It would be at least a few months, if everything went well. Only when they judged his stump thoroughly healed and in a stable shape would he be fitted with a final prosthesis.

But now he was going home. He had left the last time on March 12, 1942. That date, at least, was clear in his mind.

They are going to ask me about it, he thought, lighting a cigarette. His hand was trembling. He wondered how many things he could omit. There were a lot of things they didn't need to know.

But he thought Buck was wrong about there not being a beginning. He could tell his family about that part: November 4, 1942, when he went ashore at Lunga Point, Guadalcanal. He still had a clear picture of his boondockers piercing the cobalt sea, and he could still feel the wet seeping into his socks. Could see, still, the yards of gray sand stretching across the beach, the ordered rows of coconut palms beyond. From a distance, the place had glittered like a jewel, and he'd been fooled, at first, into thinking the jungle was beautiful.

The first Marines had landed on the Canal three months earlier, but the battle for the island was far from over that early November. He was still keeping track of the days, then, making little notes when he could in an ersatz diary. It was November 23, his nineteenth birthday, when his 8th Marines set off in a column down a too-narrow path toward their objective, Hill 83. The cloying, stinking mass of jungle seemed as though it would devour them man by man. They had been warned of lurking scorpions, centipedes, tree leeches, massive wasps and spiders. JJ flinched with every scream of a cockatoo, and shivered when a lizard slipped across the path in front of him. Mosquitoes whirred about his head. He could taste the salt of his own sweat. And then the jungle exploded into sound and fire and a hail of bullets. There was nowhere to go. The Marines dropped, returned fire.

His first time. His first time, too, seeing men die. Friends.

It must have been a relief of sorts, JJ thought, to escape so effortlessly the incessant wondering about when your end would come.

But he wouldn't talk about that, or the rest of it. Because the middle of it all was just like Buck Young said, a goddamn circus fun house.

The days rolled together: sweat, filth, stink, lice, horror, rain, sun, steam. You were a killer, for brief moments omnipotent. Afterward, you kicked the enemy to be sure he was dead and dug in his shirt pocket for the picture of himself each warrior carried, which became a souvenir for your own pocket. Moments later, you saw friends die. You were helpless to save them, and you wore your anguish on your skin. You didn't know the way out, except to keep fighting. You trusted you would die soon enough, though you would do your damndest not to.

But each man, you knew, would find his end, and then his wandering would seem so foolish. Salvation, of a kind, waited around every next corner.

For JJ, the end came on Iwo. D-Day morning, February 19, 1945.

The previous summer, he'd taken shrapnel in his back, landing on the beach they called Green 1 at Saipan, and he'd been evacuated out on a hospital ship, ending up back in Hawaii. When the Navy declared him fit again, he was reassigned to the 5th Division, 27th Marines, which was how he ended up that February morning in an LVT chugging in toward another fucking island with the sea spray wetting his face, his rifle clutched in his hand, his pack heavy on his back. A sergeant, by that time, knowing it was what he was made for. But a man never got used to it, either, and especially not approaching that black, smoking piece of real estate that looked like hell to begin with.

The day had begun hours earlier; the night before, really, because the sleep the men had managed to catch in their bunks, after a late evening spent on last checks of their gear and last stabs at writing the perfect letter to their girl or mother, was more like tiptoeing across the surface of sleep than actual sleep, and they were startled out of it at 0300 by alarm bells and a voice on the loudspeaker shouting "Reveille! Reveille!" At chow, JJ scarfed down the steak breakfast, even though it seemed to have the consistency of rubber; grinning, he told his men they'd better do the same. Soon, they were all chewing, and chewing, and chewing. It seemed like they chewed forever.

At 0630, the command came: "Land the landing force!"

Next thing JJ knew, he was sending his pack-laden, helmeted men over the side of the transport. He followed behind them, clambering down a massive net into the LST waiting below. Smaller, amphibious LVTs idled on its deck, puking blue smoke, and JJ was herding his men into one of them as the Navy's fleet of ships let go their first shells. The landing crafts were so loud that the Navy's shells were hardly audible, but one of JJ's men tugged on his elbow and pointed, and JJ saw the island shuddering under the fireballs exploding against the black sand.

Once everyone was in, packed like oysters and stinking of sweat and the disinfectant on their dungarees and the white cream they'd smeared on their faces to protect against the wall of fire it was thought the Japs might throw up when they landed, the LVT's gate was closed.

With a grinding of gears and a jolt, it began lurching toward the open gate of the LST. Still the shells screamed over their heads. When their craft crawled off the LST's deck and bounced on the swell of a wave (what a relief they weren't going to sink right to the bottom; you knew in theory these things floated, but sometimes they sure didn't look like they would), JJ saw the foot-high lettering across the ramp of one of their neighbors: TOO LATE TO WORRY. JJ's stomach flipped, but he nudged Bertinelli, pointed the lettering out to him, and the two of them smirked.

There were hundreds of LVTs in the water now, circling like street gangs about to rumble, and the shells wailed overhead. When all at once the noise stopped, the sudden silence pounded in JJ's ears. But then Navy fliers streaked in from all corners of the sky and dove screaming toward the island, firing rockets, dropping bombs, strafing the hills with machine gun fire. There must have been a hundred of them. JJ cheered them with his men; it was a hell of a show. "Won't be a damn thing left to that island when they're done!" someone shouted.

When the fliers tilted their wings in salute to the men below and circled around for their home carriers, the ships let go with a fresh bombardment. And JJ felt the mood on the LVT change. The coxswain at the helm got a scowl on his face, and pointed the craft toward the island. On all sides of them, the LVTs were forming lines. Waves. "Showtime," JJ told his men, quietly, as the craft picked up speed, heading in.

Red Beach 1 was their designated landing location: an incline steep enough it would have made a great sledding hill back behind somebody's barn in Wisconsin. But when he stepped out of the crashing surf and onto the island, the black protean sand here gave way under JJ's feet and sent him sliding back down. He scrambled up as quick as he could, volcanic dust and the stench of anxious men filling his nostrils. He glanced back over his shoulder and saw countless Marines struggling up the incline behind him, as far down the beach as he could see in either direction, as thick on the sand as fleas on an old hound. And to his left, through the haze of smoke obscuring the blue sky, loomed the giant black hump of Mount Suribachi.

There, lying on his belly in the black sand, peering up over the edge of the incline, he had a feeling of final wholeness, of the purest clarity. He felt then that the end was near. He thanked God that he'd lived to fight this long.

They advanced, dug in, taking some small arms fire. Nothing they couldn't handle.

Then the Japs ambushed them with everything they had: machine gun bursts, mortar fire, from concealed positions the Marines had already passed. JJ was conscious only of dropping to the ground, but when he looked, his left leg to mid-thigh was gone, the stump of it a gory mess. It was perplexing that he had not been immediately killed, but as it was he did not imagine he had much longer to live.

Bertinelli dumped sulfa powder on what was left of his leg and tied him a tourniquet, and together they stayed in the shell crater they'd fallen into, fighting off the enemy with the rest of their battalion, who were crouched nearby in similar craters. JJ took stock of his men when he could. His vision was clear except when the sweat off his brow leaked into his eyes. His shooting was accurate. He wanted to make something stick, in his last moments. The Marines held their ground.

He didn't know how long they'd been there when the order came to advance. Just then, four stretcher bearers scuttled up and lifted him onto a stretcher. One of them jabbed him in the thigh with a shot of morphine. JJ yelled at them to get his men first, but they ignored him. Bertinelli gave him a pat on the shoulder, then advanced with the others. JJ called out "Give 'em hell!" His voice cracked.

Jouncing along on the litter, he closed his eyes for a minute. His leg was starting to hurt like hell. The stretcher bearers, running upright because of their burden, battled the give of the black sand with every stride, dodging the bullets that zinged through the air. One grazed a button on JJ's shirt. The stretcher bearers got him to the aid station on the beach, where they dropped him, and then ran back toward the fray. "Well," said the blond Marine on the sand next to him, whose legs were missing below his knees, "looks like the end of the war for us." And he grinned, offering JJ a cigarette, as a shell burst just fifty yards behind them. "Right," JJ said, and took the cigarette, hoping it would kill the sulfurous stink that coated the insides of his nostrils. He smoked, his hands filthy, trembling.

He had always imagined death, a quick shutting away of himself, his mother hanging a gold star banner in the front window of the house where he had grown up, the neighbors bringing casseroles, the girls from his high school all wishing to themselves that they'd had the foresight to sleep with him before he left for the war. Becoming a cripple seemed to him both ineffectual and entirely unsatisfying. That this would be the answer to all he had experienced—that his life would continue, and in such a manner—was the strangest idea to grasp.

These many months later, there were still days when his mind would wrestle against the utter inadequacy of it.

"Some fucking hero," he muttered, around his cigarette, the lights of the train car blurring in his vision.

"What's that, Marine?" said the old man sitting next to him.

JJ looked over at the man, who was craggy-faced with a large red nose, cow-brown eyes, and inky hair poking out from under a crumpled fedora. JJ stubbed out his cigarette. "Nothing," he said.

It was quiet a moment, and then the old man spoke up. "If I were you," he said, "I'd make something of that brunette over there that's giving you the eye." He pointed his chin down the aisle.

JJ looked, and met the soft eyes of a woman who was standing in the aisle leaning against the side of a seat. She was wearing a white coat open over a red dress, and when she realized she had his attention, her red lips smiled. She put her hand on her hip, in the process pushing her coat out of the way so he could see her curves.

His reaction was immediate. "Nothing wrong with the old equipment," he had always assured his nurses, in case they were interested. Not that any of them had been; they weren't the type. But this brunette was looking promising. He smiled a little and winked at her, hoping he was going about this in the right way. He had not been out in the world for so long, and he had been wet behind the ears when he had left it. But he'd spent over an hour this morning getting into his freshly pressed dress uniform, lining up his medals in perfect order, polishing the Marine emblem on his cap. He figured he looked about as good as a one-legged man could look. He had shaved, too, and smelled of Aqua Velva.

She licked her bottom lip.

The old man next to him chortled.

"Next stop, Oshkosh," the conductor called, passengers parting for him as he made his way down the aisle. "Next stop, Oshkosh."

The brunette didn't take her eyes off JJ. She tossed her hair, smiling. Just looking at her, he was getting so aroused that it hurt, but he kept smiling at her, too.

As the train slowed for Oshkosh, she began making her way toward him down the aisle. His throat seized up on him. *Don't act like an idiot,* he told himself. His palms were sweating.

She came by him and looked down on him. Her smile faded, and her face went pale. He saw disgust in her eyes. She hurried past, clutching her coat to her throat.

His desire ebbed as if she'd thrown cold water on him. The pain of it remained. He forced out a laugh, and shrugged. "Hell, where does she think I got all these medals?" he said to the old man. "I was in the goddamn war."

The man just gave JJ a look of pity and turned his face toward the window, pulling his hat brim down over his eyes and leaning back as though he would sleep.

Home, JJ thought, grinding his teeth. *They'll remember me, and not look at me that way.*

As the train pulled away from the Oshkosh depot and picked up speed into the countryside, he imagined it as from above: the soft yellow light emanating from its passenger windows, its bright white headlight illuminating the skiffs of snow blowing across the track as it made its way through the rolling farmland that was iced with dainty shifting bands of snow. He imagined the brick red barns, warmed this time of night by the steaming breath of horses and cattle, the peaceful white houses each with a single lamp left burning in the front window. He remembered the electric train set he'd had when he was a kid. He used to like to run it with all the lights out, just the beam of the headlight visible as the train whirred around the track. He had not remembered that in years, and he fell asleep thinking of it, and did not dream.

Refusing assistance from the conductor and other passengers, he made his own way on his crutches down the steps of the car to the platform of the Pine Rapids depot. He was proud and exhausted when he got to the platform and looked up. His mother and father were illuminated under the depot's lights in their overcoats and hats, their breath making steam in the crisp air. His mother's face showed her dismay at the sight of him, but she quickly smiled, and brought her gloved hands to her lips.

He swallowed, straightened his spine, and made his way across the platform to them. They looked at him like they had never seen him before, but that he was the answer to their prayers. He stopped before them and, balancing on his crutches, he nudged his mother's shoulder with his knuckles. "I'm all right, Mom," he told her. "See?"

He watched the tears pooling in her eyes, and then she lunged for him and clutched him tightly to her. He remembered her holding him that way once when he was a kid and he'd gotten lost in the woods and stayed out long past dark. To his amazement, after all this time, he felt now the same surge of relief at having made it back home to his mother, and he realized that he had been mistaken. The end had not come until now, and the end would never come at all.

MINNEAPOLIS GENERAL HOSPITAL,
CADET NURSE DORMITORY
Minneapolis, Minnesota
Wednesday, November 21, 1945

As soon as the elevator dinged and the doors slid open, Elissa rushed out of it and down the hall, unbuttoning her cuffs as she went, followed on her heels by her roommate, Claire. "You'd think you had a train to catch," Claire quipped, taking long strides to keep up.

Elissa laughed. She was already feeling liberated at just the thought of spending three full days away from the hospital and the university.

The two roommates, United States Cadet Nurses in the largest and best program in the country, the University of Minnesota, had just finished a typical long Wednesday. Breakfast at six in the nurses' dining room at the hospital in their freshly pressed uniforms, then work (they were presently assigned to the obstetric ward) from seven until eleven, a run to catch the streetcar over to the U, classes all afternoon, a run to catch the streetcar back to the hospital, a quick supper at the nurses' dining room, and work again from seven until eleven. Given the schedule, Elissa had long ago been compelled to give up keeping her diary. On most Wednesdays, the cadets' day wasn't finished even after their evening shift: They would hit the books for a couple of hours after they got back to their dormitory. But not tonight—tonight Elissa was going home.

She opened the door to their room and entered. It was not an unpleasant room, but it was spartan: Each side had a desk, single bed, dresser, and closet, in that order, from window to door.

"I tell you, Cadet Mickelson," Claire said, unpinning her cap from her hair as she followed Elissa inside. "I can't say I don't envy you, getting to go home for Thanksgiving. When I'll be stuck here working a double shift."

Elissa unpinned her white cap, too. Despite the war having ended three months ago, the cadet nurses would be allowed to finish their training—as long as they stayed single. Ty wanted her to drop out the minute he got home—any day, now—so they could have their wedding. When she'd first started, she had hated it so much that she would have quit in a heartbeat. But now that she had come so far, she wasn't sure she wanted to give it up. She would graduate to senior status in four months. Her white cap would remain the same, as would her faded blue student nurse's uniform, but no matter—everyone would know she was a senior. She had worked hard enough to deserve that, she thought. And after that, she would have only a six-month senior cadet assignment at a partner hospital before her training was complete.

She regarded herself in the mirror above her dresser. Her blue eyes looked tired, but she smiled at her reflection. "Yes, Cadet Nelson, but just remember who got to go home for Thanksgiving last year, when I was left here holding the bag. Besides," she said, unknotting her necktie and unbuttoning the bodice of her uniform, "it isn't every day my brother gets home from the war."

Claire paced. She was so full of energy that most nights she would "make rounds" in the dorm, getting the lowdown on all the day's events, before finally settling in with her books. Elissa, on the other hand, would sit right down to her studies, knowing she would fall asleep over them soon enough as it was. "Some excuse," Claire joked.

"He might even be home by now," Elissa said, stepping out of her uniform dress. Her slip would stay; she didn't want to take the time to put on a fresh one. She was so anxious to get to the train, to get home. To think that JJ would be home again, after almost four years! Elissa's mother had been nearly giddy with joy in her most recent letter, discussing the quick modifications that had been done to the house: Dad's old office on the first floor made over into a bedroom, with an attached bath. JJ wouldn't be able to negotiate stairs, and they wanted him to be comfortable.

"Hand over your duds," Claire said, holding out her hand. "I'll do them up for you while you're gone." She snatched Elissa's dress and threw it in her closet with her own laundry.

"Thanks, Claire!" Elissa turned and fished her white blouse out of her closet. She would be wearing her national cadet nurse uniform tonight—it allowed a discounted rate on her train ticket. After many months of waiting for the uniforms to arrive, the cadets typically only wore them on special occasions, and when going out in the city or traveling. Elissa was always proud to wear it; but, for a brief moment, part of her wished she was putting on her comfortable pajamas instead. Her bed was neatly made, as always, but out of the corner of her eye it beckoned to her. Never mind that, though—she had a train to catch.

"You know," Claire said, "Conrad said he's working tomorrow and Friday, same shift as me."

"Yes?" Elissa said, buttoning up her blouse. Conrad, the cadet nurses had decided, was the hospital's best-looking intern. They liked his smoky gray eyes and the mysterious curve to his lips, his feathery blond hair, his shy brand of charm. And for some reason, he refused to be put off by the fact that Elissa was engaged. Not that he had tried anything untoward; he merely insisted to anyone who would listen that he was decidedly in love with Cadet Mickelson, and that he had no intention of giving his attentions to anyone else.

Claire picked up a tube of lipstick from her dresser and lifted her chin toward her mirror. "I thought I might have half a chance with him, since you're going to be gone."

Elissa laughed, and took her gray flannel uniform skirt from the closet. "Be my guest, if you want, Claire. I wish you luck."

"What do you think?" Claire said.

Elissa looked, and laughed; her friend's lips, pursed mock-seductively, were bright red. "Is that your special Rocket Red?"

"Of course," Claire said. "Want to borrow it?"

Many of the girls had purchased the lipstick, manufactured especially for the cadet nurses, but Elissa never had. She shrugged, zipping her skirt up over her hip. "All right," she said, and caught the tube that Claire lobbed to her, and set it on her dresser. She took her uniform jacket out of the closet and shrugged into it. All the girls loved the jackets with their crisp lines, red epaulets, and red cadet nurse patches on the sleeves. You couldn't help feeling a little important in it, especially when you added the beret.

Claire gave her a wolf whistle. "Don't you look the doll!"

Elissa laughed. She buttoned her jacket, put on the Rocket Red lipstick, affixed the beret atop her head, and slid her feet into her black pumps. The cadets were required to use their shoe ration stamp to furnish their own footwear, and Elissa had shopped a long while for this pair. She loved them for the way their three-inch high heels made her legs look so good.

Claire sat on her bed and chatted on about Conrad. "He just can't seem to get it through his head about you being engaged. I keep telling him. But I swear he's got his heart set on you."

"He does not."

"He does! You should hear the way he talks about you when we go out to smoke."

"It's lucky you smoke, so you can spend that extra time with him," Elissa teased.

Claire sighed. "I know. Well, maybe this weekend since you're not around, I can get him to quit moping."

"Please do. Now, how do I look?" Elissa had put on her uniform overcoat and picked up her suitcase. Her black purse hung from her shoulder.

"Fantastic, as usual. Are you sure you don't want company getting to the train?"

Elissa waved her off. "No, thanks. I'd better go, though, or I'll be late." She leaned down to give Claire a brief hug.

"You have a grand weekend," Claire said. "Say hello to your brother from me."

"I will," Elissa said, and hurried to the door. "Thank you," she said, looking back over her shoulder at Claire, who wore a curiously melancholy expression.

The night was brisk, the sky full of stars. Carrying her suitcase with one hand, Elissa clutched at the collar of her overcoat with the other to keep the cold air from sneaking in as she walked down the steps to the sidewalk, the heels of her black pumps clicking pleasingly.

It was a homesick night, she thought, feeling minuscule amidst the buildings rising high above her. She didn't have homesick nights often, anymore, not like she used to when she first came to Minneapolis. Overwhelmed by the incessant clang of streetcars and traffic, and the crowds of strangers, she used to cry herself to sleep each night, just thinking of the quiet, the hemlock trees, the burbling of the Bear Trap River. Of Ty, Muriel, her parents—yes, even her father. But she had gotten used to the city, she supposed. She had shoved all of her homesickness into a pot and put the lid on it. Now, though, with the anticipation of going home—home, for the first time in two years!—it was all bubbling over. Although the downtown street was quiet, peaceful, this time of night, she suddenly felt certain that she couldn't stand one more minute in the city, and she couldn't walk fast enough to suit her.

She reached Fourth Avenue and the streetcar stop just in time: The streetcar was approaching, its headlight blazing, quiet motors droning. Its bottom half was still adorned with the message BUY WAR BONDS & STAMPS. She climbed aboard, paid her fare, then made her way down the aisle and chose her seat. There were only a handful of other people on board; all looked as tired and as garishly exposed as Elissa felt. She was certain everyone could read the childishness, the homesickness on her face.

When the car purred to a stop in front of the depot's Washington Avenue door, she disembarked and hurried into the station, desperate with anticipation for a breath of home.

Even this late, the train was packed from one end to the other, weary travelers filling all the seats and standing shoulder to shoulder in the aisle. Elissa, not having traveled for so many months, had not expected the car to be so crowded—she had heard the stories, but not really believed them—but she was fortunate that a dimpled, gum-snapping sailor, seeing her standing in the aisle, gave up his window seat for her, making sure to brush against her with a mischievous grin as they passed. She could see where sailors got their reputation. The sailor leaned against the seat opposite with his hips thrust out casually and his arms folded across his chest; she could feel him watching her and trying to catch her eye, but she was too tired to object. She just wanted to close her eyes and be home. Clutching her ticket in her fist, she leaned her head against the cold window, taking care not to smash her beret. She was asleep by the time the train groaned out of the station.

PINE RAPIDS DEPOT
Wednesday, November 21, 1945

Nick Overby stepped off the train in Pine Rapids hungry, his knee hurting in the damp, cold air. He thought he could smell grilling hamburger, and as he straightened his khaki necktie, he licked his chops without knowing he was doing it.

He never could seem to get enough to eat, these past couple of months since he'd been back in the States, just waiting to be released from the Army. The mess they'd been fed at Camp Kilmer and Fort Sam Houston and Camp Campbell had been good, compared to the K-rations they'd subsisted on all those months in Europe, but Nick still salivated at the mere thought of hamburgers, steaks, milk shakes, hominy, white beans cooked with bacon, okra fried in butter with tomatoes, chicken and dumplings. He imagined he'd pay a hundred dollars for a pan of good fresh-baked corn bread.

So what am I doing here?

In Wisconsin, of all places. Where they wouldn't know good corn bread from chicken feed. When he could have gone home to his mother, who would have given him her world-famous corn bread for free, as much of it as he wanted.

He was still in his uniform, with his duffel slung over his shoulder, though he'd been out of the Army now for approximately thirty-seven hours.

His mother was going to kill him for sure. He'd been out-processed at Camp Campbell and had not even stopped home in Dover, just thirty-some miles away. He'd taken the train to Chicago with his buddy Hastings, and transferred trains at Union Station. "Let me know how it goes," Hastings had said when they'd parted, shaking hands. "I'll be waiting. Don't forget, it's a hundred bucks if you don't ask her. And don't think I won't come to Dover after it."

"Don't think I won't come find you for my hundred," Nick had replied, smiling a little.

The terms of the bet, worked out meticulously while the two were convalescing in the hospital in Belgium, were this: If Nick asked Elissa Mickelson to marry him within forty-eight hours of getting out of the Army, Hastings would pay him fifty bucks. If she said yes, Hastings would pay a hundred. (An embossed wedding invitation was required as proof.) If Nick failed to ask her within the prescribed amount of time, he would owe Hastings a C-note. If he asked her and she was already married, Hastings would buy Nick a beer and introduce him to his cousin Cherelle. But if she was just engaged and didn't throw over the other guy for Nick, Nick had to pay Hastings fifty bucks. Hastings had written out the terms of the agreement and both men had signed it.

Hastings was the type of man who felt that any moment in life with more than one possible outcome was an opportunity to lay some money down. He kept all his bets and their outcomes logged in a leather-bound memo book he stored in his shirt pocket. When he was wounded, he had awakened from a state of sheer unconsciousness to prevent Nick from throwing away the memo book with his bloody shirt, then had passed out again once the book was safely tucked into his belt. It was only hours later (or moments—a man could never be sure of time, in those conditions) that Nick himself was wounded. He counted himself lucky: He had already lasted a great deal longer in combat than most medics, landing at Normandy on D + 1, June 7, and pushing through France with the rest of them and into Belgium. But his wounds were not severe enough for him to be sent home; he would be sent back out to the field in a matter of weeks.

For that reason, at the time the bet was placed, the possibility of returning home at all, much less to propose to Elissa Mickelson, had seemed as remote as taking a trip to the moon. Haggling over terms had passed the time, and had taken his mind off the pain in his knee, thigh, and shoulder, where the shrapnel had gone in.

The truth was, he'd pretty near put Elissa out of his mind, until the news of the December 17 German massacre of American troops at Malmédy had spread through the ranks. Battery B, 285th Field Artillery Observation Battalion, was lined up for surrender in a snowy field, when a German officer halted two tanks passing on the road, told them to turn their guns toward the prisoners, and then gave the order to fire. Those prisoners who weren't killed immediately were sought out and beaten with rifle butts, shot with pistols. Only a slim few who played dead, lying in the snow, covering their faces and mouths with their arms so the steam of their breath in the cold air wouldn't be detected, survived to tell the tale.

It made the men's bile rise, made them want to kill. It made them determined to win. Nick was as tore up as everyone else, but, as a medic, he couldn't kill to prove it. And only a few days later, he had ended up in the hospital with plenty of time to think.

The 285th Field Artillery Observation Battalion. "This girl I knew, she was engaged to a captain in that unit," he told Hastings, who was in the bed next to Nick's, lying on top of his blankets dressed in his uniform pants, looking at an old issue of *Photoplay* and showing off his chest and the bandage around his middle to the nurses. A bullet had passed cleanly through his lower abdomen, and, after a surgeon had stitched his intestines back together again, he was in fine shape.

"Lost out to a captain, did you?" Hastings grinned. "Well, it happens to the best of 'em."

"Aw, hell," Nick said. "She was engaged when I met her. She liked me pretty good, though," he said, making things sound better than they had seemed at the time. Sure, Elissa had seemed to like him, but then her grandpa had dropped the news of her engagement, had even shown Nick a picture of her with her arms draped around the tall captain's waist. "Sorry, son," her grandpa had said. "But I thought you should know. There's a train you can catch tonight, one A.M." So Nick had gone, fuming that she had so skillfully played him. He'd gone back to Camp McCoy and thrown himself into the sheer physicality of training, every day pushing himself until he was so tired he fell into a dead sleep before even hitting his pillow. Later, in England and France and Belgium, other things had arisen to captivate his attention. Brief affairs with English lasses, endless training, and then crossing the English Channel; then, combat, alternately replete with mind-numbing terror and equally mind-numbing boredom.

Yet, when the news about the 285th came up, it brought her to his mind, and, reclining in his hospital bed, on a real pillow for the first time in months, he got started remembering the good times they'd had together. Pretty soon it seemed he couldn't think of anything else. Even a cute nurse who kept coming by to needlessly fluff his pillow didn't change matters.

And then, one sunny February day, he read in the *Stars and Stripes* that Captain Benjamin Granton of Wisconsin had been among those killed at Malmédy.

He was stricken with pain on Elissa's behalf, at first. Then, setting the paper aside, he began to look on the bright side.

Upon learning of the confirmed death of Captain Granton, Hastings had prodded Nick to write to Elissa. Nick refused. He wasn't that good a writer, and he wouldn't know how to write what he wanted to say. He didn't even know if she would remember him. "All right," Hastings told him finally, "but if we make it back to the States, you'd better go find her." Arguments ensued. Ultimately, Hastings proposed the bet. "Look," he said, "you know you want to do it. You might as well make some money off me." Put that way, it sounded so logical.

Some months later, as their troop transport approached the Statue of Liberty, and survival suddenly seemed surprisingly imminent, Nick had tried to get out of the wager by arguing that when the bet was placed he had been on pain medication and not in his right mind. Hastings had turned a deaf ear to his pleas, showing him the signed statement, still on file in his leather book.

One thing about Hastings, though, he was a romantic at heart, and Nick didn't think he would begrudge losing his money if things worked out with Elissa. One day at Camp Campbell when they went to the PX for cigarettes, he had even goaded Nick into buying a ring, which was now tucked safely in its velvet box in his shirt pocket.

He looked at his watch. He had eleven hours left to accomplish his mission.

When he glanced up, a scene taking place a car length away on the platform caught his eye. A Marine, missing his left leg and on crutches, had dismounted the train and was approaching a man and a woman. The woman lifted her hands and pressed her fingers to her lips. The man stood a step behind his wife, hands clasped behind his back, a battered old hat shadowing his face against the lights that shone down from the depot. Nick recognized them, with some astonishment, and watched as Jack and Mary Mickelson, seemingly mesmerized with agony and joy, never took their eyes off Elissa's brother as he made his way toward them. So JJ had made it! Missing a leg, sure—but Nick knew it could be much worse. For a moment, he was thrilled.

But then he looked away from the scene. It wasn't his moment to be a part of. What had he been thinking, coming here as though nothing had happened, no time had passed? And then to arrive at just the moment—

Embarrassed, he considered getting back on the train. But this train was continuing north. He would have to get a ticket for one going south.

He hitched up his duffel on his shoulder and walked across the platform, avoiding looking toward the Mickelson family reunion. He pulled open the heavy door of the depot. His chest hurt at the thought of being so close to her and then turning around, but he had to remind himself that she had played him for a fool to begin with. He thought a hundred dollars was a small price to pay to avoid making even more of an idiot of himself.

The diamond ring felt hot in his pocket, but there was little other heat in the empty, dim depot; Nick could see his breath when he exhaled. An orange glow was visible in the wood-burning stove at the center of the waiting area, where the wooden benches looked like church pews, but the stove wasn't throwing off much heat. Nick hoped he wouldn't have to wait long for a southbound train, and castigated himself again for not going directly home to his mother and his feather bed in Dover.

The ticket agent was absent from his window, and Nick smelled hamburger more strongly now, the scent emanating from the brightly lit glassed-in lunchroom at the opposite end of the building, where he and Elissa and her father had eaten his first time in town. Maybe it was warmer in there, he thought, and besides that, he could get something to eat.

He walked as quickly as his wounded knee would allow across the coffee-colored wood floor, toward the light and heat of the lunchroom.

He sat down at the counter, dropping his duffel at his feet, and ordered a hamburger, fries, and coffee from the tall stoop-shouldered woman who asked if she could help him. She brought him the coffee first, then went back to the kitchen to cook his meal. No one else was in the lunchroom, and the woman's hooded eyes spoke her fatigue.

But when she brought him his food, she leaned her angular limbs against her side of the counter, lit a cigarette, and said, "You don't sound like you're from around here, soldier." Her voice was hoarse from fatigue or smoking. Her black hair showed several strands of gray, but she had probably been pretty when she was younger.

"No, ma'am," he said. He picked up the big burger in both hands and sank his teeth in. It was good, and he relished it, leaning his elbows on the counter and holding the burger tilted up near his chin as he chewed.

She knocked the ash from her cigarette into an ashtray. "Where you headed, then?"

"Home," he said, when he'd swallowed.

"Well, isn't that nice."

He smiled, and chomped off another section of his burger.

The bell on the lunchroom door jingled. "Well, mark another one off your list, Eleanor," came a man's voice. Nick looked over. The tall thin man was dressed in the cap and coat of a ticket agent. Just the man that Nick was looking for, then. "JJ Mickelson's home," the man announced.

Nick, unsurprised, went on eating, but Eleanor straightened, and stubbed out her cigarette in the ashtray. "JJ Mickelson! Is that so? Tonight?"

"Just a few minutes ago," confirmed the ticket agent. His bug eyes darted back and forth like fish swimming in a tank.

"Well, isn't that nice!" Eleanor said, then turned to Nick. "We've been keeping track," she told him, gesturing toward the wall. "See my list? The dates of when each of the boys from town left from this depot, and now we're filling in the dates they come home." She shook her head, getting together the supplies she needed to make her notation: a black marker, a small step stool. "JJ Mickelson! He was one of the first to leave." She stepped up to eye level with her detailed chart, which listed perhaps thirty names in the left-most column. The heading of the next column was noted "Left Pine Rapids Depot for Service"; the next column was headed "Arrived Home at Pine Rapids Depot."

Eleanor went on. "See, December 12, 1941, was when he left for training. I think he came home on leave a few months later, but that doesn't count for us. This records when they get home for good. I can put today's date here."

Nick, popping a fry in his mouth, noticed that there were five gold stars in the "Arrived Home" column.

"Well, I don't know, Eleanor, now that I think of it," said the ticket agent. "Jack Mickelson said JJ has to go back to the hospital again. He's just home for Thanksgiving. Maybe we should wait, come to think of it."

From upon her step stool, marker poised, Eleanor gave the man a disappointed look. "Do you think so, Ed? He isn't staying?"

Ed shook his head. "No. Quite a family reunion they're having, though. Elissa's coming in on the red-eye from Minneapolis, and Harry got here tonight from Superior."

Nick just about choked on the bite of burger he was just swallowing. Coming in from Minneapolis! Of course. He had completely forgotten that she was going to become a cadet nurse. She had told him, but somehow, he had pictured her just staying in Pine Rapids, waiting for the war to be over. He felt like more of an idiot than ever.

Meanwhile, Eleanor had stumbled, nearly fallen from the step stool. "Harry? Harry Mickelson came home? He hasn't been home since before the war!"

Ed shoved his hands in his pants pockets; his face looked like a thunderhead. "For godsakes, Eleanor. Ain't thirty-five years enough time to carry a torch for a man who's never looked twice at you? You been after him since first grade, for Pete's sake."

Eleanor regained her footing, and stomped down from the stool. "I have not!"

"He's engaged," Ed said. "To a real hot potato. I saw her when they came in."

Eleanor turned pale.

"Excuse me?" Nick interrupted. He had been thinking, thinking, *Maybe, if I could just catch her alone, right when she gets off the train, I could at least ask her. If she's coming right here, and I'm here already, what's to stop me, even if I am a plum fool? Maybe she never cared for me, but maybe she did. I can at least ask her.* The ring felt heavy in his pocket, and he could see her pretty blue eyes, the curve of her smile.

Eleanor and Ed both looked at him, annoyed.

"What time does the red-eye get in from Minneapolis?"

Ed's eyes narrowed with distrust. "5:05 A.M.," he said. "Why?"

Nick just smiled. 5:05 A.M. He would still have nearly four hours to spare. "Thanks," he said, and took another bite of his burger.

ON THE RED-EYE TO PINE RAPIDS
Thursday, November 22, 1945

When Elissa awoke, the sailor was gone, and she was leaning on the shoulder of the soldier seated next to her. "Oh," she said, quickly sitting up, straightening her beret. "I'm so sorry."

"That's all right," said the soldier. "I didn't mind."

She was too embarrassed to look at him. "Can you tell me where we are?"

"Next stop's Pine Rapids."

"Thank goodness," Elissa said. "Thank goodness I woke up in time."

The soldier didn't say anything, but he gave her a melancholy smile when the train finally slowed and she stood.

"I'm sorry again," she told him, finally taking a look at him. He was tall and gangly, with a long face and small eyes.

He shrugged. "Happy Thanksgiving," he told her.

"Same to you," she said, and, with some difficulty, negotiated her way past his knobby knees. Fortunately, the aisle had cleared out, and it was not hard to slip past those few men dozing on their feet.

She rushed down the steps of the car and out into the clear blackness of the very early morning, inhaling the pine scent of home, the smell from the cheese factories, the brackish odor of the train heaving on the track behind her. The thin layer of snow on the platform reflected the lights that shone from the depot and the bright light of the moon.

Just then, a man in an Army uniform and service cap came around the corner of the depot. She looked over her shoulder to see who he was going to meet. But there was no one else. And as he came closer, more quickly now, his face, his deep brown eyes, became clear in the refracted light.

"Oh," she breathed. "Ty!"

"Lissa," he said, and then she was in his warm arms. He was real again, surprisingly solid, smelling like cologne and keyed-up nerves. She'd had so many dreams in which he was nothing but dissipating air, and some days she had not felt certain she would ever see him again. Her unbelieving hands hesitated before finally pulling him close to her.

"I—You're—Surprise!" he said, then grinned, leaned down, and kissed her.

THE MICKELSON HOUSE
502 W. First Street, Pine Rapids
Wednesday, August 2, 1950

When JJ awoke, he lay still a moment without opening his eyes, peaceful, savoring the lack of pain. Five or ten seconds was all he would get, his body in limbo between sleep and wakefulness, and then it would come on him again, in a quick gradation like someone was turning up the volume on it, turning it up until it screamed.

Sure enough, there it was. His head first, his gut, his goddamn leg. He opened his eyes to slits, reaching for the open bottle on the bedside table. The sky outside was gray; rain dappled the bedroom windows. He didn't know what time it was. He propped himself up on his elbow to take a swig, then set the bottle aside again and relaxed back onto the pillow with a sigh.

He liked this upstairs bedroom in his grandparents' house; it had a nice view of the river. It had some bittersweet memories, too: It was the room they'd put him in when he first got home that Thanksgiving in 1945. Yesterday, Dolly had made it up with fresh sheets, and, though they smelled a little of mothballs, the pillows were soft, and the bed was comfortable. Better than sleeping on the couch downstairs, anyway, though he'd had a hell of a time getting up the stairs last night, missing the steps with his crutches, stumbling. He'd been a little drunk.

Hell, who was he kidding? More than a little.

Since graduating college in early June, he'd spun out. All right. Was spinning. Only a matter of time before he crashed and burned.

Only a tiny part of him even considered trying to stop. The rest relished it: the first bitter swallow in the morning, the ensuing warm glow in the gut. A few more drinks and, your pain numbed, you rose to a pleasant pitch; everyone loved you and you delighted yourself. Later, when night came, you found yourself swallowing more and more of the stuff, stifling the thoughts that bounced up like bodies in a roiling ocean, swallowing more and more until consciousness dimmed and faded, an oil lamp being turned down and extinguished.

Extinguished. A fun word to say, when your lips were thick and clumsy. You could laugh at yourself then, at least for a minute, before the urge struck you again.

It has occurred to you: pillowcase over your head, thick rope around your neck. You've gauged different beams, various doorways, in the house, since arriving here a week ago. Sort of an exercise of curiosity, a project. Certain things—the transom over the pantry door, the iron curtain rod in the parlor—you know would not be strong enough to hold you. You've settled on the banister as the best option, on tying one end of the rope around the thick post at the top of the stairs and the other around your neck, and hoisting yourself over, letting yourself drop. You've heard a tale of your father finding an old vet of the Great War who'd done himself in that way, up in Stone Harbor one summer, over the banister in his house, and you think now it has a certain panache. A distinguishing extinguishing. *Something to remember me by.* A gun would be quicker, of course, and require less planning, but you worry. With your luck, you'd be like that guy you saw on the hospital ship off Saipan, shot through the head, bleeding out both ears, eyes open wide and blinking, unable to move or speak. The doctors whispering he'd live a long life, never again walking or talking.

The thing is: You're alone. Alone enough that it echoes in your head. The first time in years you've not surrounded yourself with chattering friends, hovering nurses or family; you're actually allowing the aloneness to echo through the empty house. A relief, in some ways; in others, a terror, as you remember the things you've done, the things your family would banish you for, if they knew of them.

In any case, the option has occurred to you.

The thing is: You're a goddamn monster.

You relished the killing. Not the killing you saw—the killing you did.

You can blame them for sending you in. But the little thrill that traveled up your spine when you saw, as you shot up into the tree, the sniper's head explode into the blue sky? The ecstasy in your voice when you told the guy next to you, "Got him!" On Iwo, the calm satisfaction you felt, seeing the three men you shot fall, knowing there were probably more you'd got, too, without seeing. It was like the deer hunting you'd done as a boy, only better, and you felt the calm satisfaction of a job well done.

How can you live with a monster like that? When the monster is you?

Because you have to admit, the whole thing was a hell of a thrill. Even if you were too scared to see straight half the time when you were going in. Even if you saw men who'd been buddies in life turn, in death, to creatures unspeakably grotesque, stinking things that made you have to tie a rag over your nose and mouth and turn your eyes away before you gagged. A hell of a thrill.

There are no words to describe this to your family, your friends. What you were, the things you did. There is an utter disconnect between that life and this. In fact, you have a clear memory of waking up in the hospital in Hawaii one day, as if awakening from a long nightmare. You were startled to be in a clean bed between two clean sheets. You couldn't believe you were actually clean, alive, nearly whole. You'd slept and awakened many times in the days since Iwo, but this was the first time you truly realized where you were. That it was, for you, all over.

But, if it was a nightmare you'd awakened from that morning, the nightmare hasn't left you. And the pain in that goddamn leg, you can't get around that reminder. You can't deny that you don't *have* the leg anymore, that you've exchanged the actual leg for the mere sensation of it, for the itches you can't scratch, the shooting pains, the feeling like the leg is twisted at odd angles underneath you. It feels so real, that absent leg, it makes you think you're crazy. It makes you wonder what else is imagined that you think is real, what is real that you think you've imagined. Your memories and your dreams are at times indistinguishable from one another.

But time keeps carrying you forward, despite your feeling lately that each new day can be nothing save a mistake, because time, you believe, stopped for you long ago. Yet, without your willing or quite believing it, your history has continued to develop. Four years ago, you were released from the hospital and—though you don't recall exactly how—you ended up in college. The people there thought the things in books were important, and you decided to go along with them. *What harm could it do?* you'd thought, everything seeming more doable ever since you'd discovered a way to dull the pain in your leg and the memories; there wasn't a day that went by that you weren't a little sauced. Just a little. Just enough. You kept that pleasant pitch so constant that everyone thought you were just a little wild, you had just a little gleam in your eye. They thought you were alive like them.

They knew you were a Marine, but they didn't know what you'd done, except—you couldn't hide this fact—lose your leg. You didn't want them to know more. To know that you were a monster masquerading as a real guy, as Old Joe College. In a frat with a bunch of kids too young to have fought, most of the other vets over in married housing. (You exchanged nods with them, when you saw them, but you and they both knew it was not a time for talking, for letting down the masks you wore.) You were like a big brother to all the frat kids, or so they said. They elected you president, junior and senior year both. You knew it was bullshit, but it was a little gratifying, too. You envied their innocence, the *life* in them. You kept them at bay with your laughter. You were always up for a good time, one more drink. Flirting with the coeds who fluttered their eyelashes and said they thought it was romantic you were in the war, the ones that hit you about as deep as a mosquito bite.

Always, you felt alone, hollow. Always, though, there was something to do: a party, play rehearsal, an exam to study for, someone to bullshit with. You didn't play sports, but you managed the football, basketball, and baseball teams, practicing with them when your leg allowed it. You chose history for a major because you wanted to make sense of the past, and put it all in order in your disordered mind.

Summers, you spent in Chicago under the sponsorship of your aunt Jinny, who liked the sauce and loud parties, too, though you supposed for different reasons. She got you a couple of acting gigs on the radio and pointed you in the direction of various theaters, where you were cast in a few productions. There were always plenty of people around, and glamorous women, who liked you when you were at that pleasant pitch. Sometimes, you tricked yourself into believing you felt good.

But this time: this summer. That sickness in your gut. *What am I going to do? Now? How can I go on? Why?* When the structure holding you together, that you'd relied on, was gone. Just like that. Just like your leg: It felt that sudden and violent. Gone. Though you should have known it was coming.

Aunt Jinny had a part lined up for you on her soap opera, just a couple of lines one day, but you showed up skunk-drunk and got fired. A few days later, she came home to her upscale apartment to find you passed out on her couch and every one of her dozen mirrors smashed. When you woke up, she had your bag packed for you. You tried to charm her, but she didn't fall for it.

You had to go somewhere, though you wished to go nowhere. You went to stay with a frat brother who was spending the summer with his family in Oak Park. And there was trouble there, too: the younger sister. She was all points, her elbows, knees, small breasts, freckled nose, not to mention her personality. The trouble was that you got up to use the bathroom in the night and got confused. The house had an extremely long hallway, and all the doors looked the same. You climbed into her bed. You honestly thought it was your own; you weren't even aware of her presence. But the clunk of your crutches hitting the floor woke her, and when you dropped onto the bed beside her, she let out a piercing scream, never mind that you were snoring before your head even hit her pillow.

"Sorry, man," said the frat brother, leaning on your car to bid you good-bye the next morning, while the father stood by glowering, the mother glaring, her arm around the sniffling sister. "I tried to tell them you used to do that at the frat house. Wander."

Had you? You couldn't remember.

In hindsight, you were glad that at least you hadn't climbed into bed with the father.

You weren't sure what to do next. You didn't want your mother to see you this way—she was upset enough when you got drunk at your graduation, even with everyone passing it off as an anomaly—so you visited various friends, frat brothers, even a couple of the mosquito-bite girls, trying not to wear out your welcome, though you always did. You bulldozed everything and everyone in your path, and your charm wore thin when you vomited on carpets and emptied fathers' liquor cabinets. Finally, one night on the phone, your dad said to you, "You're not doing anything this summer, are you, son?" And so, gritting your teeth, taking a swift swig from the flask you stow in the glove compartment, you pointed your car toward Pine Rapids, the old hometown you'd left behind, a couple of lifetimes ago.

"Hello? JJ?" came the voice from downstairs.

He opened his eyes, his heart racing when he recognized the voice. *Shit,* he thought, worried he hadn't had enough to drink yet to make him pleasant company. He sat up, and brought the bottle to his lips again for a couple of quick, burning swallows. He felt better as the warmth spread in his gut.

"JJ? Are you up there? Are you all right?" she called.

He put the bottle down and wiped his mouth with the back of his hand. "Be down in a minute!" he called. His voice came out hoarse, anxious. He cursed under his breath as he extricated his leg and his stump from the sheet that had twisted around him in his sleep.

He started down the stairs fifteen minutes later, having brushed his teeth, washed his face, slicked back his hair, washed and wrapped his stump, put on his leg, and dressed. He hoped he smelled all right. He wished he'd had time to shave, even bathe, but he didn't want her to worry, so he had hurried.

When he'd first arrived at his grandparents' place, he had resented the intrusion of her presence. He didn't want anything to do with her—with anyone. Or with the house, for that matter. He simply had nowhere else to go, and it was convenient to couch his presence here as a favor for his dad. He liked at least to try to look like a good guy for his family, and figured it was best to stay at a distance, to keep up the illusion. Coming to Pine Rapids to "look after the house" was the perfect charade.

But late last week, she'd actually inspired him. Maybe he could make a little difference. So he got the broken window checked out. He cleaned the bathroom, and himself. He started to realize: He loved this old house. Grandma and Grandpa's. It bothered him, what had happened. He wished he could make it right, or at least start over, and make the house come to life again.

But the last couple nights, after Dolly had left, he'd felt a fresh and galling emptiness. What did a house mean, after all? It seemed, when he thought about it, that it meant nothing. If anything, the nighttime shadows of the house seemed to beckon him toward the banister. He could almost see himself hanging there, and drank more to banish the images, wondering if there was anything to this idea of the curse. "Unlucky in love," he'd certainly been that. Perhaps the house thought it fitting that he end himself the way that unfortunate Indian princess had done. Perhaps it desired such a sacrifice; he didn't know. But something had put the thoughts in his head, and had made them persistent, too.

He supposed he could and should have called Marty, who had enlisted in the Marines with him in '41 and had ended up back home in Pine Rapids in '43 minus an eye, with shrapnel in his neck and shoulder. As far as JJ knew, Marty was still working at the service station on the corner downtown. Marty had been a good buddy, and had seen action; they could have talked without talking. JJ might not have felt so alone.

Yet: embarrassing to be such a wreck, when your friend was holding down a job and making a life. And: unbearable to think that Bob and Duke, who had enlisted with JJ and Marty, were both buried over in the Pacific. It made the whole idea of a "reunion" seem just plain shitty.

And Dolly, of course, had a husband; she couldn't very well stay all hours, playing house with him. He wouldn't even have asked her to.

So his loneliness ratcheted up to excruciating, these nights. He didn't know quite why it was worse now. He only knew it was a different feeling from that of just being alone, or feeling alone in a crowd. This was a feeling of skin scraped raw, of having just vomited out the entire contents of your guts, leaving you with the taste of gunmetal in your mouth. It was a feeling like when your leg that wasn't there began to ache, or itch, or pinch. Phantom pain. The pain of an absence; the pain you could only endure, not touch, not relieve. It was enough to make you scream.

He wanted to break things again, like he had his first night in the house. The only thing that stopped him was the thought that he would disappoint Dolly.

For that, he had to laugh at himself.

But it was true. Though in recent months he had grown almost accustomed to letting everyone down, somehow in the past few days he had come to feel he would spontaneously combust if that happened with Dolly. Her innocence was nearly palpable in those deep eyes that ranged in color from hazel, when she was happy, to dark brown, when she was sad or mad. They could swing from one to the other in a second, and JJ liked it better when they were bright and hazel. Inexplicably, keeping her eyes bright had started to mean something to him. He had been worried, yesterday, that he had made her mad, passed out on the couch when she arrived, refusing to discuss the past. He had tried to apologize, when she was on her way out, but when he'd asked her if she would come back, she had answered with a snippy "probably."

The thing was: He was drawing the line at revisiting the past. He really didn't agree that it would do any good. Besides, it was better to keep things simple with her, and make her believe that he looked nowhere but straight ahead. If she found out the truth about the past—his past—he knew she would be gone.

The thing was: She was cute as hell. He liked just watching her, her mouth, her legs, the swishing of her hips when she walked. He promised himself he wouldn't touch her, of course; he had that rule about married girls.

Unlucky in love; any way you look at it.

"Well, if it isn't my little housekeeper," he said, when from the fourth step down he saw her. She was polishing the oak frame around the front door, and turned to face him.

"Hello," she said. "Are you all right? It's past noon."

He was relieved that she didn't seem angry with him. He winked at her, continuing down the stairs. He held on tightly to the banister, determined not to fall and make an idiot of himself. "I'm fine," he said.

"Were you comfortable upstairs?"

"Yes, thanks."

She nodded, and, after watching him a moment, turned back to her dusting. "Are you hungry?" she said. "I brought you some doughnuts I picked up at the bakery. And some meat and bread and cheese and things from the store."

He felt his heart twist. "Thanks," he said. "Thanks, I am a little hungry."

He convinced her to come out on the front porch with him, though she objected that she had only just started her work. "Come on, Dolly, I won't tell," he teased her.

They settled on the front stoop, and she helped herself to a chocolate-covered doughnut when he held the bag out to her. He selected a plain one. There was a cool breeze, and a little rain was still falling from the flat gray sky, but all in all he felt, suddenly, that it was a beautiful morning. Or afternoon. Whatever.

"You slept all right, then?" she said, pinching off a piece of doughnut between her fingers.

"Fine," he said, though he filled with disgust at the thought of it. The drunken stumbling up the stairs. The whiskey-laced nightmares. The putrid taste in his furry mouth.

Her eyes widened. "What happened?"

He hadn't meant to let on. "I said it was fine, Dolly," he said.

She put the little piece of her doughnut in her mouth. When she had swallowed, she said, "You don't sleep very well, do you?"

He looked at her a moment before finally shaking his head, just slightly. He felt a little better, just giving away that much. He took a bite of his doughnut, and chewed; a sweet jolt. He felt even better, then.

"Ever?"

He laughed a little. "With help, sometimes."

"I'm worried about you, JJ. I don't think you should be living like this. Or spending all this time alone."

As he polished off his doughnut, his mouth full of the sweetness melting, his stomach began to ache. He looked at her sideways. Her eyes were warm and dark.

"Look, Dolly," he said. He took his cigarettes from his T-shirt sleeve, thinking, *This is where it starts. This is where it starts to end.* "It's no good for you to worry about me. Why don't you go home to your husband? Doesn't he wonder about you spending all this time over here?" He lit up and smoked, savoring the burning in his chest, squinting at the Bear Trap through the trees.

"I told you, he's at work all the time," she said.

He didn't look at her. "You want this house, don't you?"

". . . For him. I'm sorry."

"Do you think it would make him come home?"

He felt her flinch.

"I'm sorry," he said. "That was mean. I don't know why I said that." Then he added, "I can't imagine not wanting to come home to you."

"Don't say that," she snapped, drawing farther away from him. Then she sighed. "Besides, he's different from you. He doesn't need anybody."

"You think I do?"

"Well, don't you?"

He smoked again, and noticed his hands were shaking. "Christ, Dolly," he said. He shifted his eyes to her. The expectant look on her face crushed him. He *would* disappoint her; that much was inevitable. Better to do it sooner rather than later. The dam he'd built to keep his past in was shaky at best, anyway; it was idiotic to think it would hold forever, against the pressure of all the shit churning behind it. Maybe a controlled trickle was the answer. It would be enough to drive her away, anyway, before he got in too deep with her. "Can I tell you something?"

"All right," she said.

"You're right," he said. "I don't sleep well. I hardly sleep at all. And when I do, I have these dreams where I'm marching. I've been marching for a hundred years, but I'm not tired. And all I can hear is the boots of all these other guys in line, marching." He looked out at the Bear Trap. "Then there's a mortar attack. Heads and arms and legs go flying through the air. And blood. Everywhere. I can taste it, even; it's salty and bitter. Then I'm alone, and everything's quiet, and the only sound is the ticking of my watch. But I can't tell what time it is because my watch is covered in blood, too. Then there's this old man, off in the distance, picking his way through the bodies. Looking for watches and gold teeth. And then I'm him. I'm him, and there's lice in my long white beard, but I'm walking on two legs." In his mind, he could see the dam sealing shut again. He gave her a sharp smile. "Maybe that's the craziest thing. Walking on two legs. You ever had a dream like that, Dolly?"

"No," she said. Her eyes were wide, but she had not flinched.

He took a deep breath, then, and smoked.

She wasn't running away from him!

He felt a startling flash of relief, a mournful sort of ecstasy. Everything pooling behind the dam seemed to rise, aching for release. "I've never told anyone about that dream," he said. "I have it all the time."

She tilted her head at him, her mouth heavy, eyes dark. "I'm glad you told me," she said, her hand lighting on his for the briefest moment. But before he could speak, her hand was gone. She was gone. He heard the front door creak open, then shut behind her.

For a moment, it seemed necessary to focus all he had on breathing. Everything was clenched tight. Relaxing didn't come easy, but when it finally did, his body was too heavy to move.

He stayed there on the front stoop a long time, watching the rain fall and the Bear Trap gurgle in the distance. He leaned his head against the porch railing, from time to time pulling out another cigarette and smoking, or grabbing the flask out of his pocket for a nip. Occasionally, a car passed on the highway, slowing for the approach into town, or speeding up on its way out. Otherwise, the day was quiet but for the gentle rain and the chirping of birds in the trees. It was as pleasant as a dream of some idyllic past that had never truly been, but was nice to think of all the same. He realized he felt empty again, but this time it was a good and unfamiliar empty: almost clean.

Understand your mate. Set about that job as though
your life depended on it. Your married life
and its happiness *do* depend on it.

—*The Good Housekeeping Marriage Book*, 1939

THE MICKELSON HOUSE
502 W. First Street, Pine Rapids
Thursday, August 3, 1950

Yesterday, when JJ had told her his dream of war, Dolly had thought:
Byron! Did Byron have such things in his mind that he couldn't or
wouldn't tell her? Was this why he worked so much, stayed away
from her? Why he seemed to insist on such distance between them? It
seemed obvious now, but why had she not realized it before? That, as
JJ had so bluntly pointed out, maybe the actual house she shared with
Byron meant nothing. That, no matter how ideal their physical sur-
roundings, the distance between them would not naturally mend.
That some sort of bridge was needed, some sort of reaching out.

"Why don't you go home to your husband?" JJ had asked her. A
valid question!

"If you only knew," she wanted to tell JJ. "If you only knew what
it's like to be married and feel you're married to a stranger, or, worse,

to someone you've only imagined! You imagined him to be something, and then found that he isn't *that*, and yet you haven't found out what he *is*."

Not that she would tell JJ any such thing.

Nor would she tell him how much she hated Byron's favorite chair because it seemed to know the contours of his body so much better than she did, nor how much she resented his T-shirts for the audacious way they clung to him and absorbed the smell of his skin. (Did they not respect boundaries, for heaven's sake? Did they not appreciate that Byron, of all people, had *boundaries*?) Nor would she mention how she envied his wristwatch for all the time it got to spend with him, that wristwatch that probably knew Byron the best, since he put it on first thing in the morning and removed it just before bed. Certainly Byron had no secrets from the wristwatch, at least not if it was paying attention.

So, she was jealous of her own husband's wristwatch, and yet here was a man who would tell her of his dreams! Of his nightmares! A man whose eyes did not hide from her understanding.

It was almost too much.

She would never tell JJ, but when he had guessed yesterday that Dolly wanted the Mickelson house for her own, it was more than Byron had ever guessed about her in his life. Which was disconcerting, to say the least.

Yet, it was wonderful to feel necessary. Needed, by someone. She could see JJ's need clearly in his eyes. And, God forgive her, lapping up JJ's need for her was so satisfying. It was temporary, she knew, but, for the time being, it was so much easier than struggling to bridge that gap between her and Byron. Because whether or not she wanted Byron to need her, she realized now that she couldn't *make* him.

And so she set out again.

She was wearing her denim pedal pushers today with a sleeveless red plaid blouse and her red ballet slippers. Not exactly approved housewife-wear, but she wasn't feeling much like an approved housewife, and she wanted to be comfortable, for once, while she worked.

The sun had emerged again, and all of Pine Rapids was in bloom, the smells of backyard gardens and burgeoning lawns mixing with the petunias and cedar bushes of the more formal front gardens. Approaching the Mickelson house down First Street, Dolly thought the house was beginning to look prouder, despite its still missing shingles, the corner of the porch that was caving in, the splotches of peeling paint, the irises choking themselves in the side garden.

But when JJ answered the door, she could see in his eyes that he had been drinking again.

"My little housekeeper!" he said. "Thought I might've scared you off yesterday. I like the pants."

"Thank you," she said, brushing her way past him and into the kitchen, trying to decide what to do. She was tired, suddenly, and felt a rush of longing for the peaceful little bungalow, for Byron's constancy. At least with Byron everything always *seemed* fine. And, as much as she enjoyed JJ's attention, in some ways it was crushing to be so near such desperation.

She heard the door shut behind her, heard JJ's uneven footsteps following her.

"So, what's on the agenda today, Dolly?" he said. She turned to face him. He was grinning, but she detected the glimmer of anguish lurking in his eyes.

She did not think she could, in good conscience, leave him to his own devices. And if he needed her as much as his look had suggested, perhaps she had some leverage. "Well, I was planning to work on the pantry," she said. Then she sniffed. "But I just don't know."

His grin faded. "What's wrong?"

"I just—I don't know anymore, JJ. I want to do the right thing, and not disappoint your father, but—"

He came a step closer. "What is it, Dolly?"

"The house. It used to be such a peaceful place to come to. But now you're here, and you're drinking so much and—I don't know, JJ, seeing you—" She took a deep breath. "Seeing you destroy yourself like this, JJ, willfully destroying yourself, it makes me feel so—hopeless! I don't know if I can bear it!"

"Dolly, I'm not destroying myself."

"You are! You're drunk right now! And it isn't even noon! Every day I've seen you, you've been drinking. And you say it's worse at night? I just can't imagine!"

"I just—I—" He ran his hand over his hair, and looked up with hot eyes. "Christ, Dolly, I'm not trying to destroy myself. I'm not! I just—my leg hurts, all right?"

"Isn't there medicine you could take?"

"Nothing that works as well."

"How do you know that? You're going to kill yourself, JJ. My father's a doctor. I've seen what liquor does."

"Why don't you just mind your own business, Dolly?"

"Well," she said then, folding her arms across her chest. She hated to do it, but she knew she had to take things one step further. "You give me no choice, then. I quit."

"What?"

"I quit. I'm no longer the housekeeper. I won't stand by and be a party to your execution. Because standing by and watching would be as good as pulling the trigger. And if you refuse to save yourself, then it's hopeless for the house, too."

"You don't have to be that dramatic about it. So I drink a little."

"You can't get through a day without it."

"I could."

"I'd like to see you try."

"Christ, Dolly," he sighed. "Don't quit your job. Don't quit and disappoint my dad. I'll leave, if you want. I'll leave. That would be the best thing. I don't know why I came here in the first place."

"You wanted to help," she said, more gently, trying to backtrack; this wasn't what she had intended. "Didn't you?"

"Right. Some good I am. My dad must've felt sorry for me or something. Asking me to come here and look after the house, when he already had you."

She wrung her hands. She couldn't let a false idea that she had put in his head discourage him that way.

So, she took a deep breath and, for once in her life, told the truth.

"Well, what the hell, Dolly?" he said, when she was through explaining. A look of amusement had spread across his face. "You— broke in?"

This was not the reaction she had wanted, but she still hoped he would come to understand. "The door was open. I heard about your family from the Ladies Aid, and I was curious, I suppose, and I thought maybe I could fix the place up a little—I loved this place! I wanted to save it. I still do."

"You were being nosy," he said, laughing. "Snooping. You wanted the place for yourself."

"Well, I thought I could make my life spectacular. More glamorous. I fell in love with this house! I couldn't help it, JJ. I couldn't understand why any family could leave it like this. I wanted to understand. And I still think you should tell me what happened. Even if you'd like to forget. You say it doesn't do any good to look back at the past, but if you don't, then what do you have? And isn't it what's torturing you, besides? Leaving all that inside you to rot you from the inside out? It's the war, yes, but—this, too, isn't it? Losing your home? In every sense? Your place in the world? Your family?"

He looked up, startled. She had hit a nerve.

"See," she went on, "I *could* understand. You don't know how alone *I* am. You don't know the things I've left behind, the things *I've* given up on. Not to mention this house—do you think it can survive this kind of neglect forever?"

His smile was half a grimace. He was looking at the floor again. He pulled out a cigarette, lit it, and smoked.

She sighed, feeling disappointment descend upon her like a yoke. It was settled: She *had* been a fool, and arrogant besides, to think that God had had anything to do with her strange fascination with the house, or with JJ, when in all likelihood it was just her stupid loneliness, and her selfishness, that had spawned it.

She would not again make the mistake of horning in where she did not belong. "Well," she said. "I guess I'd better go." She turned, and walked past him toward the back door.

"Dolly," JJ said, and his voice sounded a little hoarse.

Her hand had reached the back door's knob, but she stopped, and looked at him.

"We were all over here," he said, as he limped toward her. "Thanksgiving morning. Having waffles on Grandma's gold plates, me and my mom and dad and Lissa and my uncle Harry and Anne and Grandma and Grandpa. And then there was this loud knocking at the front door." He paused, his look a peculiar mix of appeal and defiance.

Somehow, it seemed enough. She cocked her head, feeling the weight of sadness lift from her shoulders. "Well, who was it?" she said.

PART THREE

The Creation of the Wife

Romantic glamour is hard to maintain in any relationship. . . .
But once aware of the situation, wives can make adjustments.
It isn't a question of blame—often the husband is far more
to blame than the wife. It is simply that one member of
the pair must do something about it.

—"The Other Woman Is Often the Creation of the Wife,"
Look, August 2, 1949

THE MICKELSON HOUSE
502 W. First Street, Pine Rapids
Thursday, November 22, 1945

"Set an extra place for breakfast," Mary had phoned this morning to say. "Lissa has a surprise!"

An extra place! When already they were eight, and so many whom Wilma had not seen in so long. Her grandson, JJ, had been gone the longest, away at the war for almost four years. Elissa had not been home in two years. And Wilma's son Harry had not visited since 1942. Plus, he had brought a girl with him, a fiancée, Anne. Wilma had not yet adjusted to the idea of her.

Outside, the sun peeked through the thick clouds, bouncing off the sugar-icing of snow on the ground and leaping through the bay window into the dining room, making everything on the table sparkle, from the white damask tablecloth and the golden flatware, on up to the gold-rimmed plates and goblets. The effect was pleasing enough, but as she folded a gold linen napkin into a clown's hat, Wilma fretted. Mary had sounded so excited on the telephone that Wilma hadn't complained, but nine seemed an unlucky number to seat around the table.

A fold, a tuck, a tug—as she sculpted the napkins, Wilma noticed the blue veins standing out on the backs of her hands, the tissue-paper-thin skin. Her hands looked like they belonged to an old person. But she supposed that was fitting; she would be seventy in February.

Seventy years old!

Strangely, she had felt recently that she was growing younger, reverting to the child she had been. Her body, too, seemed to be shrinking into that former self—growing shorter, in fact, with tissue delicate as a newborn's, the mess of womanhood rescinded. Even the music that had plagued her mind these many years seemed to be waning. She knew she was closing like a tulip at night, but the night felt no different to her than the very early morning.

The strangest thing of all to realize was that she had lived nearly fifty years in this house. She had not felt the years passing; she had slid over them like over ice, carried along by momentum rather than will. But how things had changed, over those years! Folding the napkins now, she couldn't help but recall when her sole obligation before meals had been to sail in and out of the kitchen and dining room, giving orders, straightening a wayward fork, a misplaced goblet. Then she would sit down at the piano and play until someone summoned her. "Ma'am, do you want the flowers in the center of the table? Which sauceboat should I use for the gravy?"

But that was years and years ago. She hadn't had anyone to cook and serve meals since John had lost much of his money in the stock market crash in 1929.

She hadn't cared about the money, not really. Even fashionable clothes meant nothing to her anymore. And with clever management, hard work, and a bit of help from a woman who came two days a week to clean, she had kept the house in good enough shape, good enough at least to keep the façade from crumbling, to keep the neighbors from seeing her and her husband's failings. There seemed no point to try for more. Life had lost its luster way back in 1917 when the boys left for the war, and the light had gone out entirely when Chase was killed.

That she had never been the same went without saying. Sometimes she still could not imagine that his body had never come home: By the time she and John had received word after the war that it was safe to disinter him, it had simply seemed too late. They had decided not to disturb his rest; the grave in the Pine Rapids Cemetery that she put flowers on remained empty.

But a need to touch the ground under which her son lay had grown within her. When she found out about the government-sponsored voyages for Gold Star Mothers, she wrote to the district's congressman and within weeks was boarding a train at the Pine Rapids depot. It was the summer of 1927.

She had arrived in New York bitter, her back aching from the hours spent on the train. Yet, once on the ocean, standing at the rail of the ship with the sea spray dashing her face, watching the Statue of Liberty shrink to the aft, she began to feel her burden lightening, her decade-old frown relaxing. She began to feel a freedom she had not felt since she was a child, since the days before she had begun trying so hard to be a Proper Girl.

At first, meeting the other Gold Star Mothers, she had not known whether she would be able to find a friend. They seemed so different from her, with their gentle accents of the South and West, their nasal Eastern tones, their broken immigrant English. But, as the women unfolded themselves for the voyage, Wilma found they were all feeling the same exhilaration she felt: *This is what the boys experienced, sailing over ten years ago. Now I can begin to understand.*

And then she was standing at Chase's grave amidst the long rows and columns of white crosses that stippled the luscious green grass. The sun was high in the summer blue sky. She traced the words on the cross. CHASE G. MICKELSON, USMC. JUNE 6, 1918. All around her, hunched women in their gray suits and cloche hats, clutching hand-bags, were finding the graves of their sons, dropping to their knees. Wilma had been the one to offer comfort to a poor woman from Virginia who collapsed at a grave near to Chasey's.

I'm sorry for all I've done; I see you are at peace, she was finally able to say to her son, touching the cross to say good-bye. The bus that had borne the women to the cemetery was leaving, taking them to dinner. Life would continue. The mothers did not want to go, but they straightened their hats, brushed off their dresses. Managed teary-eyed smiles at one another, and linked arms, all of them, walking to the bus. At dinner, there was much wine, raucous laughter. Wilma yielded to the women's demands and played a mazurka on the piano in the corner. The waiter finally had to come and ask them to quiet down.

On the voyage home, she and Josie Wokowski, from Pennsylvania, were lounging in deck chairs one evening after dinner when Josie, out of the blue, advised her to treasure her remaining children and her grandchildren, to make her life surround them instead of her grief. "But I was never meant to be a mother," Wilma said, perhaps out of habit.

"But you are," Josie said fiercely. "So God meant it."

"God was punishing me, killing Chase."

"But God blessed you with three other children. God let your other son survive the war, didn't He?" Josie said.

At this, Wilma broke into sobs. Josie, unable to comfort her, finally patted her knee and left.

She must have sobbed for hours. When she finally felt it had all gone out of her, she sighed, and opened her eyes. The sun was just setting.

I'm still alive, she'd thought, with some wonder, resolving then and there to follow Josie's advice. She would stop being so selfish. Stop dreaming of her music. Live a life devoid of unsavory passions, and control the surgings of her heart.

When she returned home, she forbade herself to touch her piano; she knew it made her unruly. The freedom she'd experienced on her voyage was gone, but she was determined, and she set about making reparations with her remaining sons, her daughter, her husband. Building the relationship with her young grandchildren, trying to show them that she could be trusted, that they could count on her.

Yet the whole thing felt as treacherous as a high-wire act, and she so often slipped. No matter how she'd tried! What hurt most was that, with each failure, she felt she was letting Chase down, too. The resentment that stabbed her when she noticed her oldest son Jack's hair beginning to go gray—he had left his brother so far behind. The Christmas dinner when from her end of the table she hurled a spoon at John; she remembered how large all the eyes around the table were as the spoon pirouetted past and clattered against the marble fireplace behind him. There were more examples that she didn't care to remember.

More than twenty-eight years had passed since she had last laid eyes on Chase, and more than twenty-seven since the news of his death. His drawings, still posted on her vanity mirror, had turned yellow and brittle. Yet she still felt closer to him than to any of her other children. She heard the strain in Harry's voice whenever she spoke to him on the phone; she saw the exasperation in Jack's eyes. Her only remaining connection with Jinny was those furtive afternoons when Wilma would sneak into the living room and sink to her knees before the radio, flip on the noise, and turn the dial to WEBC and "Chesterfield Presents . . . *Damsels of My Heart.*" Her daughter, now known as Jennifer Michaels, in the major role of the vixen divorcée Roxanne Rogers, spewed out her husky lines as Wilma leaned back against the radio and let the voice vibrate through her own shallow lungs.

She had failed them all entirely, yet she kept trying. Each time she cooked a meal for John—or for any of the family who happened to visit—she considered it a penance of sorts, a peace offering. And each time she burned herself on the stove, or burned the supper and had to begin it again, she told herself, *No more than what I deserve.* Yet they never once had said to her, "This is difficult for you, isn't it? What ever happened to your love of music? Why don't you play your piano anymore?" They had not noticed the enormousness of her efforts at all.

Particularly John had not noticed. She had really tried to be a better wife to him; he seemed to take her efforts as his due. Which made continuing said efforts doubly challenging. And then one evening in June of 1940, just as they were finishing supper, his face had turned terrifyingly purple. He clutched at his chest, gasping for breath. She urged him into stumbling with her out to the Packard; he passed out as he fell into the passenger's seat. Wilma raced around to the driver's seat, fired up the engine, and peeled out of the driveway, arriving at Wausau General, more than thirty miles away, in twenty minutes, where he was rushed into emergency care.

Jack had been angry with her, hurrying into John's hospital room later that night, after John was already stable and sleeping. "Why didn't you call me, Mom? Or call the doctor? You barely know how to drive," he had said. It was true that Wilma hated to drive, and had done so relatively few times in her life. But, from her chair by John's bedside, she had looked at her son and said, "Well, I was going so fast, everyone had to get out of my way."

The truth was, she had panicked. She didn't know what she would do without John. He was the only one who always seemed able to forgive her, and though she couldn't fathom why he did, the thought of being without the one person whom she could count on for forgiveness was terrifying.

Of course, since then, she had not been as good to him as she had told herself she would be. Sometimes she still dreamed of Gust, and in those dreams she was young again, and there was always the possibility that Gust might kiss her.

She only hoped that God could not see inside her dreams; He would never let her into heaven, then. There was no amount of punishment He could dole out in this life that would discipline her heart sufficiently for being so unfaithful to her husband all these years. But she had finally realized, after so many years of seeking, that what she was seeking would not come to her until she had reached heaven.

In heaven, she imagined, she would be a child again, with all of a child's innocence. Gust would be there, but she would be content just to be near him, just to see him; she would want nothing more than that. Chasey would be there, too, a boy with a bag of marbles in his pocket, a cap pulled down low over his eyes. He wouldn't recognize her as his mother, and he would invite her to a game. They would sit cross-legged on a soft field of grass, playing marbles forever, letting each other almost win time after time, but never quite finishing the game. At least, that was what she hoped heaven would be.

Wilma was just finishing folding the ninth, unlucky napkin when Harry called from the kitchen. "Mom? Dad? They're here," he said.

She quickly finished the napkin, and went to find John in the living room. She thought she would like to be hanging on to his arm, seeing JJ for the first time.

They were flies buzzing around him, trying to help him out of the backseat, getting in the way of his maneuvering his crutches and the

Navy leg that his sister had insisted he wear. "You're going to have to get used to it, JJ," Elissa had told him that morning. She had insisted on helping him with it, and had shooed him into his new room.

His new room in the house that seemed both familiar and unfamiliar, both smaller and larger than it had been.

Mary and Jack had made over the old office off the living room into a bedroom for him with an attached bath. Mary had even decorated it with his old bedspread and curtains from upstairs, so it would look just like his old room. JJ could almost pretend he had never been gone.

Last night, after his parents brought him home from the train and his mother fed him venison stew, he had tried sleeping in the bed, but it was useless. The house was too quiet, and he was too alone, after years of sleeping in the same hole, tent, or room as two or ten or twenty other guys. The grandfather clock that stood in the corner of the living room ticked away the minutes, and chimed every quarter hour, playing longer tunes on the half hour and the hour, until his fists were clenched and ready to break it. In the hospital, when he couldn't sleep, there was always someone to talk to, a buddy, a nurse. Here, there was no one. So he got up, started drinking, chain-smoking, pacing the living room floor on his crutches, watching the photo of his dead uncle Chase hanging on the wall.

He didn't remember falling asleep in the chair, but that was where he woke up, sometime past nine. His mother was crouched next to him, a knot above her blue eyes. "JJ? It's time to get up, honey," Mary said. Her face had the hazy edges of a dream, and he blinked to try to clear his vision. "Elissa and Ty are home," she said, "and Grandma said she can't wait another minute to see you all. We're going over there for breakfast, if you'll get dressed."

He had smiled, despite the sledgehammer pounding between his eyes. *See, Mom, I'm all right?*

"You think you can order your big brother around, now that you're some hotshot cadet nurse, is that it?" JJ had grumbled, as Elissa, who had come to hug him just after Mary awakened him, coaxed him toward his room on his crutches. She took him into his private bath and had him lower himself onto the toilet seat so she could unwrap, wash, and rewrap his stump.

"This is goddamn embarrassing," he told her, as she hovered over him, winding the bandage.

"Believe me, JJ, I've seen much worse," she said, though she looked pale.

He picked up his cigarettes from the sink. "Well, I hope so," he said. He lit a cigarette, wincing a little as she finished off the bandage.

He raised himself onto his crutches, and balanced on them as she fit the prosthesis over his bandaged stump, fastened the belt around his waist. He remembered her when she was younger, how shy she used to be of him, how he could make her blush in a second, teasing her.

"So, you're actually going to marry Ty Lofgren," he said. It was the first chance he'd had to say anything to her about it: Ty had just received a call from his mother insisting that he come home for the jam he'd been supposed to bring to the Mickelsons for their breakfast, so he had gone, kissing Elissa on the cheek, saying, "You go ahead. I'll come as soon as I can, sweetheart." The idea of his sister being with a guy—even a guy who'd made a decent Gloucester in the Pine Rapids High production of *King Lear* half a lifetime ago, before the war—made JJ's stomach turn, but he supposed there was nothing he could do.

"Yes," she said, making adjustments to his leg.

"I suppose it's all right with me," he said importantly.

She smiled up at him, and quickly ducked her head, but not before he saw the tear pooling in the corner of her eye. He swallowed a lump that had sprung up in his throat, and smoked.

Now all the sentimental rot he'd felt toward his sister paled next to his anger that she had made him put the damn Navy leg on. She didn't know what it was like, having your body altered the way his had been. It had taken a lot of getting used to, not having his leg, and now he was practiced at getting around on just his crutches. But this damn thing! He felt like a sideshow freak, as he stood there on his crutches next to his dad's car, puffing from just the exertion of standing up, his medals shiny on his uniformed chest.

Sometimes he couldn't help wishing they'd sent the medals home and left him there to rot with his buddies.

Yet, no matter where JJ had gone in the world, part of him had remained here, in Grandma and Grandpa's backyard, remembering the football games they would play on Thanksgivings. Crouched in whatever mucky foxhole he had happened to be in, he could all but taste the brisk Wisconsin air that turned sweat cold the instant you stopped moving, could see the line of firs that ran the length of the yard to the west, the pink of the sky beyond them as the sun sank below the horizon over the rolling brown field. He could feel the snowflakes that sometimes drifted gently down to melt on the heat of his bare arms.

This is probably a dream, he thought now. *Maybe I've died, after all.* Because now that he was here, he could recollect as tangibly those moments of being more animal than man, reduced from a thinking creature to one surviving on instinct and sensation alone. Stomach hard with hunger, guts roiling with discontent, eyes burning from constant strain, breath polluted, rasping. Alert for predators. Prey.

But there were Grandma and Grandpa, pouring out of the back door, followed by Harry and a beautiful red-haired girl. There at JJ's side were Mom and Dad and Elissa. And everyone was grinning. Grinning at him. Rushing to him. Lining up to give him hugs, Grandma first. "Oh, JJ, don't you look grand!" she told him, tears in her eyes. Hugging him again, so tightly he was almost knocked off balance. "Thank God you're home!" she said. *Not dead yet, then,* he thought.

I've never been gone.

JJ balanced on his crutches in front of the mantel, looking at the high school portrait of his uncle Chase, studying the same mocking smile he'd studied all last night. That face followed him everywhere, always had, asking, *Are you good enough to be a hero like me?*

His grandmother had told him once that all the Mickelson boys were born heroes, and that JJ was a Mickelson boy and a hero, too.

"But Uncle Chase was the best one, right?" JJ had asked her.

There had been a slight pause as Wilma ruffled his hair. "You're the best one, JJ," she had told him, finally.

What a line of crap. Uncle Chase was the one who did it right.

His leg was hurting worse now, especially after the horrible climb up the steps into the house, but he didn't want to sit down and muss his uniform. He was clammy, sweating; the pain was twisting all the way up his misshapen spine.

Grandma called: Breakfast was ready.

Waffles. Coffee. Orange juice. Maple syrup. Toast with homemade jam. (Mrs. Lofgren's gift was unneeded; fortunately, as Ty still hadn't appeared.) JJ's grandpa waxing rhapsodically over the taste and texture of the waffles, Dad grumbling about the weather, Uncle Harry tossing out jokes and teasing Elissa to make the red-haired girl, Anne, laugh. His grandma patting his head each time she stacked a fresh waffle on his plate, his mother on his other side showering him with concerned looks. It was like a dream he might have had, once. Of course, most Thanksgivings, JJ would have just returned from a long morning out deer hunting with his buddies Bob and Duke and their dads, but nobody mentioned that now. Nobody mentioned that Bob and Duke were both dead. JJ ate until his stomach hurt, and then he ate some more.

"How are you feeling, JJ?" asked his mother quietly.

"Great! I'm great!" he said, dangling a whole waffle from his teeth, tearing off half of it and chewing, swallowing.

"Heavens, JJ!" Wilma laughed, from her customary seat at the end of the table, at his right hand.

The red-haired girl, sitting across from JJ and next to Harry, glanced at JJ, too. Anne. His aunt-to-be. She looked like goddamn Rita Hayworth, almost, only shorter, not as busty. He winked at her. She met his gaze with a calm little smile. *She thinks I'm pathetic, goddamn it.*

"So when's the wedding, Lissa, now that Ty's back?" Grandpa John asked Elissa.

"I am so sorry we couldn't wait breakfast for him, Elissa," Wilma put in, "but I was so afraid everything would get cold! Maybe we should remove his place, do you think?"

"Oh, no, Grandma, it's fine. I'm sure he'll be here any minute," Elissa said, then turned to John. "I'm not sure, exactly. He wants to have it at New Year's."

"New Year's!" exclaimed Wilma. "So soon!" There were murmurs from the others.

Elissa looked at her plate. "But I have an obligation to finish my training."

"Aw, Liss," JJ said. "The war's over. Why don't you make a soldier happy and marry him?" It seemed the thing to say.

Elissa just looked at him; her exasperated expression was familiar from years gone by. He laughed, and took another bite of waffle.

Wilma spoke up. "I left college to marry your grandfather, you know, Elissa. And Mary left college to marry your father. It's something of a family tradition. Have you decided if you're wearing my dress?"

"I told you, Grandma, Mom's made me a suit."

"A suit! In my day, we got married in a gown."

"I know, Grandma, but things are different now."

Just then, there was a loud knock at the front door.

"That must be Ty," Wilma said.

"I'll get it, Grandma," Elissa said, sliding her chair back.

"Good thing he got here now," Grandpa pronounced, "before JJ got to all the waffles."

"Look, Grandpa," JJ said with a grin, as Elissa hurried across behind Grandpa's tall chair and out of the room. "You can bet your bottom dollar I'm gonna enjoy the hell out of some waffles. I haven't had chow like this in years."

Grandpa reached for the china pitcher of maple syrup and poured a dollop on the half-eaten waffle on his plate. "Well, JJ, it sounds like you need to come down to the bank for a lesson in financial management, if you think I'd bet my bottom dollar. Speaking of that, Jack, we'd like to contribute a little something for Elissa's wedding. Maybe have the reception here, right, Wilma?"

"Oh!" said Wilma. "Certainly, I suppose."

"Now, hold on, Dad," said Jack. "Let's wait and see what Lissa wants."

John nodded, confirming his own plans. "I'll talk to her. I'm sure she can be convinced to have that wedding as soon as possible. They'll live here in Pine Rapids, of course. We can get Ty in at the bank. Way better than that insurance racket his old man runs."

JJ laughed. "You talk like it's a business deal, Grandpa. What's your interest here?" he said.

"JJ!" scolded his mother.

"JJ," added his father, who was seated to Mary's other side. JJ was glad to hear that his parents hadn't changed their tones. They had been the same since he was a child whenever he had stepped across a line: Mom shocked, Dad warning: *If you take this one step further . . .*

John's face clouded over. "My *interest*, young man, is seeing that my granddaughter is well taken care of. And since she's your sister, I would think you would have the same concern."

JJ just laughed again, and took another bite of his waffle. His stomach was about to burst, but he couldn't seem to stop eating.

"Well, of course he does, John," Wilma said. "He's just teasing, aren't you, JJ?" She reached over, patted JJ's hand, and sighed. "Ty's waffles are going to be ice if those two don't get in here." She pushed back her chair. "I'll go and make sure everything's all right."

"I'll go, Mom," Harry said, wiping his mouth with his napkin. "You just sit."

"Oh, no, Harry, I'll just run and give them a little prod." She got up, walking the length of the dining room and out into the hallway. Then there came an audible gasp.

Harry got up, went toward the door. The others followed. JJ was slowest, but he got his crutches in order, boosted himself up, and made his way toward where they had all gathered, at the door of the dining room. He almost laughed when he finally came up behind them and saw what had them all gaping. Framed by the massive oak front door, there was his sister, lip-locked to a tall blond soldier who bent over her. The soldier's one arm was fully around her waist, and the other hand was twined in her hair; she was on her tiptoes and had her arms around his neck. For a moment, everyone just stared.

"I don't think that's Ty!" Wilma whispered, finally.

"Elissa Mickelson!" Mary said.

Elissa and the soldier separated as if in slow motion, their faces flushing as he straightened up to his full height, and she turned around to see everyone watching.

"Nick!" said John, his face draining of color.

"Nick? Oh, Nick," said Wilma, recognition in her voice. Then she turned to John, noticed his pallor. "John! Are you all right?" He nodded, leaning against the wall, trying to catch his breath.

Meanwhile, Jack started forward, apparently bent on defending Elissa's honor.

The eyes of the maiden in question widened. Her hand was on the soldier's chest. It was not apparent whether she was pushing him away or trying to shield him.

"Dad, wait," she said. "Wait, please."

"What the hell are you doing here?" Jack barked at the soldier.

Suddenly, the nausea that had been plaguing JJ twisted in his gut, and he doubled over, his crutches at ski pole angle, vomiting up all the maple syrup and waffles he'd just inhaled, acid burning his throat, the pain in his leg spreading like fire up his body as he heaved all over the hallway, everyone dodging the terrible splash of liquid.

"Oh, God," someone said. JJ, still bent over, squeezed his eyes shut, his shame as searing as his pain.

Later, he would find it remarkable that his sister didn't so much as hesitate to come to his aid, despite that their father and the tall blond soldier were about to come to blows over her. When he opened his eyes, she was the one who was at his side. She had slid her arms around his waist and was all but holding him up.

"Let's get him upstairs," she said.

"We'll carry him," said his father. "Come on, Harry." JJ closed his eyes again.

His father and Uncle Harry carried him between them, his arms draped across their shoulders, their arms bracing his back. He opened his eyes long enough to smile at his mother and grandmother, not wanting them to worry.

I've never been gone, he wanted to tell them all.

They carried him through the living room and up the stairs.

Elissa's eyes swept across Nick as she followed her father and the other man carrying her brother upstairs, and Nick noticed that she still wore her engagement ring.

She must have really loved that old captain, he thought, and tried to tell himself that wasn't such a bad thing.

He could have kicked himself for falling asleep this morning. He had been determined to stay awake all night, to make sure he wouldn't miss meeting her train, but around four o'clock, with the depot swathed in utter dark and quiet, his eyes had got to feeling like someone had run sandpaper over them. He stretched out on one of those church pew waiting benches, rested his head on his duffel, and just closed his eyes for a minute. When he woke up, it was nine o'clock, the day was bright outside, and he was stiff as hell.

Shit! he thought when he looked at his watch. Nine o'clock. He'd not only missed Elissa's train, he'd just missed Hastings's deadline.

He quickly decided Hastings would be none the wiser if he was thirty minutes late with the proposal. He'd come all this way, after all.

There was a public phone at one end of the depot. Nick hurried on his stiff knee over to it, grabbed up the city directory, and flipped through the pages. He found the *M*'s, scanned over them until he found *Mickelson, John, Sr., 502 W. First Street, President, First National Bank.* Her grandpappy. The next entry, though, read *John, Jr., "Jack," 505 Rapids Avenue, Vice President, First National Bank.* He tore the page out and stuffed it in his pocket. He found Rapids Avenue on the map at the front of the book, and tore that page out, too. Then he found the restroom, shaved, and brushed his teeth. Wouldn't do to propose to a girl with breath earned by a night spent drinking too much coffee before finally dropping off to sleep on a bench in the Pine Rapids depot.

It was a hell of a walk all the way down to 505 Rapids Avenue from the depot. The Wisconsin wind bit at Nick's face, stiffened his knee, and pained his shoulder as he walked south two blocks and west three through a section of dilapidated clapboard houses and vacant lots, to the bridge that crossed the Bear Trap River. He switched his duffel from right shoulder to left and back again so that he could alternate warming his ungloved hands in his overcoat pockets. The bridge was grated steel with an arch over it; as he crossed, Nick looked down and saw the glinting gray water of the Bear Trap passing under his shoes, burbling white as it bumped into rocks and rushed on. Then he was in the downtown; a block to his right, on the corner, was the sedate brick First National Bank of Pine Rapids, its cupola peering down over the quiet street. Nick recognized Elissa's grandparents' house towering atop the hill farther down the street to the west. He hunched down against the wind and turned east. He would avoid that place if he could.

There were only four cars parked the entire five-block length of the downtown, and they were all right in front of Shorty's Pub. Nick passed the bakery, the dentist's office with its huge age-yellowed molar dangling above the sidewalk, Ralston's Furniture, Birnbaum's Department Store, Tomsovik's Flower Shop. The displays in the store windows were like placeholders in a day that time forgot. Soon, First Street began to curve with the river, and turned into Rapids Avenue. Two more blocks and, to his left, there was another arched bridge, this one leading out of town to the east. He kept on straight south, though, through three more blocks of pleasant bungalows and mid-size trees, and then he had reached the Mickelsons'.

There was no answer when he knocked. Grateful for the shelter from the wind, he waited a minute, then knocked again.

Thanksgiving Day, and nobody home. They had to be at her grandparents'.

So he set off again, his duffel slung over his shoulder. He had hoped his days of marching long distances with a heavy pack on his back were over; well, maybe after today. He hiked back up Rapids Avenue to First Street, then west again through downtown. Now there were six cars in front of Shorty's. Then he was out of downtown and there were houses on the rising hill. He kept on, finally crossing the town's westernmost avenue, to where the Mickelson house loomed.

Looking up the long flight of stairs that led from the street up to the mammoth house's front porch, he was tempted to turn around, walk back to the depot, and get himself a ticket home real quick. But, as he kept telling himself, he had come this far already; besides that, his knee hurt like hell. It would be foolish to lose a hundred dollars on top of all of this, just because he was too yellow to climb a long flight of stairs to where a girl waited for him.

Well, maybe not exactly waited for him, since she didn't know he was coming.

Nevertheless, he started up the steps. Got to the top of them, and hurried down the short path to the porch. His boots clomped noisily up the wooden porch steps. Without giving himself a chance to think twice, he bounded for the door and banged his fist on it, then, setting his duffel down, waited, hoping her grandpappy wouldn't be the one to come.

He had the best luck of his life, he thought, when she was the one standing there when the door opened. She met him with a look of astonishment. "Nick?" she said.

She remembers me!

He couldn't help breaking into a grin. She was even more beautiful than he had recalled, and it was a moment before he could speak. "Hi, Lissa," he said, finally. "I'm sorry to bust in on you like this, but I—I wanted to see you."

She said nothing.

"I don't blame you for being surprised, but I never could forget you."

"Oh!" she said.

"And I heard—or, I mean, I read about your fiancé getting killed. I'm real sorry, Lissa."

"What?"

He took a step closer, trying to judge the look on her face. She didn't seem unhappy to see him, so he went on. "Like I said, though, Lissa, I never could forget you, and when I read that Captain Granton had got killed, I mean, I was real sorry for you. To tell you the truth, I come to some decisions while I was in the hospital over in Belgium there. I tell you, going to war makes it real clear what's important and what's not. I decided I didn't care one bit if you were engaged when we met before, because I think there was really something between us." He paused, noticing she looked confused. "Didn't you think?"

"Captain Granton?" she said. "Ben Granton?"

"Sure. Your grandpappy showed me the picture of you with him. He told me about you being engaged to him. Sure, I was mad about it, and that's why I left out. But that's been some time now, and I thought, let's let bygones be gone, if you know what I mean, Lissa. Like I said, I just felt—I mean, I feel like there's something between us, never mind anything else."

In his nervousness, he just went on, pulling the black velvet box out of his shirt pocket, opening it to show the diamond ring sparkling inside. "So I done brought you a ring, Lissa, if you'll take it from me. I was hoping you might marry me instead. I mean, I know I ain't no captain, but—"

She had staggered back from him, raised her hand to cover her mouth.

He forged ahead. "But after all this time gone by, I love you," he said. "I loved you from the minute I first laid eyes on you. And after all this time, I know it even more sure now."

A little squeaking noise emitted from Elissa.

Nick snapped the ring box shut and dropped it into his pants pocket, then stepped closer to her, gently moved her hand from her mouth, leaned down, and kissed her.

He had never kissed her before, yet the instant his lips touched hers, he felt that all the moments of his life had been leading to this one and to the mingling of their breaths. Hers was sweet with promise, her lips so soft as to defy belief; his was full of all the days gone by. When he pulled back from her a little and opened his eyes, she looked up at him with sparkling blue eyes, so he leaned down and kissed her again, and rested his hands on her waist. Her finely woven sweater, warm from the heat of her skin, felt better to his hands than anything he had touched in years. He sensed her moving closer to him, surrendering just enough, reaching up to rest her hands on the back of his neck, and he slid one arm around her waist to pull her even closer, lost his other hand in the softness of her hair, and knew he had done the right thing, coming back.

Then came the angry voice: "Elissa Mickelson!" And Nick had looked up to see a crowd of people—their faces betraying all varieties of amusement, outrage, and incredulity—watching them.

He had thought for a minute that Jack Mickelson was going to kill him; JJ's sudden sickness had provided a much-needed distraction. Nick hoped that after Jack had been given a chance to cool down, Nick could explain everything, and he and Lissa would be able to get to the happily-ever-after part. He'd been waiting long enough, he figured.

But now that Lissa had gone upstairs behind Jack and JJ and Harry, with the other women all following, her grandpappy was approaching Nick, his blue eyes cold as steel. He waited until everyone else was upstairs, and then he spoke. "Nick," he boomed. "I have to insist that you leave my granddaughter alone."

Nick stood his ground at parade rest. "I'm sorry, sir," he said, "but I come all this way to see her."

John got up close enough to Nick that Nick could feel his breath when he spoke. "I said," John emphasized. "I have to *insist* upon you leaving her alone."

When Nick, accustomed to keeping a deadpan look while sergeants got in his face, didn't respond, John shook his head and stepped back, running a hand over his thinning silver hair. "Good Lord," he said. "Why you came back here—"

"I heard about Captain Granton getting killed," Nick explained.

"Oh, you heard about Captain Granton, did you?" John said. He sighed heavily, then, shaking his head. "Didn't she tell you she's planning on marrying Ty Lofgren?"

Nick felt like he'd been socked. "She's marrying someone else?" he said. "Again? Why didn't she say so?"

"Your timing's off, son, that's for certain," John said. There was a strange look in his eyes. "So what'll it take for you just to leave? How much?"

Nick looked at him a moment, puzzled; decided it had to be some kind of test. He squared his shoulders. "I don't want your money, sir. I'll stay and fight for her, if that's what it comes to."

"Nick," John said. "Don't make me do something I'll regret."

Nick was too surprised to speak.

Just then, there were voices atop the steps, and the sound of stairs creaking as the family started down. "He just overdid a little," came someone's voice. "A little!" said someone else. "Who was that man with Elissa?" whispered another voice, as legs came into view, then waists, then full bodies, faces. And five pairs of eyes, trained on Nick, in varying stages of curiosity and ire.

Nick glanced over at John, who had ironed his face into pleasantness. "How's JJ?" John boomed.

"He'll be all right," Jack said, glaring at Nick. "Liss is helping him with his leg, and he's going to stay in bed for a while. Now you can answer me, Nick. What the hell are you doing here?"

Mary came up behind Jack and touched his elbow. "Jack, please," she said.

Jack threw up his hands. "I don't have a right to know what's going on? A man who's engaged to some other girl comes in and starts fondling my daughter and I don't have a right to know what's going on?"

"He's a poor kid after our money," John said. "Throw him out on his ear."

Nick's stomach hurt. "I'm not engaged to anyone else, and I wasn't fondling her, and I'm not after your money." He pulled the velvet box from his pocket and snapped it open. "Look, I come to bring her this. And she didn't say no."

"Oh, now, that's impossible," said Wilma.

"I come because I heard Captain Granton was killed."

"Are you certain she didn't say no?"

"It sure didn't look like she did, Mom," Harry said.

"Ben Granton? What the hell does Ben Granton have to do with anything?" Jack said.

"Kid's under the impression Lissa was engaged to him," John said.

"You're the one that told me it!" Nick said. "Showed me the goldarn picture!"

"Who's Ben Granton?" Anne asked quietly.

"He's the son of a friend of Jack's," supplied Wilma. "From up near Eagle River. Jack owns part of their resort, don't you, dear?"

"Poor Ben was killed," Mary said.

"At Malmédy," Nick said. "I read about it in the *Stars and Stripes*."

"But Elissa was never engaged to him," Mary said.

"All right, so the kid got some bad information," John said.

"Now, wait," Wilma said. "I thought you said Nick was engaged to a girl back home, John."

"I saw through him back then," John said. "Same as I see through him now. He's just a poor kid out to get rich off some naïve girl like Liss."

"I've never been engaged to anyone," Nick objected. "And I don't want your money. I just came to marry Lissa."

"My goodness," Wilma said. "John, did you lie to us on purpose?"

"Mom," said Jack, with a glance at his father. "Let's leave it be. What's done is done."

"This boy hasn't done anything wrong, has he?" Wilma said.

There was quiet. John looked off into the distance.

Wilma approached Nick tentatively, like a child approaching a strange dog, pausing a moment before finally coming to his side, resting her hand lightly on his arm. "You must be hungry," she said. "Would you like some waffles?"

"Wilma!" John said.

She fixed him with a cool look. "I know you've always wanted Elissa to marry a hometown boy, John, so that she wouldn't leave you. And now she's going to. You made sure of it, didn't you? And the worst thing is, I'm not even surprised. Making up stories like that about a boy who's trying his best, John! Well, the least I can do is give him breakfast before he goes."

"Wilma," John argued, but Wilma ignored him.

With Wilma's blue eyes prodding him, Nick allowed her to take his coat and hang it on the coat tree that stood next to the door. Though he felt a little like a sheep going to the slaughter, it didn't seem he had any choice. And he was hungry, besides.

He followed her into the dining room; the others trailed along behind.

Jack called his father into the office and, once he'd closed the door behind him, lit a cigarette, and took a deep, comforting drag.

There was a time, when Jack was a teenager, that he had hated his father, had argued with every last one of his ridiculous pronouncements. The two of them had been like enraged bucks, snorting, pawing at the ground, antlers clashing.

Chase, in his quiet way, used to laugh at Jack, and tell him there was no way he was ever going to win. "Someday, I will," Jack had vowed.

But when he got back from the war, Jack didn't care anymore. He reserved his limited energy for the things that mattered: loving his wife, bringing up his kids. Now he had worked for his father for more than twenty-five years, and had let him have his way on everything. John was the boss, after all; besides, Jack was filled to his teeth with apathy about the bank, business, money in general. After what he'd seen in the war, it was hard to believe that money mattered at all.

At the same time, though, Mary and the kids needed clothes, food, a roof over their heads. They liked to be able to go to the movies, to go out for rides in the car. So Jack had provided them those things. It had all been a compromise, he was realizing. Twenty-six years of bending over and taking it. His father's selfishness had infiltrated his life to the point where he didn't even realize it anymore; perhaps it had become his own. It was likely everyone in town believed that when John died, Jack would move into the big house on the hill and be just the same. They did not know the truth of him at all, and it was Jack's own fault for having kept himself hidden in the shadow of his father all these years.

It was one thing to compromise himself, he thought, but he'd be damned if his father was going to run amuck in his daughter's life, too.

"What the hell is going on, Dad?" he said. "You lied to us. You lied to Lissa."

"I did the right thing," John snapped.

"How do you figure, Dad? Was it the fact you broke her heart then? Or the fact that now she's got two boys fighting over her and she's got to decide and break one of their hearts?" Jack tapped the dead ash from his cigarette into the ashtray on the desk. "It wasn't fair to those boys, what you did, and it wasn't fair to Liss. This is your fuck-up, Dad. You need to fix it."

John glared at Jack, his hands on his hips. "I tell you how we fix it, Jack. We get rid of that Nick."

"What's this *we*?" Jack exploded. "I'm not the one who lied to everyone. Christ, Dad! What were you thinking?"

"He isn't right for her," John insisted. "You've got to look at all the facts, Jack. A low-class boy like that—what do you think he's here for?"

"Jesus Christ, Dad! Low class? You didn't see the way Lissa was, after you told her he had a fiancée back home. It broke her heart, Dad. It killed me and Mary both to see her like that. And now we find out it wasn't true—it was all your doing!"

"He isn't right for her!" John said again. "Besides, what's the harm? She's happy with Ty now. And he's a good match for her."

"Sure, Ty's a good match for her, but she seems kind of fond of Nick! And I think you're wrong about him, Dad. I don't think he's here for the money."

"Bullhockey," John said.

"You didn't even give him a chance. You sabotaged my daughter's life for no good reason at all. I don't care if she's happy with Ty now; it wasn't your decision to make, Dad." He looked hard at his father, trying to understand; found he couldn't. "The worst thing," he said, "is that you're not even sorry."

John ran his hand across his head, and sighed. When he looked at Jack, his eyes were a watery blue. "I am sorry, Jack," he said. "You don't know how sorry I am."

Jack smoked. "So what are you going to do about it?"

Upstairs, JJ had sent everyone but Elissa out of the front bedroom almost immediately. Their mother had wanted to help, but JJ didn't think she was ready to see the way it really was. He roused himself. "Thanks, Mom. But you'll have plenty of chances later. Liss can do it today." He let his eyes drift closed, and when he opened them again, everyone was gone but Elissa.

"You're going to be all right," she told him. She handed him a cup of water. "Here, rinse your mouth."

"Right," JJ said. He did as she told him, sloshing the water around and spitting it back into the cup, handing it back to her. She set it on the bedside table. He was feeling a little better, and lifted his head to appraise himself. "Hey, I didn't get any on my uniform, did I?"

"I don't think so," she said, unknotting his tie.

She helped him sit up, and removed his uniform jacket, hanging it over the back of the chair by the window.

JJ sighed as he lay back down. "Well, this is pretty fucking embarrassing, pardon the expression. Some way to celebrate Thanksgiving, isn't it? 'Ripeness is all,' all right."

"Don't worry, JJ," she told him, as she unbuttoned his shirt. She clearly had other things on her mind.

"All right, Liss," he said. "Tell me what's going on. Who was that guy?"

When she looked up, she couldn't hold back a smile. "Nick," she said.

"Nick! You mean that's the bastard you wrote me about? I thought he had a fiancée back home."

Her brow wrinkled. "I thought he did, too, but he said the strangest thing."

"What?"

"He said Grandpa had told him that I was engaged to Ben Granton and showed Nick a picture of the two of us. I know which picture it was. It was when Mom and Dad and I went up to see Ben when he was home on leave, a few summers ago. The thing was, Ben joked all day about how if I was just a little older and if our fathers weren't such good friends—but it was just in fun. Mom and Dad and Mr. Granton were teasing us about it, because Ben kept looking at me and saying, 'Wow, you've really grown up!' Because I hadn't seen him in ages, before that. They took a picture of us, just for fun, and I gave a copy to Grandpa because he's always asking me for pictures to put on his desk and I thought it was cute. But Grandpa knew there was nothing between Ben and me! So I don't know why he'd show that picture to Nick! And then tell me that Nick had a fiancée back home."

She sighed. "Because I don't think that Nick did, JJ! And now he's come back because he read about Ben being killed. He *proposed* to me! Before I could even explain about Ty! And before I knew it, before I could say anything at all, he just kissed me and I—Oh, JJ, what am I going to do?"

JJ boosted himself up onto his elbows. "He did what? Proposed to you? I thought you were marrying Ty."

"I am, of course! Of course!" She shook her head quickly, and turned her attention back to him. "You'd better take your pants off so I can get that leg off of you."

"Turn around for a minute, then," he said. She did so, and he unfastened his belt, unbuttoned and unzipped his pants. "Jesus Christ, Lissa, you'd better tell Nick. You didn't say anything about Ty?"

"I didn't have a chance!"

He had his pants halfway off, and double-checked that his shorts weren't flapping open. "You can turn around and help me with these," he said.

She did. "I was so surprised to see him, and then—well, he had a ring and everything and he—he sort of swept me off my feet."

"Yeah, we noticed that," JJ said, cringing a little when she lifted his legs to get his pants off.

Meanwhile, in the golden dining room, Nick dug into the waffles that Wilma had piled on his plate. She had seated him at an unused place setting, then declared that she ought to get started on the dishes and get the turkey in the oven for dinner. The red-haired girl, Anne, quickly moved to help her, and soon they had the table all clear except for Nick's things. Elissa's mother, meanwhile, was out in the hallway, cleaning up where JJ had been sick.

Nick felt awful to sit there and eat while the rest of them worked, especially since he'd been the one to interrupt their breakfast, but Wilma insisted. Wilma insisted, too, that her son Harry sit and keep Nick company, so Harry lit a cigarette and smoked and drank coffee from a china cup while Nick ate. He asked how Nick knew Elissa; Nick, between bites, filled him in.

"So my dad told you that Lissa was engaged to this Ben Granton?" Harry said at the end of it, stubbing out his cigarette in a golden ashtray.

"Yes, sir. That's how come I'm back, because I read about him getting killed." Nick was beginning to feel like a broken record, explaining himself like this. He just wished Elissa would come downstairs and tell him whether or not she would marry him. If she didn't appear soon, he was about to make himself scarce. It was a real strain, being in this strange house and not knowing whether he was wanted, and he was getting powerful homesick. The Wisconsin maple syrup and the waffles were good, but they couldn't compare to his mother's corn bread.

"But she wasn't engaged to him, and you weren't engaged to anyone back home?" Harry said.

"That's right, sir. I didn't know she thought I was."

Harry narrowed his eyes. "Where did you say you're from?"

"Dover, Tennessee."

Harry took a drink of coffee. "Well, like my mom said, Dad probably just wanted to be sure Lissa married a hometown boy. He's always set a store by her. And he's never really known anyone from the South, I guess. Except—" He stopped, looked at Nick. Then he shook his head a little, smiled, and took another sip of coffee. "Well, no," he said, looking down into his cup. Then he looked up. "In any case, may I offer my apologies, whatever his motivations were. That's just my dad. He's used to getting his way. I know it isn't a good excuse, but it's the one we've always used for him."

The sound of knocking at the front door carried into the dining room.

"Ah," Harry said, raising his eyebrows. "Well, now you'll get to meet Lissa's fiancé."

Nick's stomach turned.

Under the covers in his shorts, his stump washed and rebandaged, JJ felt much better. Leaning back on the mountain of pillows Lissa had piled up for him, he reflected that there was something about the pillows in Grandma's house that made them seem softer, and cleaner, than pillows anywhere else in the world. He had always thought so, but now that he'd seen so much of the world, he could say so with certainty. This room in the front of the house had a nice view of the river through the treetops, too, just like his old upstairs room back at his mom and dad's.

"I think you should stay off your leg for a little while," Elissa said, stowing his Navy leg away in the closet. "Maybe a day. Just to give it a chance to rest."

"Hey, I wasn't even going to put that damn thing on until you made me," JJ said. "It's a temporary one and hardly fits right, anyhow. I would've been just fine on my crutches. Can I get a cigarette?"

She shut the closet door, went over to where his jacket hung on the back of the chair, and found a pack of Lucky Strikes in his pocket. She handed him the pack and his lighter. "Nevertheless," she said.

He lit a cigarette and took a long, comforting drag of it, set the pack and lighter on the bedside table. He looked at his sister through the smoke. "All right," he told her. "I'll stay off it. Guess I'll just stay the night here. Grandma won't mind.".

"Thank you."

He laughed, smoked. Just then, the sound of knocking on the front door reverberated through the house.

Elissa went white. "Can I have one of your cigarettes?" she said.

"Go ahead," he said. "I didn't know you smoked."

"I don't," she said, snatching the pack and lighter off the table, pulling out a cigarette and putting it between her lips. "I'm starting right now." She lit it, puffed, started coughing.

He burst out laughing.

She puffed again, and this time was able to stifle her cough. "Don't laugh at me. I'm going through a very difficult time."

"Yeah," JJ said, "me with my one leg, that's a piece of cake. You with your two fiancés, that's the real trouble."

She took another puff. Smoke trickled out her nose, the corners of her mouth. "I'm going to take this up," she said.

He laughed, then said, "Come on, Liss. You know you've got to tell him."

She walked away and turned to look out the window. "I know," she said. "But—" She took another drag on the cigarette, and coughed.

"Christ," JJ sighed.

When she turned to face him, tears glistened in her eyes. "I know it sounds crazy, but I don't know if I can."

THE MICKELSON HOUSE
502 W. First Street, Pine Rapids
Thursday, August 3, 1950

He had tricked her, he supposed.

The story was nothing to him, but he could drag it out, he could embellish, he could pretend. He was, among other things, an actor, after all.

He relished the way she would lean forward a little, bright-eyed, anticipating him when he paused; he judged her reactions by the curve of her mouth. Surprise: The lower lip falls. Worry: Both lips thin, and draw back. Disappointment: The left side puckers. Confusion: almost a kiss. It was gratifying—exhilarating, even—to have such an attentive audience. It was as though she really cared.

It had been some hours since he had, with the promise of the tale, hoodwinked her into coming out onto the porch with him, settling in for the afternoon. No talk of work needing to be done now. Mostly, she sat facing him, leaning back against the porch railing, her arms wrapped around one drawn-up knee, the other leg crossed under her. Every so often, she would lean forward and rest her chin on her knee. He liked her long eyelashes, and the way her dark hair curled over her ears. He liked the shadow that showed down the front of her shirt when she leaned toward him, the curves of her hips and legs as she moved this way or that, all of which kept him pleasantly aroused; better than a whiskey buzz.

He thought, *If I can just keep this story going forever.*

Because—in addition to the pleasure of Dolly's company—now that he had begun to tell his family's story, he felt an interesting peace in this exercise of reordering the past. Making sense of it. It was a relief, really. To consider so carefully so many things that he had been avoiding thinking of, or writing off as unimportant. *We don't live in Pine Rapids anymore. The end.*

He felt compelled, now, to spin the story out to its rightful end, and that she was listening actually made the task seem worthwhile. Never mind that his butt was getting sore from sitting on the porch steps, his legs stretched out before him down the stairs. Never mind that the edges of the day were softening, even the Bear Trap's babble languid and hushed. He wasn't hungry. He could stay here forever, watching the curve of her mouth. *Forever.*

She cocked her head, and reached for the pack of cigarettes he'd set between them. "So Nick and Harry are down in the dining room, your dad and grandpa are in the office arguing, and Wilma and Mary and Anne are cleaning the kitchen and the hallway, and you're upstairs with Elissa. And Ty comes to the door?"

"That's right."

A cigarette was between her lips. He reached over and lit it for her, his wrist brushing hers.

She blew out smoke, tipping up her chin. "But she'd been writing letters to Ty for two and a half years, and planning to marry him? And all that time, she was just waiting for Nick to come back?"

He corrected her; it seemed important to clarify all the details. "She didn't think he would come back. But when he did, she wasn't ready to tell him to leave."

"Goodness. What happened next?"

JJ took a deep breath. "Well—"

But Dolly had just glanced at her watch, and her eyes got wide. "I've got to get home," she said. "Byron could be getting home any minute!"

A sharp pain stabbed JJ's stomach. He could find no words.

Dolly stubbed out her cigarette in the ashtray between them, jumped to her feet, and hurried down the porch steps. She called back over her shoulder: "Can I come back tomorrow and hear the rest?"

"I thought you were quitting," he joked.

"Very funny," she said, starting down the long flight of steps to the sidewalk.

"Come back tonight," he called after her. She stopped halfway down the stairs and looked back. He grinned; appealingly, he hoped.

She frowned. "You know I can't."

"All right," he said, smiling, though his teeth were clenched. He reached for his pack of cigarettes. "Then come back tomorrow."

Dolly smiled, then ran down the steps and turned up the street. He watched her until she was out of sight. Then, contemplating the Bear Trap as it sparkled through the trees in the light of the lowering sun, he smoked one cigarette after another, until the pack was gone.

Because of women's recent growth in socially recognized
independence, any individual woman may waver between
a craving for self-sacrifice and a repugnance
to the very thought of it.

—*The Good Housekeeping Marriage Book*, 1939

HOME OF BYRON AND DOLLY MAGNUSON
406 Jefferson Avenue, Pine Rapids
Thursday, August 3, 1950

"How was your day today, Doll?" Byron asked her at dinner. Fortunately, he hadn't arrived home until seven, and by that time she'd changed into a dress and apron and had the pork chops and rice and green beans all but ready to dish up. He would never know how long she had stayed with JJ, listening to the tale of the Mickelsons.

"Good," she chirped, sawing at her pork chop. "I have a question for you." She had decided that today was as good a day as any to start trying to bridge the gap between them.

"What's that?"

"Would you tell me something about what you did in the war?"

He set down his fork and leaned back from the table. "Where's this coming from?"

She shrank a little at his coldness. "I just—thought I'd like to know something about you."

"It was a long time ago, Doll."

"I just thought maybe if I could—know more about it—about you? We've never talked about it."

He shook his head. "I want to keep you separate from all of that. It doesn't belong in our life. The life we have now. It doesn't belong." He picked up his fork again.

She was quiet a moment, then said, "I don't think that's fair. Roy was in the war with you, and, according to you, he belongs in our life."

He ignored her. "Did you go over to that house today?"

"Yes."

"You know, Doll, you're letting your obligations here slide. I didn't want to say anything this morning, but I didn't have a single clean, ironed shirt in my closet. I had to make do with the one I wore yesterday. I don't want that to happen again."

"Oh! I—I did them, Byron. I must have forgotten to bring them up from the basement." She remembered now, she'd been in such a hurry to get supper underway on Tuesday night that she had left all Byron's ironed shirts hanging downstairs. She felt guilty, though at the same time it burned her that he felt entitled to take such a disapproving tone.

"You need to cut back on your time there, Doll. Tell them you just can't give them that many hours."

"What?" It hadn't occurred to her that he might give her such orders. And she had vowed to obey him!

"You heard me, Doll."

She leaned back in her chair. She wanted to scream at him. No wonder there was such distance between them, if this was his attitude—refusing to tell her anything, scolding her as though she were a child. "Well, what about you?" she said. "You told me back in June that you would paint the bathroom, and I'm still waiting. And that wallpaper is still hideous, by the way!"

"I know, Doll. But you know how busy I've been at work."

"Well, I've been a little busy, too."

He raised one eyebrow, and looked at her.

She couldn't meet his gaze for long. She knew that her own house was supposed to be her primary concern. "I'm sorry about your shirts," she snapped, finally, then pushed her chair back from the table and got to her feet, rushing past him to head for the basement.

"Stay and have supper with me, Doll," he called after her, but she was already gone.

That night she dreamed of golden forks trailing through golden maple syrup on gold-edged plates, of standing at the upstairs bedroom door watching JJ as he leaned back on a heap of pillows and looked out with sad eyes at the Bear Trap River passing him by. In the dream, she went to him and kissed him softly, told him, "You're home now." He didn't seem to hear her, and just kept looking out at the river.

She awoke, and looked over at Byron, sleeping next to her. The shape of his forehead, his nose, his chin, and even the curve of each eyelash, all were distinct, even in the dimness. She could see his chest rising and falling as he breathed, and could feel the heat of his body under the sheet with hers. She wondered how it was possible to know someone so intimately, to have seen and touched every curve of his body, to have heard his most private moans of pleasure and pain, to know the heat of his skin while he slept, without knowing him at all. It was apt that he'd served in a tank during the war: he was like one himself, his hatch locked tight, his shell of armor thick. She loved him, of course, but never would she have imagined that he would become such an autocrat. She honestly didn't know how she would bear it, if it continued.

She clutched the sheet to her and rolled onto her side, her back to him. *It isn't as though I really kissed JJ,* she tried to convince herself, but a guilty feeling persisted.

I have to stop this. I should do what Byron asks, she told herself, though she knew deep down that she couldn't. Wouldn't, anyway.

THE MICKELSON HOUSE
502 W. First Street, Pine Rapids
Thursday, November 22, 1945

After hearing the knock at the door, Nick waited. The bite of waffle he'd taken about stuck in his throat when he swallowed. Harry lit another cigarette.

In a minute, Elissa's mother came in, with a soldier following her. "I'm so sorry, Ty," she was saying. "We went ahead and ate, and then we had a surprise visitor, and JJ got sick, and I'm afraid nothing is working out as we'd planned."

"Well, I'm sorry I was late," said the boy. "My mother and sisters wouldn't let me get away so easy." He was young, and had a gentle look despite his square jaw. Nick saw by the rank on his sleeve that he was only a PFC. Nick, a corporal, outranked him. He stood to meet him; Harry did the same.

"Are there any waffles left for Ty?" Mary asked Harry, crossing to the china cabinet. She opened the door and pulled out a gold-rimmed plate and a set of flatware.

"Sure," Harry said. "There's a couple. They're probably cold."

"Oh!" said Mary. "You haven't met Ty before, have you, Harry? This is Elissa's uncle Harry, Ty. And Harry, this is Elissa's fiancé, Ty."

"Nice to meet you."

"Nice to meet you, too," Ty said. He had noticed Nick, and was eying him curiously.

"And this is Nick," Mary said. "He's—well, an old friend of Elissa's, actually." She set a place at the head of the table, John's customary spot. Then she stood back, looked from Ty to Nick and back again. "Ty Lofgren," she said. "And Nick—What's your last name, Nick?"

"Overby," Nick said.

"Nick Overby," Mary said.

Nick reached out and shook Ty's hand. Ty had a firm handshake, and a solid, guarded look in his eye.

"You boys eat, why don't you?" Mary said. "Lissa should be down soon. I'm going to go see how JJ is."

"Is he all right?" said Ty, looking up at her as he took his seat.

"He just ate a few too many waffles," said Mary with a wan smile. She went out.

"If you boys'll excuse me a minute," Harry said, and left the room, too.

Still standing, Nick watched Ty reaching for the platter of waffles.

"So, what unit were you with?" Ty asked as he stabbed two waffles and transferred them to his plate.

Nick decided: He had made a mistake coming here. Lissa was all set to marry this nice PFC from her hometown, and her family obviously was in favor of the match. Nick fit here about as well as a penguin in a flock of turkeys. And they were bent on getting rid of him, besides. He hated to give up, but to stay would be pure foolishness. Sure, Elissa had kissed him back, but he'd had surprise on his side; he figured she'd come to her senses the minute she saw the way her family felt about him. "Sorry," he said to Ty. "I reckon I'd best be on my way."

"How do you know Lissa?"

"I knew her a long time ago. So, uh, congratulations," Nick said.

He held out his hand. Ty got to his feet and shook hands with him, still looking confused. "I reckon I come back a bit too late," Nick said.

It seemed then that Ty figured things out. "Yeah," he said, glaring at him.

Nick started out of the dining room. "Would y'all tell them I had to go? And thanks for breakfast?"

"Sure," Ty snapped.

Nick left him behind. He was careful not to make a sound as he walked out into the hallway and through the living room. After grabbing his coat off the coat tree, he shoved his arms into it, and quietly opened the heavy front door, the thinner storm door. He closed them both behind him, picked up his duffel from where he'd left it on the porch, and walked down the front porch steps, out into the rain. He pulled his service cap out of his pocket and adjusted it atop his head, trudging down the steps toward the street. He was powerful relieved to be out of that house, but it was a melancholy thought indeed that he would never see that girl again. It made his stomach hurt, in fact, and his head ache. Every cold drop of rain that hit his face burned his skin, and his pack seemed about a thousand times heavier than it had been before. Reaching the bottom of the steps, he turned down First Street, heading for the depot, kicking up water from puddles like a disappointed, wandering child.

Do you make it easy and pleasant for him to get to work on time?
Do you see that his breakfast is prepared (and if possible
shared with you) on time? Do you keep his
work clothes in order and available?

—"Making Marriage Work,"
Ladies' Home Journal, January 1950

HOME OF BYRON AND DOLLY MAGNUSON
406 Jefferson Avenue, Pine Rapids
Friday, August 4, 1950

Dolly shook off the guilt of her strange golden dream first thing in the
morning while she fixed her face, imagining what her friend Jane
would say if Dolly told her of it: "Don't be such a goose—it was just
a dream."

With makeup in place and Jane's imaginary reassurance in her
ears, Dolly felt better. She had decided not to fret overmuch about
Byron, either: She could understand that not talking about things
could get to be a habit. She would just have to keep working on him.
Meanwhile, it was only reasonable for a husband to dictate his own
schedule on household projects, not to mention expect his shirts to be
in his closet ready for him. Here she'd been so worried about the so-
called distance between them that she'd failed to keep up on her primary responsibilities, and everyone knew that for true intimacy to

occur between husband and wife, all the stars had to be aligned, and, furthermore, that the stars would never align if the husband didn't feel himself properly cared for.

With this in mind, Dolly went to the kitchen to cook Byron his favorite breakfast—three eggs, sunny side up, four sausage links, and toast with raspberry jam. When he came in, she was humming "Powder Your Face with Sunshine," and she set his plate before him. He smiled up at her and she leaned down to kiss him, enjoying the smell of his aftershave. He was wearing her favorite red necktie. She poured cups of coffee for both of them and sat down across the table from him.

"Aren't you eating, Doll?" he said.

"Oh, no, I'm not that hungry," she said, smiling, not pointing out what she thought he should know after two years of marriage—that she never ate breakfast and she hated even the smell of eggs.

He took a bite of his toast. "What do you have planned for today?"

"Oh, just things around the house, you know," she said. "You? Busy day?"

"I hope so," he said, with his cutest smile. He went on to tell her all about a sale he had made the day before and how he was trying to talk Roy into buying advertising time on a Wausau radio station. Dolly smiled and nodded appropriately, only getting up from the table when she saw he needed his coffee cup refilled.

An hour after kissing Byron good-bye at the back door, Dolly went out the front door, heading for the Mickelson house. When she had told him she would be doing things around the house, she hadn't specified which house. Technically, she had not lied at all.

The morning was warming to just-this-side-of-uncomfortable as the sun climbed the cloudless sky. As Dolly hurried north on Jefferson, she hardly noticed as she skirted the tricycles and scooters that littered the sidewalk in front of the pert little bungalows. Instead, her mind raced with questions about the Mickelsons. How had Elissa ever chosen between Nick and Ty? And what on earth did her choice have to do with the family abandoning the house?

Turning the corner onto First Street in front of Holman's Market, she almost bumped into two women who were standing together. In a blur, Dolly recognized the wild purple dress on one of them. Dolly's heart seized; her feet froze to the pavement. She said a quick prayer of thanks that she'd worn a dress today rather than her denim pedal pushers.

"Dolly," Mrs. Fryt said. A fresh red zinnia bobbed atop her hat. "You should watch where you're going."

Corinne spoke up. "Oh, Cecilia, we're standing right in the way! Are you doing some shopping today, Dolly?"

"Yes," Dolly said quickly. "I was—out of something."

They looked at her.

"Eggs!" Dolly said.

Behind her glasses, Mrs. Fryt squinted. "You aren't on your way to the Mickelson house, are you? I've seen you going there the last two days."

"Oh! Well—"

Mrs. Fryt leaned toward Dolly. "How does the house look? Do you know their plans for it yet?"

"Fine! It's fine. I don't know."

"Well, what kinds of things does he have you doing?"

Dolly took a step back, trying to get some space. "Oh, you know, just dusting. Cleaning the kitchen. Things like that."

Mrs. Fryt shook her head. "I just wish I knew what their intentions were with that place. It's like a thorn in my eye, looking at it every day."

Dolly refrained from saying that Mrs. Fryt shouldn't feel obligated to watch it so closely.

"How *is* JJ doing, Dolly?" Corinne asked.

Suddenly, Dolly was fed up with kowtowing to them. It was clear they would find out where she was going, anyway, no matter what she told them. And there was no way she was staying away from the house today. She had to find out from JJ what had happened. "You know, that reminds me, Corinne," she said. "I told JJ I'd bring him something from the bakery this morning. I guess I'd better go, or he'll know I almost forgot!"

Mrs. Fryt sniffed. "Well, I see he has you beholden to him already. Those Mickelsons. Who else would think to make a housekeeper do their personal shopping? For that matter, who else in this town would even hire a housekeeper?"

"Good-bye!" Dolly called, looking back over her shoulder to wave as she walked away. "See you at church Sunday!"

She proceeded directly to the bakery across the street and bought a half dozen doughnuts, three plain and three chocolate, the same as she'd brought him the other day. When she came out, Mrs. Fryt and Corinne were still standing on the corner. They saw her. She waved again, and set off boldly in the direction of the Mickelson house, wondering when her temper had become so short, when the ladies' opinion of her had ceased to be her primary concern.

JJ was sitting on the top front porch step, right where Dolly had left him the previous evening; he waved when he saw her coming.

She just smiled and ducked her head, worrying for a moment whether she should ask him if they could go inside—when Mrs. Fryt walked home from the market she would surely spot them on the porch. But then again, as long as Mrs. Fryt knew Dolly was coming here with doughnuts anyway, what would be the harm in her knowing that JJ Mickelson was kind enough to invite his housekeeper to sit and have a doughnut with him?

Dolly ran up the flight of steps between the street and the walk. JJ didn't seem drunk. He still looked a little bleary-eyed, even from a distance, but he had shaved and was wearing clean clothes, including a white dress shirt over his T-shirt, which he wore untucked, with the sleeves rolled up and the top buttons unbuttoned. It was too big for him. He smiled as if he were glad to see her, though his eyes were as melancholy as they'd been in her dream.

She climbed the porch steps and sat down next to him on the top step, holding the bag of doughnuts out to him. He grinned and reached into the bag for one; she followed suit.

"Tell me what happened, JJ," she said.

THE MICKELSON HOUSE
502 W. First Street, Pine Rapids
Thursday, November 22, 1945

"What do you mean you don't know if you can tell him?" JJ said to Elissa. "You've got to."

Elissa walked over to the side of his bed and stubbed out her half-smoked cigarette in the ashtray on the table. She was beginning to feel queasy. "I know," she said. Then she looked at her brother. "But he wouldn't have come here if he didn't have a good reason to, right?"

JJ shrugged.

"I mean, a boy doesn't come all the way to Pine Rapids from thousands of miles away just for fun, does he? Just to see if he can get a rise out of a girl?"

JJ blew out smoke. "Depends on what sort of a guy he is."

She put her hands on her hips. "Well, he's much more mature than you, that's for certain."

He laughed. "Look, Liss, what do you want me to tell you? That, sure, Ty would be here because he lives here, too, but for this Nick to be here really means something? Is that it?"

"Well, don't you think so?"

"Hell, I don't know, Liss. I just got home! How am I supposed to know?"

Elissa felt her lip trembling. Certainly, one wouldn't think the decision between Ty and Nick would be difficult. She supposed it could be said that she had had nothing but a short fling with Nick, while she and Ty had sustained a relationship for two and a half years, despite the war and the ocean standing between them for a good part of that time. Besides that, Ty was a hometown boy, and Nick was a foreigner. It seemed simple enough to see which boy she should choose to marry.

The problem was that when Nick had kissed her just moments ago, she'd felt like she had finally found the one thing true in the world. True like spun satin, merry-go-rounds, the Fourth of July. An electric thrill had stirred under their skins when they'd touched.

Ty was pleasantly warm, but he wasn't electric.

Or was it all her imagination? How could a girl tell? When it was her life hanging in the balance?

"You all right, there, Liss?" said her brother.

Not wanting him to see the tears pooling in her eyes, Elissa hurried out into the hall and ran toward the back of the house, where a heavy door divided the family's quarters from the servants'. She had rarely set foot back there, but she wanted to be alone. She opened the door, slipped in, and shut the door behind her.

Her grandparents had not had live-in servants since almost before Elissa was born; the cold hallway smelled stale. Elissa flung open the first door on the left, and entered a shadowy room. Along one wall was a narrow wrought-iron bed, still made up with a wool blanket; a narrow chest of drawers stood against the other, next to an old washstand and basin. She crossed to the window and stood looking out. Rain had begun to fall, and the wind spattered cold drops against the window, combining with her tears to blur the vision of her father's car parked in front of her grandparents' garage, the avenue swooping down to First Street, and Mrs. Fryt's house across the avenue, forlorn-looking in the rain.

But then she saw a khaki figure with a duffel slung over his shoulder crossing the avenue, heading for downtown. He was small in the distance. She pressed her palm against the window. "Nick!" she whispered, watching as he kicked at a puddle, jogged a few steps to get out of the way of an approaching car, hopped up onto the curb below Mrs. Fryt's house, and kept walking, holding his head high as he disappeared behind the hill. "Nick," she whispered again, then she turned from the window, and ran.

"So, Dad," Harry said nonchalantly, lighting a cigarette. The hostility between his brother, Jack, and his father, John, was as thick as the smoke that hung in the office's air. Harry could tell he had come in in the middle of something, but he had something to settle with his father, too, and he knew the nervous feeling in his stomach wouldn't go away until he did. "Guess you didn't like Nick much, Dad."

John exhaled loudly from where he sat in the large wingback chair in the corner. "Like I keep telling your brother, he's not a good match for Lissa."

Harry leaned against his father's desk next to Jack, tapped his cigarette in the ashtray. "How come, Dad?" Harry said. "Out of curiosity."

"Isn't it obvious?" John said. "Chances are, he's just after our money. Ty's a much better match for her. A nice Pine Rapids boy." He nodded, confirming his own opinion.

"Still, though, Dad," Harry pressed. "Lying to Liss about it? Giving Nick that whole story about that Granton fellow? Seems a bit officious, even for you."

"You weren't here," John grumbled.

Harry paced across the room, leaned his elbow on the upper sill of the window, and looked out at the rain. Then he looked at his brother. "What did Nick tell you about his family, Jack?" he asked.

"What the hell, Harry?" John said. "Why the hell are you asking Jack about that? Lissa's going to kick him out on his ear the minute she comes downstairs. She would have done it already, if JJ hadn't gotten sick."

"What did Nick tell you, Jack?" Harry said.

"I don't really remember," Jack said. "Seems to me his mother was a widow. He was an only child. Said he never knew his dad, that he died just before he was born. He said his father was originally from Wisconsin, come to think of it."

"Hmm," Harry said, casting a glance at his father. "Overby. We know anyone with that name, Dad?"

"Shut up, Harry," John snapped. "Just shut up with your damn hotshot reporter questions. Nick is going to be gone the minute Lissa tells him she's marrying Ty. And everyone's going to be much happier. Thanks to my intervention! And you're going around pointing fingers and judging me, when you haven't been home in three goddamn years? Why don't you go spend some time with your mother, for God's sake?"

"That sounds better than spending it with my father," Harry said. He slammed the door on his way out, and headed for the kitchen.

Elissa raced through the upstairs hall and down the front stairs, reaching the bottom slightly off balance on her high heels. She might have toppled, had Ty not come around the corner of the curved banister just then and caught her by the elbow.

"Hi, Liss," he said. "I was just about to come look for you."

"Oh—hello, Ty!" she said. "I—didn't know you were here." Not quite a lie, but almost.

"Is JJ all right?"

"Yes, he's fine."

"Are you all right?" he said. "You look pale."

"I—yes. Yes. I was just wondering—did Nick leave?"

A shadow crossed Ty's face. "Yes."

Without thinking, she blurted, "Did he say why?"

"He just said he had to go."

"Oh," she sighed. She walked out of Ty's grasp and crossed over to the seat under the front window. She sank down onto it, and looked out over her shoulder through the rain-spotted glass. She could see down First Street a little farther from this angle, but Nick was gone. "I saw him walking away," she said. "When I was upstairs."

It was foolish of her to say that, and she knew it. She didn't know why she was being so foolish. She could feel Ty looking at her. Then he said, "What's going on, Lissa?"

"I'm sorry, Ty. I'm just—not myself. I—just—I'll be all right in a minute."

"He's that guy you met at that dance back before we started dating, isn't he? I couldn't think who else you might have known with an accent like that."

"Yes," she said, looking at her hands, which were folded in her lap. If she was praying, she wasn't sure for what.

"I thought he was engaged before."

"That was a mistake. It wasn't true."

She heard him coming closer, felt his presence as he sat down next to her. "Liss, were you—happy to see him?" he asked.

"I'm sorry," she said. She thought maybe she'd marry Ty on New Year's, after all, to make this foolishness up to him. What was the point of finishing her cadet nurse training, anyway, if she was just going to move back to Pine Rapids and start a family?

"I love you," Ty said. "I guess I don't have to tell you, it was the thought of you that got me back home."

"I love you, too, Ty."

"But I'll be damned if I'm going to keep you here if you're in love with him," he said. "I'll be damned if I'll have you stay with me just because you feel obligated."

"Ty?"

"I'm not an idiot, Lissa. I saw the look on your face when you came downstairs. When you saw me was the first time you thought of me. If I hadn't come out just then, you'd be halfway downtown by now, running after him."

"No, Ty," she objected. It sounded so awful, when he put it that way.

"If I wanted to, I guess I could ignore it. He's gone, right? I win! But I know I'd always wonder. So—tell me."

She looked up into the soft brown eyes that she had missed so much the past two years. And there was no magic there at all. There was comfort, yes, and even love—but there was no magic. There was nothing at all, compared to what she felt when she looked at Nick. "Oh, Ty," she whispered.

"It's all right," he said. "It's all right." And, very gently, he unclenched her fist and slid the engagement ring off her finger.

"Ty," she said. "I'm so sorry."

He clutched the ring in his fist, leaning back from her. "You'd bet-ter hurry, or he'll be gone."

"Yes. Yes!" She jumped to her feet, grabbed her coat off the coat tree, pulled the door open, and ran out, shoving her arms into her coat as she hurried down the porch steps, her heels clicking noisily, warm tears mixing on her face with the cold rain.

Harry was almost certain he was right, but the question was, how would he prove it? And, even if he could prove it, did he want to? Maybe Nick would leave, and then what would be the point of upset-ting everyone?

When he went into the kitchen and found Anne and his mother chatting as they finished up the breakfast dishes, he decided for sure that it would be best to keep his mouth shut. His mother seemed hap-pier than he ever remembered seeing her. Happier, and older, wispier than ever, too, so tiny that a good gust of wind might blow her away. A good reason just to let things be.

He went over to Anne, sneaked his arm around her waist, and kissed her temple, smelling her jasmine-scented hair. He immediately felt better. She asked what was wrong, and he told her, "Not a thing, now, sweetheart." At which point his mother chuckled, and said how nice it was to see Harry really in love with a girl. "I can't remember the last time," she told Anne. "It was probably 1924!"

"Mom!" Harry objected, conscious of the fact that that was the year Anne had been born. But Anne just smiled.

"All right," Wilma teased. Then her brow furrowed. "Do you think I should make more waffles for those boys? You said Ty is here now?"

"He is here," Harry confirmed. "But I'm sure there are plenty of waffles. They have to save their appetite for turkey, anyway, right, Mom?"

She still looked worried. "Would you go check for me, Harry?"

So he pushed the swinging door open and looked into the dining room. There was no one there. Two syrupy plates were abandoned on the table.

Harry started to get a bad feeling about things. He turned and told his mother that the boys weren't at the table, and that he was going to go find them. He gave Anne a wink, more lighthearted than he felt.

He walked out into the hallway, and reached into his shirt pocket for a cigarette, lighting it as he walked into the living room. Still, there was no one. He smoked. And then he heard a manly sniff from the front hall. He picked up his pace. When he came around the corner of the banister, he saw Ty sitting on the front window seat, leaning his elbows on his knees, hanging his head.

"Ty!"

The boy looked up. His eyes were watery.

"What happened?"

The boy held up a ring between his thumb and forefinger.

"Cripes!" Harry said. "Where is she?"

"She went after him."

Harry felt a headache coming on. "After him? After him where?"

"He left. Guess he was going to the depot, leaving town. I asked her what she wanted, and she went after him."

"Cripes," Harry repeated, his cigarette burning unnoticed in his hand.

> Married happiness can never be taken for granted. . . . You expect
> your husband to continue his efforts to advance in his field;
> similarly you should continue your efforts to improve in
> your job as housekeeper, mother, and wife.
>
> —"Making Marriage Work,"
> *Ladies' Home Journal*, March 1950

THE MICKELSON HOUSE
502 W. First Street, Pine Rapids
Friday, August 4, 1950

"Oh, poor Ty," Dolly sighed, leaning back against the porch railing, blowing out a long stream of smoke. The sun was at high noon; she was happily languid. "I'll bet he never recovered."

JJ smiled over at her. "I heard he's starting law school this fall. I think he's just fine."

"Oh," Dolly said, disappointed. She smoked, and looked out toward the Bear Trap.

JJ laughed. "You're such a little hypocrite."

"What?"

"You pretend you want the best for everybody, but what you really want is whatever makes for good gossip."

"That isn't true!"

"Uh-oh," JJ said, pointing his chin toward the avenue. "Speaking of gossipmongers."

Dolly looked. There was Mrs. Fryt, crossing toward them, the red zinnia atop her hat bobbing in time with her step. She carried a bundle in her arms. She was watching her feet as she walked, and proceeding slowly.

Dolly panicked. She was sure it had been more than an hour since she'd seen Mrs. Fryt coming home from the market—and she was sure Mrs. Fryt had spied her sitting on the porch steps with JJ. And now she was *still* sitting on the porch with JJ! What would everyone think when they heard that she had been lounging around on the porch all day with JJ Mickelson, eating doughnuts? She lunged for the ashtray and stubbed out her cigarette, then scrambled to all fours and crawled over to the door. JJ was watching her over his shoulder, laughing.

Well, he might not care what the gossips said, but Dolly wasn't enough out of her senses to have lost *all* concern. She reached up and twisted the door handle. "She'll expect me to be working," she whispered. She slipped inside (fortunately, the heavy oak door was open already, so it was only the screen door that she had to struggle with) and latched the door behind her. She leaned against it, trying to quiet her breath.

She waited what must have been a couple of minutes before she heard Mrs. Fryt calling. "Well, mercy me, it is you, JJ Mickelson," warbled the woman, adding, "I had to come see you with my own eyes before I'd believe it. Is Dolly still here?"

"Hello, Mrs. Fryt," JJ said. "Yes, she's inside working."

Bless him, Dolly thought.

"I brought you some tomatoes out of my garden," Mrs. Fryt said. "It hasn't been the best year for them, but we do what we can with what we have. Mercy me, those steps seem taller than they used to be."

"Thank you, Mrs. Fryt," he said. Dolly pictured him reaching out to take the bundle. "It's kind of you to walk them all the way over here."

"Well, I may not be a spring chicken," she said, "but I still do get around. If I could just have the towel back when you've unpacked them."

"Of course."

A pause. "I could bring them in the kitchen and unpack them for you. Maybe Dolly needs some help."

Dolly scrambled to all fours again, prepared to crawl farther into the house. *What chore could she pretend to be in the middle of?*

"That's all right, Mrs. Fryt," JJ said smoothly. "I'm sure Dolly's doing fine. Why don't I just unpack these right here? Line them up here so they can get a little more fresh air."

"Oh, but then you'll have to carry them inside one by one and that will take you so long with your—I mean, they ought to go in the ice-box, so they'll keep."

"Oh, now, Mrs. Fryt, these are still just a little green," he said. "My grandma always said that tomatoes were best when they were ripened in the sun. They had the most flavor that way, she said."

"Your grandmother," Mrs. Fryt grumbled. "Wasn't she afraid they'd spoil?"

There was silence a moment. Dolly relaxed, and sank back down into sitting.

Then, Mrs. Fryt again: "Besides, if you want sun, you'd better bring them around to the back."

JJ said nothing.

After a moment, Mrs. Fryt spoke again. "How is your grand-mother?"

"She's fine, thank you."

Dolly pressed her fingers to her lips. She had thought that Wilma was dead!

"Will she be coming back home?"

"I don't think so," JJ said.

"Are you planning to stay?"

There was a pause. "Not sure," he said.

"I see Dolly's been taking her share of breaks," Mrs. Fryt said. "There's lipstick on some of those cigarettes. Unless you have another woman here visiting you. You aren't married, are you?"

JJ laughed. "No, I'm not married."

"I didn't think so. Dolly said she was bringing you something from the bakery, so I supposed you didn't have a wife."

"Well, you supposed right, Mrs. Fryt."

"Are you sure I can't take those into the kitchen for you?" There was a clomp: She must have taken a step up onto the porch steps. Dolly sank lower behind the door.

"No, thanks, Mrs. Fryt, they'll be fine," JJ said. "Thanks again for bringing them over."

"Mercy me, JJ, don't bother standing up," she said quickly.

"Here's your towel," said JJ.

"Thank you," she said. "Well, I'm right across the street, if you need anything."

"Thanks, Mrs. Fryt," he said. "Thanks for coming over."

"Well, that's what neighbors are *for,* isn't it?" she proclaimed.

With that, she must have gone; there was utter silence. Dolly's breath felt heavy, and she tried to catch it.

Wilma was alive!

So why on earth wasn't she here in Pine Rapids?

There was a tapping next to Dolly's ear. She reached up and un-latched the door, pushed it open an inch, and put her face up to the opening. His face was there, on level with hers. "She's gone," he whispered, making fun of her.

Dolly blushed. His blue eyes were only inches from hers.

"Maybe you should come inside to finish the story," she whis-pered. "In case she's watching."

"Then she's probably seen you out here all morning already," he whispered back.

"Still," she insisted.

He shrugged, smiled. She let the door swing closed between them.

Pine Rapids
Thursday, November 22, 1945

The cold burned in Elissa's lungs as she ran. There was burning, too, in her eyes, her throat. Just the thought of what she'd done! Was doing! Running down First Street in the rain, choking back tears and laughter at once, the sound of the river rushing in her ears, the cold rain coating her skin, flattening her hair. Her legs cold, too, in the rain, and the heels of her fashionable, pinching black pumps clicking (pounding!) against the sidewalks, the streets.

If someone saw me—they'd think I'd gone crazy.

She screamed a little, to herself, covering her mouth with her hand. No one would hear, in the rain. Even if there was anyone around. Running past Shorty's Pub, she drew the stares of two men just heading inside. She paid them no attention.

What if he doesn't want me?

She crossed First Street, pain shooting up her leg when her ankle turned sideways for a moment in a puddle. But she went on, across the bridge, the Bear Trap rushing underneath her, giving her a sense, for a moment, that she might just fly away.

But where is he? I should have caught up to him by now.

North of the bridge, it was harder to run. This part of town had been let go, since the mill burned, all those years ago. The streets were gravel, not paved like the rest of the streets in town. She was reduced to a speedy walk, and tried to catch her breath.

What if I'm too late?

What if I'm wrong?

With the depot in sight, two blocks in the distance, she broke into a jog, wincing with every step at the pinching of her shoes. She could see a train waiting on the track, belching steam. She pushed herself to run faster. What if Nick was on that train, leaving?

THE MICKELSON HOUSE
502 W. First Street, Pine Rapids
Thursday, November 22, 1945

It was all Jack's idea to join the Marines.

So John was thinking as he sank into the chair at his desk and dug in the drawer for the bottle of whiskey he kept stashed there. He didn't require it often, but if ever there was a time for it, the time was now.

John's ears strained for the noise of Harry and Jack's conversation. Perhaps they were just outside the door. He didn't know, and didn't have the energy, just now, to go and find out. Harry had interrupted them—just in time, in truth. John had felt himself on the verge of giving in to Jack, of bending under the pressure of his heavy blue eyes. Of telling him the truth. Thank God Harry had come in time, rescued John—even as, John could see, he had John's destruction on his mind. Thank God Harry was a coward, though. Thank God he was the kind of child, still, who would do anything to try to please his parents. So John had glared at him, as if to say, *Don't you dare,* and thought to himself, even as Harry pulled Jack out of the office, *That should do it. He won't say a thing.*

He took a drink from the bottle, relishing the bitterness of the whiskey going down, shivering with it. Thinking, *It was Jack's will and not mine.*

He set the bottle aside and leaned his elbows on his desk, his head in his hands, and closed his eyes. Seeing his first son at that age when he'd been so anxious to prove himself. Jack! With the miraculous bloom of immortality in his flushed cheeks, from the time he was born, the sound of his squalling filling the whole upstairs of the house. The sound, startling as a gunshot, traveling all the way to where John waited in the front hall, pacing, smoking a cigar. His ears perked, his heart quickened. *Firstborn.* Not quite conscious of his own father, Knute Mickelson, on the window seat, smoking a cigar of his own, who smiled and said, "Congratulations, son. Sounds like you're a father!" Not quite conscious of his father's eyes on him as he tossed his burning cigar into the bronze cuspidor and raced up the stairs toward the blood smell of the birth.

And into the room, to see the boy (he had known, somehow, that this, his firstborn, would be a boy, *John Junior*) swathed in white and cradled in the maid Terese's arms, the boy with his eyes squeezed shut, beating his little fists against the air with an attitude of self-righteousness, impatience. This the boy destined to take John's name, *to be what I cannot.* The insistent sound of his wailing, as though stating, *I'll be the man of this house.*

And the boy did grow up brave, to all appearances; fearless, even. From his first steps, he ran, chubby arms flailing, hurling aside whatever happened to be in his way. And always he fought with his father: John's position as king of the house was tenuous. John didn't let on that he knew.

Little wonder that a bullheaded boy like that, grown to a young man, would rush to enlist when war beckoned, and would consider enlistment just as inexorable for his younger, more circumspect brother. John, despite his misgivings, had not protested against this particular bullheaded act of Jack's, not even when Wilma had put up a fuss. He was proud of his boys, after all.

But when Chase was killed, John couldn't help thinking: *It was all Jack's idea to join the Marines!*

Wilma didn't think any of the family had suffered Chase's loss as much as she. "He wasn't born out of *your* body," she had told John once. "You didn't feel how much it meant to him to *live*. How much he struggled, just to be born! Only to have what he had worked so hard for taken away! His very life, taken away!" Of course, John had had no reply; often, when confronted with Wilma's bitterness, he was struck dumb. She typically interpreted his lack of response as an aggravating stoicism, and would turn away in a huff.

He supposed she'd had a right to believe him heartless, all those years. It was 1940 before he cried with her, awakening in the hospital in Wausau after his heart attack with her looking at him so beseechingly that he broke down. To think, she had been with him all this time! And there was so much he had never told her! So much of their hearts that they had never revealed, though they'd lived under the same roof and shared the same bed for nearly forty-five years! And so, clutching her there in Wausau General, he had vowed to start anew, now that he had been granted a second chance. Indeed, it was thought that he had *actually died* for at least an instant. His heart had *stopped beating,* then, miraculously, had started again.

He couldn't help but ask God: *Why save me, an old and bitter man, and not my son so many years ago who had his whole life in front of him?*

An old and bitter man who for the last twenty-seven years has betrayed everyone he loves (yes, loves, though sometimes he doesn't know how) and even now betrays not by a lie so much as by an omission of the truth?

Pine Rapids
Late June and early July 1918

John went back to work the day after the telegram came. He had a bank to run, after all, and there was nothing more they could do until they received the letter, which he presumed would tell them not only the circumstances of their son's death but the whereabouts of his body, which they would then make arrangements to bring home. On his lunch hour, John went to the Pine Rapids Cemetery office and paid cash for plots for Chase, himself, and Wilma.

The first three nights, Wilma refused to sleep. She stayed downstairs in the kitchen, winding balls of yarn. Each night, Harry sat with her very late, leaning forward in the chair next to her with his elbows on his knees and her skein of yarn around his wrists, while she rolled and rolled and rolled the yarn into ball after ball after ball. "The kid's exhausted, Wilma," John told her, when he came down for a glass of milk. "Why don't you let him go to sleep?"

"I'm not chaining him here," she snapped, not looking up.

Wilma had insisted they not tell anyone in town about the telegram. "Not until we know for sure," she had said, that first night, after Dr. Seguin revived her. But with Dr. Seguin, the folks at the bank, and George Schwartz down at the cemetery office, word got around. Casseroles, breads, hams piled up outside the door. When after some days their neighbor Mrs. Fryt knocked with a freshly baked pound cake, saying how sorry everyone was to hear about Chase, Wilma snapped, "Thank you, but I don't believe he's dead," and shut the door in her face. Mrs. Fryt proceeded directly to the bank and left the pound cake with John's secretary, Florence, who came right in to tell John what had happened.

"Mr. Mickelson, sir," Florence said, in her gentle Southern accent, "I know it isn't my place to say so, but don't you think your wife needs you a sight more than this bank right at the moment?"

Florence had been with him only since the previous October. She had been the most experienced of the applicants for the position, having been business assistant to her husband until his death in December 1916. But because this experience led her to think she knew something about local commerce, and because she had a tendency to say exactly what she thought, she could be an exasperating employee. Whereas John's previous assistant had taken dictation with a near-scientific exactness and a clipped "yes, sir," Florence would offer accent-honeyed criticism: "You might ought to say 'diligent' there; 'hardworking' sounds trite." The first weeks of her employ, John was (in his recollection) constantly on the verge of terminating her—the unabashed way she corrected him, as though she were the one who had been in banking her entire adult life!

So it was little surprise that she would march right into his office and tell him what he needed to do for his wife.

"I'll handle her in my own way," he told her, not looking up from his papers.

"Handle her! Begging your pardon, sir, but she isn't a horse! And she's just lost a son."

"I'm well aware of that fact," John said, and looked up to fix her with a stare.

This time, she actually backed down. Unusual. "Well, all right," she said. "Would you like a piece of this pound cake from Mrs. Fryt?"

For Florence to placate him with food was not unusual. He'd been putting on weight since she'd started working for him. The problem was her cinnamon rolls. Her husband had left her childless (she often spoke of how she envied Mr. Mickelson's fine family) and she seemed to view baking as the most significant act of creation of which she, a forty-year-old widow, was capable. John couldn't complain. There was nothing that lifted his spirits in the morning better than walking into the bank to the smell of her freshly baked rolls.

Sometimes, he imagined her alone in her small house in Pine Rapids, where she had recently made her home after years living upstairs above her husband's shop in nearby Victor. Imagined her standing in her dimly lit kitchen each evening mixing flour, sugar, milk, lard, egg, yeast, in a crockery bowl, patiently stirring in the last of the flour a sprinkle at a time. Imagined her with her pink hands, shaping the dough into a ball, covering it with a bright towel, washing her hands clean of the flour, putting away her apron, turning her back on the covered dough left there next to the sink overnight to rise. Imagined her removing the pins from her old-fashioned champagne blond hair and letting it fall to her shoulders. She was tall, ample in all the right places.

And he could imagine the next morning, the way she would come into the kitchen in her robe and slippers, hair tied with a ribbon at the nape of her neck, and uncover the risen dough. He could see her rolling it into a rectangle, lovingly drizzling butter in long yellow swoops like the earliest streaks of morning sun, then sprinkling white sugar crystals like snow across the whole landscape; finally, tap-tap-tapping the cinnamon shaker and watching the cinnamon collapse against the heat of the butter. Then, carefully, rolling the dough into a cinnamon-striped cylinder; slicing the cylinder into small disks, placing them into the pan to bake. There was no anger and no duty in her labor as he conceived of it.

For there was no anger or duty in any aspect of Florence that John could see. Some might have been bitter to have their husband taken from them in the prime of life, but Florence simply said she was grateful for the good years they had had. "I knew when I married him he was ten years older. And a Yankee, to boot. Still, it came as a surprise, so soon. But I reckon he'll always be part of me. We were married twenty years." So she would say, brushing a strand of her hair out of her eyes, turning to the file drawer to clean out, reorganize, alphabetize.

"A rolling stone gathers no moss," she always said.

John agreed. He threw himself into his work with a renewed zeal, arriving early in the morning and staying late into the evening, buoyant atop his ledgers, correspondence, meetings, like a ship on a stormy sea. Not until he stepped out of the bank each evening into the suppertime-quiet street and started trudging west toward the sinking sun and the house on the hill would he realize how heavy his feet were, how his eyes burned.

When the letter from Chase's commanding officer arrived, it was almost a relief. It said that Chase had done his duty bravely and had brought honor to himself and the Marine Corps. It said he had died when his company had led the attack on Belleau Wood. It said he was interred near the battle site along with the thousands of others who had died, and even now were dying as the battle for the woods continued. It conferred the heartfelt sympathy of the officer and the United States government.

"Well, there you have it," John told Wilma, and tried to take her in his arms. She broke away, glaring at him, and ran upstairs. He heard a door slam. Jinny and Harry stood before him like limp dolls, Harry watching his foot kicking at the floor, Jinny gazing up at John with eyes like a rolling blue storm, her lower lip trembling. Under her gaze, his knees wobbled. He reached out tentatively and cupped his daughter's little face in his big hand, watching her as a tear broke free of first one eye and then the other. None of them said a word. Finally, Jinny broke his gaze, and stepped into the parlor. John could hear her winding up the phonograph. He listened as the needle dropped and the popular martial style of tune filled the air.

Though you're leaving me today never fear
In my thoughts you'll always be ever near
There's a tear in every eye as the boys go marching by

John crossed the room quickly, went out the front door, and stood on the porch, his arms folded across his chest. He tried to catch his breath. The song wafted out through the screens.

So your mother old and gray waits to hear
I will comfort her each day never fear
We all love you and you know
That we're proud to see you go
But we're going to miss you so over here . . .
When you've won your victory
God will bring you back to me
Au revoir but not good-bye, soldier boy.

A final flourish, and then, for a moment, the empty sound of the silent record rotating steadily round and round. Then nothing at all, just the sound of leaves rustling in the summer breeze, the Bear Trap babbling in the distance.

It was the fifth of July when a letter arrived from Jack. John was back at work after the forced holiday of the day before—he and Wilma had spent the day at each other's throats, and she had refused to go see the fireworks. John had taken Jinny, and Harry had gone off with his friends. John was glad to be back at work, and only wished it wasn't a Friday. Maybe he would spend tomorrow at the creamery on the pretense of checking up on things.

Florence came rushing into John's office that afternoon, waving it in her hand. "Mr. Mickelson! A letter from your son! From Jack!"

He jumped up, holding out his hand, greedy. *He could still be dead,* he reminded himself, but his relief, his joy, was overwhelming. He snatched the envelope from Florence. And there it was, Jack's handwriting: *Mr. John Mickelson, First National Bank of Pine Rapids, First Street, Pine Rapids, Wisconsin.* John flopped back into his chair, tore open the envelope. The letter was dated June 16, and read:

Dear Mom and Dad,

I am writing with terrible news. We have been in a battle. The first day, Chase's company was one of the first to attack enemy positions. I moved closer to the front on the second day. On the way there, I saw some of the boys from Chase's company who were wounded moving toward the rear. They told me that he had been killed. They said that he was charging a machine gun nest with some others and was shot several times at once. They said that he was killed almost instantly. It was terrible to think I had not been with him. But I tell you, in the days since, I have exacted a revenge several times over on his behalf. We have been relieved now but will go back to the front again. I regret having to tell you this. I only hope that this will reach you before you hear in another way. I am sending this letter to you directly, Dad, in hopes you can break the news to Mom more gently than I can. Cannot write any more now. Chase was one of several hundred killed that day. I am sorry. We will not give up until we have taken this area. Give Mom and the Kids a hug from me,

Your son, Jack Mickelson
USMC, 2nd Div., 4th Brig., 5th Regt.,—Machine Gun Co.

"What does he say?" Florence said.

"I—" John said, and found that he couldn't form words.

"I understand," she said. "I'll leave you be." He watched her walk out. The door clicked closed behind her.

She left him undisturbed until the close of the day, not even transferring phone calls into his office. When she poked her head in to say she was going home, he was sitting at his desk staring at a ledger through a glaze of unshed tears. "Mr. Mickelson, I—" She stopped when he looked up at her. "Mr. Mickelson, are you all right?" she said, sliding into the room and shutting the door behind her.

Confronted with such tenderness, he couldn't hold in a racking sob.

"You poor man," Florence said. She crossed the room quickly and pulled the drapes shut behind him. It wouldn't do for the town to see John Mickelson not in control of himself. She stood next to his chair, rested her hand on his shoulder. "Isn't it good news that Jack is all right?"

His sobs worsened.

"Oh, dear," Florence said.

"I don't—" he choked. "What if he's—? We got a—Chase!"

"Now, now," she said, patting his shoulder.

"Got a letter from Chase—" he said, "week after he was dead. He was dead!"

"You poor man," Florence said again.

He reached out and clutched her about the waist, pulling her close, pressing his cheek between her breasts. She smelled of cinnamon rolls and powder, starch and a rosy perfume.

"Mr. Mickelson," she said gently.

He only clutched her tighter. After a moment, he felt her hand settle on the back of his head.

"Oh, my," she said afterward, quickly covering herself. She moved her leg around him and slid down off his desk. She turned her back to him and began straightening her clothing, buttoning up her blouse.

"I—I have to apologize," he said, tucking himself back into his pants and zipping up. "I wasn't myself." He fastened his belt. "It won't happen again."

She looked over her shoulder at him. "I know. It was my fault, too." She paused, looked away.

He tried to straighten the papers they'd crushed into disarray on his desk. "This won't affect your employment here in any way," he said. "We'll just pretend it didn't happen."

"Yes," she agreed, straightening her skirt.

He had been entirely helpless, he told himself as he walked home that evening. He was too wrought-up, not in his right mind. Crazy with grief and the need to prove that he lived, that he felt, that the blood was rushing through his veins. *What's done is done, but I'll be a better husband from now on,* he promised himself. It was a Friday evening—he had all weekend to prove it.

But Wilma was cold to him when he arrived home, sniping at him for working late again. When he told her about the letter from Jack, she first attacked him on the point that he had not told her about it immediately, and then, after a moment, began sobbing to the point that Harry almost called Dr. Seguin again. "Don't you dare!" she managed to choke out, slamming out the kitchen door. They watched in the dusky light as she ran to and collapsed in the earth of her untended garden. Harry moved as if he would go after her, but John stopped him with a hand on his shoulder, and told him, with more certainty than he felt, "Just let her be, son."

All that weekend, she wouldn't speak to him. When he approached her with a soft hand on her shoulder, she glared at him like he was trespassing on her private property. Saturday night, when he rolled over in bed and touched her hip to kiss her good night, she snarled, "Don't touch me." Sunday, she got angry with Jinny for playing the phonograph too loudly and dumped neighbors' casseroles onto the kitchen floor.

He was relieved when it was Monday morning and time to go back to work. He walked into the office to the aroma of Florence's fresh-baked cinnamon rolls, and that evening, after everyone else had gone home, despite all of his declarations to himself that he would *never again,* he laid her back on his desk and shuddered with the pleasure of her, wallowing in her sweet fleshy comfort. The way she smiled when he entered her, the way she met his every thrust! Crowning him again a king!

He was weak, he knew it. Rutting with her like a teenager. She enjoyed him more than Wilma ever had; every time he saw her, he tingled with it. Got careless, cupping her breast in his hand even when she came into his office in the middle of the day with customers and employees milling about in the lobby. He was invincible—no one would ever find out, he was sure.

One night, after another screaming fit of Wilma's, he went out for a walk, and found himself at her house. When she opened the door to his knock, her astonishment was plain.

"Can I come in?" he asked.

And so they had one evening of unabashed, naked pleasure in her soft widow's bed.

"I've got to stop this," he moaned as he lay back, spent, on her pillow, as she rested in the crook of his arm, tracing circles on his chest with her fingernail. "I'm getting—addicted! To you!"

"But sometime soon," she said, matter-of-factly, "you won't be needing me no more."

John and Wilma found out that they would not be able to bring Chase's body home, at least not for some time. The area where he had been buried was too close to the fighting, still.

But they started to bring flowers once a week to his Pine Rapids grave, where they'd put a simple marker. John would stand awkwardly towering over Wilma, who crouched to pull stray weeds, to replace last week's flowers with fresh ones. Harry and Jinny would stand off to the side a little, Harry kicking at the ground, Jinny complaining, "This is dumb! I don't see why we're here! He ain't *here*!"

"John," Wilma said one day, gazing up at him over her shoulder with such fathoms of emptiness in her eyes that his heart stopped a moment, and then out flooded his whole love for her, his desire to protect her, care for her, love her with all his heart as he always had, truly. "Do you suppose that he's really dead? All this time I can't help but think we're—just going through motions. Do you suppose he's really dead?"

John found he couldn't speak. A moment passed. She turned from him, and went back to pulling the weeds.

THE MICKELSON HOUSE
502 W. First Street, Pine Rapids
Thursday, November 22, 1945

Jack was relieved when Harry came into their father's office and pulled him out of what was turning into a nightmarish stalemate. With a panicked look, Harry explained that Elissa had broken off her engagement with Ty and gone chasing after Nick.

Jack nodded. "I guess I'm not surprised," he said, though he felt sorry for Ty. Getting dumped the minute you got back was almost worse than getting a "Dear John" letter while you were gone.

"But we've got to stop her!" Harry said.

"What's the matter with you, Harry?"

"Let's talk in the car," Harry said. "Come on, hurry. Get your coat."

"I'd like to tell Mary if I'm leaving," Jack said.

"We don't have time," Harry said. "Come on."

Puzzled, Jack followed along. He couldn't remember ever seeing his brother look so grim, but he couldn't imagine what Harry's concern could be. They went out the back door, Harry calling out to Wilma and Anne that they would be back soon.

"Now, what is it, Harry?" Jack said, once he was behind the wheel and had the car in gear. "What's all this fuss you're raising? You hardly met Nick." He turned on the wipers to combat the rain. "Where to, by the way?"

"The depot," Harry said. "Here's the thing, Jack. You wouldn't remember, because you were away at the war. But Dad had this secretary. Florence. I remember because it was right around the time that we found out about Chase, and Mom was nutty, and I was always trying to get out of the house, right? And sometimes I'd go down to the bank and hang around with her. She always brought in good stuff to eat. She made the best cinnamon rolls."

"What does this have to do with anything?" Jack said, stopping at the stop sign. No traffic, so he turned right onto First Street.

"Her name was Florence Overby, Jack," Harry said. "I swear I'm remembering it right. And she was from Tennessee. Had a nifty accent. And here's the thing: She was a widow. Her husband had died already. And she didn't have any children, I know for a fact. Because she used to say how much she wished she did. How much she wished she had a son like me. The thing is, it makes sense. Dad trying so hard to get rid of Nick, you know?"

Jack hardly noticed that the car was slowing down; he'd forgotten to keep pressing down on the gas. He looked at his brother, and their eyes locked. "Jesus, Harry. You're not saying what I think you're saying, are you?"

"I'm not a hundred percent sure," Harry said. "But close to ninety-nine. She left that fall. Went back home to Tennessee, as I recall it. To be closer to her family, was the story. I remember because I sure did miss those cinnamon rolls."

"So she could have been—"

"Pregnant," Harry said. "Cripes, I don't like to think it, but—did you notice how much he looks like us, Jack? How much he looks like Chase? Even the smile, for God's sake?"

"Thought it was a coincidence," Jack mumbled.

"And why else would Dad have gone to such lengths to get rid of him the first time?" Harry said. "If you think about it, it makes sense."

Jack clenched his jaw.

"We'd better hurry," Harry said. "We have to tell them. If we can find out his birthday, then we can figure it out for sure."

"Yes," Jack said, and pressed his foot down, felt the car responding.

"Dad will never admit it," Harry said.

"It will kill Mom," said Jack, swallowing back the bile that had risen in his throat. "If it's true."

PINE RAPIDS DEPOT
Thursday, November 22, 1945

Nick was getting comfortable in his seat aboard the train, and counting his blessings that he'd happened along at just the moment one was leaving for Milwaukee. He'd figure out how to get home from there; the important thing was, he wasn't going to be hanging around Pine Rapids a minute longer than necessary. Then the man in the window seat elbowed him and said, snickering, "She doesn't look half bad, for a drowned rat."

Nick looked where the man pointed, then looked again. There, approaching the train across the platform, limping a little, her coat flapping open over her sweater and skirt, her hair flattened to her head by the rain, was the girl he'd been certain he would never see again. The expression on her face was one of bewilderment, exhaustion. And a lingering hope.

He leapt to his feet, grabbed his duffel off the floor, and rushed down the aisle, just as the train lurched and began to crawl forward.

"Soldier," said the conductor, blocking the aisle. He had eyebrows like caterpillars. "Don't even think about getting off this train."

Nick pushed past him, and hurried to the door. In one motion, he tossed out his duffel, rushed down the two steps, and jumped. He landed on his hands and knees on the platform, and yelled from the pain in his knee.

He heard footsteps running toward him, and her voice: "Nick!" she cried.

He couldn't help grinning when he looked up and saw her. She landed on her knees next to him and threw her arms around him. "Nick, are you all right?"

"I reckon that isn't the most graceful thing you ever saw," he said, as he put his arms around her and pulled her close. He could hear the train behind him, picking up speed. The whistle blew. Her rain-dampened hair felt like silk under his hand. "You're all wet, sweetheart."

She leaned back from him. "I ran all the way here," she said. "Ty let me go and I ran all the way here. He knew that I loved you, Nick. He could tell just by looking at me."

His heart beat in tandem with the train as it accelerated, pulling away from the station. He kissed her. When he leaned back from her briefly, the train was gone, and all was quiet, except for the gentle sound of the rain.

Shortly, hardly noticing the cold rain running down his collar, Nick reached into his pocket for the black velvet box. He opened it, extracted the ring. "Are you certain?" he said.

"Yes."

So he slid the ring onto her finger, and took her in his arms and kissed her again. The rain on their faces and hands melded as they touched, and he couldn't exactly tell where he ended and she began.

A moment later, there was shouting from across the platform. Nick let Elissa go and looked up. There was her father, running across the platform toward them, followed closely by his brother. "Lissa! Lissa! Nick!" they shouted.

"Here we go again," Nick grumbled. They stood up; he slid his arm around her waist. Jack and Harry reached them, and stood before them, puffing, looks of horror in their matching blue eyes.

"What's wrong, Dad?" Elissa said.

"Hope you don't aim to keep this up after we get married," Nick joked. "Every time I kiss her, you come flying around the corner."

"Nick," said Jack. "What's your birthday? What month and year?"

At least Jack wasn't giving him a hard time about kissing Elissa, so this could be considered an improvement. "April sixteenth, 1919."

Jack and Harry didn't look pleased. "Count back nine months," Harry muttered to Jack. "It's July 1918. Right after Chase died. She was working for him then."

"Christ," said Jack, his eyes crunching.

"What's the matter?" Nick asked.

"What's your mother's name?" Harry said.

"Why?"

"Just—what is it?"

"Florence Overby."

"You're her only child?"

"Yes, sir."

"Who's your father?"

"Benedict Overby. He passed on a couple months before I was born."

Harry shook his head. "Your mother's tall for a woman, right? About five foot eight? Blond hair? She'd be in her sixties now?"

Nick squinted. "You knew my mother."

"She worked for our father," Harry said. "After your father died. Jack was gone at the war, but I remember her."

"What do you mean?" said Elissa.

"That can't be," Nick said. "My momma went home to Dover just as soon as my daddy died."

Jack silenced Harry with a quick gesture. "We need to ask Dad," he said.

"Ask Grandpa what?" insisted Elissa.

Nick had a bad feeling in his stomach, looking at the two brothers. He noticed for the first time that their eyes looked the same as those he saw in the mirror every day. Harry's jaw was the same shape as his own. But that didn't mean anything—did it? His mother had told him stories of Benedict Overby until Nick could recite them backward: the day she had met him at her mother's boardinghouse, their wedding day. The day she'd told him she was expecting Nick. "Your daddy loved you so much, Nick, and he would've been so proud of you!" she had always told him, and he had grown up knowing it to be true, and talking to his father, like other kids might talk to God. Looking up at the sky, knowing his every move was under surveillance. "Just like your daddy," his mother would say sometimes, shaking her head at him with a gentle smile, like when he ate too much pie and upset his stomach or went out to get the mail and came back an hour later without it. "He was always doing that," she'd say.

"He'll never admit it," Harry muttered.

"Be quiet, Harry," Jack said. "Let's just go home."

Nick blinked. The rain dripping down his collar was unbearably cold.

"What are you talking about, Dad? Uncle Harry?" said Elissa.

"Let's go home, Elissa," Jack repeated, looking at his daughter, shepherding everyone back toward the car.

THE MICKELSON HOUSE
502 W. First Street, Pine Rapids
Thursday, November 22, 1945

By the time the boys came in and asked him about it, John was drunk, and still taking frequent small pulls of whiskey from the bottle on his desk.

He denied it, of course.

"Liss is all set to marry him, Dad," Jack said. "She broke up with Ty."

John looked at his sons through bleary eyes.

"We need you to tell the truth, Dad," Jack said. "If he's your son, Lissa can't marry him."

Harry listed the evidence. The timing. The resemblance.

"You're delusional, Harry," John spat. "Accusing me of such nonsense. You think I'm the type of man to cheat on my wife? Is that what you think of your father? If that's what you think of me, you can get out of my house!"

With a glare at John, Harry slammed out.

Harry had always lacked Jack's courage, John reflected, satisfied, basking in his own drunkenness for a moment. It had been years since he had really been drunk—he couldn't recall the last time. He was appreciating the warm glow, the soft edges it gave to everything, when Jack spoke up.

"He's not saying anything illogical," he said, using the level voice that John hated. "We just need to know the truth. No one is going to judge you. It's so long ago. But—think of Lissa, Dad."

John looked at his son. Thought of all the years they'd spent working in the same office and never really knowing each other. Thought of Jack as the little boy, the willful teenager, he'd been, always so bent on tormenting his father. Pitiful to think that that brave boy had grown into this gray-haired, tired-looking man standing in front of him.

"It was your fault," John blurted. "All the pain you caused your mother. All the pain you caused me!"

Jack's brow furrowed. "What?"

"You heard me, Jack Mickelson," John said. "Why didn't you look after your brother? He never would have gone, if it weren't for you! Why didn't you look after your brother, for God's sake?"

A moment passed, father's and son's blue eyes locked in a dueling gaze, before Jack finally spoke. "He is your son, isn't he?" he said. "You fucked your secretary and used Chase as an excuse. Jesus Christ, Dad."

"Not an excuse!" John objected. "A reason!" Then a great hiccup burst from his lungs, and he felt his face turn scarlet. *I'm losing,* he realized suddenly. "You don't know what it was like!" he cried, though he knew he was dissolving into a pathetic creature, before his eldest son.

Jack shot him a withering look, turned from him, and walked out, slamming the door behind him.

John looked at the closed door, and his vision blurred. He knew he had come to the end of something. *So, Jack, you've done it.*

I always knew this day would come.

He took another bitter drink.

So they knew. And they would take everything from him. Elissa, and the sweetness in her that he treasured. And Nick, the only one of John's sons truly innocent in John's fall. The reason for it, yes, but— not his fault! And though John had done his utmost to keep Nick away, now that the truth was out, he wanted his son. He wanted to claim him, and bring him close. But it was a foolish thought: He knew the boy would never forgive him.

Besides, Wilma would hate him for it.

He felt a flare of hope: If he just let Nick go, and suffered the pain of that (as in truth he had suffered the pain of it once already, putting Nick on the train after midnight that February night in 1943, telling himself, *I am saving my family, I must sacrifice him to save the rest*), maybe Jack and Harry wouldn't tell her. They'd realize that everyone had suffered enough.

But who could tell what they might do, now that they held sway over him. His utter destruction might be the only thing that would satisfy them. And they would need only to tell Wilma.

He would explain to her! But: Would she believe it true? That, if there was lust, it had been only the product of his grief? (Perhaps, *perhaps* it was a primal instinct, in the face of death: to create, without even knowing the creation is desired! Without rationally desiring the creation at all!) And she had been so distant, had offered him no comfort at all. Surely she would recollect and acknowledge her own complicity in matters?

I sent her away, Wilma, he imagined telling his wife. She would forgive him! Such a long ago, isolated transgression. *I sent her away and never even thought of her again!*

That wasn't true, he realized, taking another drink.

He had, in fact, thought of the woman often, the first years after she had gone, wondering if what she had told him was true. Or if her sob story had been only a clever plot. Maybe she had known he was done with her; clearly, she had figured out how to get some of his money. People were always trying to get his money. He had finally convinced himself that she was a swindler, and he had been taken— seduced and taken advantage of in his grief. He had done nothing wrong, had been fortunate to survive that whole ugly patch of his life, in fact. He was not dishonorable, he had decided. It was she who was the scoundrel, taking advantage of him—a good family man—that way.

After a few years had passed, he had not thought of her much at all, only rarely, when a slant of the sun across the ledger open on his desk might remind him of a long-ago afternoon, and he would shudder with pleasure and regret.

But then: Nick. Nick Overby. One look at the boy (the man—he was nearly twenty-four years old by the time John first laid eyes on him, in 1943) and John knew.

You see, Wilma, I didn't know. For the longest time, honestly, I couldn't be sure. I didn't know that I had a son!

FIRST NATIONAL BANK OF PINE RAPIDS
101 W. First Street, Pine Rapids
October 1918

It is a glorious Friday in early October, the leaves golden on the trees, the sky a crisp, bright blue. John is closing his ledger, straightening his desk, about to call it a day so he can get home in time for a quick supper and then head out to see Harry's football game. Harry is just a sophomore, but he's already receiving for the varsity team, and tonight is their second home game of the season. It does John good to watch his son out there on the field, watching the fluid motion of his arms, legs, the determined square of his chin. John secretly thinks that Harry embodies the best qualities of his older brothers: Jack's dogged determination, Chase's ease and grace. But he would never tell Harry as much, and keeps pushing him for *more more more*.

Just two weeks before, they had received a letter from Jack that said, *I hope you get this letter from me before you get the telegram from the War Dept. I was wounded at St Mihiel, but don't worry a bit, it was only a slight wound (in my arm, and I didn't lose my arm) and I'll be right as rain in no time. I'm at the hospital now near Paris but expect to rejoin my Regiment in a matter of days. Don't worry a bit about me.*

"Oh, how *could* they send him back to the front when he's been wounded?" Wilma had said, pressing her knuckles to her mouth. But, overall, she'd taken it better than John had expected. Everyone at church had heard, of course, and that Sunday a line formed at the Mickelsons' pew, each person consoling and encouraging, telling John and Wilma how proud they were of the boys. Wilma had shaken hands, accepted kisses on the cheek, hugs, pats on the shoulder. "If there's *anything* we can do, Wilma—just ask!" the women had said earnestly. John had been proud of the way his wife met their eyes, the very picture of the sad, brave mother.

It was, in truth, a load off their minds to know that Jack was safely in the hospital for a time, away from the front. He'd been in danger all summer. John had nearly laughed with glee, reading that the wound had been a minor one. "What luck, what luck!" he'd exclaimed, waltzing Wilma around the kitchen, until she, too, miraculously, laughed.

"Perhaps that's the worst that will happen to him!" he had told Florence, who gave him a sad smile.

"I do hope so," she'd said, softly.

This crisp, bright October evening marks the three-week anniversary of the last time he broke his marriage vows with Florence. Just as she predicted, he feels less need for her now. Though his loins still tingle when he sees her, he has, these last three weeks, been able to control his desire. He has not so much as touched her, though his hands admittedly ache to, and she, seeming to sense the change in him, has kept her distance, too. He is just thinking of this, congratulating himself on his restraint, on conducting an affair that remained a secret and ended with his secretary still in his employ and not a thing the worse for it, when there is a brief knock at the door and her head peeks in.

"Can I see you for a minute?"

"Certainly," he says, keeping his tone professional. He shrugs into his coat. "I'm just on my way, though. Harry has a game tonight."

She shuts the door behind her. He looks at the curve of her neck, the way her hair curls up from it into a swirling chignon, and hopes she does not plan to try to seduce him, for just with that glance he knows he would not be able to resist.

He watches as she walks quickly across the room and draws the drapes shut with two quick motions. He steps back. "I—I shouldn't. I'm trying not—"

Her eyes are sharp when she turns to him. "I just need to talk to you. Sit down."

He obeys, watching her as she casts her eyes down, folding her hands in front of her waist. She is truly lovely, he thinks, her dress a tailored midnight blue, her ankles slim for a woman her age.

"I told you I had something personal to attend to this morning?" she says.

"Yes?"

"I went to the doctor in Wausau. I've been suspecting it for some time now. I'm going to have a baby."

He clenches his fists open and closed. "What?"

"That's right."

His eyes flash nervously toward the door.

"Everyone's gone home," she says.

He gets to his feet. "I thought you had that all taken care of. I mean—aren't you a little old?"

She laughs, looks away, her face flushed.

"Christ," he says. "This can't be happening. Are you sure it's mine?"

"Yes."

"Well, we'll just have to get it taken care of. Did the doctor in Wausau give you any place you could go?"

Her eyes flash in anger. "John Mickelson! I will not!"

He crashes his hand through his hair. "Well, you can't have it. It's as simple as that."

"I will have it!"

"Was this your plan all along?"

"No! Good Lord! What do you think I am? I—" She turns her back to him, folds her arms. "I thought I was barren. All those years, with Ben. Nothing. I thought it was me." She sighs. "And, like you said, I'm not as young as I was."

"How could you have let this happen?"

She turns to him, livid.

"Well, naturally, I thought you would have taken care of it."

"I told you. I didn't think there was any chance."

He flops heavily into his chair. "Well, you can't have my baby. Not in this town. It's as simple as that. I won't ruin everything I've worked my whole life for."

"I had a suspicion you might say such," she says. "But I told myself, well, people can surprise you sometimes, Florence. So that's why I'm giving you the chance to do the decent thing."

"The decent thing? What, in this case, is that?"

"To claim your baby, of course."

"Good God, Florence! I can't! Don't you see? My wife—"

"You might should have thought of her before."

"I won't acknowledge this child," he says. "He'll be a bastard. You can claim I'm the father and I'll deny it till I die. Who do you think everyone will believe?"

"He will not be a bastard," she says, measuring each word carefully. Tears have begun to leak from her eyes. "He'll be the child I've always wanted."

John leans over his desk, rests his head in his hands. He can smell her perfume, formerly so intoxicating. Now the smell makes him nauseous. "Leave this town," he says. "If you ever cared for me at all."

"You rotten dog," she exclaims. "If you'd ever cared for *me,* you wouldn't ask such a thing."

He looks up at her. "I can't leave my family," he snaps. "And you have the power to ruin me, thanks to your carelessness. I'm on my knees here, begging you. Do the right thing."

"I don't see you on your knees," she says, tears streaming from her eyes. "And what about you doing right by me? You left that part out."

He is a man who will do what he must. Slowly, he slides down out of his chair and sinks to his knees, turns toward her. Takes her hand in his and presses it to his cheek. Looks up at her with sorrowful eyes. He can see her softening toward him, can see her trying not to. "Please, Florence," he says, infusing his voice with emotion, fear masquerading as regret. "You have no family here, no connections. If you stay here, your reputation will be ruined, too. Everyone knows your husband died almost a year ago. Go somewhere and start over with your baby. Your baby that was conceived just before your husband tragically died? You want me to do right by you? I'll give you money. As much as you want. That's all I can do, honestly. Just, please, Florence—don't ruin me. You know I wasn't myself—I was crazy with grief and—"

"Oh, hush," she says, wiping her tears from her cheeks with the back of her hand. "Believe such if it makes you feel better. You and me both know you're just a rotten dog. I'll take your money. More than that, I have no need for you, and neither does my baby."

She pulls her hand from him and crosses to the door. He struggles to his feet. At the door, she turns. "Mr. Mickelson," she says in a clipped voice. "I'm giving you my two weeks' notice. My sister down home is sickly and she needs my help looking after her children. I'll need that money before I go." With that, she is gone, slamming the door behind her. He sinks into his chair, and is assailed with an image of a grinning towheaded toddler. He shakes off a swooning crush of disappointment, wipes his hand over his eyes. Squares his shoulders, stands, and leaves the office to go home to his family.

THE MICKELSON HOUSE
502 W. First Street, Pine Rapids
Friday, August 4, 1950

"Maybe I shouldn't be here," Dolly fretted. They were sitting in the parlor, on opposite ends of the sofa. The room was cool and dim, as the sun was just beginning to make its way around to the western sky and filter in the side window. "Mrs. Fryt warned me I'd only get into trouble. What will people think? That I'm an awful wife to Byron. Or—something worse, I don't know!"

JJ waved that off. "I wouldn't worry. Besides." He winked at her. "You're only here to get the dirt on my family."

"That is not true," she objected. "I wanted to help save the house!"

"Yes, yes," he teased her. "And you've done a lovely job, Dolly."

"But, now that you mention it, JJ—"

He laughed.

"I didn't know that your grandma—that Wilma—is still alive! Where is she?"

"In Stone Harbor, with my mom and dad," he said. "Our old summer place. They live there all the time now."

"Why on earth would she leave this house behind like that?"

"That's what I'm getting to," he said, narrowing his eyes.

Looking at him, she felt a spark of something deep within her, something that was dreadfully wrong to feel about a man who was not her husband, and her breath caught.

But then she reassured herself: It wasn't JJ, really. She liked him—was attached to him, even, in a friendly way. She wanted the best for him, hoped he would stop drinking, and find direction in his life. All of those things were true. But what had really captured her was the house, and the story of JJ's family. And Dolly had asked for the story, had asked JJ to spin a pseudo-fantasy of the past and this house for her, in lieu of facing her own reality, in lieu of going home to her own little bungalow and the problems in her own little family.

She decided then: She would stay to the end of the story, and then she would go home. Honestly. And face reality! Give up the idea that the Mickelson house could refine her marriage. Somehow work on bridging the distance between her and Byron. Stop seeking excitement in inappropriate places. Grow up! Convince Byron to take her out for dinner occasionally, or even fishing. Not that she liked fishing, but someone had to make a compromise, and if he meant as much to her as she kept telling herself he did, it might as well be her.

"Nick was my grandpa's son," JJ said.

Dolly's heart seemed to stop; her worries flew from her mind. "What?"

"That's why it was so funny about him not believing in the curse," he said. "Because that was what did him in. Cheating. It did my grandma in, too. They tried to keep it from her, but she found out."

THE MICKELSON HOUSE
502 W. First Street, Pine Rapids
Thursday, November 22, 1945

Wilma stepped out of the kitchen, wiping her hands on her apron. She had just basted the turkey, the potatoes were boiling, the yams were in the oven, the rolls were rising, and the gelatin salad was made. The pies—pumpkin and apple—she had baked yesterday.

She left Anne watching things, and thought she would go check on JJ. She wondered if he would have any appetite at all, if he would be able to come downstairs for dinner.

She started down the hall, but stopped when she heard hushed voices. Her sons. Talking in the living room. They sounded upset. She clutched her apron in her hands and stood listening.

"Did he admit it?" Harry said.

"More or less," said Jack. He sounded angry.

"So I was right? His secretary?"

There was a thud, like someone had kicked something. "He said if I hadn't dragged Chase off to the war to be killed, it never would have happened."

Wilma pressed her fingers to her lips. *Steady, steady,* she told herself. "Goddamn him."

"We're going to have to tell Nick," Jack said. "And Lissa."

"Let him tell Nick. Make him be the one to tell!"

"He's drunk."

Drunk? John? Wilma thought. *For heaven's sake!*

"I'll bring him a cup of coffee," Harry growled. After a moment, he sighed. "I'd like to keep it from Mom—I mean, she doesn't need to know, right? At this point?"

Wilma's ears perked. She began to put together what they had been saying. *His secretary. Nick. Wouldn't have happened if Chase hadn't been killed.*

But—how could it be? Her breaths were coming shorter. *I thought of Chase when I looked at him, yes, but—*

"I'll tell Nick," said Jack.

Harry exhaled in a quick puff. "I'll go with you," he said. "I'm his brother, too."

For a moment, everything before Wilma's eyes seemed to go white, and she staggered on her feet, pressing her hand to the wall to keep herself from falling. She leaned against it, gasping, as though she had forgotten how to breathe. Before her eyes it seemed that all the days of her life became distinct, and scrambled to line themselves up in rank and file, scattering their truths like dust. She saw Chase's little smile. The garden. Her knitting needles, skeins of yarn. Jinny tossing her hair. Harry sprawled on the football field, his knee twisted out of shape, his face betraying his howling pain. John waltzing her around the kitchen. The broken jar of pickles.

And she remembered Florence Overby, the woman's face popping into her mind, as clear as day after all this time. A woman she would not have known that she remembered. But she did. And, though she had been half out of her mind at the time, she remembered now all those nights, around the time Chase was killed, when John had worked late. He had said he was busier than ever, with the war, but she had known: He just didn't want to be around her. And now she knew, there had been Florence Overby.

Anger filled her like water from a spout, anger for all her wasted days and years of guilt, when her sin had not been actual so much as imagined. Rage that, compared to what she had suffered as a result of her sin, John, who bore the true shame, had not suffered a thing. She untied her apron and yanked it off over her head, throwing it to the floor. It landed with a soft *pflump,* but she had already left it behind, striding out into the living room. She saw Jack and Harry ahead of her, walking reluctantly toward Nick and Elissa in the parlor. She passed between them like a speedboat between two ships, and rushed directly to the piano, scarcely noticing Elissa and Nick, who were seated together on the sofa.

The cover over the piano's keys creaked as she lifted it and pushed it back out of the way. She touched the cool ivory, then surrendered her hands to the Sonata Pathétique—it was still in her mind, after all these years. She did not hear Jack and Harry calling to her, saying, "Mom, Mom, are you all right?"

"Cripes, she must have heard us, Jack!"

And then we knew immed., Elissa would write, much later, in her resurrected diary. *Just the look on Dad's and Uncle Harry's faces. Grandma coming in that way. (I'd never heard her play before! She'd always said it was something she used to do, before she disc. that she was nothing more or less than Mom & Grandma. & now here she was before us, a livid virtuoso.) N. and I looked at each other with absolute horror, & he pulled his hand from mine, as quickly as one pulls off a Band-Aid to keep the pain sharp and swift. I literally felt my heart exiting my fingertips, cleaving to his hand when he took it away. Absolute and utter disbelief. Grandma's music like a tirade. I couldn't take my eyes from N.'s. Heartbreak everywhere. Heartbreak like drowning.*

John lifted his head up off the desk when he heard the music. Wilma had not played in years.

So she knows, he thought immediately. *They've told her. It's the end.*

He leaned his head in his hands a moment, then rose slowly from his chair. He was a little wobbly on his feet to start, and had to lean on the desk to steady himself. It had all been speculation, before, what he might say, what she might do. But now, knowing that she knew what he had done, what he had kept from her these many years, he felt a sudden, certain conviction. He could not face her. He would not. Nor Nick. Nor Elissa, nor the rest of them.

He didn't make a sound, sneaking out through the living room, down the back hall, grabbing his coat and hat off the peg near the back door. His keys were already in his coat pocket. Quietly, he went out, blinking to clear his quivering vision as cold air and then cold rain hit his face. He stumbled down the back porch steps, then tip-toed across the snow-speckled yard to the old carriage house that had, over the years, held his father's various lacquered buggies and sleighs, then his own first Model T, on up to when he had become a Packard man, about fifteen years ago. He supposed the kids' old bi-cycles would still be up in the rafters, though he had never looked for them. That was the thing with continuity—you took it for granted that nothing would ever change. You felt you didn't have to fight, just to keep things the same, and you didn't find out how wrong you were until it was too late.

John unlatched and swung open the doors; they creaked on their hinges in the damp air. Rubbing his temple with his thick fingers, he made his way into the dark depths of the garage, along the side of his Packard Eight. The car—the only Packard in this town where most men drove Fords and Buicks—was so long that its nose came within a whisker of brushing the carriage house's front wall, while the back bumper scarcely fit inside the doors. John pulled open the car door and slid into the driver's seat. He inhaled deeply of the car's comfort-ing scents, flexing his hands on the steering wheel. This car, the sixth Packard he had owned, was a 1941 model. Like everyone else, during the war years, he'd had to live with what he had, but now he was glad. The car was a familiar old friend, a comfort in a harrowing time.

Soon, he was speeding west on Highway 46, the soothing purr of the Packard's motor vibrating under his skin, rain spattering the windshield, the road weaving before his eyes, the taste of wet metal in his mouth. He pressed the gas pedal closer and closer to the floor, imagining that maybe, given the right combination of acceleration and sheer will, he could fly.

THE MICKELSON HOUSE
502 W. First Street, Pine Rapids
Friday, August 4, 1950

"How long did Wilma play the piano?" Dolly asked.

JJ shrugged. "Hours, I guess. I don't know. I could hear it, though, from upstairs. I listened to her all afternoon, past dark." He sighed. "Meantime, I guess Nick still didn't believe it. I mean, he'd grown up his whole life believing this Ben Overby was his dad. You can understand it'd be hard to change your mind all of a sudden."

"What did he do?"

"Well, Uncle Harry got the bright idea they could try to find this Ben Overby's grave. So they could really prove it, you know. Nick knew he was buried up by Victor, and he said his mom was a Methodist. So my dad drove him and Harry and my sister around the county all afternoon in the rain to all these little cemeteries, until they found it."

"And?"

"Sure enough, good old Ben had died in 1916. Not 1918, like Nick's mom had said. There it was, carved right in stone. There was no way he could have been Nick's dad."

"Oh," Dolly said, pressing her hand to her mouth.

"So they dropped Nick off at the depot on the way back home."

"They made him leave? Just like that?"

JJ shrugged. "He insisted on it, I guess."

"Didn't he even want to face your grandpa? To get him to admit he was his father?"

"It seemed pretty clear Grandpa didn't want anything to do with him. I guess Nick didn't want to make matters worse than they already were, for Lissa's sake. But, man, when they came back to the house without him, she didn't stop crying for about three hours. Mom and Dad and Harry kept trying to calm her down, telling her it was for the best that he'd left and all. And meanwhile, here's Grandma in the parlor just playing that same sonata, over and over for hours."

"What about your grandpa? Where was he?"

"He never showed back up, so they ended up going out looking for him. They brought Liss over to her friend's house, and they brought Grandma with them. They had to practically drag her away from that piano, I guess. But they thought maybe she'd know where he'd gone. My dad called up his buddy the sheriff and got the whole county started looking for Grandpa."

"Who stayed with you?"

"Anne. She volunteered to take care of me. It turned out she had kind of a thing for me." He grinned, and reached for a cigarette. "Who could really blame her?"

Dolly raised her eyebrows. JJ decided for sure then: He would tell it his way, and make Dolly think the best of him.

Never mind that, if Anne told it, she might say something different.

THE MICKELSON HOUSE
502 W. First Street, Pine Rapids
Thursday, November 22, 1945

Anne proceeded up the front stairs carefully with a loaded plate held aloft in each of her hands. It had seemed a shame to let a whole Thanksgiving dinner go to waste, and JJ had said he was hungry. So was she, to tell the truth. She'd spent most of the day in the kitchen, smelling the turkey roasting, and hadn't eaten since breakfast. Now it was past seven, and it had certainly been a strange day. Not that she would have been hungry if she were in any of the rest of the family's positions, after what they'd found out, but, being a newcomer, she was afforded the luxury of a child's innocent carelessness. And she would keep it that way as long as possible, selfish though that was. In truth, she hoped to avoid future visits to Pine Rapids altogether. Harry wasn't himself when he was here, and the rest of the family . . . Well, she didn't like to judge, but, suffice it to say, she'd have quite some stories to tell to Linda and Janice when she got back home to Superior.

"Now," she said, as she walked into JJ's room, "I didn't give you a whole lot, because I didn't know how much you'd be able to eat. But I can always get seconds for you, all right?"

JJ was sitting up in bed, propped on a pile of pillows. He smiled. "Thanks," he said, reaching out to take the plate from her.

"Do you need more water?" she said.

"Whiskey," he said. "If you don't mind."

She laughed. "Think again," she said.

"Please?"

She sat down in the big chair over by the window. "Well, after you've eaten," she said. He was an adult, after all; she supposed she shouldn't treat him like a child.

He smiled at her, and picked up his fork.

"Are you sure it won't bother you if I eat with you?" she said.

"Hell, no," he said. "Glad for the company."

"This house is just too big," Anne said, shivering a little. "I can't get used to it. It feels so lonely with no one else here." She took a bite of her mashed potatoes.

"So they went out to look for Grandpa?" he said.

"Yes," Anne said. "Can you imagine what's happened? Your poor sister!"

"Nick's gone?"

"Yes."

"My uncle!" JJ said, laughing. "Half, anyway."

Anne shook her head. With her plate resting on her knees, she cut her turkey into bite-size pieces. "I don't see how you can laugh about it. It's awful. I can't imagine what your grandma's going to do. After all these years, to find that out!"

JJ shrugged. "Well," he said, "it isn't the worst thing I've seen, I'll put it that way."

She looked up at him. "You saw a lot of action, didn't you, in the war? Harry was telling me. What battles were you in?"

"Well, since you asked," he said. "The Canal. Tarawa. Saipan. And Iwo."

"It's a miracle you made it home at all!"

He shrugged. "Well, it makes you wonder sometimes. Why you and not the guy next to you. I think about that all the time."

"My brother says the same thing," Anne said. "And I tell him, there has to be a reason."

JJ laughed. "I don't think there's a reason for anything in this world. Life and death is just a matter of inches. Of luck."

Anne frowned. "I don't see how you can live like that," she said. "Don't you believe in God?"

"Sure, I believe in God, America, and the United States Marine Corps. Only not in that order."

"Do you wish you had been killed?"

"If I'd wanted to die, I would have," he said. "Look, Anne, for almost a year now I've been having surgeries and lying in a hospital bed and learning to walk again. Living again inch by inch. It's not like it comes back automatic. That's what I mean. Dying's a matter of inches, and so is living."

She studied him. She decided that perhaps he had lost his mind. But then, perhaps he was saner than she; she was so naïve. Perhaps he had seen life for what it was. "I'm sorry," she said finally.

He stabbed a slice of turkey. "Don't waste your time," he said. "I wouldn't trade being a Marine for anything."

Anne picked up her fork again. Her hand was trembling.

"The only thing bad about it, really," he said, "is knowing that a girl like you would never look twice at me now."

She looked up. He was looking directly at her, and she blushed. She was certain she must have mistaken the tone of his voice. "That isn't true," she said.

He raised his eyebrows. "You'd look twice at me?" he said. "At a freak like me? A half-man like me?"

She didn't know what to say. "I—"

"If you weren't engaged already, I mean," he said, with a sly smile. "Be honest."

"Well, you're very handsome."

He laughed.

"Besides, you're not a 'half-man,' as you call it. You're missing part of one leg, that's all. A lot of boys came back a lot worse off than you. A little while longer, you'll be perfectly healthy, walking around on your prosthesis, and I bet you'll hardly notice it! And neither will any girl who's got half a brain."

He just looked at her, a curious little smile on his face, as he chewed another bite.

"I mean it," she said again. She wasn't hungry anymore. She set her plate down on the floor and stood, turning to look out the front window at the dark. Raindrops sparkled on the outside surface of the glass, catching the lamplight from the room. She could see JJ reflected in the window, too, the image of him bending and breaking in the drops of water, could see and feel him, watching her.

After a minute, he took his eyes off her and went back to eating. She could hear his fork clinking against the plate. "I think you're lying," he said then, between bites.

She turned to him. "I'm not," she said.

"Look, Anne, it happened just on my way home yesterday. This girl looking at me all hot and bothered, until she realized my leg's gone. And that's the first time I've been out in the world since it happened. I just mean, my prospects aren't looking so good."

Anne folded her arms, embarrassed. "Well, maybe not every girl, then, JJ. Or maybe she'd have to get to know you first. I'm not saying that no one would be bothered by it."

"But you wouldn't?" he said.

"I don't know."

He smirked. He set his plate on the bedside table, grabbed his pack of cigarettes. He lit one.

"I just don't think it's hopeless, that's all," she said quietly, still uncomfortable. "Is that all you're going to eat?" she said, to change the subject. He had left more than half of the food she had given him.

She took their dirty plates downstairs, washed up what dishes there were, and put the food away. They'd hardly made a dent in the turkey, and there wasn't room for it in the refrigerator, so she wrapped it up well and set it on the back porch, checking to make sure the door to the outside was latched tightly to keep out any hopeful raccoons.

As she slipped back inside the kitchen, she realized she had not put the picture of JJ's blue eyes and arch smile out of her mind the entire time she'd been downstairs. She shook her head, and went to scrub the sink. She hoped that Harry would get back soon. She should have gone with him, she realized. She was going to marry him, for goodness' sake—she should be at his side. And there was something about JJ that frightened her, even as she felt his strange magnetism pulling her closer.

She scrubbed and scrubbed at the sink, the counters, the stove top, as though she could scrub off the tracks he had already made on her, as surely as if his fingertips had walked across her skin.

If I ever get out of this place, I'm not ever coming back, she thought. *Not with Harry, not at all. Ever.*

She was in the living room, just finishing reading an article in an old *LIFE* magazine about Jimmy Stewart's experience in the Army, when there came a loud banging from upstairs. She tossed the magazine onto the table and jumped up. "What is it? What's wrong?" she called, as she ran upstairs.

"Can I get that whiskey?" JJ called. "It should be in the cabinet in the dining room."

She stopped, turned around, and stomped down the stairs, found the bourbon and poured an inch of it into a tumbler, then went into the kitchen and filled the rest of the glass with water. Then she marched back up the stairs.

"You really had me worried, you know?" she told him when she went in. "All that banging and carrying on."

He shrugged. "I got strict orders from my nurse not to get out of bed."

She handed him the drink. "Well, perhaps we'll have to get you a bell," she said.

"Wanna play cards or something?"

She shrugged. "All right."

She pulled her chair up to the edge of the bed and beat him soundly at gin rummy. She was probably helped by the fact that he had her go downstairs to bring up the decanter full of whiskey, and kept pouring himself liberal drinks, not bothering to water them down. He began to get a flush in his cheeks, and laughed when she beat him a third time. He maintained that poker was his game, and when she wouldn't accept his challenge to play, he accused her of being chicken.

"You can say it," he said, grinning. "You're afraid of me."

"I am not," she said. "I just don't like playing poker."

"A likely story," he said, reaching for the decanter again.

"Don't you think you've had enough?" she blurted.

He raised his eyebrows at her, then shrugged as he poured himself another drink.

She sat on her hands, couldn't meet his eyes.

Just then, the telephone rang. Anne jumped up and ran downstairs to answer it. She was relieved to hear Harry's voice.

"Anne, sweetheart," he said. "We found Dad. Crashed into a stump at the side of the road out on County B."

"Is he all right?"

"We're at the hospital now. He's still unconscious. They're doing some tests."

"Oh, Harry, I'm so sorry."

"It's all right, sweetheart," he said. "I just wanted to tell you not to worry. I'll be home as soon as I can, but don't wait up, all right? Jack and Mary are here, too, and they already called Lissa and told her to spend the night at her friend's house. Are you doing all right? Is everything all right there with you and JJ?"

"Everything's fine."

"All right, sweetheart. I'd better go, then. I'll see you as soon as I can, all right?"

"All right."

"I love you. Sleep tight," he said, and then the line went dead.

Anne held the phone to her ear a moment, and then, when she was sure there was nothing more there, she replaced the handset gently in its cradle.

"Cripes," said JJ, when she told him, which reminded her of Harry. She was feeling so lonely she could hardly bear it. If she had known how awful this day would be at the Mickelsons', she would have stayed home in Superior and had a nice Thanksgiving with her own family. Though she knew that what had happened wasn't Harry's fault, she couldn't seem to help being a little irked that he had brought her here.

"Is he going to be all right?" JJ asked.

"I don't know anything more," Anne said.

JJ reached for the decanter again.

She folded her arms, wanting to stop him; telling herself it was none of her business, really.

"It helps the pain," he said, and when she looked at him, she saw he had sensed her discomfort.

She pursed her lips. She took a step backward, ready to excuse herself and go back downstairs.

"Make you a deal," he said, taking his hand off the decanter. "You give me a back rub, and I won't have another drink. My nurses always give me back rubs. You give your patients back rubs?"

She had told him about her Red Cross volunteer work. Still, though, she felt strange about his request, and pressed her crossed arms to her stomach. "Well, I'm not really a nurse."

"Oh, I bet you'd do fine," he said. "It sure would help my pain, too. Probably a lot better than a drink." He raised his eyebrows appealingly. "Deal?"

She hesitated.

He reached toward the decanter again, slowly, eying her.

"All right," she agreed, finally. She was responsible for him, after all, and if he was monstrously drunk when everyone got home, they probably wouldn't be too happy with her.

He grinned, and immediately pulled his T-shirt off over his head. She drew in her breath at the suddenness of it. His chest was smooth, and he was very thin, but his arms were wiry. On his biceps was a tattoo of a coiled snake, and the words DON'T TREAD ON ME. Everything below his waist was hidden under the sheets; if she hadn't already known his leg was missing, she wouldn't have been able to tell that there was anything the matter with him at all.

He grinned at her. She forced herself to stay calm as she assisted him with moving out of the way some of the pillows he'd been leaning on, and soon he was settled, lying flat on his stomach. She stood at the side of the bed, and reached toward him.

His skin was hot and dry, and his muscles gave way easily under the pressure of her fingers. He groaned with pleasure, which made her flush, but she kept on, moving her hands from his shoulders and neck down to the middle of his back, down to his waist, and back up to the middle again. She found herself watching the curve of his ear, noticing the little pinpricks of hair on the side of his neck where it had been shaved away and now was growing back.

She made herself look away.

"Do you mind switching that lamp off?" he said drowsily. "It's more relaxing with it off."

She obliged him, hoping that he would soon go to sleep. The door to the hall was partly open, and the light from out there cast a wedge onto the floor. Otherwise, all was dark. The only sound was the rain on the windowpanes.

After a few minutes, she removed her hands from him. "I'll let you get some sleep."

He rolled over onto his back, and propped himself up on one elbow. She could see his eyes shining. "Please don't leave me alone, Anne," he said, and he reached out and found her hand in the dark. "I don't like to sleep alone." He laughed a little. "Can't stand to be alone. Haven't been alone in so long, except on some damn nights when the guy next to me got killed and I didn't find anyone else till morning. Doesn't exactly make you feel good about being alone, you know?"

Her stomach felt nervous. "Would you like me to sit here in the chair next to you until you go to sleep?"

He tugged gently on her hand. "Sit down next to me, would you?" He sounded as scared and willful as a child. "My nurses always sit with me."

Anne was skeptical. "They sit on your bed with you?"

"Yes," JJ said.

He sounded so sincere that Anne didn't question him further. Carefully, she sat down on the edge of the bed next to his hip. She could almost feel the gaping space behind her where his leg should have been. He hadn't let go of her hand.

She told herself there was no need to be frightened. "You'd better get some sleep now," she told him. "You'll feel better in the morning."

"Can I ask you for one more thing?"

"What's that?"

"A little kiss good night?" he said, sounding sheepish. "I mean, like the way my mom used to kiss me good night, on the forehead? So you know that you're not alone?"

Anne considered the matter. She thought of Harry. Finally, she decided there could be no harm. And she felt sorry for JJ: This was his first night home, and his whole family had deserted him. "And then you'll go to sleep?" she said.

"Scout's honor," he said.

She bent over him, and kissed his forehead.

But as she began leaning away, she felt his arms sneaking around her, his hand pressing against the back of her head. Next thing she knew, her lips were touching his and she could taste the whiskey on his breath as he kissed her.

His hands were gentle, yet for a moment she felt strangely powerless but to stay where he held her. Then she collected herself, tried to pull away. "JJ—" she said.

"Please, Anne," he whispered, still holding her tight. "Please just kiss me. I've been so lonesome. You don't know what it's been like."

He pressed his lips to hers again. She strained against the hold he had on her, but her straining was as gentle as his kiss, and she could feel herself losing the battle. Her sympathy for him burbled like coffee in a percolator. *Just one kiss won't hurt anything, I guess,* she told herself. But when he stopped kissing her, he still clutched her close, and spoke with his lips brushing against her face, his breath hot on her skin.

"Did you know tomorrow's my birthday? Three years ago on my birthday was when I saw my first action. I saw my friends die."

She tried to pull away. "JJ—"

He held her fast. "The minute this weekend's over, I've got to go back in the hospital—"

"JJ, I'm sorry—"

"You're so nice, Anne, and you said you didn't mind about my leg."

"I don't, but—"

"Please," he said. "You don't know what it's been like."

It hadn't been easy for Anne, either, losing Bobby, but she didn't think that gave her any right to try to make anyone feel sorry for her. She had fallen in love with Harry because he hadn't tried to coddle her. He knew that everyone had their heartaches, and that there was nothing to be done about them except to keep moving forward. "I'm sorry," she said, still trying to pull away from JJ, trying to be gentle and not hurt his feelings. "I'm sorry you've had a bad time. But I'm not that kind of girl."

"Just kiss me again. Nobody would ever have to know."

"No, JJ," she said, and she managed to sit up.

But as she tried to stand, he sat up, grabbed her waist from behind, and pulled her back down on the bed. He buried his face in her neck, and kissed the spot where her neck met her shoulder. She shivered despite herself, and, while her defenses were down, he somehow pushed the sheets out of the way and pulled her down on the bed next to him. Then he was on top of her, kissing her, his hand creeping up under her sweater.

"JJ," she exclaimed, trying to push him off of her. He was too heavy, even though he had angled his body so she couldn't feel the place where his leg ended; with his good leg, he had pinned her. She was trying not to panic, but she could hardly breathe. She managed at least to shove his hand away before it reached her breast.

He stopped for a moment, and leaned up to look into her eyes. "Do you think you could ever love me, Anne?"

She gasped. "What?"

"I think you could," he whispered, leaning down to kiss her lips. She tried to twist her head away, but he pressed her face with his hand to get her mouth to line up with his again. "I really think you could. Even if maybe you don't know it right now." He kissed her again, and shifted his weight a little, so she could breathe.

"Stop it, JJ," she pleaded. Turning her head away again, she tried to appeal to his conscience. "You can't do this, JJ. I'm going to marry Harry. Your uncle!"

"Maybe you just thought you were supposed to meet Uncle Harry. Maybe you really only met him so you could meet me."

She shook her head. "An hour ago, you said you didn't believe there was a reason for anything. Let me up now."

He kissed her neck. "Maybe I was wrong, an hour ago."

She was getting desperate. She thought if she could reach the bed-side lamp, she could knock it over his head, weaken him enough so he would let her up. But when she tried to reach back over her shoulder for it, he sensed her movement, and pressed her arm back down, gentle but unyielding.

"I'm not going to hurt you, Anne," he said. "I'm sorry I'm being a little selfish, but—you won't laugh at me if I tell you something?"

She tried to appease him; he had sounded sincere. "What?"

She could see his rueful smile in the dark. "You're the first girl I've kissed in four years."

She swallowed.

"And you're the most beautiful girl I've ever seen in my life." He touched his lips to hers, and whispered, "So can you forgive me?"

She nodded once, despite herself. "But you really need to let me go now."

"Please don't make me," he said. Then he raised his head and looked in her eyes. "Will you at least let me hold you?"

The thought made her tremble, but it was clear that he wasn't going to let her get away without her granting him something. "If you get off me, I will lie here next to you until you go to sleep," she conceded, trying to console her outraged conscience with the idea that she was merely comforting a troubled veteran. A sort of extension of her Red Cross duties. It didn't stop her trembling, but after he rolled off her, she was able to take a couple of deep breaths, and she felt a little better.

He curled his body in close to hers, pulling the sheets and blankets up, tucking them around their waists. He lay down, his head an inch away from hers on the pillow. He reached out and touched her hand where it rested on her stomach.

"I'm not really sleepy," he said. "Can we talk for a while?"

He told her about his long journey home from Iwo Jima: the hospital ship, Hawaii, California, the woman on the train to Pine Rapids. After some prodding, she finally told him about her war, and when she talked about Bobby, embarrassingly, she started to cry.

He propped himself on his elbow to wipe a tear from her cheek with a gentle swipe of his thumb, and looked down on her with concern.

"I'm sorry," she said, propping herself up a little. "I haven't any right—when you've been through so much—"

He shook his head, and touched her face. "That doesn't seem to matter right now. When I'm with you."

For just a moment, she closed her eyes, loving his soft touch, the sweetness of his words. But she caught herself, shook her head, and tried to sit up. He stopped her. And when he kissed her again, she found herself kissing him back. It was as though her loneliness had taken a baseball bat to the backs of her knees: She'd lost her footing, lost all sense but pain and the crushing need for immediate succor.

Less than an hour later, Anne was folding her sweaters into her open suitcase on the bed in the guest room. She felt like she was in a nightmare. The rain outside, the spooky glow of the hall light and the guest room lamp, which even together couldn't combat the darkness in the chilly house. And the persistent recollection: "Just a little?"

"No, JJ!"

"Please, Anne?"

"Stop it!"

And yet: her fault, for letting it go so far. Drunk on loneliness, grief; relishing the comfort of such closeness, of knowing he was lonely, too. She let it go too far! Him saying, "I swear I'm in love with you. Marry me instead." A shock! Her body, beyond her control, everything spinning, him on top of her, pinning her. Could she have thrown him off her? Why didn't she try again to reach that lamp? Senseless! So afraid to hurt his feelings! His gravelly whisper in her ear. His warm breath. Letting it go so far!

Until finally all she could do was bear his weight. He would do what he would.

It was too late but to bear the consequences.

But when it was over: horror. That she had lain back and borne it! Not voicing the objection that she had felt in her soul. Not even screaming from the pain. Just bearing it! Unforgivable.

She could never marry Harry now. She couldn't stand for him to know what she had done.

The minute JJ's breathing had slowed, she'd wriggled out from under him and left him sleeping, dressing herself with trembling hands, tiptoeing out of his room, into the bathroom to try to clean herself up. She couldn't look at her reflection in the mirror; the sight of the blood made tears come to her eyes. When the worst was taken care of, she went across the hall into the guest room. Harry had shown her there when they had arrived, just last night. He had kissed her at the threshold of the door and bid her good night. Thinking of it now, as she packed her suitcase, made her want to choke.

"Anne?"

Anne looked up from her sweaters and saw JJ standing there in the door, leaning on his crutches, the wrapped stump of his leg protruding from his shorts, his clean T-shirt a bright white in the lamplight. His hair was mussed and his eyes were narrow. He was pouting like a hurt child.

"Anne, what are you doing?" he said.

"I'm leaving." She blinked to keep her tears at bay, smoothing her gray sweater atop the others in her suitcase. Her whole body was trembling.

"Anne," he said, coming closer, swinging his weight on his crutches. "Don't leave. Please."

She stood absolutely still, gazing down at her hands pressing flat against the folded sweater in her suitcase. She had already removed her engagement ring and put it on the bedside table, and her hand looked empty and sad without it.

"Look, Anne," JJ said. "I'm sorry. I really am. But I'm not sorry, too, because I meant everything I said."

She took a deep breath; it took everything she had not to start crying. "You did not."

"If I didn't, then why don't I want you to go, Anne?" His voice was frantic now.

"I don't know."

She heard his crutches clomping across the floor toward her, and then he was at her side. "Please don't leave me, Anne," he said. "I never thought I'd meet a girl like you who'd even give me the time of day."

She could no longer hold back her tears. She wiped them away with the flat of her fingers as they fell. "I can't stay here." She reached across the bed to pull her pajamas out from under the pillow where she had left them that morning—a lifetime ago.

"Anne," he said. "Don't go. I'm telling you, I've been lonely my whole life, and that's the truth. And all of a sudden, with you, I wasn't lonely anymore."

"You were just trying to get me into bed with you," she said. She closed her suitcase, zipped it.

"Look, Anne, I never—for God's sake, would you listen to me? I—all right, maybe at first I was just—well, look at you, you're goddamn Rita Hayworth here, and I've been—all right, so I was—just at first, but once I got to know you—"

"As the saying goes," Anne said, "fool me once, shame on you." She picked up her suitcase. "Fool me twice, shame on me." She dodged around him, and walked out of the room.

"Don't be like this, Anne," he called after her, his crutches clomping on the floor as he followed her out. "Please. Won't you at least give me a chance? I know I'm not—whole. But I really felt—that you—that you might love me."

She had made it to the top of the stairs, and glanced back at him. He looked miserable. But after what he'd done—to have the nerve to insist that she love him!

She wanted to hurt him the way he had hurt her. So she said the worst thing she could think of. "It's your leg," she said. "I couldn't bear it."

Devastation filled his eyes.

She turned from him, rushed down the stairs, grabbed her coat and hat. She burst out the front door into the cold rain, sobbing now, flailing down the steps to the sidewalk, puddles soaking her shoes and splashing her ankles as she turned toward downtown and the depot, clutching her coat to her chest, her suitcase bumping her knees.

Very few of us know just why we like the people to whom
we are attracted; our likes and dislikes are not rational or planned.
The people we like are not always the folk that the social
scientist would recommend for us as companions,
either for a lifetime or for a few months.

—*When You Marry*, 1948

THE MICKELSON HOUSE
502 W. First Street, Pine Rapids
Friday, August 4, 1950

He omitted certain details, and told Dolly only that Anne had lain
with him on his bed and offered comfort. Kisses on the eyes and such.
Of course, both he and Anne had wanted to go further, but they were
stopped by the strength of their respect for Harry, though Anne whispered to JJ that she'd been in love with him from the first moment she
saw him. She was just too honorable to break her engagement.
Though he would have liked to fight for Anne, he, too, had done the
honorable thing and let her go. She had insisted on it, and he cared
for her enough to respect her wishes. She left that night because she
couldn't bear to feel the way she did about him, when she was obligated to marry Harry.

His voice cracked when he told Dolly that part.

"Why, you really loved her!" Dolly said.

He was standing at the parlor window, looking out at the fir trees basking in the sun-drenched August afternoon. He shrugged, and blew out smoke, wishing he hadn't mentioned Anne at all. He didn't know why he had. "Well, that was a long time ago," he said, trying to extricate himself from his lies. He lifted his cigarette to his mouth, and smoked. He felt a little better, then, and exhaled. "Besides, I was an idiot. To even imagine a girl like her—when she just felt sorry for me, that was all."

"Goodness," said Dolly. "You are an idiot, JJ. Of course she loved you! A girl doesn't say all that just because she feels sorry for you."

JJ remembered the look in Anne's eyes when she told him she couldn't bear it about his leg, the look on her face as she packed her suitcase to leave him. Then he took another drag of his cigarette, and grinned. "Well, maybe she was just a more sympathetic girl than you."

Dolly rolled her eyes and reached for the pack of cigarettes he'd left lying on the coffee table. She drew one out; he crossed to her with his lighter and lit it for her. He let his wrist brush hers again, liking its warmth.

"So, are she and Harry together now?" she asked, leaning back on the sofa. "Or did he find out how she felt about you?"

JJ stubbed out his cigarette in the ashtray on the table. He limped around and sat down on the opposite end of the sofa from her; his leg was getting tired. He was getting tired all over, and he didn't like thinking about the letter that he had received from Anne a couple weeks after he got to the Great Lakes Naval Station Hospital.

He narrowed his eyes. "Look, Dolly, you'd better not tell anyone about this. Especially those damn church ladies, or else the whole town will know. Anne would never forgive me if she knew I'd told anyone."

"I won't say anything," Dolly assured him.

He fixed her with a glare.

"Don't worry!" she said.

He leaned back on the sofa, folding his hands across his stomach and taking a deep breath. He felt like he'd just run an obstacle course with someone shooting live ammo over his head.

Dolly leaned forward to tap the ash from her cigarette into the ashtray. He watched her, and softened at the sight of the curve of her waist and the cute plumpness of her arm. He wished he hadn't snapped at her. It seemed he couldn't stop messing everything up, no matter how he tried not to.

"Well," Dolly said. She didn't look at him. "From the way you talk, I guess it was love at first sight." She sighed. "I can't imagine giving up on that, just because you'd already agreed to marry someone else."

He could still remember the softness of Anne's skin, her sweet jasmine scent. But she was just another person he'd bulldozed, his good intentions overcome by his selfishness. "Well, I guess you just don't understand," he said finally.

They were quiet a moment.

"When I saw my husband for the first time, I knew I would end up marrying him," Dolly offered. "Of course, he didn't even know I existed, until about four years later."

JJ laughed. "You saw him and decided you'd marry him, and he didn't know you existed? Now, why doesn't that surprise me?"

Dolly made a face. She stubbed out her cigarette. "Very funny."

"So how did it happen?"

She told him how she had seen Byron at the depot in her hometown, lined up with all the boys going off to the war. "I can still see him in that red and black mackinaw, with his big red ears!" she said. "I thought he was the most attractive man I'd ever seen. And then, when he got back from the war, I managed to get his attention."

"Well," said JJ. "I guess I don't blame him for falling for you." He flashed her a smile.

"Stop it," she said, and reached for another cigarette.

THE MICKELSON HOUSE
502 W. First Street, Pine Rapids
Friday, November 23, 1945

Wilma wasn't hungry, but, after Harry woke her, she dressed herself in a pair of gardening jeans and an old blouse, pinned up her thick silver hair without looking in the mirror, and went downstairs to sit and pick at the eggs and toast he placed before her. He sat across from her, sipping coffee and looking at her so solicitously that she forced down a couple of bites. The coffee in her cup grew cold, the eggs congealed.

When Jack and Mary arrived to take JJ home, Wilma went to see them out, and then did not want to look. But she found she couldn't look away, as Jack carried his sleeping son down the stairs and out the door to the car. It would have been pleasant to watch if it had seemed JJ was a child again. Instead, he seemed old, slumping down toward death; emaciated with it, in fact. The absence of his leg was horrifying. Her eyes fixed on his mouth, hanging open in his stubbled, pinched face as he snored.

"I hope we can still have the birthday party for him tonight," Mary said, sounding worried.

"Yes, yes," Wilma said, not believing it.

Harry had packed his suitcase and was going with them, so that Jack could give him a ride to the train; something about that girl Harry had had with him yesterday. She was gone, evidently. Wilma didn't ask for details. It was enough that she was to be left alone.

"Will you be all right, Mom? For a little while?" Jack asked. "I have to go down to Wausau and check on Dad. They said we might be able to bring him home today."

"Yes, yes, fine," Wilma told him.

"Are you sure, Mom?" Harry said. "I can stay, if you need me."

"No, no, please," Wilma said, herding them out onto the back porch. As she watched them getting into Jack's car, she pressed her icy fingers to her temple to try to cool the heat there, and closed her eyes.

When she opened them again, she saw a spider, weaving its web on the corner of one of the windowpanes on the back door. She pictured the spider entwining the house in its web entirely, covering it from top to bottom with white, silky threads. Covering all the windows and doors. Outside, a gust of wind loosed several leaves from the big birch tree, and they drifted to the ground.

She went inside and meandered through the rooms of the house, running her fingers over its varied surfaces. The textured upholstery of the sofas, fraying on the arms; the cool marble of the fireplaces; the wood of the banister, worn smooth by her family's hands over the last fifty years; the almost imperceptible waves of the stained-glass window on the landing; the porcelain of the bathroom sink; the plush rug on the floor of her bedroom; the baubles on her white bedspread. She pressed her hands to the bedroom radiator, to warm them. She did not look at her reflection in her vanity mirror when she took down Chase's yellowed caricature of the family, folded it, and put it in the pocket of her jeans.

She moved on, exploring her children's old rooms, the maid's

quarters, and up to the third floor apartment that had once belonged
to John's father, Knute. Though they had moved his things out years
ago to make it a play area for the children, Wilma thought she could
still smell his cigars and the strong soap he had favored. She didn't
blame him for what had happened. She sent him a little apology for
what she was about to do.

When she finally went back downstairs, she grabbed off a hook
near the back door a heavy wool jacket that had belonged to Chase.
She had found it in the third-floor storage room perhaps a decade
ago. She imagined it still smelled like him—baseball glove leather and
pencil lead and eraser dust and adolescence—and she'd taken to
wearing it, just every so often.

She stepped into the kitchen, grabbed a book of matches out of the
drawer, and dropped them into the pocket of the coat.

Outside, the air was gray and crisp; winter was coming. Or was it
already here? She knelt stiffly in the dying grass next to the back
porch, and tried to remember back to the beginning of time. *Not the
beginning of time itself,* she told herself, crumpling a handful of yellowed leaves up from the grass. *Just, where I began.* She felt a kicking
in her stomach, something pressing against her insides. *As though he
might be born again.*

But it was death that was in the air.

Her mouth felt like silver in the cold. The leaves smelled of chalk
and earth and decay.

To everything there is a season. A time to die.

She dropped the leaves and put her hands in the pockets of Chase's
old coat. Her left hand closed on the book of matches, and she withdrew it, examined it. On its back was an advertisement for Musky
Lake Resort, Buzz Granton's place.

Clenching her teeth, she dropped the matches back in her pocket
and began gathering up leaves with both her frigid hands.

> Good meals, attractively served, go a long way
> toward keeping the family together.

> —*The New American Cook Book*, 1941

HOME OF BYRON AND DOLLY MAGNUSON
406 Jefferson Avenue, Pine Rapids
Friday, August 4, 1950

Thinking of the picture of Byron in his plaid mackinaw standing on the Battle Point depot platform inspired Dolly, and she told JJ that she had to be getting home. The final details of the Mickelson story could wait. She was going to cook Byron a fabulous dinner, wear her sexiest dress, and show him just how good life could be when they took the time to be with each other. She didn't want to find herself in a position like Wilma Mickelson had, discovering a secret about her husband years after the fact. She had to work to ensure that she and Byron would again become as close and happy as they had been on their wedding night.

Well, maybe the day after the wedding night. She had been pretty nervous on the actual night. Still, though, he had been wonderful then, and she had imagined she could never feel closer to anyone—which could only mean the potential was there to feel that way again, if she just made the effort!

By the time she got the bungalow straightened, and the beef stroganoff simmering on the stove, she had worked up quite a sweat. She went to the bedroom and stripped off her clothes in favor of her robe, then headed for the bathroom to give herself a quick sponge bath. Every time she went into the bathroom she got furious at the sight of the wallpaper and the mismatched lime-green towels, but tonight she told herself to forget about it, and concentrated on thinking about all the good things about Byron. His constancy, the security he provided her. How cute he looked with his shirt off.

She brushed her hair, rolled the ends up in curlers, and dampened them with cologne. (If she did the curlers just right, her hair looked uncannily like Elizabeth Taylor's in the new movie *Father of the Bride*.) She painted her toenails and fingernails with bright red polish, then made up her face—black mascara, red lipstick, and the whole bit. Next, she took out the curlers, combed her hair, and pinned her curls in place. She went to the bedroom and put on a bra and panty-girdle set she'd bought at Birnbaum's last month, and thigh-high silk stockings, which she attached to the garters on her girdle. She added a short slip, a black sundress with white polka dots, and her high-heeled white sandals. Looking in the mirror on her dresser, she pressed her finger to her chin, posing, trying not to resent the extra snugness of the new girdle—at least it made her stomach and her rear look flatter than her older ones did. She thought Byron would also appreciate the effect of the stylish conical bra. Though she always thought her legs were too stocky, she had to admit that, with the aid of her new undergarments, the polka-dot sundress was quite flattering.

She pulled open the bedroom door, and went out to make the noodles.

At just the minute Byron walked in, she was dumping the cooked noodles out of their pot and into a colander in the sink. The steam and the noise of pouring water obscured her vision and hearing. When she turned to put the empty pot back onto the stove, he was standing there watching her. He raised his eyebrows, but made no comment, just jingled his keys in his pocket.

"Hi, Doll," he said. "We eating?" He gestured to the kitchen table with his elbow. She usually had the table set by the time he got home.

She bit back her irritation and treated him to a smile. "Of course, Byron," she said. "But I thought we could eat in the dining room tonight." The stroganoff was already in a serving bowl, and she picked it up off the counter.

"Oh," he said. "All right." His eyes drifted to her newly enhanced chest.

She smiled sweetly, and enjoyed the swirl of her skirt as she turned to carry the stroganoff in to the candlelit table.

The evening was growing cooler, and the air that drifted in through the dining room windows was pleasant.

Byron fumbled with his fork and knife as he cut his beef. "This— uh—You look nice, Doll," he said.

She was pleased.

"Everything," he went on. "It's great. The house, and dinner, and everything."

"I thought it would be nice to make a little extra effort," Dolly said. "I was hoping we could talk."

"What about?"

"The war."

He sighed. "I already told you, I don't want to talk about it. I don't think it's something you need to know about."

"But you might feel better if you did talk about it. And maybe I would feel like I know you better."

"I don't think so, Doll. Can't we just enjoy this nice dinner?"

She sighed. "All right, Byron," she said, pouting. But, as the saying went, there was more than one way to skin a cat. After a moment, she reached her foot across under the table, found his ankle with her toes, and caressed it. She batted her eyes at him, and gave him an impish smile.

He smiled, too, the shadows clearing from his face.

He ate quickly. The minute he had cleaned up his plate, he stood, held out his hand, and led her toward the bedroom.

Ten minutes later, he kissed her cheek and stood up from the bed, straightening his clothes, zipping his pants. He'd been in such a hurry that he hadn't removed any of their clothing except her stockings and panty-girdle. (She'd had to assist him with the technicalities of both.)

She lay back on the bed, her arms stretched above her head, watching him.

"Thanks, Doll," he said, with a cute smile. "That was great. Everything."

She sighed. She craned her head to see the clock. It was almost seven-thirty, only. She had imagined that dinner would be a leisurely affair in which the two of them revealed their innermost secrets, followed by an equally languorous hours-long session in the bedroom. Well, maybe he would be more inclined to talk now that they'd been intimate physically. "Don't you want to cuddle with me?" she said.

He gave her a crestfallen look. "Doll, I'm sorry," he said. "I didn't know—The thing is, I'm meeting some guys down at Shorty's. A couple of buddies of mine and Roy's from the war. They're just passing through town, and we haven't seen them in ages. They live in Chicago, and they're heading up to the U.P. this weekend to go fishing. It's a once a year kind of thing, if that, you know? I would've told you, but—I didn't know . . ." His voice trailed off.

Dolly had begun to steam the minute he started talking, and now she was boiling over. "Fine!" she said, flouncing up off the bed, marching past him out of the bedroom. "Fine! I'll just take care of the dishes!"

"Dolly," he said, feebly, from behind her. "You—forgot your underwear."

"I don't need it!" she said. "Quicker for you to screw!" She had reached the dining room, and she picked his plate up off the table, whirled, and threw it into the kitchen with all the force of both her arms. It landed on the floor and shattered. Gray sauce, leftover swirls of noodle, and pieces of mushroom scattered to the winds.

"Dolly!" he said, coming out after her. "Dolly, settle down!" He grabbed her wrists. He was close enough that she could feel his breath on her face.

"Get your hands off me."

"It isn't like that, Doll," he said. "You know it isn't like that."

"No, Byron, I *don't*," she said, then was angry at herself for letting her desperation show in her voice.

"Don't do this, Doll."

"I'm not the one doing it, Byron."

He looked in her eyes for a moment, then let go of her wrists. He looked sideways at the floor. "I've got to go," he mumbled, jingling his keys in his pocket. "Thanks for dinner." And with that, he was gone.

She stood still until she heard the back door close behind him. Then she lunged across the table for her own plate, and threw it into the kitchen, letting out a terrible scream.

Superior, Wisconsin
Friday, November 23, 1945

Harry clutched Anne's ring in his fist as he paced back and forth on Mrs. Hanson's front porch. Sleet spat through the dusk.

He whirled, pounded on the door, and waited.

He and Jack and Mary and his mother, having left John at Wausau General for observation, had arrived back at his parents' house sometime around two—was it just this morning? It had been an hour that felt both very early and much too late. Wilma, stumbling up the back porch steps on Harry's arm, was glassy-eyed with exhaustion; Harry worried that the day's shocks had been too much for her. Once inside, he helped her off with her coat and led her through the hallway and living room and up the stairs, Jack and Mary following, at a funereal pace, toward the bright lights burning on the second floor. Astonishing, at this hour.

As they reached the top of the stairs and turned toward the source of the light, they saw JJ, stretched out on the bed in his room, propped crookedly on a pile of pillows, atop the covers, his bandaged stump protruding from his shorts, an empty decanter crooked in his arm. Mary gave a little gasp; Jack mumbled something to comfort her. Then Harry noticed: All the lights in the guest room—Anne's room—were burning, too. Uneasiness crept up his neck. He passed Wilma off to Mary, who would put her to bed, and, standing in the door to JJ's room, demanded to know where Anne was.

"Sorry, Uncle Harry," JJ said groggily. "She left."

"What do you mean she left?"

JJ's eyes glinted with drunkenness. "I'm sorry, Uncle Harry," he said again. "Guess she changed her mind."

The house was cold, but Harry felt sweat popping from his pores. "Changed her mind about what?" he demanded. He felt a hand on his shoulder: Jack's. He looked back at his older brother and saw pity in his eyes.

"I'm sorry, Uncle Harry," JJ said a third time, his eyes closing. His mouth twitched.

"What did she say?" Harry insisted, but JJ didn't answer. He appeared to have fallen asleep.

Harry found the ring on the night table in Anne's room. It figured, he thought. His luck hadn't been bound to last long.

"Tomorrow," Jack said, watching Harry from under the brim of his ragged hat, his hands folded in front of him like a night watchman's. "Tomorrow you'll go back to Superior and find out what happened."

Harry looked at him.

"Mary and I'll look after Mom," Jack told him, in that tone you didn't argue with.

Harry had slept fitfully, and Jack brought him to the train in the late morning. The day had not lost its nightmare quality, from the moment he'd found Anne was gone, to this moment, standing on her porch with the gray sleet tapping staccato on the roof.

The door opened. It was Anne's blond friend, Linda. Her eyes widened when she saw him.

"Is Anne home?" he said.

Linda nodded, and opened the door so he could come in. She shut the door behind him and, without a word, ran up the stairs and knocked on the door to Anne's room, then slipped inside. Harry watched the closed door, waiting.

HOME OF BYRON AND DOLLY MAGNUSON
406 Jefferson Avenue, Pine Rapids
Friday, August 4, 1950

Refusing to cry, or to clean up the kitchen, Dolly paced the house. She caught herself gnawing on her nails, ruining her new manicure, so she kicked the foot of the sofa, stubbing her toe. She yelled in frustration, and wished for Jane, her mother, anyone who could console her.

And then she realized: There was someone who could.

Quickly, she went to the bedroom to put on an old pair of panties, then shoved her bare feet into her red ballet slippers. She ran out the front door of the bungalow, not even bothering to lock it behind her.

"Anne, wake up. Wake up. He's here."

Anne fought her way out from under the cloud of sleep. For a blissful second upon waking, her mind was blank of yesterday, but then the memory rushed back, as quick and heavy as a wave intent on drowning her. "Harry? Harry's here?" she said, blinking against the darkness. The drapes were closed, and only a sliver of gray light made its way between them.

"Yes!" said Linda. "He looks upset."

Anne buried her face in her pillow. "I can't see him. Not now."

"Anne!"

Left in charge of the house while the other girls and Mrs. Hanson were away for Thanksgiving, Linda had come out of her room wield-

ing a baseball bat at six this morning, when the noise of Anne's suitcase dragging up the stairs awoke her. Anne burst into tears at the
sight of her, and cried while Linda took her to the kitchen and made
coffee. Linda demanded to know what had happened, as they sat
there at the table in the rising light of dawn, but Anne would tell her
only that it was something dreadful. No, Harry hadn't done anything
wrong. And with that, she burst into tears again. Linda finally took
her upstairs and put her to bed. Too tired to think anymore, too
heartbroken to move, Anne had drifted in and out of sleep all day;
she hadn't slept a wink on the train all miserable last night.

Linda shook her. "Anne, don't you think he deserves an explanation?"

"I can't. I'm so ashamed." The tears were starting again. "Please,
Lin, just tell him I'm sorry."

There was quiet for a moment, just the sound of the sleet hitting
the windowpane, and then Linda sighed. "All right," she said. "If
you're sure."

Resting her hand over her eyes, Anne listened. Linda's footsteps as
she walked out of the room, the door closing gently behind her. A
moment later, the murmur of voices.

When she heard the front door open and close again, she flopped
over onto her stomach, punched her pillow, and collapsed, sobbing.

Wanting Harry was like a cancer. It seemed to begin in her pancreas,
that day she spent in bed. In the days following, it crept steadily
through her flesh: into her stomach, the corpuscles of her lungs, the
hollows of her heart. Then it was in her blood, a sort of a tingling,
until even her hands, feet, fingertips, and toes were numb. She
couldn't walk up stairs without tripping. Her vision went cloudy; her
mouth was relentlessly dry. Even under all her quilts, she couldn't get
warm. She dreamed of JJ's weight upon her, his warm breath on her
neck, and then he turned to water and she was drowning. She woke
up choking on tears.

JJ was a prickling sensation now, under her skin. She could smell
him there, smoldering like the embers left after a forest fire has swept
through. She hated him. He had taken what she had not meant him
to have. But she couldn't stop seeing the look on his face when he

watched her leaving him. (And then she would think, *Oh, God, what have I done?*)

Sometimes she felt an inexplicable pang of wishing she might have somehow soothed him. But then she would get angry, and think, *How dare he make me feel guilty for leaving him?*

Because Harry was the one she wanted, the one whose absence was a void within her.

But when he stopped by again on Sunday, Anne still refused to see him. She couldn't bear the thought of facing him, after what she had done.

But she constantly rehearsed an imagined encounter, as she pretended to study, to iron a skirt, to wash her hair. Not meaning to rehearse, but rehearsing, all the same. *I'm sorry, Harry, but I did something that I couldn't even dare to ask you to forgive me for.*

Or: *Something was done to me. Something happened. Something happened to me. That night.*

Or: *I believed that I loved you. I believe that I love you. I love you but how can it be true when the thing that happened to me is true?*

And: *I have been thinking constantly of who is to blame. Of what is true.*

It was done to me but I did it. I did it but I love you. I couldn't ask you to forgive me. I can't.

I believed that I loved you, but how could I?

But never could she come to a satisfactory statement—she only arrived back where she had started, with more questions. And how could she meet Harry with only questions, when it was an answer that he was waiting for?

So she refused to see him, and did her best to pretend that nothing had ever happened. That she had never even met Harry. That Thanksgiving in Pine Rapids had been merely a bad dream.

Had it not been for the cancer of wanting him, she might have been able to do it.

Bobby's dead. The realization hitting her like a sledge. She thought she'd known it before, but perhaps she hadn't. Her loneliness so thick that she choked on it, on the thought of what she'd so nearly had. So nearly had, not once but twice. *Harry's dead,* she thought, and it was a moment before she realized her mistake.

. . .

On Tuesday, she got a letter.

Dear Anne, it said.

Whatever I did, I am sorry.

I'm utterly worthless without you, and I'm not kidding about that. Please, at least let me see you. I promise I'll do my best to help you forget whatever it was that I did to offend you, if you'll just give me another chance.

H.

P.S. I am sorry about my family. At least you see now what I meant about them.

She laughed a little at that, then burst into tears again.

> It's dangerous to yield to the impulse to confide in
> a masculine friend, however understanding he may be.
>
> —"Making Marriage Work,"
> *Ladies' Home Journal*, March 1950

THE MICKELSON HOUSE
502 W. First Street, Pine Rapids
Friday, August 4, 1950

Having run all the way from the stroganoff-soaked bungalow, Dolly was breathing hard when she pounded on the back door of the Mickelson house. She hoped Mrs. Fryt wouldn't spot her, but she was desperate enough to see JJ that the possibility hadn't stopped her.

After a moment, he opened the door. He smiled when he saw her, but the smile faded when he saw the look on her face. Then he said, "Want to go for a drive?"

Dolly agreed, relieved that he hadn't asked her any questions about what she was doing there. She had made such a fuss about going home to a nice dinner with her husband.

He took her to White Pine Point, which looked out on the beach and the stillness of Heron Lake. He told her it was the popular spot for high school kids to come to drink and park, that he'd come out here a lot when he was in school. It was early, though, and as JJ nosed the car up to the beach, Dolly saw they were alone. They got out and leaned against the hood of his car. As the sun dipped toward the horizon, they smoked and took nips from a flask he'd brought along.

Dolly had always thought she didn't like whiskey, but she discovered that it wasn't so bad, after you got used to it. Except for the steady chirping of crickets, all was quiet. The air smelled like the smoke of a faraway bonfire. Getting out of town had been a brilliant idea, she thought. The problems with Byron were sliding to the back of her mind, and she was feeling much better.

She lit a fresh cigarette. "You have to tell me what happened to everyone. Your family."

So he told her how Elissa had finished her cadet nurse training and then gone to work at a small hospital in South Dakota.

"So she obviously never got back together with Ty."

"No," he said. "I guess she was really in love with our uncle."

A little tipsy from her several nips at the flask, Dolly giggled at that. "So what happened to him? To Nick?"

JJ shrugged. "We never heard from him."

"Even Elissa never did?"

"No," JJ said. "At least not that she told me about."

Dolly sighed. "What about your grandpa? Did he die from that accident?"

"No. He just got knocked out, was all. Once he sobered up, he was fine. Course, his Packard's hood looked like an accordion, and he was pretty sad about that."

"Did he ever admit to being Nick's father?"

"He left him some money in his will, but we didn't know where to find Nick. I guess my dad tried writing his mother, but she wrote back and said she hadn't heard from him, either. My dad has the money in a trust for him, in case we ever find him."

"Do you think you will?"

JJ just shrugged again. He took another drink from his flask and offered it to her. She took a sip, liking the smooth burning of it going down. She wiped the back of her hand across her mouth, and handed the flask back to JJ.

He laughed. "You're a lightweight, Dolly."

"Well, so I don't drink all day long like some people," she said.

He ignored her, and said his butt was getting sore from leaning against the car. "I've got a blanket in the back, want to sit down?"

She agreed, so he got out the blanket, limping a bit on the uneven ground, and soon they were settled on it, next to the car on the grassy edge of the beach. The lake lapped quietly at the shore. He sat leaning back on his hands with his legs stretched straight out in front of him; she sat cross-legged, with her skirt carefully covering her bare legs.

"I have to ask you one more thing," she said. "If you've been in love with Anne all this time, why haven't you gone after her?"

"She married my uncle Harry."

Dolly sighed, shaking her head. "I can't believe she went through with it. When she was in love with you."

"Well, it doesn't matter anymore. They've got three kids. A dark-headed boy and two of the blondest little girls you've ever seen. Twins. They send my mom and dad a picture every Christmas."

"I can't believe it," she repeated, taking another sip of whiskey to soften the blow. She handed him back the flask, and he set it down on the grass next to him. "Well, if it was me, I would have married you," she said.

He smiled a little. "I guess it's too late for that, too."

She sat on her hands, wishing she could rewind.

He reached over to pull some grass up from past the edge of the blanket. "Tell me, Dolly, what makes a girl decide who she's going to marry? What about you and your husband?"

"Oh, I was dreadfully in love with him. Like I told you before." She felt on the verge of revealing everything, the whole terrible dinner and all. Instead, she said, "But I didn't know him, you know?"

"Well, what have you found out?"

She cocked her head, looking out at the lake. "Only the extent of my ignorance, I suppose."

JJ laughed.

"And that you're probably right about the house—I mean, that it wouldn't make any difference, where we live. Because I don't think he understands *me* at all, or even cares to. It's like I'm supposed to be this cookie-cutter wife, you know? And be there for him whenever he needs me—in just the *way* he needs me, nothing more and nothing less—and not have any needs or desires of my own."

"So what are your desires, Dolly?"

She felt a lump rise in her throat. She couldn't remember Byron ever asking her such a thing. "Well—well, adventure, of course," she stammered finally. "Romance!"

He looked at her, and in his eyes was such a mix of concern and longing that she found she couldn't speak.

And then he leaned close and kissed her, resting his fingers lightly on her face. His lips were surprisingly soft. For a moment, she was lost.

But then she realized what she was doing, and recoiled. "Oh!" she said, raising her hands to her mouth. "It's gotten me, too! The curse!"

"Me, too," he said. He moved her hands aside, and kissed her again. Goodness, he was pleasant. His formerly sour smell seemed to have sweetened. Or was it that she herself had soured?

Her tipsy brain wavered. His breath was warm on her face, and, through her dress, she felt the heat of his hand, resting on her hip. He touched his lips to hers again. "Me, too," he said again, moving closer.

It was all she could do, mustering a swell of moral fortitude, to shift her seditious body out of his grasp and struggle to her feet. "No, JJ. It can't be."

She should have known better, she saw that now. It was like Mrs. Fryt had said: You could see disaster coming. Oh, in hindsight, yes! But, like a fool, Dolly had disregarded her strange fascination for JJ, the warmth in his eyes when he looked at her—or at least she had told herself that she could keep at bay what both portended. But now this! Her own fault, too, there was no denying it: bad enough she'd spent all that time with him at the house, but to come out here with him! Was this the consequence of wanting adventure, wanting a spectacular life, wanting *more*? Glamour and fascination stripped down to nothing more than a sordid back-alley drunken tryst?

She staggered toward where the water lapped the sand. The stars had begun to emerge, pulsing pinpoints of light. Everything seemed to be spinning; she covered her eyes with her hands.

"Dolly," he called after her. After a moment, he called again. "Christ, Dolly, I'm sorry," he said. "Please."

She turned toward him. She had never seen a man so close to dying.

Anne's legs trembled as she walked up the granite stairs in the *Gazette* building, her gloved hands clutched in front of her holding her handbag. She hoped that she looked more certain of herself than she felt. She had taken special care with her hair, her hat, her plum suit and navy coat.

She had spent the past several days reviewing her options, running them over and over in her mind. Despite Harry's repeated attempts to contact her—admittedly dwindling in the last couple of weeks—she had not spoken with him since that terrible Thanksgiving Day in Pine Rapids four weeks ago. She just had not known what she would say to him. Finally, with a mix of shame and desperate happiness, she had decided. No one—not even Linda—knew what had happened with JJ. If her conscience could swallow its shame, her secret would be safe. And she loved Harry. She was more certain of it now than ever; her pain at his absence had not lessened a whit in the past weeks. She hoped that if she loved him with her whole being in the years to come—as she planned to, if he would still have her—that it would, at least in part, atone for what she had done.

The newsroom was quiet when Anne opened the door and stepped in. It was after noon; the paper had gone to press, and most of the reporters were likely out for lunch or gone for the day. Harry's secretary looked up from her typewriter, and her face registered surprise as she recognized Anne.

"Is Mr. Mickelson in?" Anne asked. Her tongue felt thick; forming the words was a struggle.

The secretary quirked her mouth, pushed her chair back from her desk. "I suppose for you he is," she said, rising and walking over to the closed door of Harry's office. She knocked.

A moment later, the door flew open, and Harry stood there. "I told you not to—" he began, but when he saw Anne, his anger faded to astonishment. "Anne!" he said.

He drew her into his office, closed the door behind them. "Anne," he said again.

"Hello, Harry," she said, feeling unsteady on her feet. She had nearly forgotten the endearing curve of his mouth, the line of his nose, his messy hair. His tie was loosened and he hadn't shaved. He looked tired. Perhaps even as tired as she. She wanted to throw her arms around him and weep, but she stood still, and waited nervously while he looked her over.

After a moment, he ran his hand over his hair. "Well, I see you've got me speechless, Miss Wallace," he said. "I was beginning to think I'd never see you again."

"I'm so sorry," she said. "I really am, Harry."

"Cripes, Anne. You've been putting me through the wringer over here, you know? It's been a month, and nothing. I really thought I'd seen the last of you. And the worst part was, I didn't know why."

She took a step toward him. "I'm so sorry."

"Tell me why."

"Oh, Harry," she said, and she felt her face crumple. "I can't. I can't explain. I just—I needed some time. I didn't know what to do."

"You left your ring on the table at my mom's house."

"I was afraid."

"Was it JJ? Did he tell you something about me? Something that made you doubt me?"

She looked down at her hands. "No."

"What was it, then, Anne? I know I shouldn't have left you alone that night, but I got so caught up with my dad—"

"It wasn't your fault, Harry. I guess I just—got scared. I'm sorry."

"I just wish you would have talked to me."

She took a deep breath. "Please, Harry, forgive me. I've come here to—"

"What?"

"To beg you. To marry me, Harry. Please. Forgive me. I want to marry you."

He looked skeptical, but the corner of his mouth twitched into a little smile.

"Please," she said, her heart racing. "I just—needed some time to be sure."

"You're sure now?"

"Yes."

He stepped toward her, slowly reached up and touched her face. Her knees nearly gave way.

"I love you, Harry," she said. "Always, I have."

"I wouldn't have minded just waiting, you know."

"I'm sorry," she said. She looked up into his eyes again, wondering if he suspected what had happened. Had JJ confessed? She had to believe that he had not. "Harry, I don't want to wait anymore. I want to marry you right away. As soon as possible."

He smiled, looking in her eyes as though to divine whatever truth was there. "All right, sweetheart," he said finally. "I've got your ring at my apartment."

He kissed her. She was shaking, and would not have kept to her feet had he not been holding her.

All kinds of wonderful qualities needed in marriage may seem
to be conspicuous in oneself chiefly by their absence, but one can
always play for time. Even if infatuated with another person,
one can hang on to what one knows is right until Time,
the mighty leveler of passion, comes to one's help.

—*The Good Housekeeping Marriage Book*, 1939

Pine Rapids
Friday, August 4, 1950

"Look, Dolly, I didn't mean that, honest," JJ told her, breaking the silence, as they sped down the dark gravel road, headlights sweeping
ahead of them around the curves, lighting the trees along the road-
side. Dolly kept having to blink to clear her vision; she had unrolled
her window, and leaned her chin on her elbow as it protruded into the
night. The fresh air blowing in her face felt good, cleansing. When he
spoke, she looked over at him for the first time since they'd gotten in
the car. His desperate grin shone white in the darkness. "It kind of
just happened," he said.

Dolly kept quiet. She didn't know what to say.

There on the beach, looking at him, she had disregarded the
warmth and pity pulsing in her, folded her arms, and said, "I need
you to take me to my husband." She'd felt the need to redeem herself,

to get her feet back on even ground. Resolving things with Byron had seemed the only way.

JJ had actually looked like a man reprieved, rushing to fold the blanket, holding the car door open for her.

But she was still shaken by the thought of what had happened.

He looked back at the road, his grin fading. "Let's just forget it," he insisted. He dug in his shirt pocket for a cigarette and his lighter. His face glowed in the flame for an instant as he lit up. "I just—I guess it got to me, being alone, and you were—I didn't mean—" He took a drag of his cigarette.

A moment passed. Dolly had the sense that he was driving much too fast. Her stomach was queasy—whether from the speed or the liquor or from what his kiss had stirred, she couldn't tell. Her mind swirled, but kept falling back on the one incontrovertible fact she knew: *I am married to Byron. Whatever else may be, I am married to Byron.*

"Christ," JJ muttered. "Seems there's nothing I can't fuck up."

She hugged herself tight, and said nothing.

"You're sure he's here?" he said a few minutes later, nosing his car into a vacant spot on First Street just a couple buildings down from Shorty's Pub.

She nodded. She felt hot and cold at once. "I didn't tell you. We had a terrible fight."

"He's lucky, then. You're a good girl."

Her skin crawled with shame. She tried to think of something to say; couldn't.

"Take it easy, Dolly. Good luck."

She exhaled; it was a relief that he was going to let her go without a fight. Just like with Anne, she realized, he was doing the honorable thing. "Thank you," she said. She was beginning to dread the task that awaited her inside Shorty's.

"You'd better go."

She opened up the car door, and watched her ballet slippers step out. First one, and then the other. She stood, closed the door behind her, and fluffed her hair with her fingers. Behind her, JJ's car backed out of the parking space; she glanced at him through the windshield, intending to wave good-bye, but he was looking over his shoulder to back up, and even when he was out of the parking spot and shifting into gear, he didn't look in her direction. She felt a sudden emptiness, watching him go, but she knew it had to be.

A man held the door open for her, giving her an appreciative going-over as she walked past him. She glared at him, then turned to survey the room for Byron. The place was packed. All the stools at the bar were occupied by men with heavy-lidded eyes and three-day stubble, clad in flannel and jeans. They were silent types, but the rest of the place was filled with laughter and chatter, the businessmen with their wives huddled around booths drinking martinis, the loose women milling about preying on the white-collared men who were there without wives. The air was thick with cigarette smoke and reeked of alcohol and grilled bratwurst. At first, Dolly didn't see Byron anywhere. As she ventured deeper into the crowded room, the stolid men on the bar stools turned their heads, watching her.

Then she recognized Roy, in a booth toward the back. A man Dolly didn't know sat next to him. She saw the side of Byron's head; he was sitting across from Roy, with his back to where Dolly had come in. They all had their hands wrapped around beer bottles, their elbows on the table. As she watched, Byron lifted his bottle to his lips and tipped his head back to take a drink.

Dolly thrust back her shoulders, feeling suddenly quite sober. *You can do this,* she told herself. She had to show him—using the cutest, most circuitous language—that he couldn't desert her this way and, moreover, that everything he would ever need was right there in their little bungalow.

She had to make him believe it, so she could believe it, too.

Just then, an ice-blond woman with red lips and a tight blue dress showing off her prominent curves sashayed out of the rear hall of the bar—there was a door back there that led to a parking lot—and went directly to Byron and Roy's table. Dolly ducked behind a tall man who was standing between tables talking to another man. She peered around him, watching.

The blond woman had one hand on her hip, and leaned the other on Byron's table. She obviously knew Byron and Roy well, and they introduced her to their friends. All the men were clearly charmed by her. Roy couldn't seem to take his eyes off her breasts, as she withdrew a cigarette from her purse and leaned over so that Byron could light it for her.

Dolly fumed. Watched as the woman reached out with her red-taloned hand and nudged Byron's shoulder. Something was raucously funny. Byron's visible ear turned bright pink.

The woman tipped back her head and blew out smoke.

Just then, the man whom Dolly had been hiding behind noticed her. He looked down at her and grinned. "Hi there," he said. "You all alone here?"

Dolly pinched her face at him, and slunk away to the end of the bar near the front door, where Byron and Roy wouldn't see her. But when she turned and looked back toward Byron's table, she was just in time to see the ice-blond woman leading him away by the hand. They disappeared down the back hall, Byron's ears glowing pink.

Dolly's hand shot to her mouth, as she tried to keep the cry that was rising in her throat from escaping. She whirled, and ran outside.

There was only one place she could think of to go.

"JJ? JJ!" she cried, again pounding on the back door of the Mickelson house. Only a couple hours had passed since she had last knocked—and she had thought things were bad then, with Byron running out on her for his friends. Now her worst fears had been realized: There was another woman. She felt old, suddenly, and all used up. She supposed her mascara had made black tracks down her cheeks. She wiped at them haphazardly with the back of her hand, but really, she didn't care.

"JJ!" she called again, still pounding. But there was no answer.

She decided to go in.

Just as on the first night, the door didn't creak when she pushed it open. Bolstered by the notion that the house didn't mind her presence, she called JJ again; no answer.

The hallway was dark, but a light burned in the living room. She moved toward it, her ballet slippers whispering on the hardwood floor. "JJ, where are you?" She ran her hand along the wall as she walked, half to keep her balance, and half to keep her senses about her, to remind her this wasn't a dream.

The lamp in the living room cast ghastly shadows on the wall. JJ was nowhere to be seen. There were no other lights on downstairs, so

Dolly tiptoed on, out of the living room, toward the staircase. She turned the corner and looked up. On the second landing, the rich colors in the stained-glass window shone in the yellow light that glowed above it. "JJ?" she called. "JJ, are you upstairs?"

He appeared at the top of the stairs then, framed in the light behind him. He had a suitcase in his hand. "Dolly?" he said. "What are you doing here?"

Tears began to leak from her eyes again. "I—I saw Byron." She stepped up one step, and then another.

JJ dropped his suitcase and started down the stairs toward her. "What happened?"

She reached the first landing, and kept going, realizing she was here for comfort, yes, and—revenge? If it came to that? But—what on earth! What was she thinking? She should turn around immediately. Two wrongs didn't make a right, wasn't that what her father always said? Oh, but had her father ever been as miserable and desperate as this? And her legs kept carrying her forward, up one step at a time.

"What happened, Dolly?" JJ asked again.

She had reached the landing in front of the stained-glass window, and looked up at him, descending toward her. Almost, she could imagine she was dreaming, the way he was silhouetted in the light coming from upstairs. Her limbs and even her head were heavy, as with sleep, and she was running on a continuous combustion of rage and a dreadful, deep loneliness, worse than anything she'd ever felt in her life.

"JJ?" she said. Her mouth felt dry. "What did Wilma do? When she found out about John and Florence?"

He took another step. "What happened with your husband, Dolly?"

"I mean, after she stopped playing the piano," Dolly insisted.

Another step. "I don't know if you should be here right now—"

She was trembling. "What did she *do,* JJ?"

THE MICKELSON HOUSE

502 W. First Street, Pine Rapids

Friday, November 23, 1945

She didn't remember dropping the match into the leaves. It was as though her neighbor's sudden grasp on her elbow awakened her from a dream.

Damn that Cecilia, is there anything she doesn't see? was Wilma's first thought.

"Give me those matches, Wilma," commanded Cecilia Fryt, towering over Wilma.

Wilma stood her ground. She sneaked a look down at the pile of leaves. A small wisp of smoke was the only evidence of the match she had dropped.

"Now, Wilma," said Cecilia, holding out her hand, palm up. "Honestly. Give them to me."

Wilma didn't answer.

Cecilia squinted at her. "Are you—ill, again, Wilma?"

"Ill? No," Wilma said. She lifted the book of matches, ripped one off and struck it. It didn't light.

"Mercy, Wilma!" Cecilia reached for the matches; there was a struggle. Cecilia was much larger, stronger. Her big hands probably could have snapped Wilma's wrists. Wilma let go.

"You have no right," Wilma snarled.

"Well, what right do *you* have, Miss High on Your Horse?" said Cecilia, pocketing the matches in her housecoat. "You think you can get away with this? I've got a good mind to call the police! Don't think I don't see what you're up to!"

"Of course!" Wilma snapped.

"Where is your family, Wilma? What have you done to your family?"

Me again! Always, it's my fault! "Enough!" Wilma screamed, pushing past her neighbor, running inside the house, through to the parlor, sobbing, finding her piano with her icy hands.

They fumble, at first. Her hands.

But the feel of the ivory under her fingertips and the exuding music soothe her, too, and, as she calms, her hands navigate the old familiar terrain of the keyboard with increasing aplomb. She is glad, then, that Cecilia stopped her; foolishly, she had not been thinking of her piano.

Over the music of her hands, she hears footsteps rushing into the room, and voices.

"Mrs. Fryt said she was piling up leaves around the foundation of the house, and dropping matches into them, Jack! She called me at home when she couldn't get you at work. I came as quickly as I could. Thank goodness you're back!"

"Mom?"

Wilma recognizes Jack's old shoes on the feet of the legs standing to the right of her stool, but she does not stop playing or look up. Immersed in a Mozart sonata, she is approaching her favorite delicate measures; all of her concentration is poised upon keeping the sixteenth notes rolling precisely from her fingers, upon keeping an unerring tempo. She is still wearing Chase's old jacket, which is uncomfortably warm, but she cannot bear to stop long enough to remove it.

"Mom, what's going on?" A pause; music fills the air. "Mom, is it true? What Mrs. Fryt told Mary?"

She will not interrupt her sonata. Let them wait. Her fingers feel perfect, dancing over the keys, though her brow is furrowed with effort. Amazing that, after so many years, she does not feel out of practice. Nor are her fingers tired, even after playing for so long yesterday.

"Mom, I brought Dad home from the hospital. He's all right, Mom. He wants to talk to you. Is that all right, Mom?"

She plays on.

Quietly: "Come on, Mary, let's leave them alone a minute."

The music swells under Wilma's hands, swells to one of its climaxes. When she notices the shoes next to her again, they have changed from Jack's shabby loafers to John's shiny Oxfords. Fingertips light upon her shoulder. She shrugs them off, and continues the precise movements of her hands. "Wilma," she hears her husband say. His voice is hoarse. "I suppose I couldn't make you understand. What it was like for me then."

Sixteenth notes cascade from her fingers.

"Although I always loved you!"

The notes are delicate, tempered, even.

"If you could just see. How lonely I was. How much I needed—to prove I was alive. After we lost Chase." A pause. "And you, Wilma, you were not a comfort to me!"

The main theme reasserts itself.

A loud sigh. "Wilma, would you listen?"

She focuses on the movement of her fingers.

"It might have—I don't know, Wilma, but you remember about the curse on this house? For God's sake, I don't think it's unreasonable to suppose that I—that it was that! Because God knows I never intended—!"

Her fingers trip. She shakes her head, rights them, and continues.

"You know I'd change it all if I could. You know I never meant to hurt anyone. Least of all you, Wilma."

Having reached the lower end of a forbidding passage, she lifts her hands from the keyboard. She looks up into the watery blue eyes of her husband, and sees reflected there all those ridiculous years of guilt, grief, subversion, penitence, following the Rules! When, all along, he had been hiding a sin more grievous than her own.

A decades-old dam breaks. And she begins to laugh. She cannot stop herself.

She collapses onto the piano, burying her head in her arms. She barely hears the footsteps running into the room. Is she laughing or sobbing? Circling around her, they can't tell. "Mom, are you all right?"

"Wilma?"

"Wilma? Wilma!"

> Few crises are filled with more insecurity and sense of loss in
> a marriage than that involved when "the other woman"
> or her male counterpart breaks the sense of unity
> so important to marital solidarity.

—*When You Marry*, 1948

THE MICKELSON HOUSE
502 W. First Street, Pine Rapids
Friday, August 4, 1950

"Why did you want to know so bad?" he said, lighting her cigarette. They were standing together on the landing in front of the stained-glass window.

She smoked, hands shaking. She had begun imagining strategies for burning down the little bungalow. Perhaps she could succeed where Wilma had not.

JJ nudged her shoulder. "Come on, Dolly, it can't be that bad."

But when she looked up at him, his brow furrowed at the pain in her eyes, and he took her into his arms. "I'm sorry, Dolly," he whispered into her hair. Deftly, he plucked the cigarette from her fingers and disposed of it in an empty glass that had been abandoned on the window seat.

. . .

Her stomach was pulsing with nausea. "Wait," she said, like a drowning woman popping above the surface for a too-brief instant, as his lips traced her neck and his hand carved out the shape of her curves, lingering on her breast, her hip.

"Are you going to leave him?" he murmured.

"Wait," she protested again, knowing this was what she had come here for, wanting it and not wanting it at once.

"You should leave him, Dolly," he whispered, pressing close.

At the thought of it, she couldn't keep her sobs at bay. JJ's hold on her seemed to grow tighter. The length of his thin body pinned her against the corner by the window. "JJ," she hiccuped, pushing at him.

But when she looked up, the set of his jaw made sweat pop from her pores. "JJ?"

He swallowed. Then his eyes and mouth softened. "Dolly," he said. "Do you think you could ever love me?"

Her mouth fell open.

He looked into her eyes a moment, then ducked his head. He let her go, and turned away. "Christ," he said. "I'm such an idiot."

Dolly hugged herself tight, pressing her back against the wall.

"'Oh, our lives' sweetness!'" he said. "'That we would hourly die / Rather than die at once!'"

"What?"

He ran his hand over his hair. "Edgar from *King Lear*. I didn't know what it meant, when I was in the play in high school. Right before the war. I just said the line, and I didn't know what it meant. Now I think about it all the time. That we would hourly die rather than die at once."

"What does it mean?"

"Think about it, Dolly."

But she couldn't think. She was trembling with dread at her own immorality, yet half of her wished he would come back and hold her again. But even as her mind reviewed the picture of Byron leaving Shorty's with that woman, her wedding ring felt so heavy that she could hardly lift her left hand. This was what she got for having been raised with moral values: a maddening inability to take satisfaction in revenge.

Glancing over his shoulder, he met her eyes. "You saw him with another woman, right? You don't have to put up with that. My grandma left my grandpa, after she found out about Nick being his."

"She did?"

He nodded. "Are you going to leave your husband?"

She closed her eyes, hardly able to register her shock. "I don't know," she said. "I don't know what I'll do."

When she opened her eyes, he was looking at the floor again. "If you did, I—I mean, Christ, I'm not much. But—"

Dolly felt her heart constrict. "Don't, JJ," she said. "You can't—can't say such things to me when I'm a married woman. You just can't. No matter what he's done. Or what I've done. I haven't made up my mind. I might be a fool, but—JJ, you said you never mess with married girls! You made me feel I was safe with you."

"I'm sorry," he mumbled. "It was just—I felt—" He looked up at the ceiling, around at the shadows. "Christ, maybe it's true about this fucking house," he said. Then he turned and started up the stairs.

She gaped at the slump of his shoulders as he ascended the stairs, stunned by the finality of his tone. She was afraid of being left alone to wither on the vine with her dreams and crazy fascinations. She realized then—her connection with JJ hadn't been only about her seeing the truth of him. He had understood her, too. She had been herself with him: angry, prideful, caring, sweet, relaxed, meticulous, demanding—an entire kaleidoscope. And he had accepted every color, every pattern, every face she showed. "JJ!" she called. "It's all right—it was a mistake! We can still—be friends! I didn't mean—Let's just—just forget about it!"

He didn't turn around. "I'm leaving," he said, making his way up the stairs, one ragged step at a time. "Do what you want with this fucking place."

For a moment, she was shocked to blankness. But then, anguish and fury mounting, she thought: *How could he?*

She called after him, but he didn't answer, just kept climbing the stairs. And suddenly, she couldn't stand the humiliation of lurking one more second in the shadows of the Mickelson house. She thundered down the stairs and burst out the front door, into the cool, dark night.

ON THE TRAIN FROM PINE RAPIDS
Monday, November 26, 1945

Wilma drew her coat tighter around her body and straightened her hat as the train picked up speed, leaving the Pine Rapids depot. She supposed John was still standing there on the platform under the gray sky, larger than life in his black overcoat, with his hat in his hands, but she didn't look back.

Following her breakdown at the piano on Friday, she had let the family put her to bed. She stayed there two days. Then she got up and packed a suitcase. Just a few things. She wouldn't need much.

He had begged her not to go, telling her she wasn't well, but she told him simply, "I'm perfectly well, and I can't stay here any longer. It's time I made something of my life."

"Made something of it? Wilma? The—children!"

Well, he would never understand. His life had been everything he wanted, whereas she had gotten on the wrong train, all those years ago. Yet, she had spent nearly fifty years wrenching faithfulness and duty out of her recalcitrant heart. Such arduous effort—and then to find out he had not reciprocated! He had expected more of her than he was willing to give.

As a consequence, she considered her obligations to him rendered null and void.

Her staggering guilt over the feelings she'd quietly harbored for Gust, too, seemed ridiculous, in light of what John had done, especially since he didn't even seem remorseful. And that he would think to blame the rumored "curse"!

She had heard a whisper or two of the curse in the early days, from the women at church, but she had never paid them any mind—she had assumed the ladies were only trying to make her more uncomfortable in her position in Pine Rapids than she already was. After the first year or so, they didn't mention it again. And, as John had never spoken of it, she had put it out of her mind. She had been surprised to hear him bring it up; apparently, he had been allowing the possibility of the curse's veracity all along.

Well, maybe there was something to it. Would God allow such a thing? Perhaps He would. Perhaps she could take comfort—as John had—in the thought that the yearnings of her heart might have been the product of something other than her own iniquity. And she could begin anew, without the yoke of guilt that had settled around her neck and weighed her down all these years.

She looked out the window at the bare trees streaming past in the gray day, and couldn't suppress a smile. Beginning anew! It was a lovely thought.

She supposed she loved John. She couldn't have lived forty-nine years with him without coming to care for him, long ago. But now his transgressions had set her free. For that, she loved him perhaps more than she ever had.

I urge wives to try to stifle their pride. A woman can't help
being hurt. But if she genuinely wants to keep
her husband, she must work at it.

—"The Other Woman Is Often the Creation of the Wife,"
Look, August 2, 1949

Pine Rapids
Friday, August 4, 1950

The dreadful realization struck Dolly a moment later: Having left the
Mickelson house, she had nowhere to go but Byron's bungalow.

The problem was, she couldn't stand the thought of one more
night in the confines of that little house, nor the thought of looking
Byron in the eye, knowing what he'd been up to behind her back.
Knowing that he didn't need or want her, either one.

To make matters worse, she was drunk. As she paced the streets of
Pine Rapids, more than once she knelt by the curb, ready to vomit.
She would wait for the urge to pass, then rise again, unsteady on her
feet, and continue on, grateful for the shroud of darkness. If the
Ladies Aid saw her now, she'd be ruined for sure.

Though she had to acknowledge it probable that she was ruined
already.

Hugging herself to keep her bare arms warm, she made so many turns and traced the four corners of so many blocks that finally she wasn't sure where she was. It really didn't matter, anyway. Even if she knew where she was, she still wouldn't know what to do. She'd been such a fool, chasing satisfaction at the Mickelson house to the exclusion of her husband, and she'd gotten what she deserved, she supposed—yet, the enormity of Byron's betrayal was impossible to swallow. And she couldn't even conceive of what had happened with JJ. Had he really implied—?

She just could not think of it.

But what was she going to do? Everything she had ever read about infidelity said that when a husband cheated it was the wife's fault, and she should woo him back afterward—but Dolly couldn't help but think that was a bunch of crap. Besides, did she really want to make such efforts to entrap herself again in such an obviously disastrous marriage?

But she couldn't *leave* Byron—could she? What would her family say? Where would she go? For everyone to know what a fool she'd been would be a nightmare.

She had always thought Byron would be the only man for her, and all the new evidence to the contrary—the sight of him with that woman, the pleasant feel of JJ's hands on her—seemed entirely too much to adjust to, all at once.

She really might have to leave Byron. As Wilma had left John!

No, she could not take any more blows to her sensibility, not on this night. So, when she was too chilled and exhausted to walk any longer, she got her bearings and dragged her feet to the bungalow.

To her surprise, when she got there, all the lights were burning. She stood for a moment to collect herself, then she walked up the front steps and pulled open the door.

Byron was sitting in his favorite chair in the living room, reading the newspaper, bathed in pleasant yellow lamplight, just as though nothing had happened. At the sight of him, it all came rushing up. She covered her mouth and raced for the bathroom, as he called after her, "Doll, what's wrong? Where have you been? What's the matter?"

She slammed the door behind her and dropped to her knees in

front of the toilet, miserably sick, until it was all gone and she was left more sobbing than heaving.

Byron knocked on the door and asked if she was all right, but she couldn't bring herself to answer him. He asked again. She pressed her fingers over her closed eyes. The smell in the bathroom was horrible, the taste in her mouth worse. She swore she would never drink whiskey again. She felt like a different person now from the one who'd admired herself in the mirror earlier in the evening. She felt like the worst creature alive.

It was a long while later when she finally wobbled out. Byron was sitting in the darkened hallway, leaning his back against the wall. He scrambled to his feet, but she lunged for the bedroom, locking the door behind her, deaf to his knocking, his supplications. Finally, he went away, which was satisfying, but also made her cry.

She lay awake a long time, clutching the sheet in her fists, staring up at the ceiling, missing the heat of Byron's body next to her, and flinching with rage at every noise she heard outside the bedroom door. She heard clanks in the kitchen, and realized he was picking up the shards of the plates she had broken. Then there was the sound of water running; amazingly, of scrubbing. Later, she heard him open the linen closet, then snap a sheet open, making up the couch. It was all she could do to keep from screaming. Finally, the noises ceased— he must have fallen asleep.

Sometime later, she, too, surrendered to a fitful sleep. She dreamed of JJ touching her face, of Byron turning his back on her, of sitting alone on the landing in the Mickelson house, choking on her tears.

> Try to figure out why he needs the other woman. . . . Don't be
> difficult, no matter how provoked you are. Be more
> cheerful and attractive than usual.
>
> —"The Other Woman Is Often the Creation of the Wife,"
> *Look*, August 2, 1949

HOME OF BYRON AND DOLLY MAGNUSON
406 Jefferson Avenue, Pine Rapids
Saturday, August 5, 1950

Dolly woke early, exhausted from her dream-filled sleep, and lay in
bed rubbing her throbbing temples. She wasn't ready to confront
Byron yet, but when he knocked on the door and said, "Doll? I've got
to get my clothes for work," she realized she had no choice but to let
him in. She dragged herself out of bed, padded over and unlocked the
door, then hurried back to bed. She had the sheet over her head by the
time he entered, and she squeezed her eyes shut tight to try to stop her
head from spinning.

A moment later, she felt him sit down on the edge of the bed. "Are
you all right, Doll?" he said. "I was really worried about you."

She cursed his charade of kindness. How could he pretend to be
concerned for her this morning, when just last night he'd been with
another woman? "I'm not speaking to you," she said.

His hand came to light on the sheet over her back. She squirmed out of its reach. She heard him sigh. "Doll, I'm really sorry about last night. I had no idea you'd be going to all that trouble with dinner and everything, and my buddies visiting kind of came up at the last minute—I came home early to try to make it up to you. I was home by ten. Where were you?"

She swallowed the bile rising in her throat. "Do you want a gold medal?"

"Doll, I guess I don't blame you for being upset. I know you're not that happy in Pine Rapids yet. I shouldn't have gone off and left you like that last night."

She flung the sheet off her and sat up. "There are a lot of things you shouldn't have done last night!"

He looked at her a moment. "Your eyes are all red. Were you drunk? Is that why you were sick?" Then he shook his head, his mouth a thin line. "You don't have to answer that. I can smell it on you. I thought I smelled it last night, but I thought there was no way—"

"I was provoked," she snapped.

"Where were you? Who were you with?"

She folded her arms, looked away. Her head was throbbing.

"I doubt those quilting friends of yours drink like that. Were you with that guy at that house?"

She looked at him, defiant, guilty. "What if I was?" she said.

He stood up as quickly as if she'd hit him. "We'll talk about this later," he said. He grabbed a shirt and pants out of the closet, underwear and socks out of his dresser. Then he was gone, slamming the door behind him.

After she heard him go out to the garage and heard the Chrysler fire up and roll out, Dolly got up and soaked in a hot bath until it cooled to tepid, washing her hair and scrubbing herself pink in the meantime, trying to get last night's residue off her. Once dressed and somewhat restored to at least the shell of her former self, she flopped on the couch with *Cherry Ames, Night Supervisor,* trying to keep her mind off things. It didn't work. She wondered what JJ was doing. She wondered what Byron would say when he got home, what she would say to him. She thought of all sorts of things that she *could* say, but nothing that seemed exactly right. Every time she recalled the picture of Byron walking out the back door of Shorty's with that woman, she felt like throwing up again.

Her swirling guilt and fury seemed too much for the little bungalow to contain. By about two o'clock, there seemed nothing to do but to return to the Mickelson house. She told herself she'd better check to see if JJ was all right. In truth, she thought going there might salve the queasy, lost feeling in her stomach. Maybe JJ would understand, and forgive her, and they could be friends again, so she wouldn't feel so alone.

But there was no answer to her knocking, and when she let herself in and glanced into the kitchen, she saw a rectangle of white paper on the butcher block. She flipped on the overhead light, and leaned over the note. She read:

Dear Dolly—

I hope you get this. I want you to know I'm sorry. Like I said, I always seem to f— things up, so I am leaving, before I can do anything more.

Your husband is probably sorry for what he did, just like my grandpa was. I would not advise doing something you might regret later, such as giving him up for me! Ha ha.

I was hoping you would look in on the house sometimes, like you were. I hope I didn't discourage you. You can write to my dad, Jack Mickelson, in Stone Harbor, Wis., about it, if there are any problems.

I would like to tell you a whole lot of things, but I'd best just tell you good-bye, and good luck.

JJ Mickelson

P.S. And thanks.

So, it was true, then. The lost queasiness. The emptiness.
She was alone, and it seemed she'd better get used to it.

She wandered farther into the house and sat on the front window seat to think. Finally, she decided that if she had anything left that was salvageable at all, it was her marriage. At the very least, it was the one thing she had stood up before God and promised to uphold, so obviously she should do her utmost to rescue it. It was shameful of her to have entertained JJ's proposal at all, even for a second, even at the back of her mind. She forced herself to shove the pictures of Byron with that woman out of her mind. She would just have to prove to him—and to herself—that they could start over.

She walked home to the bungalow and prepared potato salad and hamburgers—less challenging than her typical menus, but Byron's favorite, she was almost sure. She set the dining room table beautifully.

But when Byron arrived home, he was like a cloud entering the house. Her determination faded at the sight of him, and she was angry again, thinking, *So it's fine for him to be with that woman, but not for me to spend a Friday evening with JJ when my husband deserts me!* Of all the double standards in the world, this suddenly seemed the most galling.

They sat down to eat without a word to each other. Their burgers were nearly gone before he finally wiped his mouth and said, "I'm just disappointed in you, Doll. I don't know what you have going on—"

"Disappointed! In me! I've done nothing but try to please you!"

He looked skeptical. "You've been spending a lot of time with that JJ Mickelson guy. Roy said he's a young guy, too. My age. You haven't ever introduced him to me—like you've been keeping him to yourself. And then I find out you were drinking with him on Friday night. What am I supposed to think?"

"He's a friend. He comforted me. I was upset when you left."

Byron's jaw clenched. It was a moment before he spoke. "Comforted you?"

"Something you would know very little about," she said. "With so many *other things* on your mind." With that, she flounced up from the table with her plate and went into the kitchen. She sank the plate into the soapy dishwater, began furiously to wash it, as angry with herself as with him. Why did she always mess things up with him?

A minute later, he walked through the kitchen with a terse "I'm going out."

When the door closed behind him, she was in tears again, knowing it was comfort he sought, as well, and knowing he was going to the ice-blond woman to find it.

The specific process of learning how to face marital conflicts squarely must be carried out in a marital relationship by the couple themselves. There is no magic involved; it is a procedure of constantly trying to discover the truth about one's self, the spouse, and the relationship, no matter how distasteful that truth may be.

—*Marriage* (a textbook), 1949

HOME OF BYRON AND DOLLY MAGNUSON
406 Jefferson Avenue, Pine Rapids
Tuesday, August 8, 1950

By Tuesday morning, Dolly hated the sight of herself in the mirror. Her eyes were shadowed from lack of sleep; her forehead had broken out. Even her hair seemed lackluster, no matter how much she brushed it.

She'd been going through the motions, these last couple of days, trying to decide what to do. Saturday night after Byron had gone out and she'd finished cleaning up the kitchen, she went to bed, locking the bedroom door so that Byron would have to sleep on the couch again. Sunday morning, they went to church without speaking to each other; Dolly also managed to avoid the women of the Ladies Aid. Back home, she referred to her notes to determine Byron's least favorite entrée, and departed from her meal plan with a salmon puff for their Sunday dinner. After picking his way through it, he went out "fishing with Roy";

she stayed home and read *The Beautiful and Damned,* smoking so many cigarettes that the air in the living room turned blue and hazy. When Byron came home, he told her again that he was disappointed in her. She went to the bedroom and locked the door; he didn't even try to pursue her. Monday had proceeded similarly, the low point being when she served him warmed-over salmon puff for supper.

She knew she was supposed to be trying to win back his affections, but she still wasn't sure if she wanted him back at all.

She had to keep up appearances, though, at least until she decided what to do. So, on Tuesday afternoon, she put on her black sleeveless dress, along with a great deal of careful makeup, and, after smoking three cigarettes in quick succession, set out for Mrs. Fryt's, her sewing basket on her arm. She couldn't help but be disgusted: The weather was cheerful, the flowers in everyone's gardens chipper. The way she felt, it should be storming, with looming gray skies, bunnies and squirrels scurrying for cover.

As she tramped up the steps to Mrs. Fryt's, Dolly was queasy at the thought of facing the ladies. She'd been tempted to skip the meeting, but she feared her absence might only exacerbate gossip about her. If the ladies didn't already know that something was amiss, Dolly didn't want her behavior to betray it. But then, if Mrs. Fryt had seen her going to the Mickelson house late Friday night, or Saturday, she was already sunk.

Up on Mrs. Fryt's porch, she looked at the house across the street; she hadn't seen it since Saturday, when she'd discovered that JJ was gone. She missed the refuge it had been, the escape it had provided from the empty routine of her everyday life.

She sighed, then squared her shoulders, raised her fist, and knocked on Mrs. Fryt's door.

Dolly didn't think she was imagining that Mrs. Fryt's lips were pursed a bit tighter than usual when she came to the door. She didn't even greet Dolly, just turned and went into the parlor. Dolly followed, conscious of the sweat forming under her arms. She was too nervous to listen to the ladies' chatter as they got settled around the near-completed Wild Goose Chase quilt.

"Well, Dolly," Mrs. Fryt said, when everyone had started stitching. "How are things at the Mickelson house? You've been there enough lately."

"Fine! They're just fine!"

"I brought JJ Mickelson some tomatoes on Friday," Mrs. Fryt told the ladies.

"How nice," Corinne said.

"He was out on the front porch. I could hardly believe how pleasant he was—though he didn't invite me in. I even offered to help Dolly with the housework."

"Why would you do that, Grandma?" Judy Wasserman snickered.

"Well, it didn't matter, because he wouldn't allow it. Still, though, I was almost pleasantly surprised by his politeness. But then, I hesitate to tell you what I saw Friday night!"

Dolly froze. She would have screamed, run out of the room, anything, had terror not stricken her dumb.

"What was it, Cecilia?"

"Well, I was upstairs most of the evening, working up the agenda for the Women's Club meeting. It must have been about ten when I finished and turned out the light. I just happened to glance out the window, and I saw the most shocking thing!" She lowered her voice. "He had a woman with him. I could see their shadows through the window."

"A woman!"

"Who could it have been?"

"They were in front of the stained-glass window on the landing, so I couldn't see who she was. And what they were doing—I couldn't watch for long. It was indecent." Mrs. Fryt looked at Dolly. "The strangest thing of all is that now I haven't seen any lights on for the last couple of nights."

"It was his girlfriend from college!" Dolly blurted. "She came up on Friday and surprised him! She's really pretty. About my height. They'd had a fight before, but she came to apologize, I think. I don't know—I left when she got there. When I went back Saturday, he'd left a note saying he'd gone back with her. He asked me to look after the house."

Mrs. Fryt was taken aback. "Well, I don't know what kind of hussy girlfriend goes *by herself* to see a man, overnight!"

"I think they're engaged!" Dolly said. "They'd had a fight, that's all, and she realized she was wrong. At least, that's what I gathered before I left."

"So he's gone?" Corinne said. "He just got here. Not two weeks ago, now, was it?"

Dolly drew in a breath. "Yes, well, he never planned to stay very long. He was upset about the fight he'd had with Helen, and he needed a place to go, that was all. And then when she came to apologize, he had no reason to stay."

Mrs. Fryt shook her head, as if to say, *What did you expect?* "Helen, is it? From college, you say?"

Dolly nodded.

"Well, one thing I can say is, unlike his father before him, at least he didn't lose his smile in the war. He seemed almost cheerful!"

Dolly felt her bones turning to water. Helen!

"And the rumors about his drinking," Mrs. Fryt went on. "Well, he seemed sober to me. And you ladies will like to know: I asked him about Wilma. He said she was fine." Mrs. Fryt sighed. "I suppose that family has just gotten used to her. I suppose they had no choice."

"Mother," said Jeannette.

Mrs. Fryt gave her daughter an innocent look. "I'm only saying, when a woman tries to burn down her own house, you just know she isn't in her right mind!" She sniffed, and went back to her stitching.

"Now, Cecilia," said Thelma. "Look what she'd been through."

"Oh, yes, none of *us* had to endure such things," Mrs. Fryt sneered. "As I always say, it's a good thing I was home at the time, or she just might have succeeded. I suppose it was none of my affair, but I couldn't just sit back and watch her destroy the place, after all those years. You could look in her eyes and just see she'd gone mad. And then, a couple days later, she was gone. Off to college to study the piano! If you can believe it."

Dolly swallowed. Her heart rate was finally slowing. "Really?"

"She cut herself off from John and used the money her father had left her when he'd died years earlier. It was quite a lot, as I understand it, and she'd never breathed a word of it to John. Her father's bank had handled it all those years. Can you believe the nerve?"

"Well, she never would have left, if he hadn't had the affair," Dolly objected.

"But, mercy me, there comes a point when you just have to say 'Let bygones be bygones.' She left him twenty-seven years after the fact! She even made him drive her to the train! As if he hadn't suffered enough, all those years. She never was in her right mind!" Mrs. Fryt shook her head. "Despite that adultery *is* a sin, you do have to admit that putting up with Wilma would be enough to drive any man to the arms of another woman—"

"That isn't fair!" Dolly said.

Mrs. Fryt ignored her. "I have to say, I was a bit surprised when Wilma deigned to come home for John's funeral. It was January of 1947 when he died, wasn't it? So she had been gone for more than a year. Of all the nerve—to come back, when she was the one who drove him to his grave."

"Mother," sighed Jeannette, pressing her temple.

"More than once, he traveled down to Appleton to retrieve her, and came back empty-handed."

"She looked great at his funeral," said Corinne. "Said she loved school."

"She had the nerve to shed tears for him, that day," added Mrs. Fryt.

"Well, of course she had the right to shed tears," put in Thelma. "He was her husband."

Mrs. Fryt scoffed. "I say, when a woman leaves her husband, she gives up all claim to him. And can you imagine keeping all that money a secret that way? You had to pity John, the way he carried on after her. And the rest of the family! The way she left her children in the lurch. As though they meant nothing to her at all!"

"I wouldn't say that, Cecilia," said Corinne. "She did move up to Stone Harbor to be near Jack and Mary, when they moved there."

"Yes, it seems we're rid of the Mickelsons for good now," said Mrs. Fryt. "If JJ is, in fact, gone. Is he planning to marry that Helen, then?"

Startled, Dolly shrugged.

"Well, Jack sold the bank about the minute his father died, you know. He always did think he was too good for this town. Now he runs a charter sailboat outfit up in Stone Harbor. We hear *Wilma* teaches piano lessons."

"But what do you think she should have done?" Dolly said. "Let him get away with it?"

Mrs. Fryt fixed her with a steely glare, drawing herself up straight.

Judy Wasserman snickered. "Perhaps we've found the explanation for why Dolly's poor husband looked so awful at church on Sunday."

Of course Judy would have been watching Byron—she always did! "Leave my husband out of this," Dolly said.

"You *have* been spending a lot of time with JJ Mickelson—fiancée or no—"

"Judy, that's enough!" said Jeannette.

"I resent the insinuation," Dolly said. "I am a married woman." She picked up her sewing basket, shoved her needle into her pin cushion, threw her spool of thread in, and shut the lid, trying to hide her shaking hands, hoping her performance would hide the truth of her disastrous life.

"Oh, Dolly," said Corinne. "Judy doesn't mean anything."

"Look what you've done, Judy," scolded Jeannette.

Dolly pushed back her chair and stood. "Excuse me, Mrs. Fryt. I have to be going."

Mrs. Fryt raised her eyebrows, but said nothing.

Dolly walked home to the bungalow, but once she was there she thought she'd go crazy. She did the only thing she could think to do: sat on the back stoop and smoked one cigarette after another. She wished she could cry, but she was too miserable even for that. Was it true that, like the ladies had said about Wilma and John, Dolly had simply been too much for Byron to put up with? Was that why he'd sought out another woman?

Did Dolly want to be in the bungalow and her marriage merely *on sufferance*?

Or would people start to believe the things that Judy had insinuated about Dolly and JJ? And if they did, would she be exiled from this town, and from Byron, in disgrace?

Unable to bear the thought of starting supper, finishing the ironing, or even facing Byron when he got home from work, Dolly remembered that JJ had asked her to look in on the Mickelson house. Even though he was gone, the house could still be a refuge of sorts. Perhaps there she would be able to think straight, and decide what to do. She waited until she thought the quilting ladies would all have left Mrs. Fryt's, then set out.

When she walked into the house, its cool beauty immediately soothed her. Certainly this house could not be to blame for everything that had happened to the Mickelsons—or to Dolly herself! She wandered through the rooms and finally upstairs. Snooping more than she'd ever allowed herself to before, she ventured into Wilma and John's bedroom. On the far wall, a bay window draped in lace looked out on the line of fir trees at the edge of the property; on the near wall, there was a fireplace, just like in the dining room below it. The bed, made up in white, was an elegant four-poster of a lustrous dark wood, and there were two matching dressers, and a vanity, too.

An oval-framed sepia portrait on the wall caught her eye—she could see from where she stood that it was a wedding picture, a woman in a white dress standing behind a seated man in a dark suit. She went over to look.

Even through the haze of dust on the glass, Dolly recognized Wilma from the ladies' descriptions: her whipped-butter skin, golden piled hair, high cheekbones, and straight nose. (Her mouth, Dolly noted, had appeared on Jack.) Her high-necked, long-sleeved dress was exquisite, but so tight around the bodice that Dolly could only imagine the strain it must have been to breathe. The pointed toe of a spangled white shoe peered out from under the long skirt. Wilma was even tinier than Dolly had envisioned, her head barely clearing John's, though he was seated in front of her. Despite his obvious height and the broadness of his shoulders, there was something about him—something at the corners of his eyes—that looked insubstantial, like a good wind might blow him away. As for Wilma's eyes, they were glassy—and Dolly didn't think that was just a trick of the portrait. *Why, she almost looks as though she didn't want to marry him in the first place!*

In all of Dolly's wedding photos, she was grinning like a fool.

Well, it was a different time, she told herself. *They weren't supposed to grin in their wedding portraits.*

Moving away from the portrait, she discovered a snapshot in a small frame on the mantel. She picked it up, and recognized the girl in it immediately: Elissa. Standing next to her was a tall blond soldier: Nick, then. Both were smiling, though they looked a little awkward together. Dolly removed the back of the frame to see if there was anything written on the back of the photo. What she found was this: "1943. 'Wash me thoroughly from mine iniquity, and cleanse me from my sin. For I acknowledge my transgressions: and my sin is ever before me. Psalm 51.'"

Dolly sank to the floor, hugging the picture to her, closing her eyes.

A moment later, she began seriously to weigh her options.

She was fed up with trying to please Byron. It wasn't fair that she should give up everything for him, only to have him betray her. She knew she had been no angel, either, concerning JJ, but at least nothing too physical had happened. She decided: No matter how much everyone might think Byron's infidelity had been brought on by her wifely shortcomings, it was ample provocation for her to leave him. Wilma was proof enough of that.

But if Dolly were to leave Byron, what would she do? She had no money, only a high school education, no car, and certainly no secret inheritance like Wilma Mickelson had.

She immediately disregarded the idea of going home to Battle Point. A divorcée could hardly go back to live with her mother and father just as though nothing had happened.

Perhaps, she thought, she could live in the Mickelson house. After all, it was the only place she had ever truly felt she could be herself. She could write to JJ and his father. If JJ explained the house's needs to Jack, they would surely allow her to live in the house in exchange for its care. She could apply to work at Birnbaum's or Penney's for spending money. Staying in Pine Rapids wouldn't be so bad, if she just stopped caring what everyone thought of her.

She warmed to the idea. She would be a career woman! Eat all her meals at the café, smoke just as much as she pleased, work extra hours in order to afford flying lessons, and, someday, buy her own airplane. It was a pleasingly scandalous résumé to imagine: a divorcée/pilot living alone in the "cursed" house on the hill. Forget creating a home for her husband à la Donna Reed. She would be strong-minded and disagreeable like Bette Davis, who, in one movie Dolly had seen a few years ago, had said she'd never talked to a man for five minutes without wanting to box his ears. Dolly had always remembered the secret thrill of that line—and now she could put it to work in her own life.

Leaning back against the cool marble of the fireplace in the master bedroom, Dolly decided: She would love the house as no one else had, and pay it every attention it could desire. She would be known for her tenderness with the gardens, her finesse with paint. She would learn roofing and carpentry, and tame the derelict shingles and porches. And she wouldn't give a damn what anybody in this town said; she wouldn't even listen.

THE MICKELSON COTTAGES
Water Street, Stone Harbor, Wisconsin
Tuesday, August 8, 1950

Even after JJ told Dolly he was going to leave, he had considered staying. Maybe it wasn't too late. Maybe she would leave her husband, and JJ could convince her that he wasn't all madness and destruction.

But he couldn't even convince himself, that night. He hadn't been able to sleep; his grandparents' old house felt as cloying as the jungle. He decided there was no reason to stay and make a further ass of himself. So, very early Saturday morning, he packed up his few things, left a note for Dolly, and drove out of town, not knowing where he was headed, pressing the accelerator down hard even as his eyes lingered on his rearview mirror, watching the town fade from sight.

He'd been hoping for more. Idiot that he was, he never realized impossibility until he'd run himself smack into a wall. His mother said he was a romantic. She didn't realize he was just a drunk, half out of his mind most of the time, imagining things that never could be. Believing the things he enacted. So he'd skulked out of Pine Rapids, embarrassed and—there was no denying it—forlorn.

Feeling sorry for himself, he'd spent a couple of days at a resort near Rhinelander, where the fishing was good. He'd met a woman there, too, a waitress at the café where he ate three meals a day for three days. The food wasn't bad, and it was cheap. The waitress was blond, lonely-married, half in love with him by breakfast the second day. The third night, she came knocking on his cabin door. He was drunk; she had him almost before he realized it. He didn't remember much, just flashes—the curtain of her hair, the heat of her thighs encasing him as she moved atop him, his own snarling cries. Then, she was sprawled on the floor of his cabin, cursing him, her hair a tangle. Perhaps he had cursed her back, angry that she'd made him break his rule about not fooling around with married girls. He hadn't been doing well with that recently. In any case, he didn't know, now, what had happened, only that when he woke up, the sole evidence of her visit was a lipstick stain on the collar of his shirt. He left that morning before the dew was gone.

He wanted to be a good man, like his father, but there were so many other things he wanted, too. A little comfort; ease bordering on numbness. A sense of vitality and purpose, of being where he was meant to be, and what he was meant to be. The way he'd felt with Anne, that night all those years ago. The way he'd felt with Dolly. It was funny, he supposed, that it was only girls that weren't available that he'd ever felt that way about.

He knew better than to think it was anything that could last, but he never could stop seeking that crystalline moment of hope and forgiveness fused in a light so bright that it blinded you to pain, to memories.

In the meantime, he drank. That was another thing that could get you by.

He supposed his college degree made him employable—all he had to do was have his prof write a couple of letters and he could probably get in as a teacher at some high school—but being employable in theory was vastly different from feeling capable of settling in anywhere. He'd come so close to breaking everything in his grandparents' house. Picture him a teacher! He was liable to break some kid's head the minute he smarted off.

There was nothing that seemed possible.

But, those days at the resort, he found himself missing his family. He hadn't missed them as much when he was in Pine Rapids—he was surrounded by the evidence of their past existence, and his own—but once he left, he felt dread mounting within him, born of homelessness and vacuity. He realized that if he drowned in the lake, it would be weeks before anyone would think to look for him.

It took him a few days to convince himself to go see them. He told himself it might be better this time.

Driving over the crest of the hill and down into Stone Harbor brought a smile to his face. The bay glistened blue in the sunshine, and the village rose up on the wooded hill, white and spare with its steeples and schoolhouse and white frame houses. Following the highway as it curved along the water's edge, JJ drove by the big white hotels with their extravagant porches, then through what passed for downtown: Bronson's ice cream parlor, the village hall, the old general store. On the water side were the yacht club docks, the clubhouse. He craned his neck to try to catch a glimpse of his dad, who spent much of his time there, but he didn't see him.

The road continued straight, but the water curved away from it, making room for cottages along the shore, which was dense with cedar trees. Just as the hill started to rise again on the way out of town, JJ turned into a driveway on the left. His mom and dad's place.

He walked in the back door of his parents' cottage, calling, "Mom? Dad?" No answer. He passed through from back to front, but there was no one home. His leg was stiff and sore from driving; he couldn't keep from hobbling. He took a quick nip from the flask in his pocket.

He didn't want to be alone any longer. He stepped out onto the front porch, intending to go to his grandmother's cottage next door. Surely she would be home.

The Mickelson family cottages—fifty years old or more by this time—sat side by side on a large lawn. One cottage had belonged to his mother Mary's parents, a long time ago; JJ had always liked hearing his father tell of the summer he got back from the war and the first time he'd noticed Mary down on the dock. Surrounded by tall cedar trees on three sides, both cottages faced out toward Green Bay. Each had a large porch, perfect for watching the sunset through the trees.

J.J. felt peaceful, being here, despite the pain in his leg as he limped across the lawn. He shoved his hands in his pockets, and slowed his pace a little. There was no reason to hurry. No one was even watching to see whether he could.

He had just reached the bottom porch step at his grandmother's when the screen door banged open and out rushed Anne. She was looking down, adjusting the ribbon around the waist of her bathing suit.

He staggered, and almost lost his footing.

She didn't see him until she had reached the bottom of the porch steps and nearly run into him, and she screamed, pressing her hand to her heart. He grabbed her elbow to keep her from falling backward onto the steps.

Recognition flickered in her eyes. But she didn't move, or lose her look of fear.

He forced out his best smile. His ears were still ringing from her scream. "Sorry, Anne. I didn't mean to startle you."

"What—what are you doing here? Jack said you were in Pine Rapids."

He flushed a little, pleased, though she clearly wasn't happy to see him. At least she had been paying attention to what was said about him. "I was until just a couple days ago. I decided to come visit. I didn't know you were here."

"Yes, we're here, Harry and the children and I." She still didn't smile.

"So I'll finally get to meet my little cousins."

She blinked. Blinked again. "Yes."

A moment passed.

"Would you let go of me, please?" she said.

He hadn't realized he was still holding her elbow. He dropped it, took a step back. "Sorry," he said. His heart pounded.

"I'd better get back to the children." She squeezed past him.

He took a step after her. "Can I come? Meet them?"

She acted as though she hadn't heard him. Hugging herself tight, she walked quickly, with her head bowed, toward the steps that led down to the dock.

When she was out of sight, he slammed the banister with his fist, and cursed.

"JJ?"

He looked up. It was his grandma, poking her head out the cottage door.

"JJ, I thought that was you! I saw you out the window. For heaven's sake!"

He smiled, and shoved his hands in his pockets again. He hoped she hadn't heard him swear. "Hi, Grandma."

Superior, Wisconsin
Thursday, December 20, 1945

Late that night, after spending the afternoon and evening with Harry in bliss, planning the details of their upcoming wedding, Anne sat down at her desk to write a letter. Although she draped a blanket over her shoulders, still she shivered, unable to get warm.

Now that she was alone again, all the terror and dread that she'd been experiencing since her trip to Pine Rapids seemed to have flooded back. Her handwriting was shaky; words would scarcely come. After each sentence, she sat for several moments, just looking at the stationery glowing in the light of the desk lamp.

When she finally closed the letter and signed her name, it was past midnight. What she had written was:

Dear JJ,

I am writing to tell you that I am going to marry Harry after all.

I am so ashamed of what happened between us. I did not intend for it to happen. I have not told Harry and, for the sake of our future happiness, will not.

If you ever cared for me, as you professed to, please, you must never speak of it, to anyone. Your family must not find out, or I could never face them. If I ever see you again, remember only that I am your "aunt," and let us just forget the rest, I beg you.

Anne

As she sealed the envelope, addressed to Marine Sergeant John J. Mickelson at the Great Lakes Naval Station Hospital, the tears started again, and she dropped the envelope. It settled on the desk, facedown. She covered her eyes with one hand, cupped the other over her stomach. She was shivering so hard that her teeth chattered.

That her period had not come last week when it should have had been a terrible shock. She had counted the days, to be certain she was not mistaken, and then prayed with all her might that it was just a little delayed, and that she would soon discover a spot of blood. After five days of fervent, unanswered prayers, she had given up hope.

Though she had known from the moment when JJ sighed atop her that the consequences of what she had done were undoubtedly horrific, she had somehow not even acknowledged the possibility of this, the worst consequence imaginable. But now, she couldn't deny it. Her cycles had always been like clockwork. And the past few mornings, she had awakened feeling nauseous.

This afternoon, she and Harry had set their wedding for next Sunday, December 30. If there was a baby from JJ, it would come in August. She would just have to convince everyone—including herself—that it was five weeks early. It was the only way she would be able to live with what she had done.

It was the only way she and her child would ever have a home.

None of us can put into words why we fly. It is something
different for each of us. I can't say exactly *why* I fly but
I *know* why as I've never known anything in my life.

—"At the Twilight's Last Gleaming," by WASP Cornelia Fort,
published in *Woman's Home Companion*, July 1943

THE MICKELSON HOUSE
502 W. First Street, Pine Rapids
Tuesday, August 8, 1950

Though Dolly avoided looking at her watch, she was conscious of the
lowering light outside. This would be the first evening in the entire
history of her marriage that she had not prepared supper for Byron.
Well, not counting the once or twice that he had taken her out for a
fish fry—but for her not to even *show up* for supper? Unthinkable!
Despite that she was contemplating leaving him, she was so nervous
about committing her first wholly deliberate act of rebellion that, before she had even realized she was gnawing on her nails, she had completely ruined what was left of her manicure.

She replaced the framed snapshot of Nick and Elissa on the mantel, thinking, *But if Byron's sorry like John was—if he promises to
give that woman up—then what should I do?*

She examined the wedding portrait of John and Wilma again; it certainly appeared that Wilma had been a reluctant bride. Dolly couldn't help but think of the Byron she'd fallen in love with, the one at the Battle Point town beach with water sparkling on his eyelashes when he grinned. She thought about JJ, too. Why had she been so drawn to him, despite his destructive habits, despite her love for Byron? Was it because JJ didn't hide from her?

Was it because he had told her the truth?

Why was it so difficult for her to tell the truth, even to herself? Why could she not face up to her own inadequacies?

Maybe there was a reason for Byron's infidelity. Maybe she really had been deficient in some way, some way that she was too blind and headstrong to recognize. Should she at least give him a chance to try to explain?

Should she try to explain herself to him?

Unfortunately, the thought of it again made her feel like throwing up. She went downstairs to the parlor and sat at the piano, uncovering the keys, pressing them down one by one so gently that they barely made a sound.

Then, a knock at the front door startled her. Her heart thumped into overdrive. She jumped to her feet and looked at her watch. 6:35. *Who on earth could be knocking at the Mickelsons' door,* she wondered, but of course, she knew.

Despite herself, she was happy to see him, but the feeling was brief, as he pushed his way past her. "Where is he?"

"What do you mean?"

"JJ Mickelson." His face was flushed, and his eyes were narrow. His tie was loose, his shirt wrinkled, and a piece of his hair flopped down over his forehead. He looked exhausted. And very angry.

"What do you mean, Byron? JJ left town."

"Do I have to search this house for the son-of-a-bitch?"

"Byron! He's gone!"

"That's what you're telling everyone, then?" His eyes were ice.

"What are you talking about?"

"I went to the hardware store after work to pick up the paint for your bathroom. I was going to do something nice for you! And I ran into that red-haired woman who's in the quilting group with you— Judy, I think her name is."

Dolly's knees went weak.

"She had some very interesting things to say. Such as that you'd told them all that JJ Mickelson had hired you. You told *me* the church had arranged it and it was volunteer work. She said the church had nothing to do with it."

"I—I'm sorry, Byron. I—"

"She also told me that he's 'handsome as the devil' and that she didn't see how any woman could spend as much time with JJ Mickelson as you had, and not—what were her words—'succumb to his charms.'"

"She—she hates me—she's exaggerating. She has a crush on you!"

"You're making a fool of me in this town. Have you been screwing him?"

"Byron! No! I have not! And how dare you? I saw you! I saw you on Friday night with that woman!"

"What?"

"Don't pretend you don't know what I'm talking about. I saw everything." She mimicked the ice-blond woman's way with a cigarette. "The way she led you out by the hand."

He looked at her. "Do you mean you saw Mrs. Swanstrom?" he said finally.

"I don't care what her name is. The point is, I'm not going to stand for it."

"You're not going to stand for what?"

"Don't pretend you don't know what I mean."

"For God's sake, don't be an idiot, Doll. I sold her a car last week. Friday night she was just telling me she couldn't figure out how to get the glove box open. She wanted me to show her how to open it."

"You expect me to believe that? The way it looked?"

"It's the truth, Doll. I swear."

As his words sank in, she felt her rage collapsing into shock.

He said, "You don't honestly think I'd—?"

She pressed her hand to her throat. "A woman like that leads you out back that way," she said. "What else *could* I think?"

"If you knew me at all, Doll, it would never even cross your mind."

"But the way it looked—"

"We have to be nice to our customers around town. That's the only reason I went out to the parking lot with her. I checked her glove box and showed her how to open it. Then I went in and said good night to my buddies, and then I came home. And *you* weren't home."

She swallowed, took a step back. "How can you be so offended when I think it of you, and then—then turn around and accuse me?"

"I don't know what to think, Doll. That lady Judy said you were getting awfully cozy with this guy."

"I—well—"

"And I saw the way you got excited about this house. Like you were—in love, or something. I've been too wrapped up in my own head to consider—until Judy told me, I mean. Even though I should have known, what with all the books you read and the way you're never satisfied with just *life*. I guess I should have known that some-day you'd want more than me. I just didn't know it would be so soon. Are you in love with him?"

"Stop it. No."

"Judy said you'd told them something about how his fiancée had come last Friday, that you'd gone home and he left town. But you weren't home Friday night."

"Stop," she said. She tried to think what she could tell him. Her improvisational muscle had gone slack. But she realized: She was tired of all the lies. She would never have the spectacular life she wanted if she couldn't start being honest. With Byron, and with her-self. Hadn't she learned from JJ that not talking about things would lead them to fester, that the festering could and would destroy a per-son—or a family—from the inside out?

She took a deep breath, and started at the beginning.

By the time Dolly got to the part in the story where JJ Mickelson kissed her, she and Byron were sitting on the steps leading up to the second floor. Byron was two steps below her, leaning forward, elbows on knees, so she couldn't see his face, which made the confession a lit-tle easier. She didn't see a need for perfect honesty about this part of the tale, though, and simply told him, "So, Friday night, I was upset, and a little drunk, and I think he was, too, and—he kissed me. I stopped him, though! Almost right away."

Byron looked over his shoulder at her. He looked pale, pinched around the eyes. "Almost?"

She faltered. "You have to understand, I was under the impression that you—that you were with that woman."

She could hardly bear the heartbroken look on his face.

And yet, it was something! So much more than she had seen on his face, in his eyes, in so long.

The tragedy was that it came too late.

"Oh, Byron," she said. "I know I'm a terrible wife. Even to let it go that far. I know. I've really tried to be good to you, but I know I don't do anything the way I should. I guess I'm just not made for it. I'm so—restless! I should have realized it sooner."

"What are you saying?"

"I know you'll never forgive what I've done. I can't forgive myself."

He sighed, and turned from her again. After a moment, he said, "I don't understand why you thought where we lived would make any difference. Did you think I wasn't happy with you?"

"I didn't know. I thought I must have been doing something wrong, the way you were so distant."

"Is this why you were asking me about the war? Because this guy told you about what had happened to him?"

"Yes. A little."

A long minute passed in silence. Finally, he said, "Doll, there are things I've seen that I don't want to think about. Or talk about. I just want to leave them behind me. Maybe you can't understand that. Guys have different ways of dealing with things. I don't know what this guy JJ told you, but for me, I don't want to talk about it. I want to get on with our life."

She sighed. It seemed hopeless that he would ever understand her position. "But those things are in you, Byron. How can I really love you if I don't know half of what's in you?"

He was watching the fingers of his right hand twist his wedding band round and round on his left hand's ring finger. Dolly remembered how she had felt when she put that ring on his finger: ecstatic. Complete. "You always have. Loved me," he said. "I know you've tried. I'm sorry I haven't made you happy."

She was quiet.

"I've tried to take care of you, Doll, like you do me—I don't know what I'd do without you. That's why I went into the business with

Roy. I wanted to give us a better life—better than we ever would have had back in Battle Point with me working for my stepdad."

"But you took me away from my family. My friends. You never even asked what I wanted."

"I guess I didn't know I was supposed to." He laughed a little, ruefully.

"It never occurred to you to consider what I wanted?"

"I'm sorry, Doll. I hated living in Battle Point after the war. Everybody thinking they knew me, when they didn't. Working for my jerk of a stepfather, when next to his own son I couldn't do a damn thing right. Having to share you with your family and everything. I guess when this opportunity came up with Roy, I just thought how good it would be for me." He smiled a little. "Naturally, I figured it would be just as good for you."

She said nothing.

"I didn't want you to be unhappy, Doll. I mean, I wanted you to be happy. I thought we would be. It was my best shot, I guess, and I took it. I was really hoping you'd like the bungalow. *I* like it. It's our own, Doll, isn't that what matters? And I'll paint the bathroom this weekend. I bought the paint. I want things to be what you want them to be."

"What do you mean?" she said. "I thought—"

He smiled a little, and looked back over his shoulder and met her eyes. "Didn't you read the fine print on the marriage license? 'In case one party acts like a complete idiot, the other party gets one free pass to act like an idiot, too.'"

She looked up at the high ceiling. Cobwebs dripped from the chandelier. She could almost hear the house, urging her on: *It won't be perfect, but all life has heartache—that much I know.*

This was a wonderful house! And the Mickelsons had dared to blame it for their troubles! They had left it alone to suffer the consequences of their misdeeds and their selfishness. The "curse," she decided, had merely been an excuse for their bad behavior—including JJ's. Dolly, too, had gotten caught up in the house's mystique, and had let it entice her into imagining things that would never be. But blaming the house for that was like blaming Elizabeth Taylor for the fact that, after you'd seen her in *National Velvet*, you'd suddenly yearned for a horse.

She reached out and touched Byron's arm. He boosted himself up so he was on the same stair as she was, cupped her face in his hand, and kissed her. He was so familiar that she felt restored, and she was thrilled that maybe it wasn't too late for them, after all. At least not if a few changes were made.

"You forgive me?" he said.

"You have to start treating me like a human being. Treating me as well as you'd treat Roy, or any of your other friends. You have to listen to what I think about things. Do you know what I mean?"

"I promise, Doll."

"I can't be a cookie-cutter wife. I tried, and I just can't do it. I'm never going to look like one of those women in an appliance ad."

He laughed.

"I'm serious, Byron. I can't stay married if that's all it's going to be."

"What do you want from me, Doll? Life isn't like some movie where we can just ride off into the sunset. Did you think being married was going to be easy?"

"Yes!" She sighed. "I did. Easier than *this,* anyway."

"Well, it isn't. No matter how much we wish it was. Doll, I'm going to mess up. I can't promise you I won't. But you don't have to be like a woman in an ad. They're not real. I know that. I wouldn't want that."

She was quiet a moment, then said, "You want to know what I want?"

He nodded.

"I want you to talk to me. Tell me how you're feeling. Did you know I've been taking notes on what you say about my suppers? It's the only shred of evidence I've had!"

He hung his head. "It's not easy for me."

"Well, you said yourself, life is hard," she said. "It's just not fair that Roy knows you so much better than I do."

". . . I'll try, Doll."

"I mean, talk to me about more than just Chryslers. I want to know about your past, and what you're really thinking. About me, our life. Even the war."

He sighed. "I'll try."

"One other thing, too. I want to take flying lessons."

He looked up. "Flying lessons?"

She gave him a look.

"All right, I'm sorry. Really?"

"You don't understand what it's like never to get to *drive,* Byron. It's my own life and yet it feels like I'm just along for the ride. I want to fly. And I want to be at the controls when I do it."

"Doll, it's just—not very *wifely,* taking flying lessons. And it's dangerous."

She pointed her chin.

An awkward moment passed. Then, suddenly he took her face in both his hands, and kissed her like they weren't even married yet. It took her breath away.

He pulled back from her, and said, "Want to get something to eat? At Shorty's or something?"

She looked into his eyes. Somewhere, she heard a sonata playing. She smiled, and kissed him again. She loved the heat of his hands, the protrusion of his ears, the curve of his smile; loved that he would think to take her out for supper and not insist that they go back to the bungalow right away. Perhaps they really could forge a new path, separate from the ruts they had worn in their lives over the past few months. Maybe Pine Rapids wouldn't be so bad. Even if she was going to stay married, that didn't mean she had to care what the town thought of her. Let them talk! Starting with tonight, when they would comment on how shocking it was that her husband had had to take her out for supper on a *Tuesday.* She could hear them now: "I bet she was reading a novel all day, instead of fulfilling her obligation to the household! She's just spoiled, expects dinner out like it was her due! Why, even Wilma Mickelson always had dinner on the table for John."

Dolly took a deep breath. "Yes, let's go," she said. When they stood, she linked her arm with his.

As they walked out into the evening and she pulled the Mickelsons' front door shut behind them, she felt a little pinch around her heart. It wasn't easy, leaving the poor house behind, and with it her fanciful notions of the spectacular life she would have had living there—with Byron or without him. But she loved Byron, and even if marriage wasn't the perpetual honeymoon she'd imagined it would be, she was still determined to make it work.

In fact, walking out of the house with Byron felt good, like a new start. She was older and wiser, setting out this time, and she had made up her mind. She would not again neglect to consider her own desires, her own evolving dreams of what her life could be. To remind herself, she would visit the Mickelson house from time to time. Not for JJ, and not for Byron, but because she'd sensed within its walls the joys and costs, the possibilities and devastations, of living, and she didn't ever want to lose that part of her that she had found there.

As she walked with Byron down the front porch steps, he pulled her close to his side, leaned down, and, just for a moment, pressed his lips to the top of her head. He murmured her name, then leaned away from her, and gave her a shy smile. There was hope and longing in his voice; it was contagious. As they descended the flight of stairs to where the Chrysler waited at the curb, she felt something escape and rise from her, and she looked up over her shoulder at the house. She could almost see it—regret and yearning and used-up old dreams— sailing up past the house's waiting porch, the second floor's windows, the third floor's peaks, the chimneys, on up into the gathering sky.

THE MICKELSON COTTAGES
Water Street, Stone Harbor, Wisconsin
Tuesday, August 8, 1950

Wilma fixed JJ an iced tea (he poured in a dollop from the flask in his pocket when she wasn't looking), and they hadn't been sitting on the porch a minute when his mother, Mary, came running up from the dock. She rushed onto the porch and crouched next to JJ's chair, threw her arms around his neck, and kissed his cheek. He could tell from the look on her face as she pulled away from him that she had smelled the booze on him. He grinned disarmingly, and she smiled; she would bring it up later, he knew, but she wouldn't ruin these, their first, moments together.

She pulled up a chair and sat on the edge of it, leaning toward him, insisting he tell her everything he had been doing since she had last seen him, two months before. There was much that he omitted, and certain things that benefited from embellishment, but he liked the attention nonetheless. Freckles dusted her nose and cheeks, like they did every summer, and her honey-blond hair showed a few strands of gray around her temples. As he always found, when seeing his mother after a long absence, she was too vivid to believe.

Later, his father and Uncle Harry arrived; they had been down at the Yacht Club, working on Jack's boat. Jack looked older, his hair entirely gray, his waist thickening a little, but his eyes were bright. A shadow darkened Harry's face, and JJ wondered for an instant if Harry knew about him and Anne. *No,* he decided immediately, *he can't know, or he'd kill me.*

Jack wanted to hear about the house in Pine Rapids, so JJ told everyone about the problems: the broken windows, the missing shingles. "But there's this girl who's been coming in and cleaning this summer. Dolly. She said the door was unlocked, and she was curious about the house. She's new in town and she didn't know about us."

"That house should not have been left unlocked," Jack said.

"No, really," JJ assured them, making his voice smooth enough to cover over everything that had happened. "She's been doing a great job. It's not bad at all. We just need to get someone in there. To live, I mean. It's lonely."

Mary laughed. "A house can't be lonely, JJ."

He took a sip of his iced tea. He guessed Dolly had rubbed off on him. Or had he given away that *he* had been lonely, being there? He hoped not. He didn't want them to know how it was.

"Well, JJ's right, in any case," Jack said. "We can't just let it sit there empty and pretend it isn't an issue."

Wilma straightened. "Sell it, then, Jack," she said. "Let someone else deal with it. Sell it as it is and just be done with it."

He gave her a wounded look. "Mom."

"Why are you so sentimental, Jack? You always hated that town."

"Well, what if JJ wants to live there someday? Or Liss? Or Harry's kids? Isn't that why we've kept it this long?"

"But in the meantime, Jack—?" Wilma cocked her head at him. "Besides, your father believed that house was cursed."

"Dad?" said Jack. "Dad didn't believe in the curse."

"He did. He just didn't admit it to you. But that was his excuse for everything! Haven't I told you?"

Jack shook his head, disbelieving.

"What do you think, Mom?" Harry said. "Do you think it was cursed?"

She fixed him with a cool look. "We're happy here, aren't we? Happier than we've ever been?"

Harry was speechless.

"Dolly doesn't believe it's cursed," JJ put in. "She really loves it."

Wilma turned to him. "Who is this Dolly, JJ? You seem quite taken with her!"

His parents looked up, hopeful. He knew they wished he would settle down. But he shook his head. "No, no. She's married." But talking about her had made an ache of missing her open up in him. He was ashamed of what he had done, and yet he had been true to his desires, and he thought she had nearly seen him for what he was. Just like Anne. Thinking of it all made him want a stronger drink. And then it made him think, *Stop. You know you have to.* "She's married," he said again.

Wilma reached over and patted his good knee. "Poor JJ," she said. Then she turned to Jack. "Jack, this is our home now. There's no reason to hang on to that place. The younger generation can start over, you know. Curse or no, that house isn't exactly a bastion of happy memories."

Jack leaned back in his chair. "We were all born there, Mom."

Wilma waved him off. "Oh, you know what I mean!"

"*You* were never happy there, that's what you mean."

Wilma looked at him. "I was not a good mother, Jack. I won't pretend any different. You children deserved better. But I'm through apologizing. Haven't I told you? You can take me or leave me, now, but this is what I am. And you can't deny that that house chewed us up and spit us out—one by one. Each in our own way."

"I don't—" Jack started.

"Look," interrupted Harry, standing, gesturing toward the yard. JJ's hands went clammy when he looked and saw Anne. She had just reached the top of the stairs coming up from the dock, and was guiding two toddling girls with matching bright blond ponytails. Behind the three emerged a dark-headed boy, running circles around his mother and sisters on the lawn, making his arms into airplane wings.

His name was Tommy, JJ remembered, from the Christmas letters that had come to his mom and dad from Harry and Anne.

"For their sake, we're not going to argue anymore," Harry said, with a severe look. Taken aback, they all quieted. Then Harry bounded down the porch steps and across the lawn, approaching the boy with a roar, picking him up and swinging him in a circle until the boy squealed. Everyone's eyes softened, watching them; it did seem foolish to argue. And JJ saw there was no sense thinking about Anne, or Dolly, any longer. He hoped they would both someday forgive him, but that was out of his hands. He couldn't ask for more than what they had already given him: They had proven to him that true romantic love really did exist, by turning from him in favor of the ones they were meant for, despite his best misguided, selfish efforts to bedevil them. And if he could not quite believe that he deserved such a love, was it not enough, for the time being, to know that it existed? That it was something he could, at least, hope for?

Maybe he was a romantic, like his mother thought, after all.

He lit a cigarette. Over the water, visible above the trees, the sun was lowering toward evening, an orb of blinding golden light. He thought of Bertinelli, who was probably dead; of Buck Young, who certainly was; of the Marine with both legs blown off who'd given JJ the cigarette after the corpsmen had dropped him on the beach at Iwo. He wondered if that guy had made it. He thought of his uncle Chase, whose wartime medals and portrait had stared at JJ his whole childhood, asking, *Will you be a hero like me? Will you be worthy of your name?* Whose death still lurked at the back of JJ's father's eyes, and in the twitch of his grandmother's upper lip. It lingered, too, in the family's present palpable absences. His grandfather, whose grief-born lust had riven the family and, perhaps, hastened his own death; the half uncle, who had disappeared as quickly as he'd materialized; even JJ's own sister, who evidently hadn't been able to reconcile all her heart's accounts, at least not yet. He thought of Dolly again, and hoped she would keep the house until the rest of them could get their acts together.

JJ's leg ached. His heart ached. His head, too. But he was alive; love, hope, forgiveness—all were still possible, he supposed. As possible as the freckles on his mother's nose, the sun sparkling on the water, or the warm skin of a pretty girl: all things that, at one time, had seemed the stuff of dreams. All the things that he had to think he had been fighting for.

He blew out smoke and grinned.

His grandmother smiled. "Doesn't it feel like home here, JJ?" she said, sighing a little, reaching over to pat his knee. "Isn't it nice?"

THE MICKELSON COTTAGES
Water Street, Stone Harbor, Wisconsin
Tuesday, August 8, 1950

Later that evening, Harry found himself alone on the front porch of his mother's cottage. The sun had sunk below the horizon an hour ago, but he'd had a devil of a time getting the kids to settle down; Anne was still in their room, reading to them, having chased Harry out, saying he got them too excited. His mother had gone to bed, too, and Jack, Mary, and JJ had gone home to the other cottage, the one that had belonged to Mary's parents years ago.

The night air was pleasant, and Harry hoped Anne would soon join him. He felt like only half of himself when she wasn't beside him. The kids, too, for that matter. He loved those nights back home in Superior when there were thunderstorms—those were the only times Anne allowed the children to pile on the big bed with them, everyone's legs and arms tangling together, the tangible connection of warm skin on skin like proof of finally belonging, and no fooling this time.

Harry leaned his elbows on the porch railing, looking out at the shadowy trees, the moon glistening on the water beyond. Now that he was alone, starting to relax, he had to admit he was exhausted. It had taken all his restraint this afternoon and evening not to show his anger when his nephew, JJ, appeared. Except for at John Mickelson's funeral, Harry hadn't seen JJ in nearly five years, orchestrating his family's rare visits to Stone Harbor to ensure their paths wouldn't cross. After what Anne had told him the night before their wedding, Harry had not known how he would react to seeing JJ again.

Well, now he knew. He would shut up, preserve the peace, like he always did in this family. Shoving himself under the bus of their selfishness. Only this time, he could actually feel proud of it. This time, it was for Anne. She had tugged on his elbow, this afternoon in the yard after she'd come up from the lake, as the children swirled around them. "You won't say anything to him? Please?" Imploring him with her lovely eyes.

He did not want to see her hurt any more than she already had been, and he'd long ago come to the conclusion that JJ was too self-absorbed to think of Anne after he'd finished with her. But it still made Harry's stomach twist, thinking of the way Anne had looked the night before their wedding—telling Harry that she'd planned to deceive him but couldn't go through with it, trying again to give him back his ring. He wouldn't take it. "It isn't your fault, Anne," he'd told her. "It's my fault for leaving you alone with him. I never dreamed he would do anything like that." He'd pulled her close and held her while they both cried. Their fusion was complete. Any child of hers would be a child of his. He felt he'd have turned to dust if she had left him.

But forgiveness for his nephew had eluded him, and he had never been tested so sorely as today, seeing JJ's smug face again. He knew JJ was a war hero, and troubled—but what JJ had done to Anne was a bitter pill for Harry to swallow. Harry could not see that there was any excuse for it. He wondered what his brother Jack would say if he knew the truth about JJ. Not that Jack would ever believe it; Jack almost hadn't believed the truth about their father. Jack had that stubborn faith that everyone in the family was as heroic as he was. The truth, though, Harry thought, was that average people—and the Mickelsons *were* average, despite what some of the family might think of themselves—lived at the mercy of their own dissatisfactions and desires.

What would Jack say, Harry wondered, if he knew what Harry had seen in Virginia, Minnesota, in the summer of 1946? Harry had been up there to do a story for the paper, and had made arrangements to have lunch with Elissa, who was working at the Virginia hospital on her senior cadet assignment. After a pleasant meal—Harry had paid, relishing his role as uncle—the two walked out of the café on Main Street and were just about to part company when Harry happened to glance up at a delivery truck passing by. He recognized the driver, who looked remarkably similar to Harry himself. Harry raised an eyebrow; Elissa's face went pink. "It isn't what you think," she said, not meeting his eyes.

I can explain, she had written to Harry the following week. *He had nowhere else to go—trusted no one, you can imagine. He found me in Mpls some months ago. I haven't told anyone only because he asked me not to. We see each other regularly but, as I told you, I have been dating several of the doctors at the hospital. Uncle Harry, please don't tell anyone he is here, as N. is just trying to find himself, and get his feet under himself, as am I. We are not ready to place ourselves at the mercy of our relations, and will not be for some time, I imagine.*

Whatever Elissa meant by that, it sounded like trouble to Harry, but Anne had encouraged him not to interfere. "Just imagine what they've been through!" she'd said, so Harry had kept quiet. He had his own life to concern him, after all—Tommy was born a few weeks later. The next spring, though, after Elissa got a job in South Dakota, Harry wrote to inquire. By this time, John Mickelson was dead, and Jack had started looking for Nick, who had money coming to him from the will.

Yes, N. did come out here, too, Elissa replied. *He is working on a ranch some 30 miles from Pierre, so we see each other only occasionally. Please don't tell Dad (or Mom or anyone). N. has no interest in the money. Please don't worry, our friendship is simply the only thing that matters to either of us. I have had no trouble finding more doctors to date, thank you for asking. The trouble I have is in finding any of them remarkable enough to consider seriously.*

"That doesn't sound good," Harry said to Anne, after reading the letter to her. But still, he hadn't mentioned anything to Jack or Mary about it. As far as Harry knew now, more than three years later, Elissa and Nick were both still out there, and just tonight Mary had mentioned that Elissa still didn't have a serious boyfriend, despite all the doctors who were clamoring for the position.

Harry heard the door swing open behind him, and turned to see Anne, silhouetted in the lamplight from inside. "They're asleep, finally," she said, coming up beside him. She fit perfectly in the crook of his arm.

"Are you all right?" Harry said.

She looked up at him. "I think so."

"We can leave in the morning, if you'd like."

She sighed. "There's no need, darling. I wouldn't like for us to change our plans on his account. And I know what it means to you to be here."

He sighed, too, acknowledging that. "It's a little like being a kid again, for me. Back before Chase died. When things were okay. That's what my mom feels, too, I think. Why she likes it here so much. It's like his spirit came here to live. He always loved it here, on the water."

"Things can be okay again, Harry. Can't they? Aren't they?"

"Of course. You're right. They're perfect now," he said. "It's just that sometimes the past—it catches up to a person, you know? When you're a kid, you have all these grand ideas that nothing bad is ever going to happen to you."

"Yes, I know."

They stood a moment, absorbing the low hum of contentment that seemed to sound in such quiet times between them. It would sustain them through the next wild day and the next, come what may. Of that much, he was sure.

Suddenly, she flinched. "JJ," she whispered, pointing her chin toward the other cottage. Harry looked, and saw his nephew just shutting the door behind him as he came out onto the porch. The distance was great enough that Harry thought if he and Anne stayed perfectly still, JJ might not notice them. She evidently had the same idea; she stood frozen in place.

They watched as JJ lit a cigarette. He pulled a flask from his pocket, its silver winking in the moon. Lifted it to his lips. Then he paused, and reared back and flung it. End over end it spun across the night sky, disappearing into the shadows as it descended toward the ground, making no sound when it landed.

Harry looked down at his wife. A tear glistened in her eye. And suddenly, he felt no more anger, only sorrow for all that had been, and joy for all that would be.

Epilogue

HOME OF MRS. CECILIA FRYT
412 W. First Street, Pine Rapids
October 1950

It was one of those glorious golden fall days that took the sting out of everything's dying, and Cecilia Fryt was setting up her parlor in preparation for the second bridge club meeting of the fall. She had put the quilt frames up in the attic at the end of August, after the completion of the Wild Goose Chase quilt. On display for three weeks in September, the quilt had enticed the congregation to buy hundreds of tickets for the church bazaar raffle. When everything was tallied afterward, Cecilia was satisfied that this year's had been one of the most successful fund-raisers the church had seen. They were still just shy of enough money to buy the new organ, but Cecilia had a few ideas what to do about that.

She had just set up the fourth card table when she heard a strange buzzing sound far away outside. An airplane, again! She had heard one last week about this same time. She had to know what on earth was going on—airplanes almost never were heard above Pine Rapids. The nearest airport was in Wausau, and Pine Rapids wasn't exactly on the way anywhere.

Hurrying as fast as her aching bones would allow, Cecilia made it out to the front porch just in time to see the small red and white plane swoop low over her house, so close she could almost feel its vibrations under her skin. "Of all the nerve!" she said out loud, standing with arms akimbo, watching as the plane zoomed away, rising slightly and turning toward the west. When it turned, she could see two people inside. One almost looked like a black-haired woman, but Cecilia decided the person must just be a pretty-looking young man.

The plane tipped its wings in salute, then straightened again and headed west into the golden afternoon.

For just a moment, Cecilia watched it receding, wondering where it had been, and where it was going. When it was no bigger than a speck on the horizon, she sighed, then turned again and went back inside.

Acknowledgments

Though *Keeping the House* is entirely a work of fiction, I am grateful for the brilliant work of several historians that gave my imagination a springboard from which to leap, in particular William Manchester's *Goodbye, Darkness: A Memoir of the Pacific War* and Bill D. Ross's *Iwo Jima: Legacy of Valor*. A few more that shouldn't go unmentioned are *Calling This Place Home* by Joan M. Jensen, *Cadet Nurse Stories* by Thelma M. Robinson and Paulie M. Perry, *Over There* by Frank Freidel, *Him/Her/Self* by Peter G. Filene, and *Homeward Bound* by Elaine Tyler May. For anyone interested in the real stories of some of the events and places fictionalized in *Keeping the House,* these are all great reads.

Many people provided inspiration and support as I worked on *Keeping the House.* I wish to extend special thanks to the men and women of the World War II generation whom I met while working at the Richard I.

Bong World War II Heritage Center, for the truly inspiring stories they shared with me, and to D. J. Tice and Dorothy Youso for so graciously answering my questions about the dances at the Avalon Ballroom in La Crosse, Wisconsin, during World War II.

Thank you to Tim and Debbe at the Candlewick Inn in Merrill, Wisconsin, for sharing the story about the rumored curse on the house in Merrill, and to Linda Fournier for information on Camp McCoy.

Deepest thanks to the dear friends who reviewed early drafts and cheered me on, including Janet Murphy, Amy Tyson, Wendy Miller, Molly Holleran, and Kim Erickson. Thank you to J. Robert Lennon and Mardi Link for helping me find a mean streak, to Mike Savage for encouraging me at the outset, and to everyone at J. W. Beecroft Books & Coffee, especially Carrie Sutherland and Amanda Parker, for your continuing support.

Many, many thanks to Lara Zielin for her tireless and always insightful critiques, her unflagging support and enthusiasm, and, most important, her friendship.

Some people I just can't thank enough are my wonderful agent, Marly Rusoff, and her associates, Michael Radulescu and Julie Mosow. Deepest gratitude to Kate Medina for her enthusiasm and brilliant insight, and to the stupendous team at Random House, especially Robin Rolewicz and Abby Plesser, plus Debbie Aroff, Porscha Burke, Karen Fink, Julie Kraut, Bara MacNeill, Tom Nevins, Beth Pearson, Jessica Pearson, Lydah Pyles, Sarah Paruolo, Stephanie Sabol, and Sasha Sadikot.

Finally, thank you to my family—especially my parents, Bob and Marya, and my brother, Bill—for the constant force they are in my life, and to my husband, Jay, for providing me with support and love beyond imagining.

Keeping the House

ELLEN BAKER

A Reader's Guide

A Conversation with Ellen Baker

Random House Reader's Circle: How long did it take you to write *Keeping the House*? What kind of research did you do for it, and did it take you anywhere unexpected?

Ellen Baker: I started writing about the Mickelson family in 1996, and worked off and on for about seven years on a manuscript that dealt with their summer of 1919 in Stone Harbor, after Jack had just returned from the First World War. I finally decided that I needed to start something new, and began what would become *Keeping the House* in early 2003. I worked on it solidly for three years. I had researched World War I extensively when I was in grad school in 1998–2000, and World War II when I was working as a museum curator after that. But that really just gave me the overarching background for the story. As I wrote, I would discover details I needed and then seek them out. I traveled to North Central Wisconsin and La Crosse, and spent many hours in various libraries and archives, reading newspapers and magazines and city directories. I walked through the old Washington Avenue depot in Minneapolis, through a stand of virgin pine near Antigo, Wisconsin, and through the preserved World War II–era barracks at Fort McCoy. I interviewed several World War II veterans and even one woman who had met her husband at a dance in La Crosse. I pored over old cookbooks to plan Dolly's meals, and the War Department's 1917 advice on war gardens to plan Wilma's garden. I researched girdles and corsets, Packards and Chryslers. I can't say that any of this was really expected—I just let the story tell me where to go. I'm always fascinated by what I find, and I enjoy the challenge of weaving the details into the story.

RHRC: Speaking of research and history, readers love the excerpts that you weave throughout the book from vintage magazines, such as old issues of *Ladies' Home Journal* and *Good Housekeeping*. Which piece of advice surprised or intrigued you the most? Do you find any of the tips useful or relevant to today's modern woman?

EB: My favorite piece of advice is from the 1940 book *Popular Home Decoration*: "A house, exactly like a dog, must be loved before it will show the best side of its nature." I was so happy to find that because it seemed to go right in line with what Dolly was thinking about the Mickelson house and the bungalow. And I thought that a few of the lines from the 1939 *Good Housekeeping Marriage Book* could still be relevant today, such as the advice to really try to understand one's mate, and the idea that "all kinds of wonderful qualities needed in marriage may seem to be conspicuous in oneself chiefly by their absence, but one can always play for time." I don't know of anyone who hasn't been disappointed by their own performance in a relationship from time to time, and I like that idea of waiting out one's own bad behavior without letting the commitment waver. Some of the advice obviously seems quaint—like the lines from the cookbooks—and some of it strikes me as purely awful, particularly the stuff from the 1949 *Look* magazine article titled "The Other Woman Is Often the Creation of the Wife," and the lines from the "Making Marriage Work" column. But all of the excerpts work to set up the context that Dolly is living in, the messages she's getting from society, and why she feels bad about not living up to these expectations. In my mind, the best thing the modern woman can take from all these tips is to be conscious of the way the messages and advice one gets from today's media might be influencing one's perceptions of oneself. I know I for one can't live up to what many current women's magazines seem to expect of women.

RHRC: You've created a fascinating cast of characters in *Keeping the House,* all with such distinct personalities. Do you have a favorite? And if so, why?

EB: I love all the characters in *Keeping the House,* but if I had to pick a favorite, I think it would be Harry. He's smart, humble, a bit wounded in his own quiet way. He's more selfless than any of the other characters, more altruistic, and more honest. And he tries to do his best for his mother, despite the fact that she never really notices him. The others are fun to eavesdrop on or visit, but he's the only one I would ever want to live with.

RHRC: The conflict that Dolly feels between society's traditional wifely expectations and her own interests and passions is something that many women still struggle with today. Do you think things have really changed? Or that they need to? And did writing about Dolly's situation help you resolve any conflict in your own married life?

EB: I think this is such a complicated issue; maybe that's why I found it so fascinating to write about Dolly and Wilma and all the men and women in *Keeping the House* who are dealing with such questions in their own lives. On the one hand, there is such value in the work of keeping the house: parenting, cooking, providing a safe environment in which children can thrive, building communities. There's something about a well-kept, comfortable home that seems to suggest order and safety in a chaotic world, and those of us who are fortunate enough to have this are truly blessed. On the other hand, I think there is danger when this work of housekeeping is gendered—considered "feminine" and thus devalued. It seems to me that, for many women today, these important housekeeping tasks are piled on top of the need and desire to excel in a career, while men are more typically able to prioritize their career above the work of home and family without much angst over the issue. Maybe because women still hear so many constant messages about how that it's their job to take care of nutritious meals, clean and organize the house, nurture the kids. The real task, I think, is for communities and families to equalize the value of work both inside and outside the home and to realize that the task of keeping the house must be shared by men and women if we are to have true equality between the sexes, not to mention thrive as a society.

For me, I was appalled when I got married and people asked me why I wasn't packing my husband's lunch for him or why he occasionally had to wash the dishes or cook a meal. Even more strangely, I found myself taking on the responsibility of making sure he ate "colorful, well-balanced meals" (though I never went to the extremes that Dolly did with recording menus and responses). And I was working fifty hours a week. I was curious—and frustrated—to discover that I was wired to be a traditional wife, and that my husband seemed just as wired to be a traditional husband, despite that, if you asked us, both of us would say that our ideal was to be equal. I don't think that issues in relationships are ever resolved, but they are always in the process of evolving, and with time hopefully comes the ability to interrogate and restructure one's own unconscious expectations.

RHRC: *Keeping the House* is dedicated to your grandmothers. Did you use any of their own stories or experiences in writing this book?

EB: No, not directly. But they've both shaped my life and my thinking in significant ways.

I grew up hearing their stories. One, born in 1905, saw her farmer father killed by lightning when she was seven years old (and watched as his body was brought in from the field where he'd been working). She married young, had a child, divorced her first husband (he was never spoken of), and was a single mom for several years, working to support her daughter. She then married my grandpa, had two babies that died during the Depression (she later said she thought if she'd just been able not to work so hard doing washing, they might have survived), and finally had my dad. She was an amazing cook and housekeeper and needlewoman who also worked outside the home to earn money to send her kids to school so they could have a better life than she had (she had only an eighth-grade education), a tough and often bitter woman who embodied many contradictions. She was widowed in 1964, lived until the age of 100, and often, at the end, talked about the happiest days of her life:

when she was a child on the farm and her father was still alive. Talk about loss changing and shaping the course of a life.

My other grandma was born in 1911 in Brooklyn, the daughter of Norwegian immigrants. She earned a Master's Degree from Radcliffe College in 1935 and was married a couple of months later. My grandparents then moved to Minneapolis, Minnesota, where my grandfather soon became the president of a small college. Over the next thirty years or so, my grandma raised five daughters and worked in support of her husband's career, editing and typing his book manuscripts and hosting dinner parties for his colleagues, though she hated to cook and loved to teach and write. Hearing the stories of their lives was firsthand evidence that women typically had to choose between family and career, while men were easily able to have both. So I think these stories steered me in the direction of being interested in ideas about gender, in what society typically expects from women and from men, and started me down the path of studying history through the lens of gender.

RHRC: This is your first book; tell us a bit about your writing process and the journey to publication. Did you always want to be a writer?

EB: Yes, I did always want to be a writer. I guess I'd say I've been one my whole life. Since about the age of seven, I wrote something every day: journal entries, poetry, stories—I started my first novel when I was thirteen. It was just something I did—I always had a pen in my hand to record some secret thought. (I wrote a *Jane Eyre*-esque romance in my ninth-grade algebra notebook, for example, when I should have been paying attention to the teacher at the blackboard and her equations.) For many years I really didn't consider writing as a viable career option—it was far too personal a part of me to share with the world. But over time I discovered that there was nothing that fulfilled me the way that writing did. And once I decided not to be afraid of what the results might be, and put my whole self into not just writing for the sake of writing but writing something that other people might actually want to read, I began really studying the craft for the first time, reading more than ever, and writing and rewriting. Three years later I had a wonderful agent in New York and a book deal with Random House. Those were probably the hardest three years of work of my life, and they were absolutely the best and most rewarding, too.

RHRC: What other books would you recommend for those who enjoyed *Keeping the House*? What are some of your favorite novels?

EB: Some fantastic novels which I would recommend to people who enjoyed *Keeping the House* are *The Cape Ann* by Faith Sullivan, *The Gravedigger's Daughter* by Joyce Carol Oates, *When the Elephants Dance* by Tess Uriza Holthe, *Fried Green Tomatoes at the Whistle Stop Café* by Fannie Flagg, *Cane River* by Lalita Tademy, *The Family Tree* by Carole Cadwalladr, and *Middlesex* by Jeffrey Eugenides. Some of my other favorites include *Absalom, Absalom!* and *As I Lay Dying* by William Faulkner, *Winesburg, Ohio* by Sherwood Anderson, *Goodbye to Some* by Gordon Forbes, *The Solace of Leaving Early* by Haven Kimmel, *First Light* by Charles Baxter, *The Whistling Season* by Ivan Doig, *Wonder When You'll Miss Me* by Amanda Davis, and *The History of Love* by Nicole Krauss.

RHRC: What's next for you? Can we expect a book that's similar to *Keeping the House,* or something completely different?

EB: There are definitely certain themes that I'll come back to, just because they fascinate me: war, memory, identity, history, love, family secrets. But the setting and characters will be different. None of the women in my next book are housewives; they're farmers, artists, and World War II shipbuilders. So they're dealing with problems that are quite different from Dolly's and Wilma's in *Keeping the House*.

Questions and Topics for Discussion

1. *Keeping the House* explores the societal constraints imposed on various generations of women. Do you feel that Dolly, living as a housewife in the 1950s, has more choices and independence than Wilma did in the late 1800s? Why or why not? Do you think that American society places social constraints on women today? If so, how are the constraints similar or different?

2. The Mickelson house is such a big part of this book that it almost becomes its own character. Why do you think Dolly was initially so drawn to the house and intrigued by its history? And what do you think some of the different meanings of the title, *Keeping the House,* could be?

3. Discuss Dolly's motivations for her initial and then her continued attendance in the quilting circle. Do you think she felt compelled to go for more than just curiosity about the Mickelsons?

4. Mrs. Fryt feels quite sure she knows the Mickelsons inside out, but did you believe the stories that she and the other women in the quilting circle told? How did your opinions of the Mickelson family change when seeing them from other points of view?

5. Throughout the novel are quotes from old magazines (particularly from 1950s issues of *Ladies' Home Journal* and *Good Housekeeping*) with advice for housewives. Find a few of these quotes and discuss how these tips illustrate the change or evolution of the twentieth-century housewife. Do you think any of the tips are valid or helpful today?

6. The World Wars provide backdrop for the story. How are these conflicts portrayed? Do you believe that the hardships that John and JJ experienced in the wars excuse their treatment of women in the novel?

7. Dolly finds herself unable to stifle her desire for a more extraordinary life. Wilma, too, struggles to control her "selfish" desire to play the piano. How does each character handle her conflict between desire and duty? What could each have done to avoid the crises that arose due to her actions? Do you think the obligations that each felt were real or imagined? Do you think Wilma's and Dolly's obligations were products of the times in which they lived?

8. Discuss Dolly's desire for a child. Do you think she truly wanted to have a child, or was she attempting to conceive in order to fit the model of the "perfect housewife"? Is there such an ideal today? How has it changed?

9. Men—particularly Byron, Jack, and John—have interesting roles in this novel. Discuss how they felt about their responsibilities, and how obligations differed for men and for women. How are the roles of men and women different or the same today?

10. Do you think the rumored curse on the Mickelson house impacted the choices that members of the family made? Why or why not? Do you agree or disagree with Dolly's conclusion that the family used the curse as "an excuse for their bad behavior"? Do you think things might have gone differently for the family had there been no rumor of a curse?

11. Each character in the novel seems to have a different idea about what love is and what it means to love. In 1917, Wilma believes that "her love for [her children] had been holding her hostage in this town, this house, for more than twenty years" (page 73). What do you think Wilma learns about love over the course of the novel? Discuss what JJ, Elissa, Nick, John, Jack, Harry, Byron, and Dolly do for love in the novel, and what they learn about love. Do you think that by the end of the novel they've learned enough to stop hurting one another? Or do you think their destructive patterns will continue?

12. Weigh in on the quilting circle's argument about the Mickelsons (pages 101, 273). Who do you blame for the Mickelson family's downfall?

13. Wilma says that John "was the only one who always seemed able to forgive her" (page 348)—do you agree with her perception? Why do you think she, in turn, is unable to forgive John? What do Harry, JJ, and Anne learn about forgiveness? What do Dolly and Byron learn?

14. Despite the fact that the whole Mickelson family has left Pine Rapids, their memory is preserved in the minds of the community members, and tangible reminders of their existence remain in the house and in the bronze statue of Chase in the courthouse square. In fact, JJ is only lonely for his family after he leaves Pine Rapids, as they seem to be so present in that town. What do you think Dolly learns about the significance of storytelling and memory? What purpose do you think the Mickelson family's story serves for the people of Pine Rapids?

15. In the end, why do you think Elissa and Nick can't seem to separate from one another? Why do you think Harry keeps their secret from the rest of the family?

PHOTO: JOANN JARDINE

ELLEN BAKER was born in Grand Rapids, Minnesota, and grew up in Wisconsin and Illinois. She earned a master's degree in American studies from the University of Minnesota, worked as curator of a World War II museum, and is currently a bookseller and event coordinator at an independent bookstore. She lives with her husband in Wisconsin. Visit the author's website at www.ellenbakernovels.com.

ABOUT THE TYPE

This book was set in Sabon, a typeface designed by the well-known German typographer Jan Tschichold (1902–74). Sabon's design is based upon the original letter forms of Claude Garamond and was created specifically to be used for three sources: foundry type for hand composition, Linotype, and Monotype. Tschichold named his typeface for the famous Frankfurt typefounder Jacques Sabon, who died in 1580.